MW01166689

FABLES, FOLKLORE & ANCIENT STORIES

ARABIAN

FOLK & FAIRY TALES

FLAME TREE PUBLISHING
6 Melbray Mews, Fulham,
London SW6 3NS, United Kingdom
www.flametreepublishing.com

24 26 28 27 25
1 3 5 7 9 10 8 6 4 2

ISBN: 978-1-80417-805-8

Cover and pattern art was created by Flame Tree Studio, with elements courtesy of Shutterstock.com/svekloid/Christos Georghiou/ matrioshka. Additional interior decoration courtesy of Shutterstock.com/Ataly.

Judith John (Glossary) is a writer and editor specializing in literature and history. A former secondary school English Language and Literature teacher, she has subsequently worked as an editor on major educational projects, including *English A: Literature* for the Pearson International Baccalaureate series. Judith's major research interests include Romantic and Gothic literature, and Renaissance drama.

The text in this book is compiled and edited, with a new introduction and chapter introductions. The classic texts derive from: *Bagh O Bahar, or, Tales of the Four Darweshes*, by Mir Amman, translated by Duncan Forbes (W. H. Allen & Co., 1874); *The Bakhtyār Nāma: A Persian Romance*, translated by William Ouseley (privately printed, 1883); *The Book of Sindibād*, translated by W.A. Clouston (privately printed, 1884); *The Book of the Thousand Nights and a Night*, by Richard F. Burton (privately printed by the Kama Shastra Society, 1888); and *The Arabian Nights Entertainments*, by Andrew Lang (Longmans, Green and Co, 1918).

Due to the historical nature of the original texts, we're aware that there may be some language used which has the potential to cause offence to the modern reader. However, wishing to overall preserve the integrity of the writing, rather than imposing contemporary sensibilities, we have left it largely unaltered.

A copy of the CIP data for this book is available
from the British Library.

Designed and created in the UK | Printed and bound in China

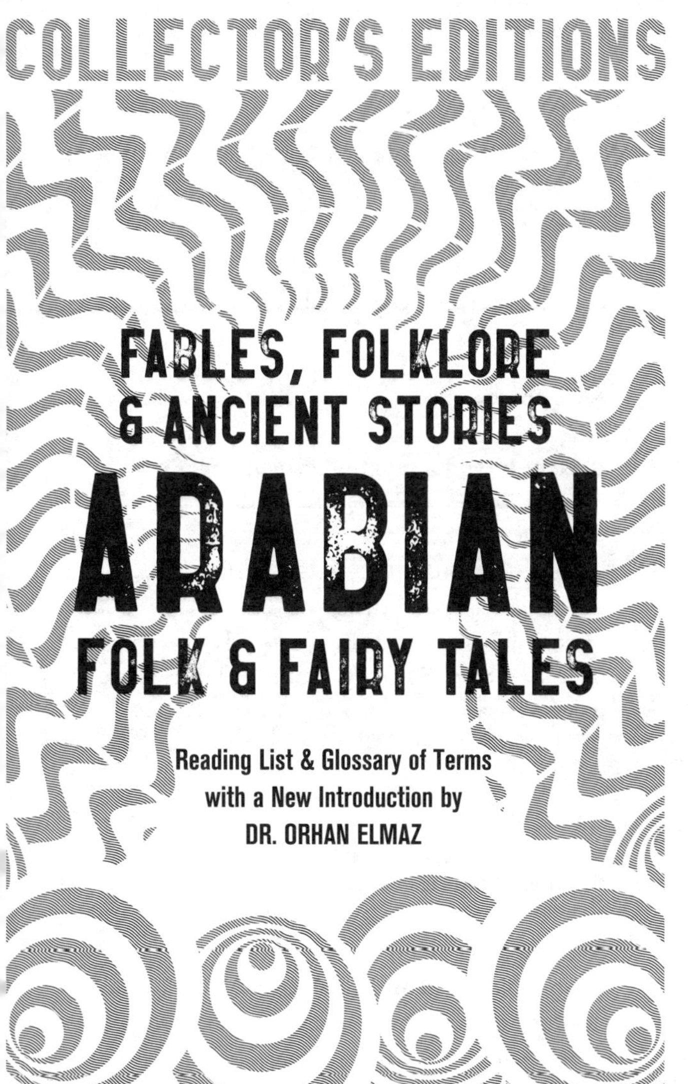

FABLES, FOLKLORE & ANCIENT STORIES

ARABIAN FOLK & FAIRY TALES

Reading List & Glossary of Terms
with a New Introduction by
DR. ORHAN ELMAZ

FLAME TREE PUBLISHING

CONTENTS

C O N T E N T S

FABLES, FOLKLORE & ANCIENT STORIES
ARABIAN
FOLK & FAIRY TALES

SERIES FOREWORD

Stretching back to the oral traditions of thousands of years ago, tales of heroes and disaster, creation and conquest have been told by many different civilizations, in ways unique to their landscape and language. Their impact sits deep within our own culture even though the detail in the stories themselves are a loose mix of historical record, the latest archaeological evidence, transformed narrative and the unwitting distortions of generations of storytellers.

Today the language of mythology lives around us: our mood is jovial, our countenance is saturnine, we are narcissistic and our modern life is hermetically sealed from others. The nuances of the ancient world form part of our daily routines and help us navigate the information overload of our interconnected lives.

The nature of a myth is that its stories are already known by most of those who hear or read them. Every era brings a new emphasis, but the fundamentals remain the same: a desire to understand and describe the events and relationships of the world. Many of the great stories are archetypes that help us find our own place, equipping us with tools for self-understanding, both individually and as part of a broader culture.

For Western societies it is Greek mythology that speaks to us most clearly. It greatly influenced the mythological heritage of the ancient Roman civilization and is the lens through which we still see the Celts, the Norse and many of the other great peoples and religions. The Greeks themselves inherited much from their neighbours, the Egyptians, an older culture that became weary with the mantle of civilization.

Of course, what we perceive now as mythology had its own origins in perceptions of the divine and the rituals of the sacred. The earliest civilizations, in the crucible of the Middle East, in the Sumer of the third millennium BCE, are the source to which many of the mythical archetypes can be traced. Over five thousand years ago, as humankind collected together in cities for the first time, developed writing and industrial scale agriculture, started to irrigate the rivers and attempted to control rather than be at the mercy of its environment, humanity began to write down its tentative explanations of natural events, of floods and plagues, of disease.

Early stories tell of gods or god-like animals who are crafty and use their wits to survive, and it is not unreasonable to suggest that these were the first rulers of the gathering peoples of the earth, later elevated to god-like status with the distance of time. Such tales became more political as cities vied with each other for supremacy, creating new gods, new hierarchies for their pantheons. The older gods took on primordial roles and became the preserve of creation and destruction, leaving the new gods to deal with more current, everyday affairs. Empires rose and fell, with Babylon assuming the mantle from Sumeria in the 1800s BCE, in turn to be swept away by the Assyrians of the 1200s BCE; then the Assyrians and the Egyptians were subjugated by the Greeks, the Greeks by the Romans and so on, leading to the spread and assimilation of common themes, ideas and stories throughout the world.

The survival of history is dependent on the telling of good tales, but each one must have the 'feeling' of truth, otherwise it will be ignored. Around the firesides, or embedded in a book or a computer, the myths and legends of the past are still the living materials of retold myth, not restricted to an exploration of historical origins. Now we have devices and global communications that give us unparalleled access to a diversity of traditions. We can find out about Indigenous American, Indian, Chinese and tribal African mythology in a way that was denied to our ancestors, we can find connections, plot the archaeology, religion and the mythologies of the world to build a comprehensive image of the human experience that is both humbling and fascinating.

The books in this series introduce the many cultures of ancient humankind to the modern reader. From the earliest migrations across the globe to settlements along rivers, from the landscapes of mountains to the vast Steppes, from woodlands to deserts, humanity has adapted to its environments, nurturing languages and observations and expressing itself through records, mythmaking stories and living traditions. There is still so much to explore, but this is a great place to start.

Jake Jackson
General Editor

FABLES, FOLKLORE & ANCIENT STORIES ARABIAN FOLK & FAIRY TALES

INTRODUCTION
& FURTHER READING

A NEW INTRODUCTION TO ARABIAN FOLK & FAIRY TALES

The Arabian Peninsula has long been a bridge between Africa, Asia and Europe. Trade routes that traversed the Arabian Peninsula, such as the Incense Route network between ancient South Arabian kingdoms and the Mediterranean, specifically the important port of Gaza, were conduits for more than just material goods. Frankincense and myrrh, harvested from trees in southern Arabia and the Horn of Africa, were highly valued for religious and secular uses. Both are still used across the globe, for example by the Catholic Church, a bulk buyer of cheaper Somalian frankincense varieties. These trade routes also facilitated a vibrant exchange of cultural practices, contributing to the development of a society that was both rich in its own traditions and receptive to external influences.

Arabian folklore encompasses a wide range of age-old stories, legends and myths that have been passed down orally through generations in the Arabic-speaking world and beyond. What characterizes them as Arabian is their reflection of the vibrant cultural heritage of Arab people, in addition to the fact that they were recorded in Arabic. Their folktales cover an array of themes. Some of the more famous and popular epic narratives include the adventures of the legendary heroes Ḥātim al-Ṭāʾī (d.

578) and Abū Zayd al-Hilālī (eleventh century), the journeys and encounters of Dhū al-Qarnayn ('the Two-Horned One', often identified with Alexander the Great), the romance of African-Arab warrior-poet ʿAntarah ibn Shaddād (d. 608) and the forbidden love of Laylā and Majnūn (identified as the seventh-century poet Qays ibn al-Mulawwaḥ). These stories are filled with honour and generosity, bravery and chivalry, the quest for knowledge and righteousness and deeply moving romance and tragedy.

ALF LAYLA WA-LAYLA

Arabian folktales today are still epitomized by the anthology known as *Alf layla wa-layla* (ألف ليلة وليلة 'One Thousand and One Nights'), often simplified to 'Arabian Nights' in English. With its blend of magic, mystery and morality, the *Nights* has captivated audiences for centuries. These timeless tales have had an immeasurable impact on the global literary landscape; their adaptations in music, art and cinema both past and present have given the collection an unparalleled afterlife. The stories within the *Nights* are diverse, ranging from fables and folktales to breathtaking adventures and love stories, not least tragedies. They start with King Shahryar who, after witnessing how his wife spectacularly cheated on him, resolves to marry a virgin each day and execute her the following morning after consummating the marriage to prevent further infidelity. This cycle is broken by Scheherazade, the vizier's daughter. She tells the king a series of enchanting and educating stories, each ending on a cliffhanger that postpones her execution by one night at a time.

The tale of Scheherazade and Shahryar works as the frame into which her stories are embedded. Her vivid characters often become narrators of their own stories with intricate plotlines, leading to a multi-dimensional narrative structure that fascinates listeners and readers alike. Of course, after sharing the marital bed for one thousand and one nights, which results in the birth of three sons, the king forgives Scheherazade for eventually running out of stories and admits his deep love for her. Thus Scheherazade's cunning plan of marrying Shahryar in order to put an end to his bloodthirsty actions, arguably driven by profound emotional pain and a desperate desire for control and revenge, succeeds.

This is a testament to the power of storytelling that shines through the narratives, making the *Nights* one of the most famous examples of embedded storytelling that has traversed the borders of language, culture and time. Yet this frame narrative is very similar to *Kathāsaritsāgara* (कथासरित्सागर, 'Ocean of the Streams of Stories'), Somadeva Bhatta's famous eleventh-century collection of Indian tales. This work is said to be an adaptation of Guṇāḍhya's unattested *Bṛhatkathā* (बृहत्कथा, 'The Great Narrative') from which the *Pañcatantra* (पञ्चतन्त्र, 'Five Treatises', *c.* third century BCE) might have also been derived. How might this be so?

LITERARY TRANSLATION

When starting to read the *Nights*, the knowledgeable reader is struck by the names of the protagonists of the frame story. Neither Scheherazade nor Shahrayar is a genuinely Arabic (or Semitic) name. Rather, they are of Persian (and thus Indo-European) extraction, probably derived from 'of noble lineage' (*čehr-āzād*) and 'holder of kingdom' (*shahr-dār*) respectively. This indicates that some of the material in the *Nights* made its way into Arabic through translation from Persian.

We are told by the tenth-century bibliographer Ibn Nadīm that the (now lost) Middle Persian *Hazār Afsān* ('Thousand Tales') or *Hazār Dastān* ('Thousand Stories') were translated into Arabic, probably in the ninth-century metropolis of Baghdad, capital of the Abbasid Empire (750–1258). The early Abbasid rulers were keen to develop the arts and sciences, building on those of the conquered lands that extended from the Iberian Peninsula and Northern Africa across the Middle East into Central Asia, and at a later stage even beyond. A translation movement was established and funded that saw significant contributions from non-Muslim bilinguals – for instance Syrian Christians, who spoke both Greek and Arabic, using Syriac as an intermediary language to prepare translations of books from ancient Greek. One of the most prolific translators was the Christian scholar Ḥunayn ibn Isḥāq. He is said to have translated over one hundred works, including medical texts and the Bible. These translators were the high earners of their time, highly valued and deservedly well-compensated for their work. Despite the name of this so-called Greco-Arabic translation movement, a significant number of works from Middle Persian, Sanskrit and Syriac were translated alongside Greek works.

In this newly emerging Islamic civilization, both arts and sciences flourished due to patronship and funding. As the language of the revelation of the Quran, Islam's holy scripture, Arabic enjoyed an elevated status as the lingua franca of the Islamic world, becoming a vehicle for the spread of its rich literary and scientific heritage. So much was this so that people learned Arabic to study fields including medicine, philosophy and even astronomy. That is hardly surprising given that the names of two out of three stars still used today originate from Arabic. In the twelfth and thirteenth centuries, at the height of the Crusades (1095–1270), the Toledo School of Translators was established. Its role was to preserve and disseminate knowledge in Arabic, Hebrew and Greek books to Western Europe through translation into medieval Latin and Castilian Spanish. Once again, Christian, Jewish and Muslim scholars collaborated across a wide array of disciplines. In so doing they laid the groundwork for modern European science, philosophy and literature, and set the stage for the Renaissance. A by-product of this translation process was the development of the Spanish language, its standardization and subsequent use as a scholarly medium.

TRADE AND CULTURAL EXCHANGE

It is not only through commissioned translation work that stories travelled. In fact Baghdad was planned and built by the Abbasid caliph al-Manṣūr in 762 to serve as the capital of the Abbasid Caliphate. Located along the Tigris River in modern-day Iraq, the city was designed on a circular plan (like ancient Babylon); it became one of the most significant cultural, economic and intellectual centres of the world. Baghdad was situated strategically along the Silk Roads network, both maritime and on land, and at the crossroads of civilizations of Africa (trans-Saharan gold and salt trade), Europe and Asia. *The Periplus of the Erythraean Sea* (Περίπλους τῆς Ἐρυθρᾶς Θαλάσσης), a Greco-Roman text in Koine Greek, details the routes and goods of the maritime trade network in the first century CE. The work highlights cosmopolitan ports such as Gerrha in the Arabian Peninsula, which acted as hubs for goods from India on their way to the Persian Empire and beyond.

The relations between the Arabian Peninsula, ancient Iran and India in antiquity pay testament to the vibrant exchange of goods, ideas and culture that has shaped our civilization. The adaptation of Indian numerals into the Arabic numeral system, which later spread to Europe, is a prime example of this exchange. The Gulf was a conduit for commerce, with merchants from the Arabian Peninsula reaching the ports of the Indus Valley, such as Lothal and Balakot, as early as the third millennium BCE. In fact, the first historically recorded maritime trade route in the world was between the Indus Valley Civilization and the civilization of Dilmun, located on the island of Bahrain and the adjacent shore of Saudi Arabia. Dilmun had acquired a monopoly on trade between the Indian subcontinent and the civilizations of Mesopotamia. This early trade was characterized by the exchange of goods such as spices, gold, ivory, pearls, precious stones and textiles. Much later, in Abbasid times, traders relied on monsoon winds to facilitate their seasonal journeys all the way to the Indonesian archipelago and southern China. Its location served to make Baghdad not only an internationally important trade hub and centre of learning, but also a cosmopolitan metropolis. Here not only were goods and ideas exchanged; stories were also told and heard.

FROM ORAL STORYTELLING TO MANUSCRIPTS AND BOOK PRINTING

Given all this, it is hardly surprising that the origins of Scheherazade's tales are as complex as some of the narratives themselves; their roots stretch back to ancient and medieval literatures, including Arabic,

Persian, Sanskrit and even Chinese. The collection as we know it today was compiled and revised over many centuries in several iterations by numerous editors across a vast geographical area, engulfed by the Mediterranean Sea to the north and the Atlantic and Indian Oceans to the west and east respectively. We are certain about iterative revisions to the texts of the *Nights* that have come down to us because they contain tales that take place in different locations across the Islamic world and beyond (not least China). Some stories feature key figures from the ninth century, while others reference historical events such as the Mongol invasions and the Crusades. Still other tales mention coffee and tobacco, enabling us to date those to the sixteenth century or even later.

The earliest physical trace of the *Nights* dates to a ninth-century Arabic paper manuscript fragment found in Cairo. By the twelfth century embedded storytelling using a frame tale had begun to influence European literature, for instance *Disciplina clericalis* ('Discipline of Clerics') by Peter Alfonsi (d. after 1121). This collection of moralizing tales translated from Arabic was framed as conversations between a Jewish philosopher and his Christian interlocutor. We find traces of embedded storytelling and the 'Tale of the Merchant and His Wife' from the frame tale of the *Nights* as early as the thirteenth century, namely in Ramon Llull's *Llibre de les bèsties* ('Book of the Beasts') in Catalan. This illustrates the fluidity of cultural boundaries and the universal nature of storytelling.

The first complete 'translation' of the *Nights* into a European language was undertaken by Antoine Galland in the early eighteenth century. His compilation in French under the title *Les Mille et Une Nuits* proved a sensation; it was soon translated into other European languages, making the stories a staple of European literary culture. Galland's work included many stories not found in the extant manuscripts in Arabic, the oldest ones dating to the fourteenth century. Either transmission strand of the Arabic text of the *Nights*, the Syrian and Egyptian strands, includes fewer than 300 nights. In order to provide enough for a whole 1001 nights, Galland included supplementary tales such as the contemporary favourites 'Aladdin's Wonderful Lamp' and 'Ali Baba and the Forty Thieves'.

The latter tale presents itself as a great example of a motif connecting Arabian folklore to others: a mountain opening to the proverbial magic formula 'open sesame'. Invoking a magic formula to open a cave is also found, for instance, in the Japanese *Konjaku Monogatarishū* (今昔物語集, 'Anthology of Tales from the Past'). This work dates from the eleventh century and contains tales from India, China and Japan. This motif is also widespread in China and the Pacific area, while it was the old Babylonians who attributed magical qualities to the sesame plant and used its oil. The story of Ali Baba is but one example of how the *Nights* blend magical and mythical elements from the diverse folkloric traditions with the real and desirable, ensuing its universal appeal.

Popularized by travelling storytellers, tales from the *Nights* were also circulating in manuscript form, although no complete Arabic manuscript has ever been found. In terms of editing these oral tales that have come down to us in manuscript form, then printing them to widen access to them, the first edition of the *Nights* was published by a certain 'Shuekh Uhmud bin Moohummud Shirwanee ool Yumunee' (Aḥmad b. Muḥammad al-Anṣārī [al-]Shirwānī al-Yamānī, 1785–1837). His edition ('Calcutta I') was commissioned by the College of Fort William in Calcutta. It was intended to be used as a textbook for learning Arabic by future officers of the British Empire. The 'Calcutta I' edition was probably based on an indirect copy of the eighteenth-century Russell manuscript (of Syrian provenance). This text contains 281 nights and is housed in the John Rylands Research Institute and Library in Manchester.

Al-Yamanī standardized the language of the manuscript, which can be characterized as mixed literary Arabic with a northern Levantine flair, making for linguistically realistic dialogues. He not only did away with this regional colouring of the tales, but he also simplified (and corrected) the grammar and published the tales of 200 nights in two volumes (1814–1818). Edward Lane (1801–1876) referred sporadically to the Arabic of 'Calcutta I' for his translation of the *Nights* into English.

The only translation of this very first print edition in Arabic into a European language, namely Danish, was produced by Jens Lassen Rasmussen (1824), who translated the first of the two volumes. Distinctly different from later editions and translations that developed an appetite for erotic content in the *Nights*, Rasmussen explicitly omitted passages that he considered 'not decent enough to be translated'. One can imagine that Shirwānī's print edition in Arabic may well have aroused the interest of adolescent students. Following Lane, almost all copies of the first volume were lost by shipwreck and thus the edition was never completed.

In Europe, the *Nights* had been in vogue since Galland. The quest for the complete text in Arabic had thus begun, characterized by adventurous anecdotes about Orientalists in quest of manuscripts (with questionable ethics). The captivating tales fed right into preconceived ideas about the exotic and lustful Orient at the beginning of the colonialization of the Middle East and North Africa, inspiring many adaptations of the *Nights* in other languages. The first definitive printed edition of the *Nights* in Arabic was published by Bulaq Press in Cairo in 1835; it was followed by the Breslau ('Habicht') edition in 1825–1843 and the second Calcutta edition in 1839–1842. All three compilations are the results of great effort, extensive research and meticulous scholarship on the various manuscripts available at the time, although the alleged complete 'Tunisian' manuscript was in fact revealed to be a work of forgery by a certain Mordechai ibn al-Najjār). They form the basis for virtually all modern editions and translations.

Today the academic study of the *Nights* is a growing field. However, the academic study of the *Nights* as literature in the Arabic-speaking world was only incepted by Suhayr al-Qalamawī (1911–1997). As one of the first five Egyptian women to graduate from Cairo University in 1941, she wrote her PhD on the *Nights*. Al-Qalamawī's work laid the foundation for her feminist ideas about achieving gender equality through education, capitalizing on Scheherazade's heroic storytelling.

EMBEDDED STORYTELLING AS COMMON LITERARY HERITAGE

It is this Scheherazadesque form of storytelling, telling stories within stories, a narrative technique that adds layers of complexity and depth to the overarching frame tale, that unites the collections selected for partial publication in this volume. All four works, the *Nights*, *Bāgh-o-Bahār*, the *Bakhtyār-nāma* and the *Seven Viziers*, employ a frame narrative structure; within this a central story serves as a framing device for a series of embedded tales, providing a context for the nested and interconnected tales. It has been widely assumed that embedded storytelling is a feature of older Indian literature in Sanskrit, especially because of the popularity of the interconnected *Pañcatantra*. In the sixth century Borzūya, a Persian physician and scholar, translated these into Middle Persian. He probably expanded them in the process, enriching Persian literature with moral and philosophical teachings from India, including political didacticism. Borzūya's translation was the basis for ʿAbdallāh ibn al-Muqaffaʿ's translation into Arabic as *Kalīla wa-Dimna* ('Kalila and Dimna') in the mid-eighth century, which then made its way into European literatures.

This chain of translation is historically factual and explains how embedded storytelling and animal fables were introduced into Middle Eastern literatures. However, some older examples of frame narratives from other cultures in the periphery of the Arabian Peninsula do exist as well. In Plato's *Sympósion* (Συμπόσιον, c. 385–370 BCE), for example, one of his philosophical dialogues about the nature of love features a framing device; the main narrative is set within a broader context. An even older instance of embedded storytelling in ancient Greek is Homer's epic *Odyssey* (Ὀδύσσεια, c. eighth century BCE). The main narrative revolves around the hero Odysseus's journey home to Ithaca after the ten-year Trojan War. Within this central narrative several instances occur in which characters within the story tell their own tales. In another, even older example, the Middle Egyptian *King Khufu and the Magicians*, also known as the 'Papyrus Westcar' (c. seventeenth century BCE), presents probably the oldest documented example of a frame tale and one of the first known examples of storytelling in antiquity. Nor, in this context, should one forget the influence of Aesop and his fables. Whether he was a legendary storyteller or a historical figure of the sixth century BCE, his work has left a lasting legacy on global literature.

BĀGH-O-BAHĀR

With its flowery title, meaning 'Garden and Spring' in English, *Bāgh-o-Bahār* (راہب و غاب) is a translation of a thirteenth-century narrative poem composed in Persian, the language of administration and literature in Mughal India (1526–1857). The poem was first translated into Urdu by Mīr Muḥammad Ḥusayn ʿAṭā Khān Taḥsīn around 1775 as *Nau Ṭarz-e Muraṣṣa*ʿ (زرط ون عصرم 'New Ornate Style'), but its language was too stylized and elevated to make for an enjoyable read. In 1801 Mir Amman, an employee of the College of Fort William in Calcutta, was commissioned to translate the original Persian, in order to acquaint future officers of the East India Company with the languages and cultures of India. He rendered the work into everyday Urdu under its common title *Bāgh-o-Bahār*, symbolizing the pursuit of love and beauty. The parallels to the publication of the first printed edition of the *Nights* in Arabic as detailed above – in 1814 and 1818, also commissioned by the College of Fort William for teaching and educational purposes – are striking.

The original poem is the thirteenth-century *Qiṣṣa-ye Chahār Darvēsh* (ۀصق راہچ شیورد 'The Tale of the Four Dervishes') by the renowned poet Amir Khusrau of Delhi (1253–1325) that circulated in various adaptations and translations. It is part of the enduring Persian literary tradition that was celebrated, at its height, in a region stretching from the eastern Mediterranean over the Caucasus and across Central Asia into the Indian subcontinent. The poem testifies to Amir Khusrau's engagement with Indian culture and literature; it shares thematic similarities and narrative devices with the Sanskrit collection of Indian tales known as *Vetālapañcaviṃśatikā* (वेतालपञ्चवशिंति, 'Vetala's Twenty-Five

Tales' to King Vikrama). By paying homage to Indian storytelling traditions, Amir Khusrau enriched Persian literature with new themes, characters and narrative techniques.

BAKHTYĀR-NĀMA (بختيارنامه)

The 'Story of Prince Bakhtyār and the Ten Viziers', also known as the 'Romance of the Ten Viziers', belongs to the realm of Persian and Turkic literatures, particularly the epic narratives of Central Asia. It exhibits similarities of motifs and themes with certain Indian literary and folk traditions, specifically the *Mahābhārata* (महाभारतम्) and the *Rāmāyaṇa* (रामायणम्). A great example of a frame story encompassing nine embedded tales, the *Bakhtyār-nāma* has been retold and adapted in various forms over the centuries. It now exists in numerous versions, featuring different variations and interpretations of the individual tales. The story serves as a vehicle for teaching virtues. It revolves around a series of moral lessons focused on leadership, making reference to honesty, integrity and humility while cautioning against vices such as greed, envy and treachery.

The story begins with the introduction of Prince Bakhtyār, a young and noble ruler who ascends to the throne after the death of his father, the king. The prince is depicted as a just and virtuous ruler, beloved by his subjects for his wisdom and compassion. He appoints ten viziers, each with unique qualities and expertise, to assist him in governing the kingdom, and they become his trusted and indispensable advisors and allies. The unfolding story examines the dynamics of power and authority within the context of governance, revealing the challenges and responsibilities that face a ruler. One of the viziers harbours jealousy and resentment towards the prince; he seeks to undermine his rule and seize power for himself. The vizier conspires with his nine colleagues to deceive and betray the prince, setting in train a series of tragic events and moral dilemmas. Prince Bakhtyār faces numerous trials and tribulations orchestrated by the viziers, including false accusations, political intrigues and personal betrayals. Despite the challenges he remains steadfast in his principles and moral integrity, refusing to compromise his values for the sake of power or revenge.

Prince Bakhtyār's virtue and righteousness eventually prevail, exposing the deceitful schemes of the viziers and restoring justice to the kingdom. Through his resilience and moral courage, the prince emerges as a triumphant hero. He has earned the admiration and loyalty of his people, a moral exemplar who upholds the principles of good governance and ethical leadership.

SEVEN VIZIERS

Also known as the *Seven Wise Masters* in Europe, this classic narrative framework shares similarities with the ancient Indian *Pañcatantra*, but is now assumed to have originated in the lost Middle Persian *Sindbād-nāma* ('Book of Sindbād'). Also known as the 'Tale of the King's Son and the Seven Viziers', it was adapted and transmitted across cultures, particularly in the Middle East and Europe. The oldest preserved versions of the 'Book of Sindbād' are the eleventh-century translations into Syriac and Greek and the tales were later popularized in Europe as the *Seven Sages of Rome* or the *Seven Sages of Greece*. The narrative contains a reflection of Potiphar's wife slandering Joseph, which is also found in the Quran (Q 12:21-29) and – as a prompt of storytelling following actual adultery – can be seen in the frame story of the *Nights* as well. Similar to the *Bakhtyār-nāma*, this collection of moralistic tales features a framing device centred around a king and his seven viziers, each of whom tells a story to impart wisdom and moral lessons to the king's son. Comparable story cycles with a frame story in the *Nights* that are modelled on *Book of Sindbād* include 'Jalî'âd and Shimâs' and the 'Craft and Malice of Women' (in the Breslau, Bulaq and Calcutta II editions), and 'Âzâdbakht and His Son' and 'Shâh Bakht and His Vizier al-Rahwân' (in the Breslau edition).

The frame tale of *Seven Viziers* consists of a king who – frustrated by his son's behaviour and lack of wisdom – seeks the counsel of his seven viziers, renowned for their wisdom and intelligence. One by one each vizier tells a story to the prince, using allegory and symbolism to convey important truths about life, virtue and human nature. The tales told by the *Seven Viziers* encompass a wide range of themes and topics, including loyalty, betrayal, friendship, love, justice and wisdom. Each story offers a distinct perspective on morality and ethics, often featuring characters who face moral dilemmas and must make difficult choices to navigate the complexities of life.

The *Seven Viziers* tales have had a profound influence on world literature and storytelling, inspiring numerous adaptations, retellings and artistic interpretations. Designed for more than entertainment, the tales also serve an educational and moralistic purpose, teaching readers important lessons about virtue, character and the consequences of one's actions. As such, they also reflect the values and ideals of their respective cultures and societies, offering insights into the moral and ethical norms of the time.

COMMON THEMES

A recurring theme in all four collections is the protagonist's quest, whether it is Scheherazade's quest to save her life through storytelling while curing Shahryār's alleged trauma, the four dervishes' journey in search of fulfilment, Bakhtyār's quest for happiness or the prince's education under the guidance of the seven viziers. Each narrative thus revolves around the protagonist's diligent pursuit of something.

Also central to all four works is the didactic nature of the incorporated stories, which aim to impart moral lessons to the audience. Whether this takes place through allegorical tales in which animals speak, parables or moral admonitions, the stories serve as vehicles for teaching ethical principles, social norms and – last but not least – ancient philosophical insights. Themes such as honesty, loyalty, justice and the consequences of one's actions are explored through the characters' experiences and dilemmas.

To some degree, the general popularity of these collections is due to blurring the lines between reality and fantasy through magic, enchantment and supernatural phenomena. From magical artefacts in the *Nights* to divine interventions in *Bāgh-o-Bahār* and mystical encounters in the *Bakhtyār-nāma*, these narratives feature fantastical elements that add depth and intrigue to the stories and captivate readers' imagination.

All four collections feature certain character archetypes and tropes that recur throughout these works. The wise counsellor, the cunning trickster, the virtuous hero and the temptress come to mind. These archetypal figures embody various virtues and vices alike; they serve as foils to the protagonist and provide triggers for moral exploration. Whether through Scheherazade's wit and intelligence, the dervishes' resilience and humility or the prince's naïveté and growth, these characters undergo journeys of transformation and self-realization.

Over the centuries these stories have been subject to cultural exchange, adaptation and reinterpretation across different regions and time periods. From their origins in the Middle East and Persia to their transmission across Asia, Europe and beyond, these tales have been translated, retold and reimagined by countless storytellers – each adding their own cultural nuances and interpretations.

The narrative techniques, motifs and stories of universal appeal shared between these four collections underscore the idea of a synthesis of literary traditions of the Middle East and Central Asia with commonalities and inspiration found in old Indian literature. This in turn led to the creation of an enriched, shared literary heritage that transcended regional boundaries and valued storytelling as a means of entertainment, learning and escape from daily life. Through their imaginative tales and cultural significance, these works continue to enchant readers across the globe, bridging the boundaries of language, space and time. It is within these narratives that we encounter the enduring power of storytelling to illuminate the human condition and discover a timeless treasure trove of wisdom. These stories address universal themes and dilemmas that continue to resonate with people today, never ceasing to remind us of literature's power to connect and inspire.

Dr. Orhan Elmaz

PUBLISHER'S NOTE

Diacritics (accents) have been removed in the stories that follow, for the sake of consistency and to provide a more uncluttered reading experience.

FURTHER READING

Allen, Roger and Donald S. Richards (eds.), *Arabic Literature in the Post-Classical Period* (Cambridge: Cambridge University Press, 2006)

Blatherwick, Helen, *Prophets, Gods and Kings in Sīrat Sayf ibn Dhī Yazan* (Leiden: Brill, 2008)

Cupane, Carolina and Bettina Krönung (eds.), *Fictional Storytelling in the Medieval Eastern Mediterranean and Beyond* (Leiden: Brill, 2016)

De Blois, François, *Burzoy's Voyage to India and the Origin of the Book of Kalīla wa Dimna* (London: The Royal Asiatic Society, 1990)

Elmaz, Orhan (ed.), *Endless Inspiration: One Thousand and One Nights in Comparative Perspective* (Piscataway, NJ, USA: Gorgias Press, 2020)

Irwin, Robert, *The Arabian Nights: A Companion* (London: Allen Lane, 1994)

Kennedy, Philip F. and Marina Warner (eds.), *Scheherazade's Children: Global Encounters with the Arabian Nights* (New York, NY: New York University Press, 2013)

Kilito, Abdelfattah, *Arabs and the Art of Storytelling: A Strange Familiarity* (Syracuse, NY: Syracuse University Press, 2014)

Kreyenbroek, Philip G. and Ulrich Marzolph (eds.), *Oral Literature of Iranian Languages: Kurdish, Pashto, Balochi, Ossetic, Persian and Tajik* (London: I.B. Tauris, 2010)

Lyons, Malcolm C., *The Arabian Epic: Heroic and Oral Story-telling* (Cambridge: Cambridge University Press, 1995)

Martin, Anna, "'Translator's Invisibility': Strategies of Adaptation in Persian Versions of Indian Tales From the Mughal Period", *Iran-Namag* 2.2 (2017), 24–37

Marzolph, Ulrich, *The Arabian Nights in Transnational Perspective* (Detroit, MI: Wayne State University Press, 2007)

Marzolph, Ulrich and Richard van Leeuwen (eds.), *Arabian Nights Encyclopedia* (Santa Barbara, CA: ABC-CLIO, 2004)

Muqaffaʿ, Ibn al- and Michael Fishbein, *Kalīlah and Dimnah: Fables of Virtue and Vice* (New York, NY: New York University Press, 2022)

Musawi, Muhsin J. al-, *The Arabian Nights in Contemporary World Cultures: Global Commodification, Translation, and the Culture Industry* (Cambridge: Cambridge University Press, 2021)

Musawi, Muhsin J. al-, *The Islamic Context of The Thousand and One Nights* (New York, NY: Columbia University Press, 2009)

Nadīm, Ibn, al-, *The Fihrist of al-Nadīm: a Tenth-Century Survey of Muslim Culture* (New York, NY: Columbia University Press, 1970)

Ouyang, Wen-Chin and Geert Jan van Gelder (eds.), *New Perspectives on Arabian Nights: Ideological Variations and Narrative Horizons* (London: Routledge, 2005)

Parasher-Sen, Aloka (ed.), *Conversations with the Animate 'Other': Historical Representations of Human and Non-Human Interactions in India* (New Delhi: Bloomsbury India, 2023)

Perry, Ben Edwin, *The Origin of the Book of Sindbad*, in: *Fabula* 3 (1960), pp. 1–94

Pinault, David, *Story-telling Techniques in the Arabian Nights* (Leiden: Brill, 1992)

Pollock, Sheldon (ed.), *Literary Cultures in History: Reconstructions from South Asia* (Berkeley, CA: University of California Press, 2003)

Reichl, Karl (ed.), *Medieval Oral Literature* (Berlin: De Gruyter, 2012)
Rubanovich, Julia (ed.), *Orality and Textuality in the Iranian World: Patterns of Interaction Across the Centuries* (Leiden: Brill, 2015)
Sharma, Sunil, *Mughal Arcadia: Persian Literature in an Indian Court* (Cambridge, MA: Harvard University Press, 2017)
Speziale, Fabrizio and Denis Hermann (eds.), *Muslim Cultures in the Indo-Iranian World during the Early-Modern and Modern Periods* (Berlin: Klaus Schwarz – IFRI, 2010)
Taylor, McComas, *The Fall of the Indigo Jackal: The Discourse of Division and Pūrṇabhadra's Pañcatantra* (Albany, NY: State University of New York Press, 2007)
Truschke, Audrey, *Culture of Encounters: Sanskrit at the Mughal Court* (New York, NY: Columbia University Press, 2016)
Tyeer, Sarah Bin and Claire Gallien (eds.), *Islam and New Directions in World Literature* (Edinburgh: Edinburgh University Press, 2022)
Wacks, David A., *Framing Iberia: Maqāmāt and Frametale Narratives in Medieval Spain* (Leiden: Brill, 2007)
Yamamoto, Kumiko, *The Oral Background of Persian Epics* (Leiden: Brill, 2021)

Dr. Orhan Elmaz (Introduction) teaches Digital Humanities and classical and modern Arabic language, literature and culture at the University of St Andrews. His research area lies at the intersection of linguistics, intellectual history and transcultural studies. He has published on the Qur'an (and its use and abuse), computational and corpus linguistics, and *One Thousand and One Nights*. Currently, he is working on the emergence and development of feminist ideas, specifically female education, contrasting different Muslim-majority and Muslim-minority communities of the Middle East, Europe and Central Asia in the nineteenth and twentieth centuries.

SELECTED TALES FROM ONE THOUSAND AND ONE NIGHTS

The tales within the *Nights* are rich with motifs of fate, morality, justice and the supernatural, especially jinnis that are distinct elements of Arabian lore. Often the motif of predestined and inevitable fate is clear; time and again, a protagonist is confronted with a situation beyond their control that requires some help or wit to overcome, highlighting human agency and intelligence over fate. Another frequently encountered theme in the *Nights* is that of personal transformation in the face of the life's vicissitudes, showing how one's status can change dramatically due to unforeseen events. The collection also contains a murder mystery that unfolds at the court of Hārūn al-Rashīd (r. 786-809) and involves three apples.

TALE OF THE TRADER AND THE JINNI

It is related that there was a merchant who had much wealth, and business in various cities. Now on a day, he mounted horse and went forth to recover monies in certain towns, and the heat sore oppressed him; so he sat beneath a tree and, putting his hand into his saddle-bags, took thence some broken bread and dry dates and began to break his fast. When he had ended eating the dates, he threw away the stones with force and lo! an Ifrit appeared, huge of stature and brandishing a drawn sword, wherewith he approached the merchant and said, "Stand up that I may slay thee, even as thou slewest my son!" Asked the merchant, "How have I slain thy son?" and he answered, "When thou atest dates and threwest away the stones they struck my son full in the breast as he was walking by, so that he died forthwith." Quoth the merchant, "Verily from Allah we proceeded and unto Allah are we returning. There is no Majesty, and there is no Might save in Allah, the Glorious, the Great! If I slew thy son, I slew him by chance medley. I pray thee now pardon me." Rejoined the Jinni, "There is no help but I must slay thee." Then he seized him and dragged him along and, casting him to the earth, raised the sword to strike him; whereupon the merchant wept, and said, "I commit my case to Allah," and began repeating these couplets:

Containeth Time a twain of days, this of blessing that of bane
And holdeth Life a twain of halves, this of pleasure that of pain.
See'st not when blows the hurricane,
sweeping stark and striking strong
None save the forest giant feels the suffering of the strain?
How many trees earth nourisheth of the dry and of the green
Yet none but those which bear the fruits for cast of stone complain.
See'st not how corpses rise and float on the surface of the tide
While pearls o' price lie hidden in the deepest of the main!
In Heaven are unnumberèd the many of the stars
Yet ne'er a star but Sun and Moon by eclipse is overta'en.
Well judgest thou the days that saw thy faring sound and well
And countedst not the pangs and pain whereof Fate is ever fain.
The nights have kept thee safe and the safety brought thee pride
But bliss and blessings of the night are 'genderers of bane!

When the merchant ceased repeating his verses the Jinni said to him, "Cut thy words short, by Allah! needs must I slay thee." But the merchant spake him thus, "Know, O thou Ifrit, that I have debts due to me and much wealth and children and a wife and many pledges in hand; so permit me to go home and discharge to every claimant his claim; and I will come back to thee at the head of the new year. Allah be my testimony and surety that I will return to thee; and then thou mayest do with me as thou wilt and Allah is witness to what I say." The Jinni took sure promise of him and let him go; so he returned to his own city and transacted his business and rendered to all men their dues, and after informing his wife and children of what had betided him, he appointed a guardian and dwelt with them for a full year. Then he arose, and made the Wuzu-ablution to purify himself before death and took his shroud under his arm and bade farewell to his people, his neighbours and all his kith and kin, and went forth despite his own nose. They then began weeping and wailing and beating their breasts over him; but he travelled until he arrived at the same garden, and the day of his arrival was the head of the new year. As he sat weeping over what had befallen him, behold, a Shaykh, a very ancient man, drew near leading a chained gazelle; and he saluted that merchant and wishing him long life said, "What is the cause of thy sitting in this place and thou alone and this be a resort of evil spirits?" The merchant related to him what had come to pass with the Ifrit, and the old man, the owner of the gazelle, wondered and said, "By Allah, O brother, thy faith is none other than exceeding faith and thy story right strange; were it graven with gravers on the eye-corners, it were a warner to whoso would be warned." Then seating himself near the merchant he said, "By Allah, O my brother, I will not leave thee until I see what may come to pass with thee and this Ifrit." And presently, as he sat and the two were at talk, the merchant began to feel fear and terror and exceeding grief and sorrow beyond relief and ever-growing care and extreme despair. And the owner of the gazelle was hard by his side; when behold, a second Shaykh approached them, and with him were two dogs both of greyhound breed and both black. The second old man after saluting them with the *salam*, also asked them of their tidings and said, "What causeth you to sit in this place, a dwelling of the Jánn?"

So they told him the tale from beginning to end, and their stay there had not lasted long before there came up a third Shaykh, and with him a she-mule of bright bay coat; and he saluted them and asked them why they were seated in that place. So they told him the story from first to last: and of no avail is a twice-told tale! There he sat down with them, and lo! a dust-cloud advanced and a mighty sand-devil appeared amidmost of the waste. Presently the cloud opened and behold, within it was that Jinni hending in hand a drawn sword, while his eyes were shooting fire-sparks of rage. He came up to them and, haling away the merchant from among them, cried to him, "Arise that I may slay thee, as thou slewest my son, the life-stuff of my liver." The merchant wailed and wept, and the three old men began sighing and crying and weeping and wailing with their companion. Presently the first old man (the owner of the gazelle) came out from among them and kissed the hand of the Ifrit and said, "O Jinni, thou Crown of the Kings of the Jann! were I to tell thee the story of me and this gazelle and thou shouldst consider it wondrous, wouldst thou give me a third part of this merchant's blood?" Then quoth the Jinni "Even so, O Shaykh! if thou tell me this tale, and I hold it a marvellous, then will I give thee a third of his blood." Thereupon the old man began to tell:

The First Shaykh's Story

Know O Jinni! that this gazelle is the daughter of my paternal uncle, my own flesh and blood, and I married her when she was a young maid, and I lived with her well-nigh thirty years, yet was I not blessed with issue by her. So I took me a concubine, who brought to me the boon of a male child fair as the full moon, with eyes of lovely shine and eyebrows which formed one line, and limbs of perfect design. Little by little he grew in stature and waxed tall; and when he was a lad fifteen years old, it became needful I should journey to certain cities, and I travelled with great store of goods. But the daughter of my uncle (this gazelle) had learned gramarye and egromancy and clerkly craft from her childhood; so she bewitched that son of mine to a calf, and my handmaid (his mother) to a heifer, and made them over to the herdsman's care. Now when I returned after a long time from my journey and asked for my son and his mother, she answered me, saying, "Thy slave-girl is dead, and thy son hath fled, and I know not whither he is sped." So I remained for a whole year with grieving heart and streaming eyes until the time came for the Great Festival of Allah. Then sent I to my herdsman bidding him choose for me a fat heifer; and he brought me one which was the damsel, my handmaid, whom this gazelle had ensorcelled. I tucked up my sleeves and skirt and, taking a knife, proceeded to cut her throat, but she lowed aloud and wept bitter tears. Thereat I marvelled and pity seized me and I held my hand, saying to the herd, "Bring me other than this." Then cried my cousin, "Slay her, for I have not a fatter nor a fairer!" Once more I went forward to sacrifice her, but she again lowed aloud, upon which in truth I refrained and commanded the herdsmen to slay her and flay her. He killed her and skinned her but found in her neither fat nor flesh, only hide and bone; and I repented when penitence availed me naught. I gave her to the herdsman and said to him, "Fetch me a fat calf;" so he brought my son ensorcelled.

When the calf saw me, he broke his tether and ran to me, and fawned upon me and wailed and shed tears; so that I took pity on him and said to the herdsman, "Bring me a heifer and let this calf go!" Thereupon my cousin (this gazelle) called aloud at me, saying, "Needs must thou kill this calf; this is a holy day and a blessed, whereon naught is slain save what be perfect-pure; and we have not amongst our calves any fatter or fairer than this!" Quoth I, "Look thou upon the condition of the heifer which I slaughtered at thy bidding and how we turn from her in disappointment and she profited us on no wise; and I repent with an exceeding repentance of having killed her: so this time I will not obey thy bidding for the sacrifice of this calf." Quoth she, "By Allah the Most Great, the Compassionating, the Compassionate! there is no help for it; thou must kill him on this holy day, and if thou kill him not to me thou art no man and I to thee am no wife." Now when I heard those hard words, not knowing her object, I went up to the calf, knife in hand, but saw it weeping. My heart relented and I said to the herdsman, "Keep the calf among my cattle."

O Lord of the Kings of the Jann, this much took place and my uncle's daughter, this gazelle, looked on and saw it, and said, "Butcher me this calf, for surely it is a fat one;" but I bade the herdsman take it away and he took it and turned his face homewards. On the next day, as I was sitting in my own house, lo! the herdsman came and, standing before me said, "O my master, I will tell thee a thing which shall gladden thy soul, and shall gain me the gift of good tidings." I answered, "Even so." Then said he, "O merchant, I have a daughter, and she learned magic in her childhood from an old woman who lived with us. Yesterday when thou gavest me the calf, I went into the house to her, and she looked upon it and veiled her face; then she wept and laughed alternately, and at last she said: O my father, hath mine honour become so cheap to thee that thou bringest in to me strange men? I asked her: Where be these strange men and why wast thou laughing, and crying?; and she answered, Of a truth this calf which is with thee is the son of our master, the merchant; but he is ensorcelled by his stepdame who bewitched both him and his mother: such is the cause of my laughing; now the reason of his weeping is his mother, for that his father slew her unawares. Then I marvelled at this with exceeding marvel and hardly made sure that day had dawned before I came to tell thee."

When I heard, O Jinni, my herdsman's words, I went out with him, and I was drunken without wine, from the excess of joy and gladness which came upon me, until I reached his house. There his daughter welcomed me and kissed my hand, and forthwith the calf came and fawned upon me as before. Quoth I to the herdsman's daughter, "Is this true that thou sayest of this calf?" Quoth she, "Yea, O my master, he is thy son, the very core of thy heart." I rejoiced and said to her, "O maiden, if thou wilt release him thine shall be whatever cattle and property of mine are under thy father's hand." She smiled and answered, "O my master, I have no greed for the goods nor will I take them save on two conditions; the first that thou marry me to thy son and the second that I may bewitch her who bewitched him and imprison her, otherwise I cannot be safe from her malice and malpractices." Now when I heard, O Jinni, these, the words of the herdsman's daughter, I replied, "Beside what thou askest all the cattle and the household stuff in thy father's charge are thine and, as for the daughter of my uncle, her blood is lawful to thee." When I had spoken, she took a cup and filled it with water: then she recited a spell over it and sprinkled it upon the calf, saying, "If Almighty Allah created thee a calf, remain so shaped, and change not; but if thou be enchanted, return to thy whilom form, by command of Allah Most Highest!" and lo! he trembled and became a man. Then I fell on his neck and said, "Allah upon thee, tell me all that the daughter of my uncle did by thee and by thy mother." And when he told me what had come to pass between them I said, "O my son, Allah favoured thee with one to restore thee, and thy right hath returned to thee." Then, O Jinni, I married the herdsman's daughter to him, and she transformed my wife into this gazelle, saying: Her shape is a comely and by no means loathsome. After this she abode with us night and day, day and night, till the Almighty took her to Himself. When she deceased, my son fared forth to the cities of Hind, even to the city of this man who hath done to thee what hath been done; and I also took this gazelle (my cousin) and wandered with her from town to town seeking tidings of my son, till Destiny drove me to this place, where I saw the merchant sitting in tears. Such is my tale!

Quoth the Jinni, "This story is indeed strange, and therefore I grant thee the third part of his blood." Thereupon the second old man, who owned the two greyhounds, came up and said, "O Jinni, if I recount to thee what befell me from my brothers, these two hounds, and thou see that it is a tale even more wondrous and marvellous than what thou hast heard, wilt thou grant to me also the third of this man's blood?" Replied the Jinni, "Thou hast my word for it, if thine adventures be more marvellous and wondrous." Thereupon he thus began:

The Second Shaykh's Story

Know, O lord of the Kings of the Jann! that these two dogs are my brothers and I am the third. Now when our father died and left us a capital of three thousand gold pieces, I opened a shop with my share, and bought and sold therein, and in like guise did my two brothers, each setting up a shop. But I had been in business no long while before the elder sold his stock for a thousand dinars, and after buying outfit and merchandise, went his ways to foreign parts. He was absent one whole year with the caravan; but one day as I sat in my shop, behold, a beggar stood before me asking alms, and I said to him, "Allah open thee another door!" Whereupon he answered, weeping the while, "Am I so changed that thou knowest me not?" Then I looked at him narrowly, and lo! it was my brother, so I rose to him and welcomed him; then I seated him in my shop and put questions concerning his case. "Ask me not," answered he; "my wealth is awaste and my state hath waxed un-stated!" So I took him to the Hammám-bath and clad him in a suit of my own and gave him lodging in my house. Moreover, after looking over the accounts of my stock-in-trade and the profits of my business, I found that industry had gained me one thousand dinars, while my principal, the head of my wealth, amounted to two thousand. So I shared the whole with him, saying, "Assume that thou hast made no journey abroad but hast remained at home; and be not cast down by thine ill-luck." He took the share in great glee and opened for himself a shop; and matters went on quietly for a few nights and days. But presently my second brother (yon other dog), also setting his heart upon travel, sold off what goods and stock-in-trade he had, and albeit we tried to stay him, he would not be stayed: he laid in an outfit for the journey, and fared forth with certain wayfarers. After an absence of a whole year he came back to me, even as my elder brother had come back; and when I said to him, "O my brother, did I not dissuade thee from travel?" he shed tears and cried, "O my brother, this be destiny's decree: here I am a mere beggar, penniless and without a shirt to my back." So I led him to the bath, O Jinni, and clothing him in new clothes of my own wear, I went with him to my shop and served him with meat and drink. Furthermore, I said to him, "O my brother, I am wont to cast up my shop-accounts at the head of every year, and whatso I shall find of surplusage is between me and thee." So I proceeded, O Ifrit, to strike a balance and, finding two thousand dinars of profit, I returned praises to the Creator (be He extolled and exalted!) and made over one half to my brother, keeping the other to myself. Thereupon he busied himself with opening a shop and on this wise we abode many days. After a time my brothers began pressing me to travel with them; but I refused, saying, "What gained ye by your voyage that I should gain thereby?" As I would not give ear to them we went back each to his own shop where we bought and sold as before. They kept urging me to travel for a whole twelvemonth, but I refused to do so till full six years were past and gone when I consented with these words, "O my brothers, here am I, your companion of travel: now let me see what monies you have by you." I found, however, that they had not a doit, having squandered their substance in high diet and drinking and carnal delights. Yet I spoke not a word of reproach; so far from it I looked over my shop accounts once more, and sold what goods and stock-in trade were mine; and, finding myself the owner of six thousand ducats, I gladly proceeded to divide that sum into halves, saying to my brothers, "These three thousand gold pieces are for me and for you to trade withal," adding, "Let us bury the other moiety underground that it may be of service in case any harm befall us, in which case each shall take a thousand wherewith to open shops." Both replied, "Right is thy recking;" and I gave to each one his thousand gold pieces, keeping the same sum for myself, to wit, a thousand dinars. We then got ready suitable goods and hired a ship and, having embarked our merchandise, proceeded on our voyage, day following day, a full month, after which we arrived at a city, where we sold our venture; and for every piece of gold we gained ten. And as we turned again to our voyage we found on the shore of the sea a maiden clad in worn and ragged gear, and she kissed my hand and said, "O master, is there kindness in thee and charity? I can make thee a fitting return for them." I answered, "Even so; truly in me are benevolence and good works, even though thou render me no return." Then she said, "Take me to wife, O my master, and carry me to thy city, for I have given myself to thee; so do me a kindness and I am of those who be meet for good works and charity: I will make thee a fitting return for these and be thou not shamed by my condition." When I heard her words, my heart yearned towards her, in such sort as willed it Allah (be He extolled and exalted!); and took her and clothed her and made ready for her a fair resting-place in the vessel, and honourably entreated her.

So we voyaged on, and my heart became attached to her with exceeding attachment, and I was separated from her neither night nor day, and I paid more regard to her than to my brothers. Then they were estranged from me, and waxed jealous of my wealth and the quantity of merchandise I had, and their eyes were opened covetously upon all my property. So they took counsel to murder me and seize my wealth, saying, "Let us slay our brother and all his monies will be ours;" and Satan made this deed seem fair in their sight; so when they found me in privacy (and I sleeping by my wife's side) they took us both up and cast us into the sea. My wife awoke startled from her sleep and, forthright becoming an Ifritah, she bore me up and carried me to an island and disappeared for a short time; but she returned in the morning and said, "Here am I, thy faithful slave, who hath made thee due recompense; for I bore thee up in the waters and saved thee from death by command of the Almighty. Know that I am a Jinniyah, and as I saw thee my heart loved thee by will of the Lord, for I am a believer in Allah and in His Apostle (whom Heaven bless and preserve!). Thereupon I came to thee conditioned as thou sawest me and thou didst marry me, and see now I have saved thee from sinking. But I am angered against thy brothers and assuredly I must slay them." When I heard her story I was surprised and, thanking her for all she had done, I said, "But as to slaying my brothers this must not be." Then I told her the tale of what had come to pass with them from the beginning of our lives to the end, and on hearing it quoth she, "This night will I fly as a bird over them and will sink their ship and slay them." Quoth I, "Allah upon thee, do not thus, for the proverb saith, O thou who doest good to him that doth evil, leave the evil doer to his evil deeds. Moreover, they are still my brothers." But she rejoined, "By Allah, there is no help for it but I slay them." I humbled myself before her for their pardon, whereupon she bore me up and flew away with me till at last she set me down on the terrace-roof of my own house. I opened the doors and took up what I had hidden in the ground; and after I had saluted the folk, I opened my shop and bought me merchandise. Now when night came on I went home, and there I saw these two hounds tied up; and, when they sighted me, they arose and whined and fawned upon me; but ere I knew what happened my wife said, "These two dogs be thy brothers!" I answered, "And who hath done this thing by them?" and she rejoined, "I sent a message to my sister and she entreated them on this wise, nor shall these two be released from their present shape till ten years shall have passed." And now I have arrived at this place on my way to my wife's sister that she may deliver them from this condition, after their having endured it for half a score of years. As I was wending onwards I saw this young man, who acquainted me with what had befallen him, and I determined not to fare hence until I should see what might occur between thee and him. Such is my tale! Then said the Jinni, "Surely this is a strange story and therefore I give thee the third portion of his blood and his crime." Thereupon quoth the third Shaykh, the master of the mare-mule, to the Jinni, "I can tell thee a tale more wondrous than these two, so thou grant me the remainder of his blood and of his offence," and the Jinni answered, "So be it!" Then the old man began:

The Third Shaykh's Story

Know, O Sultan and head of the Jann, that this mule was my wife. Now it so happened that I went forth and was absent one whole year; and when I returned from my journey I came to her by night, and saw a black slave lying with her on the carpet-bed, and they were talking, and dallying, and laughing, and kissing and playing the close-buttock game. When she saw me, she rose and came hurriedly at me with a gugglet of water; and, muttering spells over it, she besprinkled me and said, "Come forth from this thy shape into the shape of a dog;" and I became on the instant a dog. She drove me out of the house, and I ran through the doorway nor ceased running until I came to a butcher's stall, where I stopped and began to eat what bones were there. When the stall-owner saw me, he took me and led me into his house, but as soon as his daughter had sight of me she veiled her face from me, crying out, "Dost thou bring men to me and dost thou come in with them to me?" Her father asked, "Where is the man?" And she answered, "This dog is a man whom his wife hath ensorcelled and I am able to release him." When her father heard her words, he said, "Allah upon thee, O my daughter, release him." So she took a gugglet of water and, after uttering words over it, sprinkled upon me a few drops, saying, "Come forth from that form into thy former form." And I returned to my natural shape. Then I kissed her hand and said, "I wish thou wouldest transform my wife even as she transformed me." Thereupon she gave me some water, saying, "As soon as thou see her asleep, sprinkle this liquid upon her and speak what words thou heardest me utter, so shall she become whatsoever thou desirest." I went to my wife and found her fast asleep; and, while sprinkling the water upon her, I said, "Come forth from that form into the form of a mare-mule." So she became on the instant a she-mule, and she it is whom thou seest with thine eyes, O Sultan and head of the Kings of the Jann! Then the Jinni turned towards her and said, "Is this sooth?" And she nodded her head and replied by signs, "Indeed, 'tis the truth: for such is my tale and this is what hath befallen me." Now when the old man had ceased speaking, the Jinni shook with pleasure and gave him the third of the merchant's blood.

When the third old man told a tale to the Jinni more wondrous than the two preceding, the Jinni marvelled with exceeding marvel; and, shaking with delight, cried, "Lo! I have given thee the remainder of the merchant's punishment and for thy sake have I released him." Thereupon the merchant embraced the old men and thanked them, and these Shaykhs wished him joy on being saved and fared forth each one for his own city.

THE STORY OF THE FISHERMAN

There was once upon a time a fisherman so old and so poor that he could scarcely manage to support his wife and three children. He went every day to fish very early, and each day he made a rule not to throw his nets more than four times. He started out one morning by moonlight and came to the seashore. He undressed and threw his nets, and as he was drawing them towards the bank he felt a great weight. He thought he had caught a large fish, and he felt very pleased. But a moment afterwards, seeing that instead of a fish he only had in his nets the carcass of an ass, he was much disappointed.

Vexed with having such a bad haul, when he had mended his nets, which the carcass of the ass had broken in several places, he threw them a second time. In drawing them in he again felt a great weight, so that he thought they were full of fish. But he only found a large basket full of rubbish. He was much annoyed.

"O Fortune," he cried, "do not trifle thus with me, a poor fisherman, who can hardly support his family!"

So saying, he threw away the rubbish, and after having washed his nets clean of the dirt, he threw them for the third time. But he only drew in stones, shells, and mud. He was almost in despair.

Then he threw his nets for the fourth time. When he thought he had a fish he drew them in with a great deal of trouble. There was no fish however, but he found a yellow pot, which by its weight seemed full of something, and he noticed that it was fastened and sealed with lead, with the impression of a seal. He was delighted. "I will sell it to the founder," he said; "with the money I shall get for it I shall buy a measure of wheat."

He examined the jar on all sides; he shook it to see if it would rattle. But he heard nothing, and so, judging from the impression of the seal and the lid, he thought there must be something precious inside. To find out, he took his knife, and with a little trouble he opened it. He turned it upside down, but nothing came out, which surprised him very much. He set it in front of him, and whilst he was looking at it attentively, such a thick smoke came out that he had to step back a pace or two. This smoke rose up to the clouds and, stretching over the sea and the shore, formed a thick mist, which caused the fisherman much astonishment. When all the smoke was out of the jar, it gathered itself together and became a thick mass in which appeared a genius, twice as large as the largest giant. When he saw such a terrible-looking monster, the fisherman would like to have run away, but he trembled so with fright that he could not move a step.

"Great king of the genii," cried the monster, "I will never again disobey you!"

At these words the fisherman took courage.

"What is this you are saying, great genius? Tell me your history and how you came to be shut up in that vase."

At this, the genius looked at the fisherman haughtily. "Speak to me more civilly," he said, "before I kill you."

"Alas! why should you kill me?" cried the fisherman. "I have just freed you; have you already forgotten that?"

"No," answered the genius; "but that will not prevent me from killing you; and I am only going to grant you one favour, and that is to choose the manner of your death."

"But what have I done to you?" asked the fisherman.

"I cannot treat you in any other way," said the genius, "and if you would know why, listen to my story.

"I rebelled against the king of the genii. To punish me, he shut me up in this vase of copper, and he put on the leaden cover his seal, which is enchantment enough to prevent my coming out. Then he had the vase thrown into the sea. During the first period of my captivity I vowed that if anyone should free me before a hundred years were passed, I would make him rich even after his death. But that century passed, and no one freed me. In the second century I vowed that I would give all the treasures in the world to my deliverer; but he never came.

"In the third, I promised to make him a king, to be always near him, and to grant him three wishes every day; but that century passed away as the other two had done, and I remained in the same plight. At last I grew angry at being captive for so long, and I vowed that if anyone would release me I would kill him at once, and would only allow him to choose in what manner he should die. So you see, as you have freed me today, choose in what way you will die."

The fisherman was very unhappy. "What an unlucky man I am to have freed you! I implore you to spare my life."

"I have told you," said the genius, "that it is impossible. Choose quickly; you are wasting time."

The fisherman began to devise a plot.

"Since I must die," he said, "before I choose the manner of my death, I conjure you on your honour to tell me if you really were in that vase?"

"Yes, I was," answered the genius.

"I really cannot believe it," said the fisherman. "That vase could not contain one of your feet even, and how could your whole body go in? I cannot believe it unless I see you do the thing."

Then the genius began to change himself into smoke, which, as before, spread over the sea and the shore, and which, then collecting itself together, began to go back into the vase slowly and evenly till there was nothing left outside. Then a voice came from the vase which said to the fisherman, "Well, unbelieving fisherman, here I am in the vase; do you believe me now?"

The fisherman, instead of answering, took the lid of lead and shut it down quickly on the vase.

"Now, O genius," he cried, "ask pardon of me, and choose by what death you will die! But no, it will be better if I throw you into the sea whence I drew you out, and I will build a house on the shore to warn fishermen who come to cast their nets here, against fishing up such a wicked genius as you are, who vows to kill the man who frees you."

At these words the genius did all he could to get out, but he could not, because of the enchantment of the lid.

SELECTED TALES FROM 'THE PORTER AND THE THREE LADIES OF BAGHDAD'

Introduction

Once upon a time there was a Porter in Baghdad, who was a bachelor and who would remain unmarried. It came to pass on a certain day, as he stood about the street leaning idly upon his crate, behold, there stood before him an honourable woman in a mantilla of Mosul silk, broidered with gold and bordered with brocade; her walking-shoes were also purfled with gold and her hair floated in long plaits. She raised her face-veil and, showing two black eyes fringed with jetty lashes, whose glances were soft and languishing and whose perfect beauty was ever blandishing, she accosted the Porter and said in the suavest tones and choicest language, "Take up thy crate and follow me." The Porter was so dazzled he could hardly believe that he heard her aright, but he shouldered his basket in hot haste saying in himself, "O day of good luck! O day of Allah's grace!" and walked after her till she stopped at the door of a house. There she rapped, and presently came out to her an old man, a Nazarene, to whom she gave a gold piece, receiving from him in return what she required of strained wine clear as olive oil; and she set it safely in the hamper, saying, "Lift and follow." Quoth the Porter, "This, by Allah, is indeed an auspicious day, a day propitious for the granting of all a man wisheth." He again hoisted up the crate and followed her; till she stopped at a fruiterer's shop and bought from him Shámi apples and Osmáni quinces and Omani peaches, and cucumbers of Nile growth, and Egyptian limes and Sultáni oranges and citrons; besides Aleppine jasmine, scented myrtle berries, Damascene nenuphars, flower of privet and camomile, blood-red anemones, violets, and pomegranate-bloom, eglantine and narcissus, and set the whole in the Porter's crate, saying, "Up with it." So he lifted and followed her till she stopped at a butcher's booth and said, "Cut me off ten pounds of mutton." She paid him his price and he wrapped it in a banana-leaf, whereupon she laid it in the crate and said "Hoist, O Porter." He hoisted accordingly, and followed her as she walked on till she stopped at a grocer's, where she bought dry fruits and pistachio-kernels, Tihámah raisins, shelled almonds and all wanted for dessert, and said to the Porter, "Lift and follow me." So he up with his hamper and after her till she stayed at the confectioner's, and she bought an earthen platter, and piled it with all kinds of sweetmeats in his shop, open-worked tarts and fritters scented with musk and "soap-cakes," and lemon-loaves and melon-preserves, and "Zaynab's combs," and "ladies' fingers," and "Kazi's tit-bits" and goodies of every description; and placed the platter in the Porter's crate. Thereupon quoth he (being a merry man), "Thou shouldest have told me, and I would have brought with me a pony or a she-camel to carry all this market-stuff." She smiled and gave him a little cuff on the nape saying, "Step out and exceed not in words for (Allah willing!) thy wage will not be wanting." Then she stopped at a perfumer's and took from him ten sorts of waters, rose scented with musk, orange-flower, water-lily, willow flower, violet and five others; and she also bought two loaves of sugar, a bottle for perfume-spraying, a lump of male incense, aloe-wood, ambergris and musk, with candles of Alexandria wax; and she put the whole into the basket, saying, "Up with thy crate and after me." He did so and followed until she stood before the greengrocer's, of whom she bought pickled safflower and olives, in brine and in oil; with tarragon and cream-cheese and hard Syrian cheese; and she stowed them away in the crate saying to the Porter, "Take up thy basket and follow me." He did so and went after her till she came to a fair mansion fronted by a spacious court, a tall, fine place to which columns gave strength and grace: and the gate thereof had two leaves of ebony inlaid with plates of red gold. The lady stopped at the door and, turning her face-veil sideways, knocked softly with her knuckles whilst the Porter stood behind her, thinking of naught save her beauty and loveliness. Presently the door swung back and both leaves were opened, whereupon he looked to see who had opened it; and behold, it was a lady of tall figure, some five feet high; a model of beauty and loveliness, brilliance and symmetry and perfect grace. Her forehead was flower-white; her cheeks like the anemone ruddy bright; her eyes were those of the wild heifer or the gazelle, with eyebrows like the crescent-moon which ends Sha'abán and begins Ramazán; her mouth was the ring of Sulayman, her lips coral-red, and her teeth like a line of strung pearls or of camomile petals. Her throat recalled the antelope's, and her breasts, like two pomegranates of even size, stood at bay as it were; her body rose and fell in waves below her dress like the rolls of a piece of brocade, and her navel would hold an ounce of benzoin ointment. In fine she was like her of whom the poet said:

On Sun and Moon of palace cast thy sight
Enjoy her flower-like face, her fragrant light:
Thine eyes shall never see in hair so black
Beauty encase a brow so purely white:
The ruddy rosy cheek proclaims her claim
Though fail her name whose beauties we indite:
As sways her gait I smile at hips so big
And weep to see the waist they bear so slight.

When the Porter looked upon her his wits were waylaid, and his senses were stormed so that his crate went nigh to fall from his head, and he said to himself, "Never have I in my life seen a day more blessed than this day!" Then quoth the lady-portress to the lady-cateress, "Come in from the gate and relieve this poor man of his load." So the provisioner went in, followed by the portress and the Porter, and went on till they reached a spacious ground-floor hall, built with admirable skill and beautified with all manner of colours and carvings; with upper balconies and groined arches and galleries and cupboards and recesses whose curtains hung before them. In the midst stood a great basin full of water surrounding a fine fountain, and at the upper end, on the raised dais, was a couch of juniper-wood set with gems and pearls, with a canopy like mosquito-curtains of red satin-silk looped up with pearls as big as filberts and bigger. Thereupon sat a lady bright of blee, with brow beaming brilliancy, the dream of philosophy, whose eyes were fraught with Babel's gramarye and her eyebrows were arched as for archery; her breath breathed ambergris and perfumery and her lips were sugar to taste and carnelian to see. Her stature was straight as the letter ا, and her face shamed the noon-sun's radiancy; and she was even as a galaxy, or a dome with golden marquetry or a bride displayed in choicest finery or a noble maid of Araby. Right well of her sang the bard when he said:

Her smiles twin rows of pearls display
Chamomile-buds or rimey spray
Her tresses stray as night let down
And shames her light the dawn o' day.

The third lady, rising from the couch, stepped forward with graceful swaying gait till she reached the middle of the saloon, when she said to her sisters, "Why stand ye here? take it down from this poor man's head!" Then the cateress went and stood before him, and the portress behind him while the third helped them, and they lifted the load from the Porter's head; and, emptying it of all that was therein, set everything in its place. Lastly, they gave him two gold pieces, saying, "Wend thy ways, O Porter." But he went not, for he stood looking at the ladies and admiring what uncommon beauty was theirs, and their pleasant manners and kindly dispositions (never had he seen goodlier); and he gazed wistfully at that good store of wines and sweet-scented flowers and fruits and other matters. Also, he marvelled with exceeding marvel, especially to see no man in the place and delayed his going; whereupon quoth the eldest lady, "What aileth thee that goest not; haply thy wage be too little?" And, turning to her sister the cateress, she said, "Give him another dinar!" But the Porter answered, "By Allah, my lady, it is not for the wage; my hire is never more than two dirhams; but in very sooth my heart and my soul are taken up with you and your condition. I wonder to see you single with ne'er a man about you and not a soul to bear you company; and well you wot that the minaret toppleth o'er unless it stand upon four, and you want this same fourth; and women's pleasure without man is short of measure, even as the poet said:

Seest not we want for joy four things all told
The harp and lute, the flute and flageolet;
And be they companied with scents four-fold
Rose, myrtle, anemone and violet;
Nor please all eight an four thou wouldst withhold
Good wine and youth and gold and pretty pet.

You be three and want a fourth who shall be a person of good sense and prudence; smart witted, and one apt to keep careful counsel." His words pleased and amused them much; and they laughed at him and said, "And who is to assure us of that? We are maidens and we fear to entrust our secret where it may not be kept, for we have read in a certain chronicle the lines of one Ibn al-Sumam:

Hold fast thy secret and to none unfold
Lost is a secret when that secret's told:
An fail thy breast thy secret to conceal
How canst thou hope another's breast shall hold?
And Abu Nowás said well on the same subject:
Who trusteth secret to another's hand
Upon his brow deserveth burn of brand!"

When the Porter heard their words he rejoined, "By your lives! I am a man of sense and a discreet, who hath read books and perused chronicles; I reveal the fair and conceal the foul and I act as the poet adviseth:

None but the good a secret keep
And good men keep it unrevealed:
It is to me a well-shut house
With keyless locks and door ensealed."

When the maidens heard his verse and its poetical application addressed to them they said, "Thou knowest that we have laid out all our monies on this place. Now say, hast thou aught to offer us in return for entertainment? For surely we will not suffer thee to sit in our company and be our cup-companion, and gaze upon our faces so fair and so rare without paying a round sum. Wottest thou not the saying:

Sans hope of gain
Love's not worth a grain?"

Whereto the lady-portress added, "If thou bring anything thou art a something; if no thing, be off with thee, thou art a nothing;" but the procuratrix interposed, saying, "Nay, O my sisters, leave teasing him, for by Allah he hath not failed us this day, and had he been other he never had kept patience with me, so whatever be his shot and scot I will take it upon myself." The Porter, overjoyed, kissed the ground before her and thanked her saying, "By Allah, these monies are the first fruits this day hath given me." Hearing this they said, "Sit thee down and welcome to thee," and the eldest lady added, "By Allah, we may not suffer thee to join us save on one condition, and this it is, that no questions be asked as to what concerneth thee not, and frowardness shall be soundly flogged." Answered the Porter, "I agree to this, O my lady, on my head and my eyes be it! Lookye, I am dumb, I have no tongue." Then arose the provisioneress and, tightening her girdle, set the table by the fountain and put the flowers and sweet herbs in their jars, and strained the wine and ranged the flasks in row and made ready every requisite. Then sat she down, she and her sisters, placing amidst them the Porter who kept deeming himself in a dream; and she took up the wine flagon, and poured out the first cup and drank it off, and likewise a second and a third. After this she filled a fourth cup which she handed to one of her sisters; and, lastly, she crowned a goblet and passed it to the Porter, saying:

Drink the dear draught, drink free and fain
What healeth every grief and pain.

He took the cup in his hand and, louting low, returned his best thanks and improvised:

Drain not the bowl save with a trusty friend
A man of worth whose good old blood all know:
For wine, like wind, sucks sweetness from the sweet
And stinks when over stench it haply blow:

Adding:

Drain not the bowl, save from dear hand like thine
The cup recalls thy gifts; thou, gifts of wine.

After repeating this couplet he kissed their hands and drank and was drunk and sat swaying from side to side and pursued:

All drinks wherein is blood the Law unclean
Doth hold save one, the bloodshed of the vine:

Fill! fill! take all my wealth bequeathed or won
Thou fawn! a willing ransom for those eyne.

Then the cateress crowned a cup and gave it to the portress, who took it from her hand and thanked her and drank. Thereupon she poured again and passed to the eldest lady who sat on the couch, and filled yet another and handed it to the Porter. He kissed the ground before them; and, after drinking and thanking them, he again began to recite:

Here! Here! by Allah, here!
Cups of the sweet, the dear!
Fill me a brimming bowl
The Fount o' Life I speer

Then the Porter stood up before the mistress of the house and said, "O lady, I am thy slave, thy Mameluke, thy white thrall, thy very bondsman;" and he began reciting:

A slave of slaves there standeth at thy door
Lauding thy generous boons and gifts galore:
Beauty! may he come in awhile to 'joy
Thy charms? for Love and I part nevermore!

She said to him, "Drink; and health and happiness attend thy drink." So he took the cup and kissed her hand and recited these lines in sing-song:

I gave her brave old wine that like her cheeks
Blushed red or flame from furnace flaring up:

She bussed the brim and said with many a smile
How durst thou deal folk's cheek for folk to sup?
"Drink!" (said I) "these are tears of mine whose tinct
Is heart-blood sighs have boilèd in the cup."

She answered him in the following couplet:

"And tears of blood for me, friend, thou hast shed
Suffer me sup them, by thy head and eyes!"

Then the lady took the cup, and drank it off to her sisters' health, and they ceased not drinking (the Porter being in the midst of them), and dancing and laughing and reciting verses and singing ballads and ritornellos. All this time the Porter was carrying on with them, kissing, toying, biting, handling, groping, fingering; whilst one thrust a dainty morsel in his mouth, and another slapped him; and this cuffed his cheeks, and that threw sweet flowers at him; and he was in the very paradise of pleasure, as though he were sitting in the seventh sphere among the Houris of Heaven. They ceased not doing after this fashion until the wine played tricks in their heads and worsted their wits; and, when the drink got the better of them, the portress stood up and doffed her clothes till she was mother-naked. However, she let down her hair about her body by way of shift, and throwing herself into the basin disported herself and dived like a duck and swam up and down, and took water in her mouth, and spurted it all over the Porter, and washed her limbs, and between her breasts, and inside her thighs and all around her navel. Then she came up out of the cistern and throwing herself on the Porter's lap said, "O my lord, O my love, what callest thou this article?" pointing to her slit, her solution of continuity. "I call that thy cleft," quoth the Porter, and she rejoined, "Wah! wah! art thou not ashamed to use such a word?" and she caught him by the collar and soundly cuffed him. Said he again, "Thy womb, thy vulva;" and she struck him a second slap crying, "O fie, O fie, this is another ugly word; is there no shame in thee?" Quoth he, "Thy coynte;" and she cried, "O thou! art wholly destitute of modesty?" and thumped him and bashed him. Then cried the Porter, "Thy clitoris," whereat the eldest lady came down upon him with a yet sorer beating, and said, "No;" and he said, "'Tis so," and the Porter went on calling the same commodity by sundry other names, but whatever he said they beat him more and more till his neck ached and swelled with the blows he had gotten; and on this wise they made him a butt and a laughing-stock. At last he turned upon them asking, "And what do you women call this article?" Whereto the damsel made answer, "The basil of the bridges." Cried the Porter, "Thank Allah for my safety: aid me and be thou propitious, O basil of the bridges!" They passed round the cup and tossed off the bowl again, when the second lady stood up; and, stripping off all her clothes, cast herself into the cistern and did as the first had done; then she came out of the water and throwing her naked form on the Porter's lap pointed to her machine and said, "O light of mine eyes, do tell me what is the name of this concern?" He replied as before, "Thy slit;" and she rejoined, "Hath such term no shame for thee?" and cuffed him and buffeted him till the saloon rang with the blows. Then quoth she, "O fie! O fie! how canst thou say this without blushing?" He suggested, "The basil of the bridges;" but she would not have it and she said, "No! no!" and struck him and slapped him on the back of the neck. Then he began calling out all the names he knew, "Thy slit, thy womb, thy coynte, thy clitoris;" and the girls kept on saying, "No! no!" So he said, "I stick to the basil of the bridges;" and all the three laughed till they fell on their backs and laid slaps on his neck and said, "No! no! that's not its proper name." Thereupon he cried, "O my sisters, what is its name?" and they replied, "What sayest thou to the husked sesame-seed?" Then the cateress donned her clothes and they fell again to carousing, but the Porter kept moaning, "Oh! and Oh!" for his neck and shoulders, and the cup passed merrily round and round again for a full hour. After that time the eldest and handsomest lady stood up and stripped off her garments, whereupon the Porter took his neck in hand, and rubbed and shampoo'd it, saying, "My neck and shoulders are on the way of Allah!" Then she threw herself into the basin, and swam and dived, sported and washed; and the Porter looked at her naked figure as though she had been a slice of the moon and at her face with the sheen of Luna when at full, or like the dawn when it brighteneth, and he noted her noble stature and shape, and those glorious forms that quivered as she went; for she was naked as the Lord made her. Then he cried "Alack! Alack!" and began to address her, versifying in these couplets:

"If I liken thy shape to the bough when green
My likeness errs and I sore mistake it;
For the bough is fairest when clad the most
And thou art fairest when mother-naked."

When the lady heard his verses she came up out of the basin and, seating herself upon his lap and knees, pointed to her genitory and said, "O my lordling, what be the name of this?" Quoth he, "The basil of the bridges;" but she said, "Bah, bah!" Quoth he, "The husked sesame;" quoth she, "Pooh, pooh!" Then said he, "Thy womb;" and she cried, "Fie, Fie! art thou not ashamed of thyself?" and cuffed him on the nape of the neck. And whatever name he gave declaring "'Tis so," she beat him and cried "No! no!" till at last he said, "O my sisters, and what is its name?" She replied, "It is entitled the Khan of Abu Mansur;" whereupon the Porter replied, "Ha! ha! O Allah be praised for safe deliverance! O Khan of Abu Mansur!" Then she came forth and dressed and the cup went round a full hour. At last the Porter rose up, and stripping off all his clothes, jumped into the tank and swam about and washed under his bearded chin and armpits, even as they had done. Then he came out and threw himself into the first lady's lap and rested his arms upon the lap of the portress, and reposed his legs in the lap of the cateress and pointed to his prickle and said, "O my mistresses, what is the name of this article?" All laughed at his words till they fell on their backs, and one said, "Thy pintle!" But he replied, "No!" and gave each one of them a bite by way of forfeit. Then said they, "Thy pizzle!" but he cried "No," and gave each of them a hug – And Shahrazad perceived the dawn of day and ceased saying her permitted say.

Now when it was the Tenth Night, quoth her sister Dunyazad, "Finish for us thy story;" and she answered, "With joy and goodly gree." It hath reached me, O auspicious King, that the damsels stinted not saying to the Porter, "Thy prickle, thy pintle, thy pizzle," and he ceased not kissing and biting and hugging until his heart was satisfied, and they laughed on till they could no more. At last one said, "O our brother, what, then, is it called?" Quoth he, "Know ye not?" Quoth they, "No!" "Its veritable name," said he, "is mule Burst-all, which browseth on the basil of the bridges, and muncheth the husked sesame, and nighteth in the Khan of Abu Mansur." Then laughed they till they fell on their backs, and returned to their carousal, and ceased not to be after this fashion till night began to fall. Thereupon said they to the Porter, "Bismillah, O our master, up and on with those sorry old shoes of thine and turn thy face and show us the breadth of thy shoulders!" Said he, "By Allah, to part with my soul would be easier for me than departing from you: come let us join night to day, and tomorrow morning we will each wend our own way." "My life on you," said the procuratrix, "suffer him to tarry with us, that we may laugh at him: we may live out our lives and never meet with his like, for surely he is a right merry rogue and a witty." So they said, "Thou must not remain with us this night save on condition that thou submit to our commands, and that whatso thou seest, thou ask no questions thereanent, nor enquire of its cause." "All right," rejoined he, and they said, "Go read the writing over the door." So he rose and went to the entrance and there found written in letters of gold wash; "WHOSO SPEAKETH OF WHAT CONCERNETH HIM NOT, SHALL HEAR WHAT PLEASETH HIM NOT!" The Porter said, "Be ye witnesses against me that I will not speak on whatso concerneth me not." Then the cateress arose, and set food before them and they ate; after which they changed their drinking-place for another, and she lighted the lamps and candles and burned ambergris and aloes-wood, and set on fresh fruit and the wine service, when they fell to carousing and talking of their lovers. And they ceased not to eat and drink and chat, nibbling dry fruits and laughing and playing tricks for the space of a full hour when lo! a knock was heard at the gate. The knocking in no wise disturbed the seance, but one of them rose and went to see what it was and presently returned, saying, "Truly our pleasure for this night is to be perfect." "How is that?" asked they; and she answered, "At the gate be three Persian Kalandars with their beards and heads and eyebrows shaven; and all three blind of the left eye – which is surely a strange chance. They are foreigners from Roum-land with the mark of travel plain upon them; they have just entered Baghdad, this being their first visit to our city; and the cause of their knocking at our door is simply because they cannot find a lodging. Indeed one of them said to me: Haply the owner of this mansion will let us have the key of his stable or some old outhouse wherein we may pass this night; for evening had surprised them and, being strangers in the land, they knew none who would give them shelter. And, O my sisters, each of them is a figure o' fun after his own fashion; and if we let them in we shall have matter to make sport of." She gave not over persuading them till they said to her, "Let them in, and make thou the usual condition with them that they speak not of what concerneth them not, lest they hear what pleaseth them not." So she rejoiced and going to the door presently returned with the three monoculars whose beards and mustachios were clean shaven. They salam'd and stood afar off by way of respect; but the three ladies rose up to them and welcomed them and wished them joy of their safe arrival and made them sit down. The Kalandars looked at the room and saw that it was a pleasant place, clean swept and garnished with flowers; and the lamps were burning and the smoke of perfumes was spiring in air; and beside the dessert and fruits and wine, there were three fair girls who might be maidens; so they exclaimed with one voice, "By Allah, 'tis good!" Then they turned to the Porter and saw that he was a merry-faced wight, albeit he was by no means sober and was sore after his slappings. So they thought that he was one of themselves and said, "A mendicant like us! whether Arab or foreigner." But when the Porter heard these words, he rose up, and fixing his eyes fiercely upon them, said, "Sit ye here without exceeding in talk! Have you not read what is writ over the door? surely it befitteth not fellows who come to us like paupers to wag your tongues at us." "We crave thy pardon, O Fakír," rejoined they, "and our heads are between thy hands." The ladies laughed consumedly at the squabble; and, making peace between the

Kalandars and the Porter, seated the new guests before meat and they ate. Then they sat together, and the portress served them with drink; and, as the cup went round merrily, quoth the Porter to the askers, "And you, O brothers mine, have ye no story or rare adventure to amuse us withal?" Now the warmth of wine having mounted to their heads they called for musical instruments; and the portress brought them a tambourine of Mosul, and a lute of Irák, and a Persian harp; and each mendicant took one and tuned it; this the tambourine and those the lute and the harp, and struck up a merry tune while the ladies sang so lustily that there was a great noise. And whilst they were carrying on, behold, someone knocked at the gate, and the portress went to see what was the matter there. Now the cause of that knocking, O King (quoth Shahrazad) was this, the Caliph, Hárún al-Rashíd, had gone forth from the palace, as was his wont now and then, to solace himself in the city that night, and to see and hear what new thing was stirring; he was in merchant's gear, and he was attended by Ja'afar, his Wazir, and by Masrúr his Sworder of Vengeance. As they walked about the city, their way led them towards the house of the three ladies; where they heard the loud noise of musical instruments and singing and merriment; so quoth the Caliph to Ja'afar, "I long to enter this house and hear those songs and see who sing them." Quoth Ja'afar, "O Prince of the Faithful; these folk are surely drunken with wine, and I fear some mischief betide us if we get amongst them." "There is no help but that I go in there," replied the Caliph, "and I desire thee to contrive some pretext for our appearing among them." Ja'afar replied, "I hear and I obey;" and knocked at the door, whereupon the portress came out and opened. Then Ja'afar came forward and kissing the ground before her said, "O my lady, we be merchants from Tiberias-town: we arrived at Baghdad ten days ago; and, alighting at the merchants' caravanserai, we sold all our merchandise. Now a certain trader invited us to an entertainment this night; so we went to his house and he set food before us and we ate: then we sat at wine and wassail with him for an hour or so when he gave us leave to depart; and we went out from him in the shadow of the night and, being strangers, we could not find our way back to our Khan. So haply of your kindness and courtesy you will suffer us to tarry with you this night, and Heaven will reward you!" The portress looked upon them and seeing them dressed like merchants and men of grave looks and solid, she returned to her sisters and repeated to them Ja'afar's story; and they took compassion upon the strangers and said to her, "Let them enter." She opened the door to them, when said they to her, "Have we thy leave to come in?" "Come in," quoth she; and the Caliph entered, followed by Ja'afar and Masrur; and when the girls saw them they stood up to them in respect and made them sit down and looked to their wants, saying, "Welcome, and well come and good cheer to the guests, but with one condition!" "What is that?" asked they, and one of the ladies answered, "Speak not of what concerneth you not, lest ye hear what pleaseth you not." "Even so," said they; and sat down to their wine and drank deep. Presently the Caliph looked on the three Kalandars and, seeing them each and every blind of the left eye, wondered at the sight; then he gazed upon the girls and he was startled and he marvelled with exceeding marvel at their beauty and loveliness. They continued to carouse and to converse and said to the Caliph, "Drink!" but he replied, "I am vowed to Pilgrimage;" and drew back from the wine. Thereupon the portress rose and spreading before him a table-cloth worked with gold, set thereon a porcelain bowl into which she poured willow flower water with a lump of snow and a spoonful of sugar-candy. The Caliph thanked her and said in himself, "By Allah, I will recompense her tomorrow for the kind deed she hath done." The others again addressed themselves to conversing and carousing; and, when the wine got the better of them, the eldest lady, who ruled the house rose and making obeisance to them, took the cateress by the hand, and said, "Rise, O my sister and let us do what is our devoir." Both answered "Even so!" Then the portress stood up and proceeded to remove the table-service and the remnants of the banquet; and renewed the pastiles and cleared the middle of the saloon. Then she made the Kalandars sit upon a sofa at the side of the estrade, and seated the Caliph and Ja'afar and Masrur on the other side of the saloon; after which she called the Porter, and said, "How scant is thy courtesy! now thou art no stranger; nay, thou art one of the household." So he stood up and, tightening his waist-cloth, asked, "What would ye I do?" and she answered, "Stand in thy place." Then the procuratrix rose and set in the midst of the saloon a low chair and, opening a closet, cried to the Porter, "Come help me," So he went to help her and saw two black bitches with chains round their necks; and she said to him, "Take hold of them;" and he took them and led them into the middle of the saloon. Then the lady of the house arose and tucked up her sleeves above her wrists and, seizing a scourge, said to the Porter, "Bring forward one of the bitches." He brought her forward, dragging her by the chain, while the bitch wept, and shook her head at the lady who, however, came down upon her with blows on the sconce; and the bitch howled and the lady ceased not beating her till her forearm failed her. Then, casting the scourge from her hand, she pressed the bitch to her bosom and, wiping away her tears with her hands, kissed her head. Then said she to the Porter, "Take her away and bring the second;" and, when he brought her, she did with her as she had done with the first. Now the heart of the Caliph was touched at these cruel doings; his chest straitened and he lost all patience in his desire to know why the two bitches were so beaten. He threw a wink at Ja'afar wishing him to ask, but the Minister, turning towards him, said by signs, "Be silent!" Then quoth the portress to the mistress of the house, "O my lady, arise and go to thy place that I in turn may do my devoir." She answered, "Even so," and, taking her seat upon the couch of juniper-wood, pargetted with gold and silver, said to the portress and cateress, "Now do ye what ye have to do." Thereupon the portress sat upon a low seat by the couch side; but the procuratrix, entering a closet, brought out of it a bag of satin with green fringes and two tassels of gold. She stood up before the lady of the house and shaking the bag drew out from it a lute which she tuned by tightening its pegs; and when it was in perfect order, she began to sing these quatrains:

Ye are the wish, the aim of me
And when, O love, thy sight I see
The heavenly mansion openeth;
But Hell I see when lost thy sight.
From thee comes madness; nor the less
Comes highest joy, comes ecstasy:
Nor in my love for thee I fear
Or shame and blame, or hate and spite.
When Love was throned within my heart
I rent the veil of modesty;
And stints not Love to rend that veil
Garring disgrace on grace to alight;
The robe of sickness then I donned
But rent to rags was secrecy:
Wherefore my love and longing heart
Proclaim your high supremest might;

The tear-drop railing adown my cheek
Telleth my tale of ignomy:
And all the hid was seen by all
And all my riddle ree'd aright.
Heal then my malady, for thou
Art malady and remedy!
But she whose cure is in thy hand
Shall ne'er be free of bane and blight;
Burn me those eyne that radiance rain
Slay me the swords of phantasy;
How many hath the sword of Love
Laid low, their high degree despite?
Yet will I never cease to pine
Nor to oblivion will I flee.
Love is my health, my faith, my joy
Public and private, wrong or right.
O happy eyes that sight thy charms
That gaze upon thee at their gree!
Yea, of my purest wish and will
The slave of Love I'll aye be hight.

When the damsel heard this elegy in quatrains she cried out "Alas! Alas!" and rent her raiment, and fell to the ground fainting; and the Caliph saw scars of the palm-rod on her back and welts of the whip; and marvelled with exceeding wonder. Then the portress arose and sprinkled water on her and brought her a fresh and very fine dress and put it on her. But when the company beheld these doings their minds were troubled, for they had no inkling of the case nor knew the story thereof; so the Caliph said to Ja'afar, "Didst thou not see the scars upon the damsel's body? I cannot keep silence or be at rest till I learn the truth of her condition and the story of this other maiden and the secret of the two black bitches." But Ja'afar answered, "O our lord, they made it a condition with us that we speak not of what concerneth us not, lest we come to hear what pleaseth us not." Then said the portress, "By Allah, O my sister, come to me and complete this service for me." Replied the procuratrix, "With joy and goodly gree;" so she took the lute; and leaned it against her breasts and swept the strings with her finger-tips, and began singing:

Give back mine eyes their sleep long ravishèd
And say me whither be my reason fled:
I learnt that lending to thy love a place
Sleep to mine eyelids mortal foe was made.
They said, "We held thee righteous, who waylaid
Thy soul?" "Go ask his glorious eyes," I said.
I pardon all my blood he pleased to spill
Owning his troubles drove him blood to shed.
On my mind's mirror sun-like sheen he cast
Whose keen reflection fire in vitals bred
Waters of Life let Allah waste at will
Suffice my wage those lips of dewy red:
An thou address my love thou'lt find a cause
For plaint and tears or ruth or lustihed.
In water pure his form shall greet your eyne
When fails the bowl nor need ye drink of wine.

Then she quoted from the same ode:

I drank, but the draught of his glance, not wine;
And his swaying gait swayed to sleep these eyne:

'Twas not grape-juice gript me but grasp of Past
'Twas not bowl o'erbowled me but gifts divine:
His coiling curl-lets my soul ennetted
And his cruel will all my wits outwitted.

After a pause she resumed:

If we 'plain of absence what shall we say?
Or if pain afflict us where wend our way?
An I hire a truchman to tell my tale
The lovers' plaint is not told for pay:
If I put on patience, a lover's life
After loss of love will not last a day:
Naught is left me now but regret, repine
And tears flooding cheeks for ever and aye:
O thou who the babes of these eyes hast fled
Thou art homed in heart that shall never stray;
Would heaven I wot hast thou kept our pact
Long as stream shall flow, to have firmest fay?
Or hast forgotten the weeping slave
Whom groans afflict and whom griefs waylay?
Ah, when severance ends and we side by side
Couch, I'll blame thy rigours and chide thy pride!

Now when the portress heard her second ode she shrieked aloud and said, "By Allah! 'tis right good!"; and laying hands on her garments tore them, as she did the first time, and fell to the ground fainting. Thereupon the procuratrix rose and brought her a second change of clothes after she had sprinkled water on her. She recovered and sat upright and said to her sister the cateress,

"Onwards, and help me in my duty, for there remains but this one song." So the provisioneress again brought out the lute and began to sing these verses:

How long shall last, how long this rigour rife of woe
May not suffice thee all these tears thou seest flow?
Our parting thus with purpose fell thou dost prolong
Is't not enough to glad the heart of envious foe?
Were but this lying world once true to lover-heart
He had not watched the weary night in tears of woe:
Oh pity me whom overwhelmed thy cruel will
My lord, my king, 'tis time some ruth to me thou show:
To whom reveal my wrongs, O thou who murdered me?
Sad, who of broken troth the pangs must undergo!
Increase wild love for thee and phrenzy hour by hour
And days of exile minute by so long, so slow;
O Moslems, claim vendetta for this slave of Love
Whose sleep Love ever wastes, whose patience Love lays low:
Doth law of Love allow thee, O my wish! to lie
Lapt in another's arms and unto me cry "Go!"?
Yet in thy presence, say, what joys shall I enjoy
When he I love but works my love to overthrow?

When the portress heard the third song she cried aloud; and, laying hands on her garments, rent them down to the very skirt and fell to the ground fainting a third time, again showing the scars of the scourge. Then said the three Kalandars, "Would Heaven we had never entered this house, but had rather nighted on the mounds and heaps outside the city! for verily our visit hath been troubled by sights which cut to the heart." The Caliph turned to them and asked, "Why so?" and they made answer, "Our minds are sore troubled by this matter." Quoth the Caliph, "Are ye not of the household?" and quoth they, "No; nor indeed did we ever set eyes on the place till within this hour." Hereat the Caliph marvelled and rejoined, "This man who sitteth by you, would he not know the secret of the matter?" and so saying he winked and made signs at the Porter. So they questioned the man but he replied, "By the All-might of Allah, in love all are alike! I am the growth of Baghdad, yet never in my born days did I darken these doors till today and my companying with them was a curious matter." "By Allah," they rejoined, "we took thee for one of them and now we see thou art one like ourselves." Then said the Caliph, "We be seven men, and they only three women without even a fourth to help them; so let us question them of their case; and, if they answer us not, fain we will be answered by force." All of them agreed to this except Ja'afar who said, "This is not my recking; let them be; for we are their guests and, as ye know, they made a compact and condition with us which we accepted and promised to keep: wherefore it is better that we be silent concerning this matter; and, as but little of the night remaineth, let each and every of us gang his own gait." Then he winked at the Caliph and whispered to him, "There is but one hour of darkness left and I can bring them before thee tomorrow, when thou canst freely question them all concerning their story." But the Caliph raised his head haughtily and cried out at him in wrath, saying, "I have no patience left for my longing to hear of them: let the Kalandars question them forthright." Quoth Ja'afar, "This is not my rede." Then words ran high and talk answered talk; and they disputed as to who should first put the question, but at last all fixed upon the Porter. And as the jangle increased the house-mistress could not but notice it and asked them, "O ye folk!

on what matter are ye talking so loudly?" Then the Porter stood up respectfully before her and said, "O my lady, this company earnestly desire that thou acquaint them with the story of the two bitches and what maketh thee punish them so cruelly; and then thou fallest to weeping over them and kissing them; and lastly they want to hear the tale of thy sister and why she hath been bastinado'd with palm-sticks like a man. These are the questions they charge me to put, and peace be with thee." Thereupon quoth she who was the lady of the house to the guests, "Is this true that he saith on your part?" and all replied, "Yes!" save Ja'afar who kept silence. When she heard these words she cried, "By Allah, ye have wronged us, O our guests, with grievous wronging; for when you came before us we made compact and condition with you, that whoso should speak of what concerneth him not should hear what pleaseth him not. Sufficeth ye not that we took you into our house and fed you with our best food? But the fault is not so much yours as hers who let you in." Then she tucked up her sleeves from her wrists and struck the floor thrice with her hand crying, "Come ye quickly;" and lo! a closet door opened and out of it came seven negro slaves with drawn swords in hand to whom she said, "Pinion me those praters' elbows and bind them each to each." They did her bidding and asked her, "O veiled and virtuous! is it thy high command that we strike off their heads?"; but she answered, "Leave them awhile that I question them of their condition, before their necks feel the sword." "By Allah, O my lady!" cried the Porter, "slay me not for other's sin; all these men offended and deserve the penalty of crime save myself. Now by Allah, our night had been charming had we escaped the mortification of those monocular Kalandars whose entrance into a populous city would convert it into a howling wilderness." Then he repeated these verses:

How fair is ruth the strong man deigns not smother!
And fairest fair when shown to weakest brother:
By Love's own holy tie between us twain,
Let one not suffer for the sin of other.

When the Porter ended his verse the lady laughed. And after laughing at the Porter despite her wrath, she came up to the party and spake thus, "Tell me who ye be, for ye have but an hour of life; and were ye not men of rank and, perhaps, notables of your tribes, you had not been so froward and I had hastened your doom." Then said the Caliph, "Woe to thee, O Ja'afar, tell her who we are lest we be slain by mistake; and speak her fair before some horror befal us." "'Tis part of thy deserts," replied he; whereupon the Caliph cried out at him saying, "There is a time for witty words and there is a time for serious work." Then the lady accosted the three Kalandars and asked them, "Are ye brothers?"; when they answered, "No, by Allah, we be naught but Fakirs and foreigners." Then quoth she to one among them, "Wast thou born blind of one eye?"; and quoth he, "No, by Allah, 'twas a marvellous matter and a wondrous mischance which caused my eye to be torn out, and mine is a tale which, if it were written upon the eye-corners with needle-gravers, were a warner to whoso would be warned." She questioned the second and third Kalandar; but all replied like the first, "By Allah, O our mistress, each one of us cometh from a different country, and we are all three the sons of Kings, sovereign Princes ruling over suzerains and capital cities." Thereupon she turned towards them and said, "Let each and every of you tell me his tale in due order and explain the cause of his coming to our place; and if his story please us let him stroke his head and wend his way." The first to come forward was the Hammál, the Porter, who said, "O my lady, I am a man and a porter. This dame, the cateress, hired me to carry a load and took me first to the shop of a vintner; then to the booth of a butcher; thence to the stall of a fruiterer; thence to a grocer who also sold dry fruits; thence to a confectioner and a perfumer-cum-druggist and from him to this place where there happened to me with you what happened. Such is my story and peace be on us all!" At this the lady laughed and said, "Rub thy head and wend thy ways!"; but he cried, "By Allah, I will not stump it till I hear the stories of my companions." Then came forward one of the Monoculars and began to tell her:

The First Kalandar's Tale

Know that the cause of my beard being shorn and my eye being out-torn was as follows. My father was a King and he had a brother who was a King over another city; and it came to pass that I and my cousin, the son of my paternal uncle, were both born on one and the same day. And years and days rolled on; and, as we grew up, I used to visit my uncle every now and then and to spend a certain number of months with him. Now my cousin and I were sworn friends; for he ever entreated me with exceeding kindness; he killed for me the fattest sheep and strained the best of his wines, and we enjoyed long conversing and carousing. One day, when the wine had gotten the better of us, the son of my uncle said to me, "O my cousin, I have a great service to ask of thee; and I desire that thou stay me not in whatso I desire to do!" And I replied, "With joy and goodly will." Then he made me swear the most binding oaths and left me; but after a little while he returned leading a lady veiled and richly apparelled with ornaments worth a large sum of money. Presently he turned to me (the woman being still behind him) and said, "Take this lady with thee and go before me to such a burial ground," (describing it, so that I knew the place), "and enter with her into such a sepulchre and there await my coming." The oaths I swore to him made me keep silence and suffered me not to oppose him; so I led the woman to the cemetery and both I and she took our seats in the sepulchre; and hardly had we sat down when in came my uncle's son, with a bowl of water, a bag of mortar and an adze somewhat like a hoe. He went straight to the tomb in the midst of the sepulchre and, breaking it open with the adze, set the stones on one side; then he fell to digging into the earth of the tomb till he came upon a large iron plate the size of a wicket-door; and on raising it there appeared below it a staircase, vaulted and winding. Then he turned to the lady and said to her, "Come now and take thy final choice!" She at once went down by the staircase and disappeared; then quoth he to me, "O son of my uncle, by way of completing thy kindness, when I shall have descended into this place, restore the trap-door to where it was, and heap back the earth upon it as it lay before; and then of thy great goodness mix this unslaked lime which is in the bag with this water which is in the bowl and, after building up the stones, plaster the outside so that none looking upon it shall say: This is a new opening in an old tomb. For a whole year have I worked at this place whereof none knoweth but Allah, and this is the need I have of thee;" presently adding, "may Allah never bereave thy friends of thee nor make them desolate by thine absence, O son of my uncle, O my dear cousin!" And he went down the stairs and disappeared for ever. When he was lost to sight I replaced the iron plate and did all his bidding till the tomb became as it was before; and I worked almost unconsciously for my head was heated with wine. Returning to the palace of my uncle, I was told that he had gone forth a-sporting and hunting; so I slept that night without seeing him; and, when the morning dawned, I remembered the scenes of the past evening and what happened between me and my cousin;

I repented of having obeyed him when penitence was of no avail, I still thought, however, that it was a dream. So I fell to asking for the son of my uncle; but there was none to answer me concerning him; and I went out to the graveyard and the sepulchres, and sought for the tomb under which he was, but could not find it; and I ceased not wandering about from sepulchre to sepulchre, and tomb to tomb, all without success, till night set in. So I returned to the city, yet I could neither eat nor drink; my thoughts being engrossed with my cousin, for that I knew not what was become of him; and I grieved with exceeding grief and passed another sorrowful night, watching until the morning. Then went I a second time to the cemetery, pondering over what the son of mine uncle had done; and, sorely repenting my hearkening to him, went round among all the tombs, but could not find the tomb I sought. I mourned over the past, and remained in my mourning seven days, seeking the place and ever missing the path. Then my torture of scruples grew upon me till I well nigh went mad, and I found no way to dispel my grief save travel and return to my father. So I set out and journeyed homeward; but as I was entering my father's capital, a crowd of rioters sprang upon me and pinioned me. I wondered thereat with all wonderment, seeing that I was the son of the Sultan, and these men were my father's subjects and amongst them were some of my own slaves. A great fear fell upon me, and I said to my soul, "Would heaven I knew what hath happened to my father!" I questioned those that bound me of the cause of their so doing, but they returned me no answer. However, after a while one of them said to me (and he had been a hired servant of our house), "Fortune hath been false to thy father; his troops betrayed him and the Vizier who slew him now reigneth in his stead and we lay in wait to seize thee by the bidding of him." I was well-nigh distraught and felt ready to faint on hearing of my father's death, when they carried me off and placed me in presence of the usurper. Now between me and him there was an olden grudge, the cause of which was this. I was fond of shooting with the stone-bow, and it befell one day, as I was standing on the terrace-roof of the palace, that a bird lighted on the top of the Vizier's house when he happened to be there. I shot at the bird and missed the mark; but I hit the Vizier's eye and knocked it out as fate and fortune decreed. Even so saith the poet:

We tread the path where Fate hath led
The path Fate writ we fain must tread:
And man in one land doomed to die
Death nowhere else shall do him dead.

And on like wise saith another:

Let Fortune have her wanton way
Take heart and all her words obey:
Nor joy nor mourn at anything
For all things pass and no things stay.

Now when I knocked out the Vizier's eye he could not say a single word, for that my father was King of the city; but he hated me ever after and dire was the grudge thus caused between us twain. So when I was set before him hand-bound and pinioned, he straightway gave orders for me to be beheaded. I asked, "For what crime wilt thou put me to death?"; whereupon he answered, "What crime is greater than this?" pointing the while to the place where his eye had been. Quoth I, "This I did by accident, not of malice prepense;" and quoth he, "If thou didst it by accident, I will do the like by thee with intention." Then cried he, "Bring him forward," and they brought me up to him, when he thrust his finger into my left eye and gouged it out; whereupon I became one-eyed as ye see me. Then he bade bind me hand and foot, and put me into a chest and said to the sworder, "Take charge of this fellow, and go off with him to the waste lands about the city; then draw thy scymitar and slay him, and leave him to feed the beasts and birds." So the headsman fared forth with me, and when he was in the midst of the desert, he took me out of the chest (and I with both hands pinioned and both feet fettered) and was about to bandage my eyes before striking off my head. But I wept with exceeding weeping until I made him weep with me and, looking at him, I began to recite these couplets:

I deemed you coat-o'-mail that should withstand
The foeman's shafts; and you proved foeman's brand;
I hoped your aidance in mine every chance
Though fail my left to aid my dexter hand:
Aloof you stand and hear the railer's gibe
While rain their shafts on me the giber-band:
But an ye will not guard me from my foes
Stand clear, and succour neither these nor those!

And I also quoted:

I deemed my brethren mail of strongest steel
And so they were – from foes to fend my dart!
I deemed their arrows surest of their aim;
And so they were – when aiming at my heart!

When the headsman heard my lines (he had been sworder to my sire and he owed me a debt of gratitude) he cried, "O my lord, what can I do, being but a slave under orders?" presently adding, "Fly for thy life and nevermore return to this land, or they will slay thee and slay me with thee, even as the poet said:

Take thy life and fly whenas evils threat;
Let the ruined house tell its owner's fate:
New land for the old thou shalt seek and find
But to find new life thou must not await.
Strange that men should sit in the stead of shame,
When Allah's world is so wide and great!
And trust not other, in matters grave
Life itself must act for a life beset:
Ne'er would prowl the lion with maned neck,
Did he reckon on aid or of others reck."

Hardly believing in my escape, I kissed his hand and thought the loss of my eye a light matter in consideration of my escaping from being slain. I arrived at my uncle's capital; and, going in to him, told him of what had befallen my father and myself; whereat he wept with sore weeping and said, "Verily thou addest grief to my grief, and woe to my woe; for thy cousin hath been missing these many days; I wot not what hath happened to him, and none can give me news of him." And he wept till he fainted. I sorrowed and condoled with him; and he would have applied certain medicaments to my eye, but he saw that it was become as a walnut with the shell empty. Then said he, "O my son, better to lose eye and keep life!" After that I could no longer remain silent about my cousin, who was his only son and one dearly loved, so I told him all that had happened. He rejoiced with extreme joyance to hear news of his son and said, "Come now and show me the tomb;" but I replied, "By

Allah, O my uncle, I know not its place, though I sought it carefully full many times, yet could not find the site." However, I and my uncle went to the graveyard and looked right and left, till at last I recognized the tomb, and we both rejoiced with exceeding joy. We entered the sepulchre and loosened the earth about the grave; then, upraising the trap-door, descended some fifty steps till we came to the foot of the staircase, when lo! we were stopped by a blinding smoke. Thereupon said my uncle that saying whose sayer shall never come to shame, "There is no Majesty and there is no Might, save in Allah, the Glorious, the Great!" and we advanced till we suddenly came upon a saloon, whose floor was strewed with flour and grain and provisions and all manner of necessaries; and in the midst of it stood a canopy sheltering a couch. Thereupon my uncle went up to the couch and inspecting it found his son and the lady who had gone down with him into the tomb, lying in each other's embrace; but the twain had become black as charred wood; it was as if they had been cast into a pit of fire. When my uncle saw this spectacle, he spat in his son's face and said, "Thou hast thy desserts, O thou hog! this is thy judgment in the transitory world, and yet remaineth the judgment in the world to come, a durer and a more enduring."

My uncle struck his son with his slipper as he lay there, a black heap of coal. I marvelled at his hardness of heart and, grieving for my cousin and the lady, said, "By Allah, O my uncle, calm thy wrath: dost thou not see that all my thoughts are occupied with this misfortune, and how sorrowful I am for what hath befallen thy son, and how horrible it is that naught of him remaineth but a black heap of charcoal? And is not that enough, but thou must smite him with thy slipper?" Answered he, "O son of my brother, this youth from his boyhood was madly in love with his own sister; and often I forbade him from her, saying to myself: They are but little ones. However, when they grew up sin befell between them; and, although I could hardly believe it, I confined him and chided him and threatened him with the severest threats; and the eunuchs and servants said to him: Beware of so foul a thing which none before thee ever did, and which none after thee will ever do; and have a care lest thou be dishonoured and disgraced among the Kings of the day, even to the end of time. And I added: Such a report as this will be spread abroad by caravans, and take heed not to give them cause to talk, or I will assuredly curse thee and do thee to death. After that I lodged them apart and shut her up; but the accursed girl loved him with passionate love, for Satan had got the mastery of her as well as of him and made their foul sin seem fair in their sight. Now when my son saw that I separated them, he secretly built this subterrain and furnished it and transported to it victuals, even as thou seest; and, when I had gone out a-sporting, came here with his sister and hid from me. Then His righteous judgment fell upon the twain and consumed them with fire from Heaven; and verily the last judgment will deal them durer pains and more enduring!" Then he wept and I wept with him; and he looked at me and said, "Thou art my son in his stead." And I bethought me awhile of the world and of its chances, how the Vizier had slain my father and had taken his place and had put out my eye; and how my cousin had come to his death by the strangest chance: and I wept again and my uncle wept with me. Then we mounted the steps and let down the iron plate and heaped up the earth over it; and, after restoring the tomb to its former condition, we returned to the palace. But hardly had we sat down ere we heard the tom-toming of the kettle-drum and tantara of trumpets and clash of cymbals; and the rattling of war-men's lances; and the clamours of assailants and the clanking of bits and the neighing of steeds; while the world was canopied with dense dust and sand-clouds raised by the horses' hoofs. We were amazed at sight and sound, knowing not what could be the matter; so we asked and were told us that the Vizier who had usurped my father's kingdom had marched his men; and that after levying his soldiery and taking a host of wild Arabs into service, he had come down upon us with armies like the sands of the sea; their number none could tell and against them none could prevail. They attacked the city unawares; and the citizens, being powerless to oppose them, surrendered the place: my uncle was slain and I made for the suburbs, saying to myself, "If thou fall into this villain's hands he will assuredly kill thee." On this wise all my troubles were renewed; and I pondered all that had betided my father and my uncle and I knew not what to do; for if the city people or my father's troops had recognized me they would have done their best to win favour by destroying me; and I could think of no way to escape save by shaving off my beard and my eyebrows. So I shore them off and, changing my fine clothes for a Kalandar's rags, I fared forth from my uncle's capital and made for this city; hoping that peradventure someone would assist me to the presence of the Prince of the Faithful, and the Caliph who is the Viceregent of Allah upon earth. Thus have I come hither that I might tell him my tale and lay my case before him. I arrived here this very night, and was standing in doubt whither I should go, when suddenly I saw this second Kalandar; so I *salam*'d to him, saying: I am a stranger! and he answered: I too am a stranger! And as we were conversing behold, up came our companion, this third Kalandar, and saluted us saying: I am a stranger! And we answered: We too be strangers! Then we three walked on and together till darkness overtook us and Destiny drove us to your house. Such, then, is the cause of the shaving of my beard and mustachios and eyebrows; and the manner of my losing my right eye.

The Second Kalandar's Tale

Know, O my lady, that I was not born one-eyed and mine is a strange story; an it were graven with needle-graver on the eye-corners, it were a warner to whoso would be warned. I am a King, son of a King, and was brought up like a Prince. I learned intoning the Koran according to the seven schools; and I read all manner of books, and held disputations on their contents with the doctors and men of science; moreover I studied star-lore and the fair sayings of poets and I exercised myself in all branches of learning until I surpassed the people of my time; my skill in calligraphy exceeded that of all the scribes; and my fame was bruited abroad over all climes and cities, and all the kings learned to know my name. Amongst others the King of Hind heard of me and sent to my father to invite me to his court, with offerings and presents and rarities such as befit royalties. So my father fitted out six ships for me and my people; and we put to sea and sailed for the space of a full month till we made the land. Then we brought out the horses that were with us in the ships; and, after loading the camels with our presents for the prince, we set forth inland. But we had marched only a little way, when behold, a dust-cloud up-flew, and grew until it walled the horizon from view. After an hour or so the veil lifted and discovered beneath it fifty horsemen, ravening lions to the sight, in steel armour dight. We observed them straightly and lo! they were cutters-off of the highway, wild as wild Arabs. When they saw that we were only four and had with us but the ten camels carrying the presents, they dashed down upon us with lances at rest. We signed to them, with our fingers, as it were saying, "We be messengers of the great King of Hind, so harm us not!" but they answered on likewise, "We are not in his dominions to obey nor are we subject to his sway." Then they set upon us and slew some of my slaves and put the lave to flight; and I also fled after I had gotten a wound, a grievous hurt, whilst the Arabs were taken up with the money and the presents which were with us. I went forth unknowing whither I went, having become mean as I was mighty; and I fared on until I came to the crest of a mountain where I took shelter for the night in a cave. When day arose I set out again, nor ceased after this fashion till I arrived at a fair city and a well-filled. Now it was the season when winter was turning away with his rime and to greet the world with his flowers came Prime, and the young blooms were springing and the streams flowed ringing, and the birds were sweetly singing, as saith the poet concerning a certain city when describing it:

A place secure from every thought of fear
Safety and peace for ever lord it here:
Its beauties seem to beautify its sons
And as in Heaven its happy folk appear.

I was glad of my arrival for I was wearied with the way, and yellow of face for weakness and want; but my plight was pitiable and I knew not whither to betake me. So I accosted a Tailor sitting in his little shop and saluted him; he returned my salam, and bade me kindly welcome and wished me well and entreated me gently and asked me of the cause of my strangerhood. I told him all my past from first to last; and he was concerned on my account and said, "O youth, disclose not thy secret to any: the King of this city is the greatest enemy thy father hath, and there is blood-wit between them and thou hast cause to fear for thy life." Then he set meat and drink before me; and I ate and drank and he with me; and we conversed freely till nightfall, when he cleared me a place in a corner of his shop and brought me a carpet and a coverlet. I tarried with him three days; at the end of which time he said to me, "Knowest thou no calling whereby to win thy living, O my son?" "I am learned in the law," I replied, "and a doctor of doctrine; an adept in art and science, a mathematician and a notable penman." He rejoined, "Thy calling is of no account in our city, where not a soul understandeth science or even writing or aught save money-making." Then said I, "By Allah, I know nothing but what I have mentioned;" and he answered, "Gird thy middle and take thee a hatchet and a cord, and go and hew wood in the wold for thy daily bread, till Allah send thee relief; and tell none who thou art lest they slay thee." Then he bought me an axe and a rope and gave me in charge to certain woodcutters; and with these guardians I went forth into the forest, where I cut fuel-wood the whole of my day and came back in the evening bearing my bundle on my head. I sold it for half a dinar, with part of which I bought provision and laid by the rest. In such work I spent a whole year and when this was ended I went out one day, as was my wont, into the wilderness; and, wandering away from my companions, I chanced on a thickly grown lowland in which there was an abundance of wood. So I entered and I found the gnarled stump of a great tree and loosened the ground about it and shovelled away the earth. Presently my hatchet rang upon a copper ring; so I cleared away the soil and behold, the ring was attached to a wooden trap-door. This I raised and there appeared beneath it a staircase. I descended the steps to the bottom and came to a door, which I opened and found myself in a noble hall, strong of structure and beautifully built, where was a damsel like a pearl of great price, whose favour banished from my heart all grief and cark and care; and whose soft speech healed the soul in despair and captivated the wise and ware. Her figure measured five feet in height; her breasts were firm and upright; her cheek a very garden of delight; her colour lively bright; her face gleamed like dawn through curly tresses which gloomed like night, and above the snows of her bosom glittered teeth of a pearly white. As the poet said of one like her:

Slim-waisted loveling, jetty hair-encrowned
A wand of willow on a sandy mound:

And as saith another:

Four things that meet not, save they here unite
To shed my heart-blood and to rape my sprite:
Brilliantest forehead; tresses jetty bright;
Cheeks rosy red and stature beauty-dight.

When I looked upon her I prostrated myself before Him who had created her, for the beauty and loveliness He had shaped in her, and she looked at me and said, "Art thou man or Jinni?" "I am a man," answered I, and she, "Now who brought thee to this place where I have abided five-and-twenty years without even yet seeing man in it." Quoth I (and indeed I found her words wonder-sweet, and my heart was melted to the core by them), "O my lady, my good fortune led me hither for the dispelling of my cark and care." Then I related to her all my mishap from first to last, and my case appeared to her exceeding grievous; so she wept and said, "I will tell thee my story in my turn. I am the daughter of the King Ifitamus, lord of the Islands of Abnús, who married me to my cousin, the son of my paternal uncle; but on my wedding night an Ifrit named Jirjís bin Rajmús, first cousin that is, mother's sister's son, of Iblís, the Foul Fiend, snatched me up and, flying away with me like a bird, set me down in this place, whither he conveyed all I needed of fine stuffs, raiment and jewels and furniture, and meat and drink and other else. Once in every ten days he comes here and lies a single night with me, and then wends his way, for he took me without the consent of his family; and he hath agreed with me that if ever I need him by night or by day, I have only to pass my hand over yonder two lines engraved upon the alcove, and he will appear to me before my fingers cease touching. Four days have now passed since he was here; and, as there remain six days before he come again, say me, wilt thou abide with me five days, and go hence the day before his coming?" I replied "Yes, and yes again! O rare, if all this be not a dream!" Hereat she was glad and, springing to her feet, seized my hand and carried me through an arched doorway to a Hammam-bath, a fair hall and richly decorate. I doffed my clothes, and she doffed hers; then we bathed and she washed me; and when this was done we left the bath, and she seated me by her side upon a high divan, and brought me sherbet scented with musk. When we felt cool after the bath, she set food before me and we ate and fell to talking; but presently she said to me, "Lay thee down and take thy rest, for surely thou must be weary." So I thanked her, my lady, and lay down and slept soundly, forgetting all that had happened to me. When I awoke I found her rubbing and shampooing my feet; so I again thanked her and blessed her and we sat for a while talking. Said she, "By Allah, I was sad at heart, for that I have dwelt alone underground for these five-and-twenty years; and praise be to Allah, who hath sent me someone with whom I can converse!" Then she asked, "O youth, what sayest thou to wine?" and I answered, "Do as thou wilt." Whereupon she went to a cupboard and took out a sealed flask of right old wine and set off the table with flowers and scented herbs and began to sing these lines:

Had we known of thy coming we fain had dispread
The cores of our hearts or the balls of our eyes;
Our cheeks as a carpet to greet thee had thrown
And our eyelids had strown for thy feet to betread.

Now when she finished her verse I thanked her, for indeed love of her had gotten hold of my heart and my grief and anguish were gone. We sat at converse and carousal till nightfall, and with her I spent the night – such night never spent I in all my life! On the morrow, delight followed delight till midday, by which time I had drunken wine so freely that I had lost my wits, and stood up, staggering to the right and to the left, and said "Come, O my charmer, and I will carry thee up from this underground vault and deliver thee from the spell of thy Jinni." She laughed and replied "Content thee and hold thy peace: of every ten days one is for the Ifrit and the other nine are thine." Quoth I (and in good sooth drink had got the better of me), "This very instant will I break down the alcove whereon is graven the talisman and summon the Ifrit that I may slay him, for it is a practise of mine to slay Ifrits!" When she heard my words her colour waxed wan and she said, "By Allah, do not!" and she began repeating:

This is a thing wherein destruction lies
I rede thee shun it an thy wits be wise.

And these also:

O thou who seekest severance, draw the rein
Of thy swift steed nor seek o'ermuch t' advance;
Ah stay! for treachery is the rule of life,
And sweets of meeting end in severance.

I heard her verse but paid no heed to her words, nay, I raised my foot and administered to the alcove a mighty kick.

But when, O my mistress, I kicked that alcove with a mighty kick, behold, the air starkened and darkened and thundered and lightened; the earth trembled and quaked and the world became invisible. At once the fumes of wine left my head: I cried to her, "What is the matter?" and she replied, "The Ifrit is upon us! did I not warn thee of this? By Allah, thou hast brought ruin upon me; but fly for thy life and go up by the way thou camest down!" So I fled up the staircase; but, in the excess of my fear, I forgot sandals and hatchet. And when I had mounted two steps I turned to look for them, and lo! I saw the earth cleave asunder, and there arose from it an Ifrit, a monster of hideousness, who said to the damsel, "What trouble and pother be this wherewith thou disturbest me? What mishap hath betided thee?" "No mishap hath befallen me" she answered, "save that my breast was straitened and my heart heavy with sadness: so I drank a little wine to broaden it and to hearten myself; then I rose to obey a call of Nature, but the wine had gotten into my head and I fell against the alcove." "Thou liest, like the whore thou art!" shrieked the Ifrit; and he looked around the hall right and left till he caught sight of my axe and sandals and said to her, "What be these but the belongings of some mortal who hath been in thy society?" She answered, "I never set eyes upon them till this moment: they must have been brought by thee hither cleaving to thy garments." Quoth the Ifrit, "These words are absurd; thou harlot! thou strumpet!" Then he stripped her stark naked and, stretching her upon the floor, bound her hands and feet to four stakes, like one crucified; and set about torturing and trying to make her confess. I could not bear to stand listening to her cries and groans; so I climbed the stair on the quake with fear; and when I reached the top I replaced the trap-door and covered it with earth. Then repented I of what I had done with penitence exceeding; and thought of the lady and her beauty and loveliness, and the tortures she was suffering at the hands of the accursed Ifrit, after her quiet life of five-and-twenty years; and how all that had happened to her was for cause of me. I bethought me of my father and his kingly estate and how I had become a woodcutter; and how, after my time had been awhile serene, the world had again waxed turbid and troubled to me. So I wept bitterly and repeated this couplet:

What time Fate's tyranny shall most oppress thee
Perpend! one day shall joy thee, one distress thee!

Then I walked till I reached the home of my friend, the Tailor, whom I found most anxiously expecting me; indeed he was, as the saying goes, on coals of fire for my account. And when he saw me he said, "All night long my heart hath been heavy, fearing for thee from wild beasts or other mischances. Now praise be to Allah for thy safety!" I thanked him for his friendly solicitude and, retiring to my corner, sat pondering and musing on what had befallen me; and I blamed and chided myself for my meddlesome folly and my frowardness in kicking the alcove. I was calling myself to account when behold, my friend, the Tailor, came to me and said, "O youth, in the shop there is an old man, a Persian, who seeketh thee: he hath thy hatchet and thy sandals which he had taken to the woodcutters, saying, I was going out at what time the Mu'azzin began the call to dawn-prayer, when I chanced upon these things and know not whose they are; so direct me to their owner. The woodcutters recognised thy hatchet and directed him to thee: he is sitting in my shop, so fare forth to him and thank him and take thine axe and sandals." When I heard these words I turned yellow with fear and felt stunned as by a blow; and, before I could recover myself, lo! the floor of my private room clove asunder, and out of it rose the Persian who was the Ifrit. He had tortured the lady with exceeding tortures, natheless she would not confess to him aught; so he took the hatchet and sandals and said to her, "As surely as I am Jirjis of the seed of Iblis, I will bring thee back the owner of this and these!" Then he went to the woodcutters with the pretence aforesaid and, being directed to me, after waiting a while in the shop till the fact was confirmed, he suddenly snatched me up as a hawk snatcheth a mouse and flew high in air; but presently descended and plunged with me under the earth (I being aswoon the while), and lastly set me down in the subterranean palace wherein I had passed that blissful night. And there I saw the lady stripped to the skin, her limbs bound to four stakes and blood welling from her sides. At the sight my eyes ran over with tears; but the Ifrit covered her person and said, "O wanton, is not this man thy lover?" She looked upon me and replied, "I wot him not nor have I ever seen him before this hour!" Quoth the Ifrit, "What! this torture and yet no confessing;" and quoth she, "I never saw this man in my born days, and it is not lawful in Allah's sight to tell lies on him." "If thou know him not," said the Ifrit to her, "take this sword and strike off his head." She hent the sword in hand and came close up to me; and I signalled to her with my eyebrows, my tears the while flowing adown my cheeks. She understood me and made answer, also by signs, "How couldest thou bring all this evil upon me?" and I rejoined after the same fashion, "This is the time for mercy and forgiveness." And the mute tongue of my case spake aloud saying:

Mine eyes were dragomans for my tongue betied
And told full clear the love I fain would hide:

When last we met and tears in torrents railed
For tongue struck dumb my glances testified:
She signed with eye-glance while her lips were mute
I signed with fingers and she kenned th' implied:
Our eyebrows did all duty 'twixt us twain;
And we being speechless Love spake loud and plain.

Then, O my mistress, the lady threw away the sword and said, "How shall I strike the neck of one I wot not, and who hath done me no evil? Such deed were not lawful in my law!" and she held her hand. Said the Ifrit, "'Tis grievous to thee to slay thy lover; and, because he hath lain with thee, thou endurest these torments and obstinately refusest to confess. After this it is clear to me that only like loveth and pitieth like." Then he turned to me and asked me, "O man, haply thou also dost not know this woman;" whereto I answered, "And pray who may she be? assuredly I never saw her till this instant." "Then take the sword," said he "and strike off her head and I will believe that, thou wottest her not and will leave thee free to go, and will not deal hardly with thee." I replied, "That will I do;" and, taking the sword went forward sharply and raised my hand to smite. But she signed to me with her eyebrows, "Have I failed thee in aught of love; and is it thus that thou requitest me?" I understood what her looks implied and answered her with an eye-glance, "I will sacrifice my soul for thee." And the tongue of the case wrote in our hearts these lines:

How many a lover with his eyebrows speaketh
To his beloved, as his passion pleadeth:
With flashing eyne his passion he inspireth
And well she seeth what his pleading needeth.

How sweet the look when each on other gazeth;
And with what swiftness and how sure it speedeth:
And this with eyebrows all his passion writeth;
And that with eyeballs all his passion readeth.

Then my eyes filled with tears to overflowing and I cast the sword from my hand saying, "O mighty Ifrit and hero, if a woman lacking wits and faith deem it unlawful to strike off my head, how can it be lawful for me, a man, to smite her neck whom I never saw in my whole life. I cannot do such misdeed though thou cause me drink the cup of death and perdition." Then said the Ifrit, "Ye twain show the good understanding between you; but I will let you see how such doings end." He took the sword, and struck off the lady's hands first, with four strokes, and then her feet; whilst I looked on and made sure of death and she farewelled me with her dying eyes. So the Ifrit cried at her, "Thou whorest and makest me a wittol with thine eyes;" and struck her so that her head went flying. Then turned he to me and said, "O mortal, we have it in our law that, when the wife committeth advowtry it is lawful for us to slay her. As for this damsel, I snatched her away on her bride-night when she was a girl of twelve and she knew no one but myself. I used to come to her once in every ten days and lie with her the night, under the semblance of a man, a Persian; and when I was well assured that she had cuckolded me, I slew her. But as for thee I am not well satisfied that thou hast wronged me in her; nevertheless I must not let thee go unharmed; so ask a boon of me and I will grant it." Then I rejoiced, O my lady, with exceeding joy and said, "What boon shall I crave of thee?" He replied, "Ask me this boon; into what shape I shall bewitch thee; wilt thou be a dog, or an ass or an ape?" I rejoined (and indeed I had hoped that mercy might be shown me), "By Allah, spare me, that Allah spare thee for sparing a Moslem and a man who never wronged thee." And I humbled myself before him with exceeding humility, and remained standing in his presence, saying, "I am sore oppressed by circumstance." He replied, "Talk me no long talk, it is in my power to slay thee; but I give thee instead thy choice."

TALE OF THE THREE APPLES

They relate that the Caliph Harun al-Rashid summoned his Vizier Ja'afar one night and said to him, "I desire to go down into the city and question the common folk concerning the conduct of those charged with its governance; and those of whom they complain we will depose from office, and those whom they commend we will promote." Quoth Ja'afar, "Hearkening and obedience!" So the Caliph went down with Ja'afar and Eunuch Masrur to the town and walked about the streets and markets and, as they were threading a narrow alley, they came upon a very old man with a fishing net and crate to carry small fish on his head, and in his hand a staff; and, as he walked at a leisurely pace, he repeated these lines:

They say me: Thou shinest a light to mankind
With thy lore as the night which the Moon doth uplight!
I answer, "A truce to your jests and your gibes;
Without luck what is learning? – a poor-devil wight!
If they take me to pawn with my lore in my pouch,
With my volumes to read and my ink-case to write,
For one day's provision they never could pledge me;
As likely on Doomsday to draw bill at sight:"
How poorly, indeed, doth it fare wi' the poor,

With his pauper existence and beggarly plight:
In summer he faileth provision to find;
In winter the fire-pot's his only delight:
The street-dogs with bite and with bark to him rise,
And each losel receives him with bark and with bite:
If he lift up his voice and complain of his wrong,
None pities or heeds him, however he's right;
And when sorrows and evils like these he must brave
His happiest homestead were down in the grave.

When the Caliph heard his verses he said to Ja'afar, "See this poor man and note his verses, for surely they point to his necessities." Then he accosted him and asked, "O Shaykh, what be thine occupation?" and the poor man answered, "O my lord, I am a fisherman with a family to keep and I have been out between midday and this time; and not a thing hath Allah made my portion wherewithal to feed my family. I cannot even pawn myself to buy them a supper and I hate and disgust my life and I hanker after death." Quoth the Caliph, "Say me, wilt thou return with us to Tigris's bank and cast thy net on my luck, and whatsoever turneth up I will buy of thee for an hundred gold pieces?" The man rejoiced when he heard these words and said, "On my head be it! I will go back with you;" and, returning with them river-wards, made a cast and waited a while; then he hauled in the rope and dragged the net ashore and there appeared in it a chest padlocked and heavy. The Caliph examined it and lifted it finding it weighty; so he gave the fisherman two hundred dinars and sent him about his business, whilst Masrur, aided by the Caliph, carried the chest to the palace and set it down and lighted the candles. Ja'afar and Masrur then broke it open and found therein a basket of palm leaves corded with red worsted. This they cut open and saw within it a piece of carpet which they lifted out, and under it was a woman's mantilla folded in four, which they pulled out; and at the bottom of the chest they came upon a young lady, fair as a silver ingot, slain and cut into nineteen pieces. When the Caliph looked upon her he cried, "Alas!" and tears ran down his cheeks and, turning to Ja'afar, he said, "O dog of Viziers, shall folk be murdered in our reign and be cast into the river to be a burden and a responsibility for us on the Day of Doom? By Allah, we must avenge this woman on her murderer and he shall be made to die the worst of deaths!" And presently he added, "Now, as surely as we are descended from the Sons of Abbas, if thou bring us not him who slew her, that we do her justice on him, I will hang thee at the gate of my palace, thee and forty of thy kith and kin by thy side." And the Caliph was wroth with exceeding rage. Quoth Ja'afar, "Grant me three days delay;" and quoth the Caliph, "We grant thee this." So Ja'afar went out from before him and returned to his own house, full of sorrow and saying to himself, "How shall I find him who murdered this damsel, that I may bring him before the Caliph? If I bring other than the murderer, it will be laid to my charge by the Lord: in very sooth I wot not what to do." He kept his house three days, and on the fourth day the Caliph sent one of the Chamberlains for him and, as he came into the presence, asked him, "Where is the murderer of the damsel?" to which answered Ja'afar, "O Commander of the Faithful, am I inspector of murdered folk that I should ken who killed her?" The Caliph was furious at his answer and bade hang him before the palace gate and commanded that a crier cry through the streets of Baghdad, "Whoso would see the hanging of Ja'afar, the Barmaki, Vizier of the Caliph, with forty of the Barmecides, his cousins and kinsmen, before the palace gate, let him come and let him look!" The people flocked out from all the quarters of the city to witness the execution of Ja'afar and his kinsmen, not knowing the cause. Then they set up the gallows and made Ja'afar and the others stand underneath in readiness for execution, but whilst every eye was looking for the Caliph's signal, and the crowd wept for Ja'afar and his cousins of the Barmecides, lo and behold! a young man fair of face and neat of dress and of favour like the moon raining light, with eyes black and bright, and brow flower-white, and cheeks red as rose and young down where the beard grows, and a mole like a grain of ambergris, pushed his way through the people till he stood immediately before the Vizier and said to him, "Safety to thee from this strait, O Prince of the Emirs and Asylum of the poor! I am the man who slew the woman ye found in the chest, so hang me for her and do her justice on me!" When Ja'afar heard the youth's confession he rejoiced at his own deliverance, but grieved and sorrowed for the fair youth, and whilst they were yet talking, behold, another man well stricken in years pressed forwards through the people and thrust his way amid the populace till he came to Ja'afar and the youth, whom he saluted, saying, "Ho thou the Vizier and Prince sans-peer! believe not the words of this youth. Of a surety none murdered the damsel but I; take her wreak on me this moment; for, an thou do not thus, I will require it of thee before Almighty Allah." Then quoth the young man, "O Vizier, this is an old man in his dotage who wotteth not whatso he saith ever, and I am he who murdered her, so do thou avenge her on me!" Quoth the old man, "O my son, thou art young and desirest the joys of the world and I am old and weary and surfeited with the world; I will offer my life as a ransom for thee and for the Vizier and his cousins. No one murdered the damsel but I, so Allah upon thee, make haste to hang me, for no life is left in me now that hers is gone."

The Vizier marvelled much at all this strangeness and, taking the young man and the old man, carried them before the Caliph, where, after kissing the ground seven times between his hands, he said, "O Commander of the Faithful, I bring thee the murderer of the damsel!" "Where is he?"; asked the Caliph and Ja'afar answered, "This young man saith, I am the murderer, and this old man giving him the lie saith, I am the murderer, and behold, here are the twain standing before thee." The Caliph looked at the old man and the young man and asked, "Which of you killed the girl?" The young man replied, "No one slew her save I;" and the old man answered, "Indeed none killed her but myself." Then said the Caliph to Ja'afar, "Take the twain and hang them both;" but Ja'afar rejoined, "Since one of them was the murderer, to hang the other were mere injustice." "By Him who raised the firmament and dispread the earth like a carpet," cried the youth, "I am he who slew the damsel;" and he went on to describe the manner of her murder and the basket, the mantilla and the bit of carpet, in fact all that the Caliph had found upon her. So the Caliph was certified that the young man was the murderer; whereat he wondered and asked him, "What was the cause of thy wrongfully doing this damsel to die, and what made thee confess the murder without the bastinado, and what brought thee here to yield up thy life, and what made thee say Do her wreak upon me?" The youth answered, "Know, O Commander of the Faithful, that this woman was my wife and the mother of my children; also my first cousin and the daughter of my paternal uncle, this old man who is my father's own brother. When I married her she was a maid and Allah blessed me with three male children by her; she loved me and served me and I saw no evil in her, for I also loved her with fondest love. Now on the first day of this month she fell ill with grievous sickness and I fetched in physicians to her; but recovery came to her little by little and, when I wished her to go to the Hammam-bath, she said: There is a something I long for before I go to the bath and I long for it with an exceeding longing. To hear is to comply, said I. And what is it? Quoth she, I have a queasy craving for an apple, to smell it and bite a bit of it. I replied: Hadst thou a thousand longings I would try to satisfy them! So I went on the instant into the city and sought for apples but could find none; yet, had they cost a gold piece each, would I have bought them. I was vexed at this and went home and said: O daughter of my uncle, by Allah I can find none! She was distressed, being yet very weakly, and her weakness increased greatly on her that night, and I felt anxious and alarmed on her account. As soon as morning dawned I went out again and made the round of the gardens, one by one, but found no apples anywhere. At last there met me an old gardener, of whom I asked about them and he answered: O my son, this fruit is a rarity with us and is not now to be found save in the garden of the Commander of the Faithful at Bassorah, where the gardener keepeth it for the Caliph's eating. I returned to my house troubled by my ill-success; and my love for my wife and my affection moved me to undertake the journey. So I got me ready and set out and travelled fifteen days and nights, going and coming, and brought her three apples, which I bought from the gardener for three dinars. But when I went in to my wife and set them before her, she took no pleasure in them and let them lie by her side; for her weakness and fever had increased on her and her malady lasted without abating ten days, after which time she began to recover health. So I left my house and, betaking me to my shop, sat there buying and selling; and about midday, behold, a slave, long as a lance and broad as a bench, passed by my shop holding in hand one of the three apples, wherewith he was playing. Quoth I: O my good slave, tell me whence thou tookest that apple, that I may get the like of it? He laughed and answered: I got it from my mistress, for I had been absent and on my return I found her lying ill with three apples by her side, and she said to me: My horned wittol of a husband made a journey for them to Bassorah and bought them for three dinars. So I ate and drank with her and took this one from her. When I heard such words from the slave, O Commander of the Faithful, the world grew black before my face, and I arose and locked up my shop and went home beside myself for excess of rage. I looked for the apples and, finding only two of the three, asked my wife: O my cousin, where is the third apple?; and raising her head languidly, she answered: I wot not, O son of my uncle, where 'tis gone! This convinced me that the slave had spoken the truth, so I took a knife and, coming behind her, got upon her breast without a word said and cut her throat. Then I hewed off her head and her limbs in pieces and, wrapping her in her mantilla and a rag of carpet, hurriedly sewed up the whole, which I set in a chest and, locking it tight, loaded it on my he-mule and threw it into the Tigris with my own hands. So Allah upon thee, O Commander of the Faithful, make haste to hang me, as I fear lest she appeal for vengeance on Resurrection Day. For, when I had thrown her into the river and none knew aught of it, as I went back home I found my eldest son crying and yet he knew naught of what I had done with his mother. I asked him: What hath made thee weep, my boy?; and he answered: I took one of the three apples which were by my mammy and went down into the lane to play with my brethren when, behold, a slave snatched it from my hand and said: Whence hadst thou this? Quoth I: My father travelled far for it, and brought it from Bassorah for my mother, who was ill, and two other apples for which he paid three ducats. He took no heed of my words, and I asked for the apple a second and a third time, but he cuffed me and kicked me and went off with it. I was afraid lest my mother should swinge me on account of the apple, so for fear of her I went with my brother outside the city and stayed there till evening closed in upon us; and indeed I am in fear of her; and now by Allah, O my father, say nothing to her of this or it may add to her ailment!

When I heard what my child said, I knew that the slave was he who had foully slandered my wife, the daughter of my uncle, and was certified that I had slain her wrongfully. So I wept with exceeding weeping, and presently this old man, my paternal uncle and her father, came in; and I told him what had happened and he sat down by my side and wept, and we ceased not weeping till midnight. We have kept up mourning for her these last five days and we lamented her in the deepest sorrow for that she was unjustly done to die. This came from the gratuitous lying of the slave, and this was the manner of my killing her; so I conjure thee, by the honour of thine ancestors, make haste to kill me and do her justice upon me, as there is no living for me after her!" The Caliph marvelled at his words and said, "By Allah the young man is excusable; I will hang none but the accursed slave, and I will do a deed which shall comfort the ill-at-ease and suffering, and which shall please the All-glorious King."

Then he turned to Ja'afar and said to him, "Bring before me this accursed slave who was the sole cause of this calamity; and, if thou bring him not before me within three days, thou shalt be slain in his stead." So Ja'afar fared forth weeping and saying, "Two deaths have already beset me, nor shall the crock come off safe from every shock. In this matter craft and cunning are of no avail; but He who preserved my life the first time can preserve it a second time. By Allah, I will not leave my house during the three days of life which remain to me and let the Truth (whose perfection be praised!) do e'en as He will." So he kept his house three days, and on the fourth day he summoned the Kazis and legal witnesses, and made his last will and testament, and took leave of his children, weeping. Presently, in came a messenger from the Caliph and said to him, "The Commander of the Faithful is in the most violent rage that can be, and he sendeth to seek thee, and he sweareth that the day shall certainly not pass without thy being hanged unless the slave be forthcoming." When Ja'afar heard this he wept, and his children and slaves and all who were in the house wept with him. After he had bidden adieu to everybody except his youngest daughter, he proceeded to farewell her; for he loved this wee one, who was a beautiful child, more than all his other children; and he pressed her to his breast and kissed her and wept bitterly at parting from her, when he felt something round inside the bosom of her dress and asked her, "O my little maid, what is in thy bosom pocket?"; "O my father," she replied, "it is an apple with the name of our Lord the Caliph written upon it. Rayhán our slave brought it to me four days ago and would not let me have it till I gave him two dinars for it." When Ja'afar heard speak of the slave and the apple, he was glad and put his hand into his child's pocket and drew out the apple and knew it and rejoiced, saying, "O ready Dispeller of trouble!" Then he bade them bring the slave and said to him, "Fie upon thee, Rayhan! Whence haddest thou this apple?" "By Allah, O my master," he replied, "though a lie may get a man once off, yet may truth get him off, and well off, again and again. I did not steal this apple from thy palace nor from the gardens of the Commander of the Faithful. The fact is that five days ago, as I was walking along one of the alleys of this city, I saw some little ones at play and this apple in hand of one of them. So I snatched it from him and beat him, and he cried and said: O youth, this apple is my mother's and she is ill. She told my father how she longed for an apple, so he travelled to Bassorah and bought her three apples for three gold pieces, and I took one of them to play withal. He wept again, but I paid no heed to what he said and carried it off and brought it here, and my little lady bought it of me for two dinars of gold. And this is the whole story." When Ja'afar heard his words he marvelled that the murder of the damsel and all this misery should have been caused by his slave; he grieved for the relation of the slave to himself, while rejoicing over his own deliverance, and he repeated these lines:

If ill betide thee through thy slave,
Make him forthright thy sacrifice:
A many serviles thou shalt find,
But life comes once and never twice.

Then he took the slave's hand and, leading him to the Caliph, related the story from first to last, and the Caliph marvelled with extreme astonishment, and laughed till he fell on his back, and ordered that the story be recorded and be made public amongst the people.

SELECTED TALES FROM BAGH O BAHAR, OR, TALES OF THE FOUR DERVISHES

The enchanting *Bāgh-o-Bahār* blossomed in the literary landscape of Mughal India. The story revolves around a sorrowful king with the Persian name Azad Bakht who resides at Constantinople. He has turned forty years of age, has no male heir and – to make matters even worse – discovers a grey hair on his head. One night, clad in rags, the king escapes the palace in search of advice. He comes across four dervishes who have been unhappy in love; they have renounced the world and each tells him a story. The four interconnected tales feature adventure, romance and moral lessons, as well as several other embedded stories. At the end of the fourth dervish's tale King Azad Bakht learns that one of his wives has given birth to his son, ending the cycle of depression and anxiety, which makes for a strong parallel to the *Nights*. To share his joy, the king arranges a great feast to celebrate the wedding of all separated lovers, so that in the end everyone's dreams and desires are fulfilled. The narrative showcases themes of love, bravery, perseverance and the eventual triumph of good over evil. It is characterized by vivid storytelling, rich imagery and moral lessons that reflect the customs and traditions of Mughal India.

INTRODUCTION

I now commence my tale; pay attention to it, and be just to its merits. In the "Adventures of the Four Dervish", it is thus written, and the narrator has related, that formerly in the Empire of Rum there reigned a great king, in whom were innate justice equal to that of Naushirwan, and generosity like that of Hatim. His name was Azad Bakht, and his imperial residence was at Constantinople (which they call Istanbul). In his reign the peasant was happy, the treasury full, the army satisfied, and the poor at ease. They lived in such peace and plenty, that in their homes the day was a festival, and the night was a *shabi barat.* Thieves, robbers, pickpockets, swindlers, and all such as were vicious and dishonest, he utterly exterminated, and no vestige of them allowed he to remain in his kingdom. The doors of the houses were unshut all night, and the shops of the bazaar remained open. The travellers and wayfarers chinked gold as they went along, over plains and through woods; and no one asked them, "How many teeth have you in your mouth," or "Where are you going?"

There were thousands of cities in that king's dominions, and many princes paid him tribute. Though he was so great a king, he never for a moment neglected his duties or his prayers to God. He possessed all the necessary comforts of this world; but male issue, which is the fruit of life, was not in the garden of his destiny, for which reason he was often pensive and sorrowful, and after the five regulated periods of prayer, he used to address himself to his Creator and say, "O God! thou hast, through thy infinite goodness blest thy weak creature with every comfort, but thou hast given no light to this dark abode. This desire alone is unaccomplished, that I have no one to transmit my name and support my old age. Thou hast everything in thy hidden treasury; give me a living and thriving son, that my name and the vestiges of this kingdom may remain."

In this hope the king reached his fortieth year; when one day he had finished his prayers in the Mirror Saloon, and while telling his beads, he happened to cast his eyes towards one of the mirrors, and perceived a white hair in his whiskers, which glittered like a silver wire; on seeing it, the king's eyes filled with tears, and he heaved a deep sigh, and then said to himself, "Alas! thou hast wasted thy years to no purpose, and for earthly advantages thou hast overturned the world. And all the countries thou hast conquered, what advantage are they to thee? Some other race will in the end squander these riches.

Death hath already sent thee a messenger; and even if thou livest a few years, the strength of thy body will be less. Hence, it appears clearly from this circumstance, that it is not my destiny to have an heir to my canopy and throne. I must one day die, and leave everything behind me; so it is better for me to quit them now, and dedicate the rest of my days to the adoration of my Maker."

Having in his heart made this resolve, he descended to his lower garden. Having dismissed his courtiers, he ordered that no one should approach him in future, but that all should attend the Public Hall of Audience, and continue occupied in their respective duties. After this speech the king retired to a private apartment, spread the carpet of prayer, and began to occupy himself in devotion: he did nothing but weep and sigh. Thus the king, Azud Bakht, passed many days; in the evening he broke his fast with a date and three mouthfuls of water, and lay all day and night on the carpet of prayer. Those circumstances became public, and by degrees the intelligence spread over the whole empire, that the king, having withdrawn his hand from public affairs, had become a recluse. In every quarter enemies and rebels raised their heads, and stepped beyond the bounds of obedience; whoever wished it, encroached on the kingdom, and rebelled; wherever there were governors, in their jurisdictions great disturbance took place; and complaints of mal-administration arrived at court from every province. All the courtiers and nobles assembled, and began to confer and consult.

At last it was agreed, "that as his Highness the Vizier is wise and intelligent, and in the king's intimacy and confidence, and is first in dignity, we ought to go before him, and hear what he thinks proper to say on the occasion," All the nobles went to his Highness the Vizier, and said: "Such is the state of the king and such the condition of the kingdom, that if more delay takes place, this empire, which has been acquired with such trouble, will be lost for nothing, and will not be easily regained." The Vizier was an old, faithful servant, and wise; his name was Khiradmand, a name self-significant. He replied, "Though the king has forbidden us to come into his presence, yet go you: I will also go – may it please God that the king be inclined to call me to his presence." After saying this, the Vizier brought them all along with him as far as the Public Hall of Audience, and leaving them there, he went into the Private Hall of Audience, and sent word by the eunuch to the royal presence, saying, "this old slave is in waiting, and for many days has not beheld the royal countenance; he is in hopes that, after one look, he may kiss the royal feet, then his mind will be at ease." The king heard this request of his Vizier, and inasmuch as his majesty knew his length of services, his zeal, his talents, and his devotedness, and had often followed his advice, after some consideration, he said, "call in Khiradmand." As soon as permission was obtained, the Vizier appeared in the royal presence, made his obeisance, and stood with crossed arms. He saw the king's strange and altered appearance, that from extreme weeping and emaciation, his eyes were sunk in their sockets, and his visage was pale.

Khiradmand could no longer restrain himself, but without choice, ran and threw himself at the king's feet. His majesty lifted up the Vizier's head with his hands, and said, "There, thou hast at last seen me; art thou satisfied? Now go away, and do not disturb me more – do thou govern the empire." Khiradmand, on hearing this, gnashing his teeth, wept and said, "This slave, by your favour and welfare, can always possess a kingdom; but ruin is spread over the empire from your majesty's such sudden seclusion, and the end of it will not be prosperous. What strange fancy has possessed the royal mind! If to this hereditary vassal your majesty will condescend to explain yourself, it will be for the best – that I may unfold whatever occurs to my imperfect judgment on the occasion. If you have bestowed honours on your slaves, it is for this exigency, that your majesty may enjoy yourself at your ease, and your slaves regulate the affairs of the state; for if your imperial highness is to bear this trouble, which God forbid! of what utility are the servants of the state?" The king replied, "Thou sayest true; but the sorrow which preys on my mind is beyond cure.

"Hear, O Khiradmand! my whole age has been passed in this vexatious career of conquest, and I am now arrived at these years; there is only death before me; I have even received a message from him, for my hairs are turned white. There is a saying; 'We have slept all night, and shall we not awake in the morning?' Until now I have not had a son, that I might be easy in mind; for which reason my heart is very sorrowful, and I have utterly abandoned everything. Whoever wishes, may take the country and my riches. I have no use for them. Moreover, I intend some day or other, to quit everything, retire to the woods and mountains, and not show my face to anyone.

In this manner I will pass this life of at best but a few days' duration. If some spot pleases me, I shall sit down on it; and by devoting my time in prayers to God, perhaps my future state will be happy; this world I have seen well, and have found no felicity in it." After pronouncing these words, the king heaved a deep sigh, and became silent.

Khiradmand had been the Vizier of his majesty's father, and when the king was heir-apparent he had loved him; moreover, he was wise and zealous. He said (to Azad Bakht), "It is ever wrong to despair of God's grace; He who has created the eighteen thousand species of living beings by one fiat, can give you children without any difficulty. Mighty sire, banish these fanciful notions from your mind, or else all your subjects will be thrown into confusion, and this empire, with what trouble and pains your royal forefathers and yourself have erected it, will be lost in a moment, and, from want of care, the whole country will be ruined; God forbid that you should incur evil fame! Moreover, you will have to answer to God, in the day of judgment, when he will say, 'Having made thee a king, I placed my creatures under thy care; but thou hadst no faith in my beneficence, and thou hast afflicted thy subjects by abandoning thy charge.' What answer will you make to this accusation? Then even your devotion and prayers will not avail you, for the heart of man is the abode of God, and kings will have to answer only for the justice of their conduct. Pardon your slave's want of respect, but to leave their homes, and wander from forest to forest, is the occupation of hermits, but not that of kings. You ought to act according to your allotted station: the remembering of God, and devotion to him, are not limited to woods or mountains: your majesty has undoubtedly heard this verse, 'God is near him, and he seeks him in the wilderness; the child is in his arms, and there is a proclamation of its being lost throughout the city.'

"If you will be pleased to act impartially, and follow this slave's advice, in that case the best thing is, that your Majesty should keep God in mind every moment, and offer up to him your prayers. No one has yet returned hopeless from his threshold. In the day, arrange the affairs of state, and administer justice to the poor and injured; then the creatures of God will repose in peace and comfort under the skirt of your prosperity. Pray at night; and after beseeching blessings for the pure spirit of the Prophet, solicit assistance from recluse Dervishes and holy men, who are abstracted from worldly objects and cares; bestow daily food on orphans, prisoners, poor parents of numerous children, and helpless widows. From the blessings of these good works and benevolent intentions, if God please, it is to be fervently hoped that the objects and desires of your heart will all be fulfilled, and the circumstances for which the royal mind is afflicted, will likewise be accomplished, and your noble heart will rejoice! Look towards the favour of God, for he can in a moment do what he wishes." At length, from such various representations on the part of Khiradmand the Vizier, Azad Bakht's heart took courage, and he said, "Well, what you say is true; let us see to this also; and hereafter, the will of God be done."

When the king's mind was comforted, he asked the Vizier what the other nobles and ministers were doing, and how they were. He replied, that "all the pillars of state are praying for the life and prosperity of your majesty; and from grief for your situation, they are all in confusion and dejected. Show the royal countenance to them, that they may be easy in their minds. Accordingly, they are now waiting in the *Diwani Amm*." On hearing this, the king said, "If God please, I will hold a court tomorrow: tell them all to attend." Khiradmand was quite rejoiced on hearing this promise, and lifting up his hands, blessed the king, saying, "As long as this earth and heaven exist, may your majesty's crown and throne remain. Then taking leave of the king, he retired with infinite joy, and communicated these pleasing tidings to the nobles. All the nobles returned to their homes with smiles and gladness of heart. The whole city rejoiced, and the subjects became boundless in their transports at the idea that the king would hold a general court the next day. In the morning, all the servants of state, noble and menial, and the pillars of state, small and great, came to the court, and stood each according to his respective place and degree, and waited with anxiety to behold the royal splendour.

When one *pahar* of the day had elapsed, all at once the curtain drew up, and the king, having ascended, seated himself on the auspicious throne. The sounds of joy struck up in the *Naubat-Khana*, and all the assembly offered the *nazars* of congratulation, and made their obeisance in the hall of audience. Each was rewarded according to his respective degree and rank, and the hearts of all became joyful and easy. At midday his majesty arose and retired to the interior of the palace; and after enjoying the royal repast, retired to rest. From that day the king made this an established rule, viz., to hold his court every morning, and pass the afternoons in reading and in the offices of devotion; and after expressing penitence, and beseeching forgiveness from God, to pray for the accomplishment of his desires.

One day, the king saw it written in a book, that if anyone is so oppressed with grief and care as not to be relieved by any human contrivance, he ought to commit his sorrows to Providence, visit the tombs of the dead, and pray for the blessing of God on them, through the mediation of the Prophet; and conceiving himself nothing, keep his heart free from the thoughtlessness of mankind; weep as a warning to others, and behold with awe the power of God, saying, "Anterior to me, what mighty possessors of kingdoms and wealth have been born on earth! but the sky, involving them all in its revolving circle, has mixed them with the dust." It is a byword, that, "on beholding the moving handmill, Kabira, weeping, exclaimed, 'Alas! nothing has yet survived the pressure of the two millstones.'"

"Now, if you look for those heroes, not one vestige of them remains, except a heap of dust. All of them, leaving their riches and possessions, their homes and offsprings, their friends and dependants, their horses and elephants, are lying alone! All these worldly advantages have been of no use to them; moreover, no one by this time knows even their names, or who they were; and their state within the grave cannot be discovered (for worms, insects, ants, and snakes have eaten them up); or who knows what has happened to them, or how they have settled their accounts with God? After meditating on these words in his mind, he should look on the whole of this world as a perfect farce; then the flower of his heart will ever bloom, and it will not wither in any circumstance." When the king read this admonition in the book, he recollected the advice of Khiradmand the Vizier, and found that they coincided. He became anxious in his mind to put this in execution; "but to mount on horseback, said his majesty to himself, and take a retinue with me, and go like a king, is not becoming; it is better to change my dress, and go at night and alone to visit the graves of the dead, or some godly recluse, and keep awake all night; perhaps by the mediation of these holy men, the desires of this world and salvation in the next, may be obtained."

Having formed this resolution, the king one night put on coarse and soiled clothes, and taking some money with him, he stole silently out of the fort, and bent his way over the plain; proceeding onwards, he arrived at a cemetery, and was repeating his prayers with a sincere heart. At that time, a fierce wind continued blowing, and might be called a storm. Suddenly the king saw a flame at a distance which shone like the morning star; he said to himself, "In this storm and darkness this light cannot shine without art, or it may be a talisman; for if nitre and sulphur be sprinkled in the lamp, around the wick, then let the wind be ever so strong, the flame will not be extinguished – or may it not be the lamp of some holy man which burns? Let it be what it may, I ought to go and examine it; perhaps by the light of this lamp, the lamp of my house also may be lighted, and the wish of my heart fulfilled." Having formed this resolution, the king advanced in that direction; when he drew near, he saw four erratic fakirs, with *kafnis* on their bodies, and their head reclined on their knees; sitting in profound silence, and senselessly abstracted. Their state was such as that of a traveller, who, separated from his country and his sect, friendless and alone, and overwhelmed with grief, is desponding and at a loss. In the same manner sat these four Fakirs, like statues, and a lamp placed on a stone burnt brightly; the wind touched it not, as if the sky itself had been its shade, so that it burnt without danger of being extinguished.

On seeing this sight, Azad Bakht was convinced and said to himself that "assuredly thy desires will be fulfilled, by the blessing resulting from the footsteps of these men of God; and the withered tree of thy hopes shall revive by their looks, and yield fruit. Go into their company, and tell thy story, and join their society; perhaps they may feel pity for thee, and offer up for thee such a prayer as may be accepted by the Almighty." Having formed this determination, he was about to step forward, when his judgment told him, O fool, do not be hasty! Look a little before thee. What dost thou know as to who they are, from whence they have come, and where they are going? How can we know but they may be Devs or Ghuls of the wilderness, who, assuming the appearance of men, are sitting together? In every way, to be in haste, and go amongst them and disturb them, is improper. At present, hide thyself in some corner, and learn the story of these Dervishes." At last the king did so, and hid himself in a corner with such silence, that no one heard the sound of his approach; he directed his attention towards them to hear what they were saying amongst themselves. By chance one of the Fakirs sneezed, and said, "God be praised." The other three Kalandars, awakened by the noise he made, trimmed the lamp; the flame was burning bright, and each of them sitting on his mattress, lighted their *hukkas*, and began to smoke. One of these Azads said, "O friends in mutual pain, and faithful wanderers over the world! we four persons, by the revolution of the heavens, and changes of day and night, with dust on our heads, have wandered for some time, from door to door. God be praised, that by the aid of our good fortune, and the decree of fate, we have today met each other on this spot. The events of tomorrow are not in the least known, nor what will happen; whether we remain together, or become totally separated; the night is a heavy load, and to retire to sleep so early is not salutary. It is far better that we relate, each on his own part, the events which have passed over our heads in this world, without admitting a particle of untruth in our narrations; then the night will pass away in words, and when little of it remains, let us retire to rest." They all replied, "O leader, we agree to whatever you command. First you begin your own history, and relate what you have seen; then shall we be edified."

ADVENTURES OF THE FIRST DERVISH

The first Dervish, sitting at his ease, began thus to relate the events of his travels:

"Beloved of God, turn towards me, and
hear this helpless one's narrative.
Hear what has passed over my head with attentive ears,
Hear how Providence has raised and depressed me.
I am going to relate whatever misfortunes I have
suffered; hear the whole narrative."

O my friends, the place of my birth, and the country of my forefathers, is the land of Yaman; the father of this wretch was Maliku-t-Tujjar, a great merchant, named Khwaja Ahmad. At that time no merchant or banker was equal to him. In most cities he had established factories and agents, for the purchase and sale (of goods); and in his warehouses were *lakhs* of *rupis* in cash, and merchandise of different countries. He had two children born to him; one was this pilgrim, who, clad in the *kafni* and *saili*, is now in your presence, and addressing you, holy guides; the other was a sister, whom my father, during his lifetime, had married to a merchant's son of another city; she lived in the family of her father-in-law. In short, what bounds could be set to the fondness of a father, who had an only son, and was so exceedingly rich! This wanderer received his education with great tenderness under the shadow of his father and mother; and began to learn reading and writing, and the science and practice of the military profession; and likewise the art of commerce, and the keeping of accounts. Up to the age of fourteen years, my life passed away in extreme delight and freedom from anxiety; no care of the world entered my heart. All at once, even in one year, both my father and mother died by the decree of God.

I was overwhelmed with such extreme grief, that I cannot express its anguish. At once I became an orphan! No elder of the family remained to watch over me. From this unexpected misfortune I wept night and day; food and drink were utterly disregarded. In this sad state I passed forty days: on the fortieth day, after the death of my parents, my relations and strangers of every degree assembled to perform the rites of mourning. When the *Fatiha* for the dead was finished, they tied on this pilgrim's head the turban of his father; they made me understand, that, "In this world the parents of all have died, and you yourself must one day follow the same path. Therefore, have patience, and look after your establishment; you are now become its master in the room of your father; be vigilant in your affairs and transactions." After consoling me in this friendly manner, they took their leave. All the agents, factors and employees of my late father came and waited on me; they presented their *nazars*, and said, "Be pleased to behold with your own auspicious eye the cash in the coffers, and the merchandise in the warehouses." When all at once my sight fell on this boundless wealth, my eyes expanded. I gave orders for the fitting up of a *diwan-khana*; the *farrashes* spread the carpets, and hung up the *pardas* and magnificent *chicks*. I took handsome servants into my service; and caused them to be clothed in rich dresses out of my treasury. This mendicant had no sooner reposed himself in the vacant seat of his father than he was surrounded by fops, coxcombs, "thiggars and sornars," liars and flatterers, who became his favourites and friends. I began to have them constantly in my company. They amused me with the gossip of every place, and every idle, lying tittle tattle; they continued urging me thus: "In this season of youth, you ought to drink of the choicest wines, and send for beautiful mistresses to participate in the pleasures thereof, and enjoy yourself in their company."

In short, the evil genius of man is man: my disposition changed from listening constantly to their pernicious advice. Wine, dancing, and gaming occupied my time. At last matters came to such a pitch, that, forgetting my commercial concerns, a mania for debauchery and gambling came over me. My servants and companions, when they perceived my careless habits, secreted all they could lay hand on; one might say a systematic plunder took place. No account was kept of the money which was squandered; from whence it came, or where it went:

"When the wealth comes gratuitously, the heart has no mercy on it."

Had I possessed even the treasures of Karun, they would not have been sufficient to supply this vast expenditure. In the course of a few years such became all at once my condition, that, a bare skull cap for my head, and a rag about my loins, were all that remained. Those friends who used to share my board, and who so often swore to shed their blood by the spoonful for my advantage, disappeared; yea, even if I met them by chance on the highway, they used to withdraw their looks and turn aside their faces from me; moreover, my servants, of every description, left me, and went away; no one remained to enquire after me, and say, "what state is this you are reduced to?" I had no companion left but my grief and regret.

I now had not a half-farthing's worth of parched grain to grind between my jaws, and give a relish to the water I drank: I endured two or three severe fasts, but could no longer bear the cravings of hunger. From necessity, covering my face with the mask of shamelessness, I formed the resolution of going to my sister; but this shame continued to come into my mind, that, since the death of my father, I had kept up no friendly intercourse with her, or even written her a single line; nay, further, she had written me two or three letters of condolence and affection, to which I had not deigned to make any reply in my inebriated moments of prosperity. From this sense of shame my heart felt no inclination to go to my sister, but except her house, I had no other to which I could resort. In the best way I could, on foot, empty-handed, with much fatigue and a thousand toils, having traversed the few intervening stages, I arrived at the city where my sister lived, and reached her house. My sister, seeing my wretched state, invoked a blessing upon me, embraced me with affection, and wept bitterly; she distributed the customary offerings to the poor on the occasion of my safe arrival, such as oil, vegetables, and small coins, and said to me, "Though my heart is greatly rejoiced at this meeting, yet, brother, in what sad plight do I see you?" I could make her no reply, but shedding tears, I remained silent. My sister sent me quickly to the bath, after having ordered a splendid dress to be sewn for me. I, having bathed and washed, put on these clothes. She fixed on an elegant apartment, near her own, for my residence. I had in the morning *sharbat*, and various kinds of sweetmeats for my breakfast; in the afternoon, fresh and dried fruits for my luncheon; and at dinner and supper she having procured for me *pulaos*, *kebabs*, and bread of the most exquisite flavour and delicious cookery; she saw me eat them in her own presence; and in every manner she took care of me. I offered thousands upon thousands of thanksgivings to God for enjoying such comfort, after such affliction as I had suffered. Several months passed in this tranquillity, during which I never put my foot out of my apartment.

One day, my sister, who treated me like a mother, said to me, "O brother, you are the delight of my eyes, and the living emblem of the dead dust of our parents; by your arrival the longing of my heart is satisfied; whenever I see you, I am infinitely rejoiced; you have made me completely happy; but God has created men to work for their living, and they ought not to sit idle at home. If a man becomes idle and stays at home, the people of the world cast unfavourable reflections on him; more especially the people of this city, both great and little, though it concerns them not, will say, on your remaining with me and doing nothing, 'That having lavished and spent his father's worldly wealth, he is now living on the scraps from his brother-in-law's board.' This is an excessive want of proper pride, and will be our ridicule, and the subject of shame to the memory of our parents; otherwise I would keep you near my heart, and make you shoes of my own skin, and have you wear them. Now, my advice is that you should make an effort at travelling; please God the times will change, and in place of your present embarrassment and destitution, gladness and prosperity may be the result." On hearing this speech my pride was roused; I approved of her advice, and replied, very well, you are now in the place of my mother, and I will do whatever you say. Having thus received my consent, she went into the interior of her house, and brought out, by the assistance of her female slaves and servants, fifty *toras* of gold and laid them before me, saying, "A caravan of merchants is on the point of setting out for Damascus. Do you purchase with this money some articles of merchandise. Having put them under the care of a merchant of probity, take from him a proper receipt for them: and do you also proceed to Damascus. When you arrive there in safety, receive the amount sales of your goods, and the profit which may accrue from your merchant, or sell them yourself as may be most convenient or advantageous." I took the money and went to the bazaar; and having bought articles of merchandise, I delivered them over in charge to an eminent merchant, and set my mind at ease on receiving a satisfactory receipt from him. The merchant embarked with the goods on board a vessel, and set off by sea, and I prepared to go by land. When I took leave of my excellent sister, she gave me a rich dress and a superb horse with jewelled harness; she put some sweetmeats in a leather bag and hung it to the pummel of my saddle, and she suspended a flask of water from the crupper; she tied a sacred rupee on my arm, and having marked my forehead with *tika*, "Proceed," said she, suppressing her tears, "I have put thee under the protection of God; thou showest thy back in going, in the same happy state show me soon your face." I also said, after repeating the prayer of welfare, "God be your protector also. I obey your commands." Coming out from thence, I mounted my horse, and having placed my reliance on the protection of the Almighty, I set forward, and throwing two stages into one, I soon reached the neighbourhood of Damascus.

In short, when I arrived at the city gate, the night was far advanced, and the door-keepers and guards had shut them. I made much entreaty, and added, "I am a traveller, who has come a long journey, at a great rate; if you would kindly open the gates, I could get into the city and procure some refreshment for myself and my horse." They rudely replied from within, "There is no order to open the gates at this hour; why have you come so late in the night?" When I heard this plain answer of theirs, I alighted from my horse under the walls of the city, and spreading my housing, I sat down; but to keep awake, I often rose up and walked about. When it was exactly midnight, there was a dead silence. What do I see but a chest descending slowly from the walls of the fortress! When I beheld this strange sight, I was filled with surprise, thinking what talisman is this! perhaps God, taking pity on my perplexity and my misfortunes, has sent me here some bounty from his hidden treasure. When the chest rested on the ground, I approached it with much fear, and perceived it was of wood. Instigated by curiosity, I opened it; I beheld in it a beautiful lovely woman (at the sight of whom the senses would vanish), wounded and weltering in her blood, with her eyes closed, and in extreme agonies. By degrees her lips moved, and these sounds issued slowly from her mouth, "O faithless wretch! O barbarous tyrant! Is this deed which thou hast done, the return I merited for all my affection and kindness! Well, well! give me another blow and complete thy cruelty: I entrust to God the executing of justice between myself and thee." After pronouncing these words, even in that insensible state, she drew the end of her *dopatta* over her face; she did not look towards me.

Gazing on her, and hearing her exclamations, I became torpid. It occurred to me, what savage tyrant could wound so beautiful a lady! what demon possessed his heart, and how could he lift his hand against her! she still loves him, and even in this agony of death, she recollects him! I was muttering this to myself; the sound reached her ear; drawing at once her veil from her face, she looked at me. The moment her look met mine, I nearly fainted, and my heart throbbed with difficulty; I supported myself by a strong effort, and taking courage, I asked her, "tell me true, who art you, and what sad occurrence is this I see; if you will explain it, then it will give ease to my heart." On hearing these words, though she had scarce strength to speak, yet she slowly uttered, "I thank you! how can I speak? my condition, owing to my wounds, is what you see; I am your guest for a few moments only; when my spirit shall depart, then, for God's sake, act like a man, and bury unfortunate me in some place, in this chest; then I shall be freed from the tongue of the good and bad, and you will earn for yourself a future reward." After pronouncing these words, she became silent.

In the night I could apply no remedy; I brought the chest near me, and began to count the *gharis* of the remaining night. I determined, when the morning came, to go into the city and do all in my power for the cure of this beautiful woman. The short, remaining night became so heavy a load, that my heart was quite restless. At last, after suffering much uneasiness, the morning approached – the cock crowed, and the voices of men were heard. After performing the morning prayer, I enclosed the chest in a coarse canvas sack, and just as the gates opened, I entered the city. I began to enquire of every man and shopkeeper where I could find a mansion for hire; and after much search, I found a convenient, handsome house, which I rented. The first thing I did, was to take that beautiful woman out of the chest, and lay her on a soft bed made up of flocks of cotton, which I had removed to a corner. I then placed a trusty person near her, and went in search of a surgeon. I wandered about, asking of everyone I met who was the cleverest surgeon in the city, and where he lived. One person said, "There is a certain barber who is unique in the practice of surgery, and the science of physic; and in these arts is quite perfect. If you carry a dead person to him, by the help of God, he will apply such remedies as will bring him to life. He dwells in this quarter of the city, and his name is *'Isa.*"

On hearing this agreeable intelligence, I went in search of him, and after several enquiries, I found out his abode from the directions I had received. I saw a man with a white beard sitting under the portico of his door, and several men were grinding materials for plasters beside him. For the sake of complimenting him, I made him a respectful *salam*, and said, "having heard of your name and excellent qualities, I am come to solicit your assistance. The case is this: I set out from my country for the purpose of trade, and took my wife with me, from the great affection I had for her; when I arrived near this city, I halted at a little distance, as the evening had set in. I did not think it safe to travel at night in an unseen country; I therefore rested under a tree on the plains. At the last quarter of the night, I was attacked by robbers; they plundered me of all the money and the property they could find, and wounded my wife, from avidity for her jewels. I could make no resistance, and passed the remainder of the night as well as I could. Early in the morning I came into this city, and rented a house; leaving her there, I am come to you with all speed. God has given you this perfection in your profession; favour this unfortunate traveller, and come to his humble dwelling; see my wife, and if her life should be saved, then you will acquire great fame, and I will be your slave as long as I live." *'Isa*, the surgeon, was very humane and devout; he took pity on my misfortune, and accompanied me to my house. On examining the wounds, he gave me hopes, and said, "By the blessing of God, this lady's wounds will be cured in forty days; and I will then cause to be administered to her the ablution of cure."

In short, the good man having thoroughly washed all the wounds with the decoction of *nim*, he cleansed them; those that he found fit for stitching, he sewed up; and on the others he laid lint and plasters, which he took out of his box, and tied them up with bandages, and said with much kindness, "I will continue to call morning and evening; be thou careful that she remain perfectly quiet, so that the stitches may not give way; let her food be chicken broth administered in small quantities at a time, and give her often the spirit of *Bed-Mushk*, with rose water, so that her strength may be supported." After giving these directions, he took his leave. I thanked him much with joined hands, and added, "From the consolation you have bestowed, my life also has been restored; otherwise, I saw nothing but death before me; God keep you safe." And after giving him *'Itr* and *betel*, I took leave of him. Night and day I attended on that beautiful lady with the utmost solicitude; rest to myself I renounced as impious, and in the threshold of God I daily prayed for her cure.

It came to pass that the merchant who had charge of my merchandise, arrived, and delivered over to me the goods I had entrusted to his care. I sold them as occasion required, and began to spend the amount in medicines and remedies. The good surgeon was regular in his attendance, and in a short time all the wounds filled up, and began to heal; a few days after she performed the ablution of cure. Joy of a wonderful nature arose in my heart! A rich *khil'at*, and a purse of gold pieces I laid before *'Isa*, the surgeon. I ordered elegant carpets to be spread for that fair one, and caused her to sit upon the *masnad*. I distributed large sums to the poor on the joyous occasion, and that day I was as happy as if I had gained possession of the sovereignty of the seven climes. On that beautiful lady's cure, such rosy, pure colour appeared in her complexion, that her face shone like the sun, and sparkled with the lustre of the purest gold. I could not gaze on her without being dazzled with her beauty. I devoted myself entirely to her services, and zealously performed whatever she commanded. In the full pride of beauty and consciousness of high rank, if ever she condescended to cast a look on me, she used to say, "Take care, if my good opinion is desirable to you, then never breathe a syllable in my affairs; whatever I order, perform without objection; never utter a breath in my concerns, otherwise you will repent." It appeared, however, from her manners, that the return due to me for my services and obedience, was fully impressed on her mind. I also did nothing without her consent, and executed her commands with implicit obedience.

A certain space of time passed away in this mystery and submission – I instantly procured for her whatever she desired. I spent all the money I had from the sale of my goods, both principal and interest. In a foreign country where I was unknown, who would trust me? that by borrowing, affairs might go on. At last, I was distressed for money, even for our daily expenses, and thence my heart became much embarrassed. With this anxious solicitude I pined daily, and the colour fled from my face; but to whom could I speak for aid? What my heart suffered, that it must suffer. "The grief of the poor man preys on his own soul." One day the beautiful lady, from her own penetration, perceived my distressed state and said, "O youth! my obligations to you for the services you have rendered me are engraven on my heart as indelible as on stone; but their return I am unable to make at present. If there be anything required for necessary expenses, do not be distressed on that account, but bring me a slip of paper, pen, and ink." I was then convinced that this fair lady must be a princess of some country, or else she would not have addressed me with such boldness and haughtiness. I instantly brought her the writing materials, and placed them before her – she having written a note in a fair hand, delivered it to me, and said, "There is a *Tirpauliya* near the fort; in the adjoining street is a large mansion, and the master of that house is called Sidi Bahar; go and deliver this note to him."

I went according to her commands, and by the name and address she had given me, I soon found out the house; by the porter I sent word of the circumstance of my having brought a letter. The moment he heard my message, a handsome young negro, with a flashy turban on his head, came out to me; though his colour was dark, his countenance was full of animation. He took the note from my hand, but said nothing, asked no questions, and at the same pace without a pause entered the house. In a short time he came out, accompanied by slaves, who carried on their heads eleven sealed trays covered with brocade. He told the slaves, "Go with this young man, and deliver these trays." I, having made my salutation, took my leave of him, and brought the slaves with their burdens to our house. I dismissed the men from the door, and carried in the trays entrusted to me to the presence of the fair lady. On seeing them she said, "Take these eleven bags of gold pieces and appropriate the money to necessary expenses; God is most bountiful." I took the gold, and began to lay it out in immediate necessaries. Although I became more easy in my mind, yet this perplexity continued in my heart. "O God, said I to myself, what a strange circumstance is this! that a stranger, whose person is unknown to me, should, on the mere sight of a bit of paper, have delivered over to me so much money without question or enquiry. I cannot ask the fair lady to explain the mystery, as she has beforehand forbidden me." Through fear, I was unable to breathe a syllable.

Eight days after this occurrence, the beloved fair one thus addressed me: "God has bestowed on man the robe of humanity which may not be torn or soiled; and although tattered clothes are no disparagement to his manhood, yet in public, in the eyes of the world he has no respect paid to him if shabbily clothed. So take two bags of gold with thee, and go to the *chauk*, to the shop of Yusuf the merchant, and buy there some sets of jewels of high value, and two rich suits of clothes, and bring them with thee." I instantly mounted my horse, and went to the shop described. I saw there a handsome young man, clothed in a saffron-coloured dress, seated on a cushion; his beauty was such, that a whole multitude stopped in the street from his shop as far as the bazaar to gaze at him. I approached him with perfect pleasure, having made my "*salam 'alaika*." I sat down, and mentioned the articles required. My pronunciation was not like that of the inhabitants of that city. The young merchant replied with great kindness, "Whatever you require is ready, but tell me, sir, from what country are you come, and what are the motives of your stay in this foreign city? If you will condescend to inform me on these points, it will not be remote from kindness." It was not agreeable to me to divulge my circumstances, so I made up some story, took the jewels and the clothes, paid their price, and begged to take my leave. The young man seemed displeased and said, "O sir, if you wished to be so reserved, it was not necessary to show such warmth of friendly greeting in your first approach. Amongst well-bred people these amicable greetings are of much consideration." He pronounced this speech with such elegance and propriety, that it quite delighted my heart, and I did not think it courteous to be unkind and leave him so hastily; therefore, to please him, I sat down again and said, I agree to your request with all my heart, and am ready to obey your commands.

He was greatly pleased with my compliance, and smiling he said, "If you will honour my poor mansion with your company today, then having a party of pleasure, we shall regale our hearts for some hours in good cheer and hilarity." I had never left the fair lady alone since we first met, and recollecting her solitary situation, I made many excuses, but that young man would not accept any; at last, having extorted from me a promise to return as soon as I had carried home the articles I had purchased, and having made me swear to that effect, he gave me leave to depart. I, having left the shop, carried the jewels and the clothes to the presence of the fair lady. She asked the price of the different articles, and what passed at the merchant's. I related all the particulars of the purchase, and the teasing invitation I had received from him. She replied, "It is incumbent on man to fulfil whatever promise he may make; leave me under the protection of God, and fulfil your engagement; the law of the prophet requires we should accept the offers of hospitality." I said, "My heart does not wish to go and leave you alone, but such are your orders, and I am forced to go; until I return, my heart will be attached to this very spot." Saying this, I went to the merchant's: he, seated on a chair, was waiting for me. On seeing me, he said, "Come, good sir, you have made me wait long."

He instantly arose, seized my hand, and moved on; proceeding along, he conducted me to a garden; it was a garden of great beauty; in the basons and canals, fountains were playing; fruits of various kinds were in full bloom, and the branches of the trees were bent down with their weight; birds of various species were perched on the boughs, and sung their merry notes, and elegant carpets were spread in every apartment of the grand pavilion which stood in the centre of the garden. There on the border of the canal, we sat down in an elegant saloon; he got up a moment after and went out, and then returned richly dressed. On seeing him, I exclaimed, "Praised be the Lord, may the evil eye be averted!" On hearing this, exclamation, he smiled, and said, "It is fit you, too, should change your dress." To please him, I also put on other clothes. The young merchant, with much sumptuousness, prepared an elegant entertainment, and provided every article of pleasure that could be desired; he was warm in his expressions of attachment to me, and his conversation was quite enchanting. At this moment a cupbearer appeared with a flask of wine and a crystal cup, and delicious meats of various kinds were served up. The salt-cellars were set in order, and the sparkling cup began to circulate. When it had performed three or four revolutions, four young dancing boys, very beautiful, with loose, flowing tresses, entered the assembly, and began to sing and play. Such was the scene, and such the melody, that had Tan-Sen been present at that hour, he would have forgot his strains; and Baiju-Ba,ora would have gone mad. In the midst of this festivity, the young merchant's eyes filled suddenly with tears, and involuntarily two or three drops trickled down his cheeks; he turned round and said to me, "Now between us a friendship for life is formed; to hide the secrets of our hearts is approved by no religion. I am going to impart a secret to you, in the confidence of friendship and without reserve. If you will give me leave I will send for my mistress into our company, and exhilarate my heart with her presence; for in her absence, I cannot enjoy any pleasure."

He pronounced these words with such eager desire, that though I had not seen her, yet my heart longed for her. I replied, "Your happiness is essential to me, what can be better than what you propose; send for her without delay; nothing, it is true, is agreeable without the presence of the beloved one." The young merchant made a sign towards the *chick* and shortly a black woman, as ugly as an ogress, on seeing whom one would die without the intervention of fate, approached the young man and sat down. I was frightened at her sight, and said within myself, is it possible this she-demon can be beloved by so beautiful a young man, and is this the creature he praised so highly, and spoke of with such affection! I muttered the form of exorcism, and became silent. In this same condition, the festive scene of wine and music continued for three days and nights; on the fourth night, intoxication and sleep gained the victory; I, in the sleep of forgetfulness, involuntarily slumbered; next morning the young merchant wakened me, and made me drink some cups of a cooling and sedative nature. He said to his mistress, "To trouble our guest any longer would be improper."

He then took hold of both my hands, and we stood up. I begged leave to depart; well pleased with my complaisance, he gave me permission to return home. I then quickly put on my former clothes, and bent my way homewards, waited on the angelic lady. But it had never before occurred in my case, to leave her by herself and remain out all night. I was quite ashamed of myself for being absent three days and nights, and I made her many apologies, and related the whole circumstances of the entertainment, and his not permitting me to come home sooner. She was well acquainted with the manners of the world, and smiling said, "What does it signify, if you had to remain to oblige your friend; I cheerfully pardon you, where is the blame on your part; when a man goes on occasions of this sort to any person's house, he returns when the other pleases to let him. But you having eaten and drunk at his entertainments for nothing, will you remain silent, or give him a feast in return? Now I think it proper you should go to the young merchant, and bring him with you, and feast him two-fold greater than he did you. Give yourself no concern about the materials for such an entertainment; by the favour of God, all the requisites will soon be ready, and in an excellent style, the hospitable party will obtain splendour." According to her desire, I went to the jeweller, and said to him, "I have complied with your request most cheerfully, now do you also in the way of friendship, grant my request." He said, "I will obey you with heart and soul."

Then I said, "If you will honour your humble servant's house with a visit, it will be the essence of condescension." That young man made many excuses and evasions, but I would not give up the point. When at length he consented, I brought him with me to my house; but on the way I could not avoid making the reflection, that if I had had the means, I could receive my guest in a style which would be highly gratifying to him. Now I am taking him with me, let us see what will be the result. Absorbed in these apprehensions, I drew near my house. Then how was I surprised to see a great crowd and bustle at the door; the street had been swept and watered; silver mace and club bearers were in waiting. I wondered greatly at what I saw, but knowing it to be mine own house, I entered, and perceived that elegant carpets befitting every apartment, were spread in all directions, and rich *masnads* were laid out. *Betel* boxes, *gulab-pashes*, *'itr-dans*, *pik-duns* flower pots, narcissus-pots, were all arranged in order. In the recesses of the walls, various kinds of oranges and confectionery of various colours were placed. On one side variegated screens of *talk*, with lights behind them were displayed, and on the other side tall branches of lamps in the shape of cypresses and lotuses, were lighted up. In the hall and alcove, camphorated candles were placed in golden candlesticks, and rich glass shades were placed over thorn; every attendant waited at his respective post. In the kitchen the pots continued jingling; and in the *abdar-khana* there was a corresponding preparation; jars of water, quite new, stood on silver stands, with percolators attached, and covered with lids. Further on, on a platform, were placed spoons and cups, with salvers and covers; *kulfis* of ice were arranged, and the goglets were being agitated in saltpetre.

In short, every requisite becoming a prince was displayed. Dancing girls and boys, singers, musicians and buffoons, in rich apparel, were in waiting, and singing in concert. I led the young merchant in, and seated him on the *masnad*; I was all amazement and said to myself "O God, in so short a time how have such preparations been made?" I was staring around and walking about in every direction, but I could nowhere perceive a trace of the beautiful lady; searching for her, I went into the kitchen, and I saw her there, with an upper garment on her neck, slippers on her feet, and a white handkerchief thrown over her head, plain and simply dressed, and without any jewels.

"She on whom God hath bestowed beauty has no need of ornaments;
Behold how beautiful appears the moon, without decorations."

She was busily employed in the superintendence of the feast, and was giving directions for the eatables, saying, "have a care that this dish may be savoury, and that its moisture, its seasoning and its fragrance, may be quite correct." In this toil that rose-like person was all over perspiration.

I approached her with reverence, and having expressed my admiration of her good sense, and the propriety of her conduct, I invoked blessings upon her. On hearing my compliments, she was displeased, and said, "various deeds are done on the part of human beings which it is not the power of angels to perform: what have I done that thou art so much astonished? Enough, I dislike much talk; but say, what manners is this to leave your guest alone, and amuse yourself by staring about; what will he think of your behaviour? return quickly to the company, and attend to your guest, and send for his mistress, and make her sit by him." I instantly returned to the young merchant, and showed him every friendly attention. Soon after, two handsome slaves entered with bottles of delicious wine, and cups set with precious stones, and served us the liquor. In the meantime, I then observed to the young merchant, "I am in every way your friend and servant; it were well that your handsome mistress, to whom your heart is attached, should honour us with her presence; it will be perfectly agreeable to me, and if you please, I will send a person to call her." On hearing this, he was extremely pleased, and said, "Very well, my dear friend, you have by your kind offer spoken the wish of my heart." I sent a eunuch to bring her. When half the night was past, that foul hag, mounted on an elegant *chaudol*, arrived like an unexpected evil.

To please my guest, I was compelled to advance, and receive her with the utmost kindness, and place her near the young man. On seeing her, he became as rejoiced as if he had received all the delights of the world. That hag also clung round the neck of that angelic youth. The ludicrous sight appeared, in plain truth, such as when over the moon of the fourteenth night, an eclipse comes. As many people as were in the assembly began to put their fore-fingers between their teeth, saying to themselves "How could such a hag subdue the affections of this young man!" The eyes of all were turned in that direction. Disregarding the amusements of the entertainment, they began to attend only to this strange spectacle. Some apart observed, "O friends, there is an antagonism between love and reason! what judgment cannot conceive, this cursed love will show. You must behold Laili with the eyes of Majnun." All present exclaimed, "Very true, that is the fact."

According to the directions of the lady, I devoted myself to attending on my guests; and although the young merchant pressed me to eat and drink equally with himself, yet I refrained from fear of the fair one's displeasure, and did not give myself up to eating and drinking, or the pleasures of the entertainment. I pleaded the duties of hospitality as my excuse for not joining him in the good cheer. In this scene of festivity three nights and days passed away. On the fourth night, the young merchant said to me with extreme fondness, "I now beg to take my leave; for your good sake I have utterly neglected my affairs these three days, and have attended you. Pray do you also sit near me for a moment, and rejoice my heart," I in my own heart imagined that if I do not comply with his request at this moment, then he will be grieved; and it is necessary I should please my new friend and guest; on which account I replied, "it is a pleasure to me to obey the command of your honour;" for "a command is paramount to ceremony." On hearing this, the young merchant presented me a cup of wine, and I drank it off; then the cup moved in such quick successive rounds, that in a short time all the guests in the assembly became inebriated and stupefied; I also became senseless.

When the morning came, and the sun had risen the height of two spears, my eyes opened, but I saw nothing of the preparations, the assembly, or the beautiful lady – only the empty house remained – but in a corner of the hall something lay folded up in a blanket; I unfolded it, and saw the corpses of the young merchant and of his black woman, with their heads severed from their bodies. On seeing this sight, my senses forsook me, and my judgment was of no avail in explaining to me what this was and what had happened. I was staring about me, in every direction with amazement, when I perceived a eunuch (whom I had seen in the preparations of the entertainment). I was somewhat comforted on seeing him, and asked him an explanation of these strange events. He replied briefly, "What goodwill it do thee to hear an explanation of what has happened, that thou askest it?"

I also reflected in my mind, that what he said was true; however, after a short pause, I said to the eunuch, well, do not tell it to me; but inform me in what apartment is the beloved lady. He answered, "Certainly; whatever I know I will relate to thee; but I am surprised that a man like thee, possessed of understanding, should, without her ladyship's permission, and without fear or ceremony, have indulged in a wine-drinking party after an intimacy of only a few days. What does all this mean?"

I became much ashamed of my folly and felt the justice of the eunuch's reprobation. I could make no other reply than to say, "indeed I have been guilty, pardon me." At last the eunuch, becoming gracious, pointed out the beloved lady's abode, and took his leave; he himself went to bury the two beheaded bodies. I was free from any participation in that crime, and was anxious to meet the beautiful lady. After a painful and difficult search, I arrived at eventide in that street, where she then was according to the eunuch's direction; and in a corner near the door I passed the whole night in a state of agitation. I did not hear the sound of any person's footsteps, nor did anyone ask me about my affairs. In this forlorn state the morning came; when the sun rose, the lovely fair one looked at me from a window in the balcony of the house. My heart only knows the state of joy I felt at that moment. I praised the goodness of God.

In the meanwhile, a eunuch came up to me, and said, "Go and stay in this adjoining mosque; perhaps your wishes may, in that place, be accomplished, and you may yet gain the desires of your heart." According to his advice I got up from the place where I had passed the night, and went to the mosque; but my eyes remained fixed in the direction of the door of the house, to see what might appear from behind the curtain of futurity. I waited for the arrival of evening with the anxiety of a person who keeps the fast of *Ramadan*. At last the evening came, and the heavy day was removed from my heart. All at once the same eunuch who had given me the directions to find out the lady's house, came to the mosque. After finishing the evening prayer, having come up to me, that obliging person, who was in all my secrets, gave me much comfort, and taking me by the hand, led me along with him, proceeding onwards at last having made me sit down in a small garden, he said: "Stay here until your desire of seeing your mistress be accomplished." Then he himself having taken his leave, went, perhaps, to impart my wishes to the beautiful lady. I amused myself with admiring the beauty of the flowers of the garden, and the brightness of the full moon, and the play of the fountains in the canals and rivulets, a display like that of the mouths of *Sawan* and *Bhadon*; but when I beheld the roses, I thought of the beautiful rose-like angel, and when I gazed on the bright moon, I recollected her moon-like face. All these delightful scenes without her were so many thorns in my eyes.

At last God made her heart favourable to me. After a little while that lovely fair one entered from the garden door adorned like the full moon, wearing a rich dress, enriched with pearls, and covered from head to feet with an embroidered veil; she stepped along the garden walk, and stood at a little distance from me. By her coming, the beauties of that garden, and the joy of my heart revived. After strolling for a few minutes about the garden, she sat down in the alcove on a richly-embroidered *masnad*. I ran, and like the moth that flutters around the candle, offered my life as a sacrifice to her, and like a slave stood before her with folded arms. At this moment the eunuch appeared, and began to plead for my pardon and restoration to her favour. Addressing myself to him, I said, I am guilty, and culpable; whatever punishment is fixed on me, let it be executed. The lady, though she was displeased, said with hauteur, "The best thing that can be done for him now is that he should receive a hundred bags of gold pieces, and having got his property all right, let him return to his native country."

On hearing these words, I became a block of withered wood; if anyone had cut my body, not a drop of blood would have issued; all the world began to appear dark before my sight; a sigh of despair burst involuntarily from my heart, and the tears flowed from my eyes. I had at that time no hope from anyone except God; driven to utter despair, I ventured to say, "Well, cruel fair, reflect a moment, that if to this unfortunate wretch there had been a desire for worldly wealth, he would not have devoted his life and property to you. Are the acknowledgments due to my services, and my having devoted my life to you, flown all of a sudden from this world, that you have shown such disfavour to a wretch like me? It is all well; to me life is no longer of any use; to the helpless, half-dead lover there is no resource against the faithlessness of the beloved one."

On hearing these words, she was greatly offended, and frowning with anger, she exclaimed, "Very fine indeed! What, thou art my lover! Has the frog then caught cold? O fool, for one in thy situation to talk thus is an idle fancy; little mouths should not utter big words: no more – be silent – repeat not such presumptuous language; if any other had dared to behave so improperly, I vow to God, I would have ordered his body to be cut in pieces, and given to the kites of the air; but what can I do? Your services ever come to my recollection. Thou hadst best now take the road to thy home; thy fate had decreed thee food and drink only until now in my house!" I then, weeping, said, "If it has been written in my destiny that I am not to attain the desires of my heart, but to wander miserably through woods and over mountains, then I have no remedy left." On hearing these words, she became vexed and said, "These hints and this flattering nonsense are not agreeable to me; go and repeat them to those who are fit to hear them." Then, getting up in the same angry mood, she returned to her house. I beseeched her to hear me, but she disregarded what I said. Having no resource, I likewise left the place, sad and hopeless.

In short, for forty days this same state of things continued. When I was tired of pacing the lanes of the city, I wandered into the woods, and when I became restless there, I returned to the lanes of the city like a lunatic. I thought not of nourishment during the day, or sleep at night; like a washerman's dog, that belongs neither to the house nor the *ghat*. The existence of man depends on eating and drinking; he is the worm of the grain. Not the least strength remained in my body. Becoming feeble, I went and lay down under the wall of the same mosque; when one day the eunuch aforementioned came there to say his Friday prayers, and passed near me; I was repeating at the time, slow from weakness, this verse:

"Give me strength of mind to bear these pangs of the heart,
or give me death;
Whatever may have been written in my destiny, O God! let it
come soon."

Though in appearance my looks were greatly altered, and my face was such that whoever had seen me formerly would not have recognized me to be the same person; yet the eunuch, hearing the sounds of grief, looked at me, and regarding me with attention, pitied me, and with much kindness addressed me, saying, "At last to this state thou hast brought thyself." I replied, "What was to occur has now happened; I devoted my property to her welfare, and I have sacrificed my life likewise; such has been her pleasure; then what shall I do?"

On hearing this, he left a servant with me, and went into the mosque; when he finished his prayers, and heard the *Khutba*, he returned to me, and putting me into a *miyana*, had me carried along to the house of that indifferent fair, and placed me outside the *chik* of her apartment. Though no trace of my former self remained, yet as I had been for a long while constantly with the lovely fair one, she must have recognized me; however, though knowing me perfectly, she acted as a stranger, and asked the eunuch who I was. That excellent man replied, "This is that unfortunate, ill-fated wretch who has fallen under the displeasure and reprehension of your highness; for this reason his appearance is such; he is burning with the fire of love; how much soever he endeavours to quench the flame with the water of tears, yet it burns with double force. Nothing is of the least avail; moreover he is dying with the shame of his fault." The fair lady jocosely said, "Why dost thou tell lies? I received from my intelligencers, many days ago, the news of his arrival in his own country; God knows who this is of whom you speak." Then the eunuch, putting his hands together, said, "If security be granted to my life, then I will be so bold as to address your highness." She answered, "Speak; your life is secure." The eunuch said, "Your highness is by nature a judge of merit; for God's sake lift up the screen from between you, and recognize him, and take pity on his lamentable condition. Ingratitude is not proper. Now whatever compassion you may feel for his present condition is amiable and meritorious – to say more would be to outstep the bounds of respect; whatever your highness ordains, that assuredly is best."

On hearing this speech of the eunuch, she smiled and said, "Well, let him be who he will, keep him in the hospital; when he gets well, then his situation shall be enquired into." The eunuch answered, "If you will condescend to sprinkle rose-water on him with your own royal hands, and say a kind word to him, then there may be hopes of his living; despair is a bad thing; the world exists through hope." Even on this, the fair one said nothing to console me. Hearing this dialogue, I also continued becoming more and more tired of existence. I fearlessly said, "I do not wish to live any longer on these terms; my feet are hanging in the grave, and I must soon die; my remedy is in the power of your highness; whether you may apply it or not, that you only know." At last the Almighty softened the heart of that stony-hearted one; she became gracious and said, "Send immediately for the royal physicians." In a short time they came and assembled around me; they felt my pulse and examined my urine with much deliberation; at last it was settled in their prognosis, that "this person is in love with someone; except the being united with the beloved object, there is no other cure; whenever he possesses her he will be well." When from the declaration of the physicians my complaint was thus confirmed, the fair lady said, "Carry this young man to the warm bath, and after bathing him and dressing him in fine clothes, bring him to me." They instantly carried me out, and after bathing me and clothing me well, they led me before the lovely angel; then that beautiful creature said with kindness, "Thou hast constantly, and for nothing, got me censured and dishonoured; now what more dost thou wish? Whatever is in thy heart, speak it out quite plainly?"

O, Dervishes! at that moment my emotions were such that I thought I should have died with joy, and I swelled so greatly with pleasure that my *jama* could hardly contain me, and my countenance and appearance became changed; I praised God, and said to her, this moment all the art of physic is centred in you, who have restored a corpse like me to life with a single word; behold, from that time to this, what a change has taken place in my circumstances by the kindness you have shown." After saying this, I went round her three times, and standing before her, I said, "your commands are that I should speak whatever I have in my heart; this boon is more precious to your slave than the empire of the seven climes; then be generous and accept this wretch! keep me at your feet and elevate me," On hearing this ejaculation, she became thoughtful for a moment; then regarding me askance, she said, "Sit down; your services and fidelity have been such that whatever you say becomes you; they are also engraven on my heart. Well, I comply with your request."

The same day, in a happy hour, and under a propitious star the Kazi quite privately performed the marriage rites. After so much trouble and afflictions, God showed me this happy day, when I gained the desires of my heart; but in the same degree that my heart wished to possess this angelic lady, it felt equally anxious and uneasy to know the explication of those strange events which had occurred; for, up to that day I knew nothing about who she was; or who was that brown, handsome negro, who on seeing a bit of paper, delivered to me so many bags of gold; and how that princely entertainment was prepared in the space of one *pahar*; and why those two innocent persons were put to death after the entertainment; and the cause of the anger and ingratitude she showed me after all my services and kindnesses; and then all at once to elevate this wretch to the height of happiness.. In short, I was so anxious to develop these strange circumstances and doubts, that for eight days after the marriage ceremonies, notwithstanding my great affection for her, I did not attempt to consummate the rites of wedlock. I merely slept with her at night, and got up in the morning "re non effectâ".

One morning I desired an attendant to prepare some warm water in order that I might bathe. The princess smiling, said, "Where is the necessity for the hot water?" I remained silent; but she was perplexed to account for my conduct; moreover, in her looks the signs of anger were visible; so much so, that she one day said to me, "Thou art indeed a strange man; at one time so warm before, and now so cold! what do people call this conduct? If you had not manly vigour, then why did you form so foolish a wish? I then having become fearless, replied, "O, my darling, justice is a positive duty; no person ought to deviate from the rules of justice." She replied, "What further justice remains to be done? whatever was to happen has taken place." I answered, "In truth, that which was my most earnest wish and desire I have gained; but, my heart is uneasy with doubts, and the man whose mind is filled with suspicions is ever perplexed; he can do nothing, and becomes different from other human creatures. I had determined within myself that after this marriage, which is my soul's entire delight, I would question your highness respecting sundry circumstances which I do not comprehend, and which I cannot unravel; that from your own blessed lips I might hear their explanation; then my heart would be at ease." The lovely lady frowning, said, "How pretty! you have already forgotten what I told you; recollect, many times I have desired you not to search into my concerns, or to oppose what I say; and is it proper in you to take, contrary to custom, such liberties?" I, laughing, replied, "As you have pardoned me much greater liberties, forgive this also." That angelic fair, changing her looks and getting warm, became a whirlwind of fire, and said, "You presume too much; go and mind your own affairs; what advantage can you derive from the explanation of these circumstances?" I answered, "the greatest shame in this world is the exposure of our person; but we are conversant with one another in that respect, hence as you have thought it right to lay aside this repugnance with me, then why conceal any other secrets from me?"

Her good sense made her comprehend my hint, and she said, "This is true; but I am very apprehensive if I, wretched, should divulge my secrets; it may be the cause of great trouble." I answered, "What strange apprehensions you form! do not conceive in your heart such an idea of me, and relate without restraint all the events of your life; never, never, shall they pass from my breast to my lips; what possibility, then, of their reaching the ear of another?" When she perceived that, without satisfying my curiosity she should have no rest, being without resource, she said, "Many evils attend the explanation of these matters, but you are obstinately bent upon it. Well, I must please you; for which reason I am going to relate the events of my past life – take care; it is equally necessary for you to conceal them from the world; my information is on this condition."

In short, after many injunctions, she began the relation of her life as follows: "The unfortunate wretch before you is the daughter of the King of Damascus; he is a great sovereign among sultans; he never had any child except me. From the day I was born I was brought up with great delicacy and tenderness, in joy and happiness under the eye of my father and mother. As I grew up I became attached to handsome and beautiful women; so that I kept near my person the most lovely young girls of noble families, and of my own age; and handsome female servants of the like age, in my service. I ever enjoyed the amusements of dancing and singing, and never had a care about the good or evil of the world. Contemplating my own condition thus free from care, except the praises of God, nothing else occupied my thoughts.

"It so happened that my disposition became suddenly of itself so changed, that I lost all relish for the company of others, nor did the gay assembly afford me any pleasure; my temper became melancholic, and my heart sad and confused; no one's presence was agreeable to me, nor did my heart feel inclined for conversation. Seeing this sad condition of mine, all the female servants were overwhelmed with sorrow and fell at my feet begging to know the cause of my gloom. This faithful eunuch, who has long been in my secrets, and from whom no action of my life is concealed, seeing my melancholy, said, 'If the princess would drink a little of the exhilarating lemonade, it is most probable that her cheerful disposition would be restored; and gladness return to her heart.' On hearing him say so, I had a desire to taste it, and ordered some to be prepared immediately.

"The eunuch went out to make it up, and returned, accompanied by a young boy, who brought a goblet of the lemonade, carefully prepared and cooled in ice. I drank it, and perceived it produced the good effect ascribed to it; for this piece of service I bestowed on the eunuch a rich *khil'at*, and desired him to bring me a goblet of the same every day at the same hour. From that day it became a regular duty, that the eunuch came, accompanied by the boy who brought the lemonade, and I drank it. When its inebriating quality took effect, I used in the elevation of my spirits to jest and laugh with the boy, and beguile my time. When his timidity wore off, he began to utter very agreeable speeches, and related many pleasant anecdotes; moreover, he began to heave sighs and sobs. His face was handsome and worth seeing; I began to like him beyond control. I, from the affections of my heart, and the relish I felt for his playful humour, every day gave him rewards and gratuities; but the wretch always appeared before me in the same clothes that he had been accustomed to wear, and they even were dirty and soiled.

"One day I said to him, you have received a good deal of money from the treasury, but your appearance is as wretched as ever; what is the cause of it? have you spent the money, or do you amass it?" When the boy heard these encouraging words, and found that I enquired into his condition, he said with tears in his eyes, 'Whatever you have bestowed on this slave, my preceptor has taken from me; he did not give me one *paisa* for myself; with what shall I make up other clothes, and appear better dressed before you? it is not my fault, and I cannot help it.' At this humble statement of his, I felt pity for him; I instantly ordered the eunuch to take charge of the boy from that day, to educate him under his own eye, and give him good clothes, and not to allow him to play and skip about with other boys; moreover, that my wish was, he should be taught a respectful mode of behaviour, to fit him for my own princely service, and to wait on me. The eunuch obeyed my orders, and perceiving how my inclinations leaned, he took the utmost care of him. In a little time, from ease and good living, his colour and sleekness changed greatly, like a snake's throwing off its slough; I restrained my inclinations as much as I could, but the handsome form of that rogue was so engraven on my heart, that I fondly wished to keep him clasped to my bosom, and never take my eyes off him for a moment.

"At last, I made him enter into my companionship, and dressing him in a variety of rich clothes and all kinds of jewels, I used to gaze at him. In short, by being always with me, my longing eyes were satisfied and my heart comforted; I every moment complied with his wants and wishes; at last, my condition was such, that if on any urgent occasion he was absent for a moment from my sight, I became quite uneasy. In a few years he became a youth, and the down appeared on his cheeks; his body and limbs were well formed! then there began to be a talk about him out of doors among the courtiers. The guards of all descriptions began to forbid him from coming and going within the palace. At length, his entrance into it was quite stopped, and without him I had no rest; a moment of absence on his part, was an age of pain on mine. When I heard these tidings of despair, I was as distracted as if the day of judgment had burst over me; and such was my condition that I could not speak a word to express my wishes: nor yet could I live separated from him. I had no means of relief; O God, what could I do; a strange kind of uneasiness came over me, and in consequence of my distraction I addressed myself to the same eunuch who was in all my secrets, and said to him, 'I wish to take care of this youth. In fact, the best plan is for you to give him a thousand gold pieces, to set him up in a jeweller's shop in the *chauk*, that he may from the profit of his trade live comfortably; and to build him a handsome house near my residence; to buy him slaves, and hire him servants and fix their pay, that he may in every way live at his ease.' The eunuch furnished him with a house, and set up a jeweller's shop for him to carry on the traffic, and prepared everything that was requisite. In a short time, his shop became so brilliant and showy, that whatever rich *khil'ats* or superb jewels were required for the king and his nobles, could only be procured there; and by degrees his shop so flourished, that all the rarities of every country were to be found there; and the daily traffic of all other jewellers became languid in comparison with his. In short, no one was able to compete with him in the city, nor was his equal to be found in any other country.

"He made a great deal of money by his business; but grief for his absence daily preyed on my mind, and injured my health; no expedient could be hit upon by which I might see him, and console my heart. At last, for the purpose of consultation, I sent for the same experienced eunuch, and said to him, 'I can devise no plan by which I may see the youth for a moment, and inspire my heart with patience. There remains only this method, which is to dig a mine from his house and join the same to the palace.' I had no sooner expressed my wish, than such a mine was dug in a few days, so that on the approach of evening the eunuch used to conduct the young man through that same passage, in silence and secrecy to my apartment. We used to pass the whole night in eating and drinking, and every enjoyment; I was delighted to meet him, and he was rejoiced to see me. When the morning star appeared, and the Muwazzin gave notice of the time for morning prayers, the eunuch used to lead the youth by the same way to his house. No fourth person had any knowledge of these circumstances; it was known only to the eunuch and two nurses who had given me milk, and brought me up.

"A long period passed in this manner; but it happened one day that when the eunuch went to call him, according to custom, then he perceived that the youth was sitting sorrowful and silent. The eunuch asked him, 'Is all well today? why are you so sad? Come to the princess; she has sent for you.' The youth made no reply whatever, nor did he move his tongue. The eunuch returned alone with a similar face, and mentioned to me the young man's condition. As the devil was about to ruin me, even after this conduct I could not banish him from my heart; if I had known that my love and affection for such an ungrateful wretch would have at last rendered me infamous and degraded, and would have destroyed my fame and honour; then I should have at that moment shrunk back from such a proceeding, and should have done penance; I never again should have pronounced his name, neither should I have devoted my heart to the shameless fellow. But it was to happen so; for this reason I took no heed of his improper conduct, and his not coming I imagined to be the affectation and airs of those who are conscious of being beloved; its consequences I have sadly rued, and thou art now also informed of these events without hearing or seeing them; or else where were you, and where was I? Well, what has happened is past. Bestowing not a thought on the conceited airs of that ass, I again sent him word by the eunuch, saying, 'if thou wilt not come to me now, by some means or other I will come to thee; but there is much impropriety in my coming there; if this secret is discovered, thou wilt have cause to rue it; so do not act in a manner that will have no other result than disgrace; it is best that thou comest quickly to me, otherwise imagine me arrived near thee. When he received this message, and perceived that my love for him was unbounded, he came with disagreeable looks and affected airs.

"When he sat down by me, I asked him, 'what is the cause of your coolness and anger today; you never showed so much insolence and disrespect before, you always used to come without making any excuses.' To this he replied, 'I am a poor nameless wretch; by your favour, and owing to you, I am arrived to such power, and with much ease and affluence I pass my days. I ever pray for your life and prosperity; I have committed this fault in full reliance on your highness's forgiveness, and I hope for pardon. As I loved him from my soul and heart, I accepted his well-turned apology, and not only overlooked his knavery, but even asked him again with affection, what great difficulty has occurred that you are so thoughtful? mention it, and it shall be instantly removed.'

"In short, in his humble way, he replied, 'Everything is difficult to me; before your highness, all is easy,' At last, from the purport of his discourse and conversation, it appeared that an elegant garden, with a grand house in it, together with reservoirs, tanks and wells, of finished masonry, was for sale, situated in the centre of the city and near his house; and that with the garden a female slave was to be sold, who sung admirably and understood music perfectly. But they were to be sold together, and not the garden alone, 'like the cat tied to the camel's neck,' and that whoever purchased the garden must also buy the slave; the best of it was, the price of the garden was five thousand rupees, and the price of the slave five hundred thousand. He concluded saying, 'Your devoted slave cannot at present raise so large a sum.' I perceived that his heart was greatly bent on buying them, and that for this reason he was thoughtful, and embarrassed in mind; although he was seated near me, yet his looks were pensive and his heart sad: as his happiness every hour and moment was dear to me, I that instant ordered the eunuch to go in the morning and settle the price of the garden and the slave, get their bills of sale drawn up, and deliver them to this person, and pay the price to their owner from the royal treasury.

"On hearing this order, the young man thanked me, tears of joy came upon his face; and we passed the night as usual in laughing and delight; in the morning he took leave. The eunuch, agreeably to my orders, bought and delivered over to him the garden and the slave. The youth continued his visits at night, according to custom and retired in the morning. One day in the season of spring, when the whole place was indeed charming, the clouds were gathering low, and the rain drizzling fell, the lightning also continued to flash through the murky clouds, and the breeze played gently through the trees – in short, it was a delightful scene. When in the *taks* the liquors of various colours, arranged in elegant phials, fell upon my sight; my heart longed to take a draught. After I had drunk two or three cupfuls, instantly the idea of the newly purchased garden struck me. An irrepressible desire arose within me, when in that state, that for a short time I should enjoy a walk in that garden. When the stream of misfortune flows against us, we struggle in vain against the tide. I involuntarily took a female servant with me, and went to the young man's house by the way of the mine; from thence I proceeded to the garden, and saw that the delightful place was in truth equal to the Elysian fields. As the raindrops fell on the fresh green leaves of the trees, one might say they were like pearls set in pieces of emerald, and the carnation of the flowers, in that cloudy day, appeared as beautiful as the ruddy crepuscle after the setting sun; the basons and canals, full of water, seemed like sheets of mirrors, over which the small waves undulated.

"In short, I was strolling about in every direction in that garden, when the day vanished and the darkness of night became conspicuous. At that moment, the young man appeared on a walk in the garden; and on seeing me, he approached with respect and great warmth of affection, and taking my hand in his, led me to the pavilion. On entering it, the splendour of the scene made me entirely forget all the beauty of the garden. The illuminations within were magnificent; on every side, gerandoles, in the shape of cypresses, and various kinds of lights in variegated lamps were lighted up; even the *shabi barat*, with all its moonlight and its illuminations, would appear dark in comparison to the brightness which shone in the pavilion; on one side, fire-works of every description were displayed.

"In the meantime, the clouds dispersed, and the bright moon appeared like a lovely mistress clothed in a lilac-coloured robe, who suddenly strikes our sight. It was a scene of great beauty; as the moon burst forth, the young man said, 'Let us now go and sit in the balcony which overlooks the garden.' I had become so infatuated, that whatever the wretch proposed I implicitly obeyed; now he led me such a dance, that he dragged me up to the balcony. That building was so high, that all the houses of the city and the lights of the bazaar, appeared as if they were at the foot of it. I was seated in a state of delight, with my arms round the youth's neck; meanwhile, a woman, quite ugly, without form or shape, entered as it were from the chimney, with a bottle of wine in her hand; I was at that time greatly displeased at her sudden entrance, and on seeing her looks, my heart became alarmed. Then, in confusion, I asked the young man, 'who is this precious hag; from whence have you grubbed her up?' Joining his hands together, he replied, 'This is the slave who was bought with the garden through your generous assistance.' I had perceived that the simpleton had bought her with much eager desire, and perhaps his heart was fixed on her; for this reason, I, suppressing my inward vexation, remained silent; but my heart from that moment was disturbed and displeasure affected my temper; moreover, the wretch had the impudence to make this harlot our cup-bearer. At that moment I was drinking my own blood with rage, and was as uneasy as a parrot shut up in the same cage with a crow: I had no opportunity of going away, and did not wish to stay. To shorten the story, the wine was of the strongest description, so that on drinking it a man would become a beast. She plied the young man with two or three cups in succession of that fiery liquor, and I also bitterly swallowed half a cupful at the importunity of the youth; at last, the shameless harlot likewise got beastly drunk, and took very unbecoming liberties with that vile youth; and the mean wretch also, in his intoxication, having become regardless, began to be disrespectful, and behave indecently.

"I was so much ashamed, that had the earth opened at the moment I would have willingly jumped into it; but in consequence of my passion for him, I, infatuated, even after all these circumstances, remained silent. However, he was completely a vile wretch, and did not feel the value of my forbearance. In the fervour of intoxication, he drank off two cups more, so that his little remaining sense vanished, and he completely drove from his heart all respect for me. Without shame, and in the rage of lust, the barefaced villain consummated before me his career of infamous indecency with his hideous mistress, who, in that posture, began to play off all the blandishments of love, and kissing and embracing took place between the two. In that faithless man no sense of honour remained; neither did modesty exist in that shameless woman; 'as the soul is, so are the angels.' My state of mind at the time was like that of a songstress who, having lost the musical time, sings out of tune. I was invoking curses on myself for having come there, saying that I was properly punished for my folly. At last, how could I bear it? I was on fire from head to foot, and began to roll on live coals. In my rage and wrath I recollected the proverb, that 'It is not the bullock that leaps, but the sack; whoever has seen a sight like this?' in saying this to myself, I came away thence.

"That drunkard in the depravity of his heart thought, if I was offended now, what then would be his treatment the next day, and what a commotion I should raise. So he imagined it best to finish my existence whilst he had me in his power. Having formed this resolution in his mind with the advice of the hag, he put his *patka* round his neck and fell at my feet, and taking off his turban from his head, began to supplicate my forgiveness in the humblest manner. My heart was infatuated towards him; whithersoever he turned I, turned; and like the handmill I was entirely under his control. I implicitly complied with all he desired; some way or other he pacified me, and persuaded me to retake my seat. He again took two or three cupfuls of the fiery liquor, and he induced me to drink some also. I, in the first place, was already inflamed with rage, and secondly, after drinking such strong liquor I soon became quite senseless – no recollection remained. Then that unfeeling, ungrateful, cruel wretch wounded me with his sword; yea, further, he thought he had completely killed me. At that moment, my eyes opened, and I uttered these words, 'Well, as I have acted, so I have been rewarded; but do thou screen thyself from the consequences of shedding unjustly my blood. Let it not so happen that some tyrant should seize thee; do thou wash off my blood from thy garment; what has happened is past.'

"Do not divulge this secret to anyone; I have not been wanting to thee even with loss of life. Then placing him under the protection of God's mercy, I fainted from the loss of blood, and knew nothing of what afterwards happened. Perhaps, that butcher, conceiving me dead, put me into the chest, and let me down over the walls of the fortress, the same as you yourself saw, I wished no one ill; but these misfortunes were written in my destiny, and the lines of fate cannot be effaced. My eyes have been the cause of all these calamities: if I had not had a strong desire to behold beautiful persons, then that wretch would not have been my bane. God so ordained that He made thee arrive there; and, He made thee the means of saving my life. After undergoing these disgraces, I am ashamed to reflect that I should yet live and show my face to anyone. But what can I do? the choice of death is not in our hands; God, after killing me, hath restored me to life; let us see what is written in my future fate. In all appearance, your exertions and zeal have been of use, so that I have been cured of such wounds. Thou hast been ready to promote my wishes with thy life and property, and whatever were thy means, thou hast offered them cheerfully. In those days, seeing thee without money and sad, I wrote the note to Sidi Bahar, who is my cashier. In that note, I mentioned that I was in health and safety in such a place, and I said, "convey the intelligence of me unfortunate to my excellent mother."

"The Sidi sent by thee those trays of gold for my expenses; and when I sent thee to the shop of Yusuf the merchant, to purchase *khil'ats* and jewels, I felt confident that the weakminded wretch, who soon becomes friends with everyone, conceiving you a stranger, would certainly form an intimacy with you, and indulging his conceit, invite you to a feast and entertainment. This stratagem of mine turned out right, and he did exactly what I had imagined in my heart. Then, when you promised him to return, and came to me and related the particulars of his insisting upon it, I was heartily pleased with the circumstance; for I knew that if you went to his house, and there ate and drank, you would invite him in return, and that he would eagerly come; for this reason, I sent thee back quickly to him. After three days, when you returned from the entertainment, and, quite abashed, made me many apologies for staying away so long, to make you easy in your mind, I replied, 'it is of no consequence; when he gave you leave then you came away; but to be without delicacy is not proper, and we should not bear another's debt of gratitude without an idea of paying it; now do you go and invite him also, and bring him along with you.' When you went away to his house, I saw that no preparations could be got ready for the entertainment at our house, and if he should all at once come, what could I do? but it fortunately happened that from time immemorial, the custom of this country has been for the kings to remain out for eight months in the year, to settle the affairs of the provinces, and collect the revenues, and for four months, during the rains, to stay in the city in their auspicious palaces. In those days, the king, this unfortunate wretch's father, had gone into the provinces some two or four months previously to arrange the affairs of the kingdom.

"Whilst you were gone to bring the young merchant to the entertainment, Sidi Bahar imparted the particulars of my present ituation to the queen (who is the mother of me impure). Again I, ashamed of my guilty conduct, went to the queen and related to her all that happened to me. Although she, from motherly affection and good sense, had used every means to conceal the circumstance of my disappearance, saying, 'God knows what may be the end of it,' she onceived it wrong to make public my disgrace for the present, and or my sake she had concealed my errors in her maternal breast; but she had all along been in search of me.

"When she saw me in this condition, and heard all the ircumstances of my misfortune, her eyes filled with tears, and she aid, 'O unfortunate wretch! thou hast knowingly destroyed the onour and glory of the throne; a thousand pities that thou hadst ot perished also; if instead of thee I had been brought to bed of stone, I should have been patient; even now it is not too late to epent; whatever was in thy unfortunate fate has happened; what ilt thou do next? Wilt thou live or die?' I replied, with excessive hame, that in this worthless wretch's fate it was so written, that I hould live in such disgrace and distress after escaping such various dangers; it would have been better to have perished; though the mark of infamy is stamped on my forehead, yet I have not been guilty of such an action as can disgrace my parents.

"The great pain I now feel is, that those base wretches should escape my vengeance, and enjoy their crime in each other's company, whilst I have suffered such affliction from their hands: it is a pity that I can do nothing in order to punish them. I hope one favour from your majesty, that you would order your steward to prepare all the necessary articles for an entertainment at my house, that I may, under the pretence of an entertainment, send for those two wretches, and punish them for their deeds and also inflict vengeance for myself. In the same manner that he lifted his hand upon me and wounded me, may I be enabled to cut them to pieces; then my heart will be soothed; otherwise I must continue glowing in this fire of resentment, and ultimately I must be burnt to cinders. On hearing this speech, my excellent mother became kind from maternal fondness, and concealed my guilt in her own breast, and sent all the necessaries for the entertainment by the same eunuch who is in my secrets. Every necessary attendant came also, and each was ready in his own appropriate occupation. In the time of evening, you brought the base villain who is now dead; I wished the harlot should likewise come.

"For this reason I earnestly desired you to send for her; when she also came and the guests were assembled, they all became thoroughly intoxicated and senseless by drinking largely of wine; you also got drunk along with them, and lay like a corpse. I ordered a Kilmakini to cut off both their heads with a sword; she instantly drew her sword and cut off both their heads, and dyed their bodies with their blood. The cause of my anger towards thee was this, that I had given thee permission for the entertainment, but not to become an associate in wine-drinking, with people thou hadst only known for a few days. Assuredly this folly on thy part was anything but pleasing to me; for when you drank till you became senseless, then what hopes of aid from you remained? But the claims of thy services so cling around my neck, that, notwithstanding such conduct, I forgive thee. And now, behold, I have related to thee all my adventures from the beginning to the end; do you yet desire in your heart any other explanations? In the same manner that I have, in compliance with your wishes, granted all you requested, do you also in like manner perform what I desire; my advice on this occasion is, that it is no longer proper either for you or me to remain in this city. Henceforward you are master."

O devoted to God! the princess having spoken thus far, remained silent. I, who with heart and soul considered her wishes paramount to everything, and was entangled in the net of her affections, replied, "whatever you advise, that is best, and I will without hesitation carry the same into effect." When the princess found me obedient, and her servant, she ordered two swift and high-mettled horses (which might vie with the wind in speed), to be brought from the royal stables, and kept in readiness. I went and picked out just such beautiful and high spirited horses as she required, and had them saddled and brought to our house. When a few hours of the night remained, the princess put on men's clothes, and arming herself with the five weapons, mounted on one of the horses; I got on the other, completely armed, and we set out in the same direction.

When night was over, and the dawn began to appear, we arrived on the banks of a certain lake; alighting from our horses, we washed our hands and faces; having breakfasted in great haste, we mounted again and set off. Now and then the princess spoke, and said, "I have for your sake left fame, honour, wealth, country and parents all behind me; now, may it not so happen, that you also should behave to me like that faithless savage." Sometimes I talked of different matters to beguile the journey, and sometimes replied to her questions and doubts, saying "O princess, all men are not alike; there must have been some defect in that base villain's parentage, that by him such a deed was done; but I have sacrificed my wealth and devoted my life to you, and you have dignified me in every way. I am now your slave without purchase, and if you should make shoes of my skin and wear them, I will not complain." Such conversation passed between us, and day and night to travel onward was our business. If through fatigue we sometimes dismounted somewhere, we then used to hunt down the beasts and birds of the woods, and having lawfully slain them, and applied salt from the salt-cellar, and having struck fire with steel (from a flint), we used to broil and eat them. The horses we let loose to graze, and they generally found sufficient to satisfy their hunger from the grass and leaves.

One day we reached a large even plain, where there was no trace of any habitation, and where no human face could be seen; even in this solitary and dreary scene, owing to the princess's company, the day appeared festive and the nights joyful. Proceeding on our journey, we came suddenly to a large river, the sight of which would appal the firmest heart. As we stood on its banks, as far as the eye could reach, nothing was to be seen but water; no means of crossing was to be found. O God, cried I, how shall we pass this sea! we stood reflecting on this sad obstacle for a few moments, when the thought came into my mind to leave the princess there, and to go in search of a boat; and that until I could find some means to pass over, the princess would have time to rest. Having formed this plan, I said "O princess, if you will allow me, I will go and look out for a ferry or ford." She replied, "I am greatly tired, and likewise hungry and thirsty; I will rest here a little, whilst thou findest out some means to pass over the river."

On that spot was a large *pipal* tree, forming a canopy of such extent, that if a thousand horsemen sheltered themselves under its wide-spread branches, they would be protected from the sun and rain. Leaving there the princess, I set out, and was looking all around to find somewhere or other on the ground, or the river, some trace of a human being. I searched much, but found the same nowhere. At last, I returned hopeless, but did not find the princess under the tree; how can I describe the state of my mind at that moment! my senses forsook me, and I became quite distracted. Sometimes I mounted the tree, and looked for her in every individual leaf and branch; sometimes, letting go my hold, I fell on the ground, and went round the roots of the tree as one who performs the *tasadduk*. Sometimes I wept and shrieked at my miserable condition; now I ran from west to east, then from north to south. In short, I searched everywhere, but could not find any trace of the rare jewel I had lost; when, at last, I found I could do nothing, then weeping and throwing dust over my head, I looked for her everywhere.

This idea came into my mind, that perhaps some of the jinns had carried her away, and had inflicted on me this wound; or else that someone had followed her from her country, and finding her alone, had persuaded her to return to Damascus. Distracted with these fancies, I threw off and cast away my clothes, and becoming a naked fakir, I wandered about in the kingdom of Syria from morn until eve, and at night lay down to rest in any place I could find. I wandered over the whole region, but could find no trace of my princess, nor hear anything of her from anyone, nor could I ascertain the cause of her disappearance. Then this idea came into my mind, that since I could find no trace of that beloved one, even life itself was a weariness. I perceived a mountain in some wilderness; I ascended it, and formed the design of throwing myself headlong from its summit, that I might end my wretched existence in a moment, by dashing my head to pieces against the stones, then would my soul be freed from a state of affliction.

Having formed this resolution within myself, I was on the point of precipitating myself from the mountain, and had even lifted up my foot, when someone laid hold of my arm. In the meanwhile, I regained my senses, and looking round, I saw a horseman clothed in green, with a veil thrown over his face, who said to me, "Why dost thou attempt to destroy thy life; it is impious to despair of God's mercy; whilst there is breath, so long there is hope. Three Dervishes will meet thee a few days hence, in the empire of Rum, who are equally afflicted with thyself, entangled in the same difficulties, and who have met with adventures similar to thine; the name of the king of that country is Azad Bakht; he is also in great trouble; when he meets you and the other three Dervishes, then the wishes and desires of the heart of each of you will be completely fulfilled."

I instantly laid hold of the stirrup of this guardian angel, and kissed it, and exclaimed, "O messenger of God, the few words you have pronounced have consoled my afflicted heart; but tell me, for God's sake, who you are, and what is your name." He replied, "My name is Murtaza 'Ali, and my office is this, that to whomsoever there occurs a danger or difficulty, I am at hand to afford relief." Having said this much, he vanished from my sight. In short, having set my heart at ease from the happy tidings I received from my spiritual guide Murtaza 'Ali, "the remover of difficulties," I formed the design of proceeding to Constantinople. On the road I suffered all those misfortunes which were decreed me by fate; with the hopes of meeting the princess. Through the assistance of God, I am come here, and by good fortune I have become honoured by your presence. The promised meeting has taken place between us, and we have enjoyed each other's society and conversation; now it only remains for us to be known to, and acquainted with, the king Azad Bakht.

Assuredly after this, we five shall attain the desires of our hearts. Do you also beseech the blessings of God, and say amen. O ye holy guides! such have been the adventures which have befallen this bewildered wanderer, which have been faithfully related in your presence; now let us look forward to the time when my trouble and sorrows will be changed into joy and gladness by the recovery of the princess. Azad Bakht, concealed in silence in his corner, having heard with attention the story of the first Dervish, was greatly pleased; then he betook himself to listen to the adventures of the next Dervish.

ADVENTURES OF THE SECOND DERVISH

When it came to the turn of the second Dervish to speak, he placed himself at his ease, and said,

"O friends, to this fakir's story listen a little;
I will tell it to you, from first to the last, listen;
Whose cure no physician can perform;
My pain is far beyond remedy – listen."

O ye clothed in the *dalk*! this wretch is the prince of the kingdom of Persia; men skilled in every science are born there, for which reason the Persian proverb "*Isfahan nisfi Jahan,*" or "Ispahan is half the world," has become well known. In the seven climes, there is no kingdom equal to that ancient kingdom; the star of that country is the sun, and of all the seven constellations it is the greatest. The climate of that region is delightful, and the inhabitants are of enlightened minds, and refined in their manners. My father (who was the king of that country), in order to teach me the rules and lessons of government, made choice of very wise tutors in every art and science, and placed them over me for my instruction from my infancy. So, having received complete instruction in every kind of knowledge, I am now learned. With the favour of God, in my fourteenth year I had learned every science, polite conversation, and polished manners; and I had acquired all that is fit and requisite for kings to know; moreover, my inclinations night and day, led me to associate with the learned, and hear the histories of every country, and of ambitious princes and men of renown.

One day, a learned companion, who was well versed in history, and had seen a great deal of the world, said to me, "That though there is no reliance on the life of man, yet such excellent qualities are often found in him, that owing to them, the name of some men will be handed down with praise on people's tongues to the day of judgment." I begged of him to relate circumstantially a few instances on that score, that I might hear them, and endeavour to act accordingly. Then that person began to relate as follows, some of the adventures of Hatim Ta'i. "That there lived in the time of Hatim, a king of Arabia, named Naufal, who bore great enmity towards Hatim, on account of his renown, and having assembled many troops, he went up to give him battle. Hatim was a God-fearing and good man; he thus conceived, that, "If I likewise prepare for battle, then the creatures of God will be slaughtered, and there will be much bloodshed; the punishment of heaven for which will be recorded against my name." Reflecting on this, he quite alone, taking merely his life with him, fled and hid himself in a cave in the mountains. When the news of Hatim's flight reached Naufal, he confiscated all the property and dwellings of Hatim, and proclaimed publicly that whoever would look out for him and seize him, should receive from the king's treasury five hundred pieces of gold. On hearing this proclamation, all became eager, and began to make diligent search for Hatim.

"One day, an old man and his wife, taking two or three of their young children with them, for the purpose of picking up wood, strayed near the cave where Hatim was concealed; and began to gather fuel in that same forest. The old woman remarked, 'If our days had been at all fortunate, we should have seen and found Hatim somewhere or other, and seizing him, we should have carried him to Naufal; then he would give us five hundred pieces of gold, and we should live comfortably, and be released from this toil and care,' The old woodman said, 'What art thou prating about? it was decreed in our fate, that we should pick up wood every day, place it on our heads, and sell it in the bazaar, and with its produce procure bread and salt; or one day the tiger of the woods will carry us off: peace, mind thy work; why should Hatim fall into our hands, and the king give us so much money?' The old woman heaved a cold sigh, and remained silent.

"Hatim had heard the words of the two old people, and conceived it unmanly and ungenerous to conceal himself to save his life, and not to conduct those helpless ones to the object of their desire. True it is, that a man without pity is not a human being, and he in whose heart there is no feeling is a butcher.

'Man was created to exercise compassion,
Otherwise, angels were not wanting for devotion.'

In short, Hatim's manly mind would not allow him to remain concealed, after what he had with his own ears heard from the woodman; he instantly came out, and said to the old man, 'O friend, I myself am Hatim, lead me to Naufal; on seeing me, he will give thee whatever amount of money he has promised.' The old woodman replied, 'It is true that my welfare and advantage certainly consist in doing so, but who knows how he will treat thee; if he should put thee to death, then what shall I do? This, on my part, can never be done – that I should deliver over thee to thine enemy for the sake of my own avarice. In a few days I shall spend the promised wealth, and how long shall I live? I must die at last; then what answer shall I give to God?' Hatim implored him greatly, and said, 'Take me along with thee – I say so of my own pleasure; I have ever desired that, should my wealth and life be of use to someone or other of my fellow creatures, then so much the better.' But the old man could not in any way be persuaded to carry Hatim along with him, and receive the proclaimed reward. At last, becoming hopeless, Hatim said, 'If you do not carry me in the way I wish, then I will go of myself to the king, and say, this old man concealed me in a cave in the mountains,' The old man smiled and said, 'If I am to receive evil for good, then hard will be my fate.' During this conversation, other men arrived, and a crowd assembled around them; perceiving the person they saw to be Hatim, they instantly seized him and carried him along; the old man also, a little in the rear, followed them in silent grief. When they brought Hatim before Naufal, he asked, 'Who has seized and brought him here?' A worthless, hard-hearted boaster answered, 'Who could have performed such a deed except myself? This achievement belongs to my name, and I have planted the standard of glory in the sky.' Another vaunting fellow clamoured, 'I searched for him many days in the woods, and caught him at last, and have brought him here; have some consideration for my labour, and give me what has been promised.' In this manner, from avidity for the promised pieces of gold, everyone said he had done the deed. The old man, in silence, sat apart in a corner, and heard all their boastings, and wept for Hatim. When each had recounted his act of bravery and enterprise, then Hatim said to the king, 'If you ask for the truth, then it is this; that old man, who stands aloof from all, has brought me here; if you can judge from appearances, then ascertain the fact, and give him for my seizure what you have promised; for in the whole body the tongue is a most sacred member. It is incumbent upon a man to perform what he has promised; for in other respects God has given tongues to brutes likewise; then what would have been the difference between a man and other animals?'

"Naufal called the old wood-cutter near him, and said, 'Tell the truth; what is the real state of the matter; who has seized and brought Hatim here?' The honest fellow related truly all that had occurred from beginning to end, and added, 'Hatim is come here of his own accord for my sake.' Naufal, on hearing this manly act of Hatim's, was greatly astonished, and exclaimed, 'How surprising is thy liberality! even thy life thou hast not feared to risk for the good of others!' With regard to all those who laid false claims to having seized Hatim, the king ordered them to have their hands tied behind their backs, and instead of five hundred pieces of gold, to receive each five hundred strokes of a slipper on their heads, so that their lives might perish under the punishment. Instantly, the strokes of the slippers began to be laid on in such a style, that in a short time their heads became quite bald. True it is, that to tell an untruth is such a guilt, that no other guilt equals it; may God keep everyone free from this calamity, and not give him a propensity for telling lies;

many people persevere in uttering falsehoods, but at the moment of detection they meet with their dessert.

"In short, Naufal having rewarded all of them according to their desserts, thought it contrary to gentlemanly conduct and manliness of character to harbour enmity and strife towards a man like Hatim, from whom multitudes received happiness, and who, for the sake of the necessitous, did not even spare his own life, and was entirely devoted to the ways of God. He instantly seized Hatim's hand with great cordiality and friendship, and said to him, 'Why should it not be the case? such a man as you are can perform such an action.' Then the king, with great respect and attention, made Hatim sit down near him, and he instantly restored to him the lands and property, and the wealth and moveables, he had confiscated; and bestowed on him anew the chieftainship of the tribe of *Ta,i*, and ordered the five hundred pieces of gold to be given to the old man from the treasury, who, blessing the king, went away."

When I had heard the whole of this adventure of Hatim's, a spirit of rivalry came into my mind; and this idea occurred to me, viz., "Hatim was the only chief of his own tribe of Arabs. He, by one act of liberality has gained such renown, that to this day it is celebrated; whilst I am, by the decree of God, the king of all Iran; and it would be a pity if I were to remain excluded from this good fortune. It is certain that in this world no quality is greater than generosity and liberality; for whatever a man bestows in this world, he receives its return in the next. If anyone sows a single seed, then how much does he reap from its produce! With these ideas impressed upon my mind, I called for the lord of the buildings, and ordered him to erect, as speedily as possible, a grand palace without the city, with forty high and wide gates. In a short time, even such a grand palace as my heart wished for, was built and got ready, and in that place every day at all times, from morning till night, I used to bestow pieces of silver and gold on the poor and helpless; whoever asked for anything in charity, I granted it to the utmost of his desire.

In short, the necessitous entered daily through the forty gates, and received whatever they wanted. It happened one day that a fakir came in from the front gate and begged some alms. I gave him a gold piece; then the same person entered through the next gate, and asked two pieces of gold; though I recollected him to be the same fakir, I passed over the circumstance and gave them. In this manner he came in through each gate, and increased a piece of gold in his demand each time; and I knowingly appeared ignorant of the circumstance, and continued supplying him according to his demand. At last he entered by the fortieth gate, and asked forty pieces of gold – this sum I likewise ordered to be given him. After receiving so much, the fakir re-entered from the first gate and again begged alms: his conduct appeared to me highly impudent, and I said, "Hear, O avaricious man, what kind of a fakir art thou, that dost not even know the meaning of the three letters which compose the word *fakr* (poverty); a fakir ought to act up to them. He replied, "Well, generous soul, explain them yourself." I answered, "*Fe* means *faka* (fasting); *kaf* signifies *kina'at* (contentment); and *re* means *riyazat* (devotion); whoever has not these three qualities, is not a fakir. All this which you have received, eat and drink with it, and when it is done, return to me, and receive whatever thou requirest. This charity is bestowed on thee to relieve immediate wants and not for the purpose of accumulation. O avidious! from the forty gates thou hast received from one piece of gold up to forty; add up the amount, and see by the rule of arithmetical progression how many pieces of gold it comes to; and even after all this, thy avarice hath brought thee back again through the first gate. What wilt thou do after having accumulated so much money? A real fakir ought only to think of the wants of the passing day; the following day the great Provider of necessaries will afford thee a new pittance. Now evince some shame and modesty; have patience, and be content; what sort of mendicity is this that thy spiritual guide hath taught thee?"

On hearing these reproaches of mine, he became displeased and angry, and threw down on the ground all the money he had received from me, and said, "Enough, sir, do not be so warm; take back your gifts and keep them, and do not again pronounce the word generosity. It is very difficult to be generous; you are not able to support the weight of generosity, when will you attain to that station? you are as yet very far from it. The word *sakhi* (generous), is also composed of three letters; first act up to the meaning of those three letters, then you will be called generous." On hearing this I became uneasy, and said to the fakir, well, holy pilgrim, explain to me the meaning of those three letters. He replied, "from *sin* is derived *sama,i* (endurance); from *khe* comes *khaufi Ilahi* (fear of God); and from *ye* proceeds *yad* (remembrance of one's birth and death). Until one is possessed of these three qualities, he should not mention the name of generosity; and the generous man has also this happiness, that although he acts amiss in other points, yet he is dear to his Maker on account of his generosity. I have travelled through many countries, but except the princess of Basra, I have not seen a person really generous. The robe of generosity God hath shaped out on the person of that woman; all others desire the name, but do not act up to it." On hearing this, I made much entreaty, and conjured him by all that was sacred to forgive my rebuke, and take whatever he required. He would not, on any account, accept my proffered gifts, but went away repeating these words, "Now if thou wert to give all thy kingdom, I would not spit upon it, nor would I even—"

The pilgrim went away, but having heard such praises of the princess of Basra, my heart became quite restless, and no way could I be easy. Now this desire arose within me, that by some means or other I must go to Basra and take a look at her.

In the meantime, the king, my father, died, and I ascended the throne. I got the empire, but the idea I had formed of going to Basra did not leave me. I held a consultation with the vizier and nobles, who were the support of the throne, and the pillars of the empire, saying, I wish to make a journey to Basra. Do ye remain steady in your respective stations; if I live, then the duration of the journey will be short; I will soon be back. No one seemed pleased at the idea of my going; in my helplessness, my heart continued to become more and more sorrowful. One day, without consulting anyone, I privately sent for the resourceful vizier, and made him regent and plenipotentiary during my absence, and placed him at the head of the affairs of the empire. I then put on the ochre-coloured habit of a pilgrim, and, assuming the appearance of a fakir, I took the road to Basra alone. In a few days, I reached its boundaries, and constantly began to witness this scene; wherever I halted for the night, the servants of the princess advanced to receive me, and made me halt at some elegant house, and they used to provide me in perfection with all the requisites of a banquet, and to remain in attendance on me all night with the utmost respect. The following day, at the next stage, I experienced the same reception. In this comfort I journeyed onwards for months; at last I entered the city of Basra. I had no sooner entered it, than a good-looking young man, well dressed, and well-behaved, who carried wisdom in his looks, came up to me, and said with extreme sweetness of address, "I am the servant of pilgrims; I am always on the look out to conduct to my house all travellers, whether pilgrims or men of the world, who come to this city; except my house alone, there is no other place here for a stranger to put up at; pray, holy sir, come with me, bestow honour on my abode, and render me exalted.

I asked him, "what is the noble name of your honour?" He replied, "they call the name of this nameless one Bedar Bakht." Seeing his good qualities and affable manners, I went along with him and came to his house. I saw a grand mansion fitted up in a princely style – he led me to a grand apartment, and made me sit down; and sending for warm water, he caused the attendants to wash my hands and feet; and having caused the *dastar-khwan* to be spread, the steward placed before me alone a great variety of trays and dishes, and large quantities of fruit and confectionery. On seeing such a grand treat, my very soul was satiated, and taking a mouthful from each dish, my stomach was filled; I then drew back my hand from eating.

The young man became very pressing, and said, "Sir, what have you eaten? all the dinner remains as it were for a deposit; eat some more without ceremony." I replied, there is no shame in eating; God prosper your house, I have eaten as much as my stomach can contain, and I cannot sufficiently praise the relish of your feast, and even now my tongue smacks with their flavour, and every belch I make is absolutely perfumed, now pray take them away. "When the *dastar-khwan* was removed, they spread a carpet of *kashani* velvet, and brought to me ewers and basins of gold, with scented soap and warm water, wherewithal I might wash my hands; then *betel* was introduced, in a box set with precious stones, and spices of various kinds; whenever I called for water to drink, the servants brought it cooled in ice. When the evening came, camphorated candles were lighted up in the glass shades; and that friendly young man sat down near me and entertained me with his conversation. When one watch of the night had elapsed, he said to me, "be pleased to sleep in this bed, in front of which are curtains and screens." I said, "O, Sir, for us pilgrims a mat or a deer-skin is sufficient; this luxury God has ordained for you men of the world."

He replied, "All these things are for pilgrims; they do not in the least belong to me." On his pressing me so urgently, I went and lay down on the bed which was softer than even a bed of flowers. Pots of roses and baskets of flowers were placed on both sides of the bedstead, and aloes and other perfumes were burning; to whichever side I turned, my senses were intoxicated with fragrance; in this state I slept. When the morning came, the attendants placed before me for breakfast, almonds, pistachio nuts, grapes, figs, pears, pomegranates, currants, dates, and *sharbat* made of fruit. In this festive manner I passed three days and nights. On the fourth day I requested leave to depart. The young man said, with joined hands, "Perhaps I have been deficient in my attentions to you, for which reason you are displeased." I replied with astonishment, "For God's sake, what a speech is this? the rules of hospitality require one to stay three days – these have I fulfilled; to remain longer would be improper; and besides this, I have set out to travel, and if I remain merely at one place, then it will not suit; for which reason I beg leave to depart; in other respects, your kindness is such that my heart does not wish to be separated from you."

He then said, "Do as you please; but wait a moment, that I may go to the princess and in her presence mention the circumstance; and as you wish to depart be it known to you, that all the wearing apparel and bedding, also the vessels of silver and gold, and the jewelled vessels in this guest's apartment, are your property; whatever directions you may give for the purpose of taking them away, an arrangement to that effect shall be made." I answered, "cease to talk in this manner; I am a pilgrim, and not a strolling bard; if such avarice had a place in my heart, then why should I have turned pilgrim; and where would be the evil of my leading a worldly life?" That kind young man replied, "If the princess should hear of this circumstance of your refusal, she will discharge me from my employment, and God knows what other punishment I shall receive; if you are so indifferent to possess them, then lock up all these articles in a room, and put your seal on the door, and you may hereafter dispose of them as you please."

I would not accept his offer, and he would not submit to me. At last, this plan was adopted, I locked them all up in a room, and put my seal on the door, and waited with impatience for leave of departing. In the meantime a confidential eunuch, having on his head an aigrette, and a short robe round his loins, and a golden mace studded with gems in his hand, accompanied by several other respectable attendants, filling various offices, came near me with this splendour and pomp. He addressed me with such kindness and complaisance that I cannot express it, and added, "O, sir, if showing kindness and benevolence, you do me the favour to dignify my humble dwelling with your presence, then it will not be far from courtesy and condescension.

Perhaps the princess will hear that a traveller had been here, and no one had received him with courtesy and politeness; and that he had gone away as he came; for this reason God knows what punishment she will inflict on me, or how far her displeasure will be raised; yea more, it is a matter affecting my life," I refused to listen to his request, but through dint of solicitations he overcame my resistance, and conducted me to another house, which was better than the first. Like the former host, he entertained me twice a day for three days and nights, with the same kind of meals, and in the morning and afternoon, sherbet and fruits for passing away the time, and he told me that I was the master of all the rich gold and silver dishes, carpets, etc., and that I might do with them whatever I pleased.

On hearing these strange proposals, I was quite confounded, and wished that I might by some means take my leave and escape from this place. On perceiving my embarassed countenance, the eunuch said, "O creature of God, whatever your wants or wishes may be, impart them to me, that I may lay them before the princess." I replied, "in the garb of a pilgrim, how can I desire the riches of this world, which you offer me unasked, and which I refuse?" He then said, "The desire of worldly goods forsakes the heart of no one, for which reason some poet has composed these verses:

"I have seen ascetics with nails unpared;
I have seen others with hair thickly matted;
I have seen jogis *with their ears split,*
Having their bodies covered with ashes;
I have seen the maunis *who never speak;*
I have seen the sevras *with heads shaved;*
I have seen the people sporting,
In the forest of Ban-khandi;
I have seen the brave, I have seen heroes;
I have seen the wise and the foolish, all;
I have seen those filled with delusion,
Continuing in forgetfulness amidst their wealth;
I have seen those who were happy from first to last.
I have seen those who were afflicted from their birth;
But never have I seen those men
In whose minds avarice did not exist."

On hearing these lines, I replied, what you say is true, but I want nothing; if you will permit, I will write out a note and send it which will express my wish, and which you will convey to the presence of the princess, it will be doing me a great favour, as if I had received all the riches in the world. The eunuch said, "I will do it with pleasure, there is no difficulty in it." I immediately wrote a note to the following purport: first, I began with the praise of God; I then related my circumstances and situation, saying, "that this creature of God had, some days since, arrived in the city, and from the munificence of her government, had been taken care of in every way; that I had heard such accounts of her highness's generosity and munificence, as had raised in me an ardent desire to see her, and that I had found those qualities four-fold greater than they had been represented. Your nobles now tell me to set forth before you whatever wants or wishes I may have; for this reason I beg to represent to you without ceremony the wishes of my heart. I am not in want of the riches of this world. I am also the king of my own country; my sole reason for coming so far and undergoing such fatigues, was the ardent desire I had to see you, which motive only has conducted me here in this manner quite alone. I now hope through your benevolence to attain the wishes of my heart; I shall then be satisfied. Any further favours will rest with your pleasure; but if the request of this wretch is not granted, then he will wander about in this same manner, encountering hardships, and sacrifice his restless life to the passion he feels for you. Like Majnun and Farhad, he will end his life in some forest or mountain."

Having written my wishes, I gave the note to the eunuch; he carried it to the princess. After a short while, he returned and called me, and conducted me to the door of the seraglio. On arriving there, I saw an elderly and respectable woman dressed in jewels, sitting on a golden stool, and many eunuchs and other servants richly clothed, were standing before her with arms across. I, imagining her to be the superintendent of affairs, and regarding her as a venerable person, made her my obeisance; the old lady returned my salute with much civility, and said, "Come and sit down, you are welcome; it is you who wrote an affectionate note to the princess." I, feeling ashamed, hung down my head and remained sitting silent.

After a short pause, she said, "O, young man, the princess has sent you her *salam*, and said thus, 'There is nothing wrong in my taking a husband; you have solicited me in marriage; but to speak of your kingdom, and to conceive yourself a king in this mendicant state, and to be proud of it, is quite out of place; for this reason, that all men among each other are certainly equal; although superior consideration ought to be due to those who are of the religion of Muhammad. I also have wished for a long while to marry, and as you are indifferent to worldly riches, to me likewise God has given such wealth as cannot be counted. But there is one condition, that first of all you procure my marriage portion.' The marriage-gift of the princess," added the old lady, "is a certain task to perform, if you can fulfil it." I replied, "I am ready in every way, and I shall not be sparing of my wealth or life; tell me what the task is, that I may hear it. The old woman then said, "Remain here today, and tomorrow I will tell it to you." I accepted her proposal with pleasure, and taking my leave, I came out.

The day had in the meantime passed away, and when the evening came, a eunuch called upon me, and conducted me to the seraglio. On entering, I saw that the nobles, the learned, the virtuous, and the sages of the divine law were present. I likewise joined the assembly and sat down. In the meantime the cloth for the repast was spread, and eatables of every variety, both sweet and salt, were laid out. They all began to eat, and with courtesy solicited me to join them.

When dinner was over, a female servant came out from the interior of the seraglio and asked, "Where is Bahrawar? call him." The servants in waiting brought him immediately; his appearance was very respectable, and many keys of silver and gold were suspended from his waist. After saluting me, he sat down by me. The same female servant said, "O, Bahrawar, whatever thou hast seen, relate it fully to this stranger."

Bahrawar, addressing himself to me, began the following narration: "O, friend! our princess possesses thousands of slaves, who are established in trade; among them I am one of the humblest of her hereditary servants. She sends them to different countries with goods and merchandise, worth *lakhs* of rupees, of which they have the charge; when these return from the respective countries to which they were sent to trade, then the princess, in her own presence, enquires of them the state and manners of such country, and hears their different accounts. Once it so happened that this meanest of her slaves went to the country and city of Nimroz to trade, and perceiving that all the inhabitants were dressed in black, and that they sighed and wept every moment, and it appeared to me that some sad calamity had befallen them. From whomsoever I asked the reason of these strange circumstances, no one would answer my enquiry. One day, the moment the morning appeared, all the inhabitants of the city, little and great, young and old, poor and rich, issued forth. They went out and assembled on a plain; the king of the country went there also mounted on horseback, and surrounded by his nobles; then they all formed a regular line, and stood still.

"I also stood among them to see the strange sight, for it clearly appeared that they were waiting for the arrival of someone. In an hour's time a beautiful young man, of an angelic form, about fifteen or sixteen years of age, uttering a loud noise, and foaming at the mouth, and mounted on a dun bull, holding something in one hand, approached from a distance, and came up in front of the people; he descended from the bull, and sat down oriental fashion on the ground, holding the halter of the animal in one hand, and a naked sword in the other; a rosy-coloured, beautiful attendant was with him; the young man gave him that which he held in his hand; the slave took it, and went along showing it to all of them from one end of the line to the other; but such was the nature of the object, that whoever saw it, the same involuntarily wept aloud and bitterly at the strange sight. In this way he continued to show it to everyone, and made everyone weep; then passing along the front of the line, he returned to his master again.

"The moment he came near him, the young man rose up, and with the sword severed the attendant's head from his body, and having again mounted his bull, galloped off towards the quarter from whence he had come. All present stood looking on. When he disappeared from their sight, the inhabitants returned to the city. I was anxiously asking everyone I met the real meaning of this strange occurrence; yea, I even held out the inducement of money and beseeched and flattered them to get an explanation, who the young man was, and why he committed the deed I had seen, and from whence he came, and where he went, but no one would give me the slightest information on the subject, nor could I comprehend it. When I returned here, I related to the princess the astonishing circumstance I had seen. Since then, the princess herself has been amazed at the strange event, and anxious to ascertain its real cause. For which reason she has been fixed on this very point as her marriage portion, that whatever man will bring her a true and particular account of that strange circumstance, she will accept him in marriage; and he shall be the master of all her wealth, her country, and herself."

Bahrawar concluded by saying, "You have now heard every circumstance; reflect within yourself if you can bring the intelligence which is required respecting the young man, then undertake the journey towards the country of Nimroz, and depart soon, or else refuse the conditions and the attempt, and return to your home." I answered, "If God please, I will soon ascertain all the circumstances relating to the strange event, and return to the princess with success; or if my fate be unlucky, then there is no remedy; but the princess must give me her solemn promise she will not swerve from what she engages to perform. And now an uneasy apprehension arises in my heart; if the princess will have the benevolence to call me before her, and allow me to sit down outside the *parda*, and hear with her own ears the request I have made, and favour me with an answer from her own lips; then my heart will be at ease, and everything will be possible for me." These my requests the female servant related to the fairy-formed princess. At last, by way of condescension, she ordered me to be called before her.

The same female returned, and conducted me to the apartment where the princess was; what a display of beauty I saw! Handsome female slaves and servants, and armed damsels, from Kilmak, Turkistan, Abyssinia, Uzbak Tartary and Kashmir, were drawn up in two lines, dressed in rich jewels, with their arms folded across, and each standing in her appropriate station. Shall I call this the court of Indra? or is it a descent on the part of the fairies? an involuntary sigh of rapture escaped from my breast, and my heart began to palpitate; but I forcibly restrained myself. Regarding them all around, I advanced on; but my feet became each as heavy as a hundred *mans*. Whenever I gazed on one of those lovely women, my heart was unwilling to proceed farther

On one side of the saloon a screen was suspended, and a stool set with precious stones was placed near it, as well as a chair of sandal-wood; the female servant made me a sign to sit down on the jewelled stool; I sat down upon it, and she seated herself on the sandal-wood chair; she said, "Now, whatever you have to say, speak it fully and from the heart."

I first extolled the princess's excellent qualities, also her justice and liberality; I then added, that "ever since I have entered the limits of this country, I saw at every stage accommodations for travellers and lofty buildings; and found everywhere servants of all grades appointed to attend upon travellers and necessitous persons. I have likewise spent three days at every halting place, and the fourth day, when I wished to take my leave, no one said with goodwill, "You may depart;" and whatever articles and furniture had been applied to my use at those places, such as chequered carpets, etc., etc., I was told that they were all mine, and that I might either take them away or lock them up in a room, and put my seal on it; that, should it be my pleasure, whenever I came back I might take them away. I have done so; but the wonder is, that if a lonely pilgrim like me has met with such a princely reception, then there must be thousands of such pilgrims who will resort to your dominions; and if everyone is hospitably received in the same manner as myself, sums incalculable must be spent. Now, whence comes the great wealth of which there is such an expenditure, and of what nature is it? The treasures of Karun would not be equal to it; and if we look at the princess's territories, it would appear that their revenues would hardly suffice to defray the kitchen charges, setting the other expenses aside. If the princess would condescend to explain this seeming wonder with her own lips, then, my mind being set at ease, I shall set out for the country of Nimroz; and reaching it by some means or other, after having learned all the particulars of the strange circumstance, I will return, if God should spare my life, to the presence of the princess, and attain the desires of my heart."

On hearing these words, the princess herself said, "O youth, if you have a strong desire to know the exact nature of these circumstances, then stay here today also. I will send for you in the evening, and the account of my vast riches shall be unfolded to you without any reservation." After this assurance, I retired to my place of residence, and waited anxiously, saying, "when will the evening arrive, that my curiosity may be gratified?" In the meantime a eunuch brought some covered trays on the heads of porters, and laid them before me, and said, "The princess has sent you a dinner from her own table; partake of it." When he uncovered the trays before me, the rich fragrance of the meats intoxicated my brains, and my soul became satiated. I ate as much as I could, and sent away the rest, and returned my grateful thanks to the princess. At last, when the sun, the traveller of the whole day, wearied and fatigued, reached his home, and the moon advanced from her palace, attended by her companions, then the female servant came to me and said, "Come, the princess has sent for you."

I went along with her; she led me to the private apartment; the effect of the lights was such that the *shabi kadr* was nothing to it. A *masnad*, covered with gold, was placed on rich carpets, with a pillow studded with jewels; over it an awning of brocade was stretched, with a fringe of pearls on silver poles studded with precious stones; and in front of the *masnad* artificial trees formed of various jewels, with flowers and leaves attached (one would say they were nature's own production), were erected in beds of gold; and on the right and left, beautiful slaves and servants were in waiting with folded arms and downcast eyes, in respectful attitude. Dancing women and female singers, with ready-tuned instruments, attended to begin their performances. On seeing such a scene and such splendid preparations, my senses were bewildered. I asked the female servant who came with me "there is here such gay splendour in the scene of the day, and such magnificence in that of the night, that the day may very justly be called *'Id*, and the night *shabi barat*; moreover, a king who possessed the whole world could not exhibit greater splendour and magnificence. Is it always so at the princess's court? The servant replied, "The princess's court ever displays the same magnificence you see now; there is no abatement or difference, except that it is sometimes greater: sit you here; the princess is in another apartment; I will go and inform her of your arrival."

Saying this, the nurse went away and quickly returned; he desired me to come to the princess. The moment I entered her apartment I was struck with amazement. I could not tell where the door was, or where the walls, for they were covered with Aleppo mirrors, of the height of a man, all around, the frames of which were studded with diamonds and pearls. The reflection of one fell on the other, and it appeared as if the whole room was inlaid with jewels. At one end a *parda* was hung, behind which the princess sat. The female servant seated herself close to the *parda*, and desired me to sit down also; then she began the following narrative, according to the princess's commands: "Hear, O intelligent youth! The sultan of this country was a potent king; he had seven daughters born in his house. One day, the king held a festival, and these seven daughters were standing before him superbly dressed, with each sixteen jewels, twelve ornaments, and in every hair an elephant pearl. Something came into the king's mind, and he looked towards his daughters and said, 'If your father had not been a king, and you had been born in the house of some poor man, then who would have called you princesses? Praise God that you are called princesses; all your good fortune depends on my life.'

"Six of his daughters, being of one mind, replied, 'Whatever your majesty says, is true, and our happiness depends on your welfare alone.' But the princess now present, though she was younger than all her sisters, yet even in sense and judgment, even at that age, she was superior to them all. She stood silent, and did not join her sisters in the reply they made; for this reason, that to say so was impious. The king looked towards her with anger, and said, 'Well, my lady, you say nothing; what is the cause of this?' Then the princess, tying both her hands with a handkerchief, humbly replied, 'If your majesty will grant me safety of my life, and pardon my presumption, then this humble slave will unfold the dictates of her heart.' The king said, 'Speak what thou hast to say.' Then the princess said, 'Mighty king, you must have heard, that the voice of truth is bitter; for which reason, disregarding life at this moment, I presume to address your majesty; whatever the great Writer has written in the book of my destiny, no one can efface, and in no way can it be evaded. "Whether you bruise your feet by depending on your own exertions, or lay your head on the carpet in prayer, your fate written on the forehead, whatever it be, shall come to pass."

"'That Almighty Ruler, who has made you a king, He indeed also has made me a princess. In the arsenal of his omnipotence, no one has power. You are my sovereign and benefactor, and if I should apply the dust which lies under your auspicious feet, as a colyrium for my eyes, then it would become me; but the destinies of everyone are with everyone.' The king, on hearing this speech, became angry; the reply displeased him highly, and he said with wrath, 'What great words issue from a little mouth! Now let this be her punishment, that you strip off whatever jewels she has on her hands and feet, and let her be placed in a sedan-chair, and set down in such a wilderness, where no human traces can be found; then we shall see what is written in her destinies.'

"According to the king's commands, at that midnight hour, when it was the very essence of darkness, the princess (who had been reared with such delicacy and tenderness), and had seen no other place except her own apartments, was carried by the porters in a litter, and set down in a place where not even a bird ever flapped its wing, much less did human creatures there exist; they left her there and returned. The princess's heart was all at once in such a state as cannot be conceived; reduced to what she was, from what she had been! Then in the threshold of God, she offered up her prayers, and said, "Thou art so mighty O Lord, that what thou hast wished, Thou hast done; and whatever Thou willest, Thou dost; and whatever Thou mayest wish, that Thou wilt do: whilst life remains in my nostrils, I shall not be hopeless of thy protection'. Impressed with these thoughts, she fell asleep. When the morn appeared, the eyes of the princess opened; she called for water to perform her ablutions. Then, all at once, the occurrences of last night came to her recollection; she said to herself, 'Where art thou, and where this speech?' Saying this to herself, she got up, and performed the *tayammum*, said her prayers, and poured forth the praises of her Maker! O youth, the heart is torn with anguish to reflect on the princess's sad condition at that time. Ask that innocent and inexperienced heart what it felt.

"In short, she sat in the litter, and putting her trust in God, she repeated to herself at that moment these verses:

"When I had no teeth, then thou gavest milk;
When thou hast given teeth, wilt thou not grant food!
He who takes care of the fowls of the air,

And of all the animals of the earth,
He will also take care of thee.
Why art thou sad, simple-minded one!
By being sorrowful thou'lt get nothing;
He who provides for the fool, for the wise, and for the whole world,
Will likewise provide for thee.'

"It is true, that when no resource remains, then God is remembered, or else everyone in his own plans, thinks himself a Lukman, and a Bu' Ali Sina. Now listen to the surprising ways of God. In this manner three days clear passed away, during which a grain of food did not enter the princess's mouth; her flower-like frame became quite withered as a dry thorn; and her colour, which hitherto shone like gold, became yellow as turmeric; her mouth became rigid, and her eyes were petrified, but still a faint respiration remained passing and re-passing. Whilst there is life, there is hope. In the morning of the fourth day, a hermit appeared of bright countenance, in appearance like Khizr, and of an enlightened heart. Seeing the princess in that state, he said, 'O daughter, though your father is a king, yet these sorrows were decreed in thy destiny. Now, conceive this old hermit your servant, and think day and night of your Maker. God will do what is right.' And whatever morsels the hermit had in his wallet, he laid them before the princess; then he went in search of water; he saw a well, but where were the wheel and bucket by means of which he might draw the water? He pulled off some leaves from a tree, and made a cup, and taking off his sash, he fastened the cup to it, and drew up some water, and gave it to the princess. At last she regained her senses. The holy man, seeing her helpless and solitary state, gave her every consolation, and cheered her heart; and he himself began to weep. When the princess saw his sympathetic grief, and heard his kind assurances, she became easy in her mind. From that day, the old man made this an established rule, that in the morning he went to the city to beg, and brought to the princess whatever scraps or morsels he received.

"In this way a few days passed. One day the princess designed to put some oil in her hair, and comb it; just as she opened the plaits of her hair, a pearl round and brilliant dropped out. The princess gave it to the hermit, and desired him to sell it in the city, and bring her the amount. He sold that pearl, and brought back the money received for it to the princess. Then the princess desired that a habitation fit for her residence might be erected on that spot. The hermit replied, 'O daughter, do you dig the foundation for the walls, and collect some earth; I will, some of these days, bring some water, knead the clay for the bricks, and erect a room for you.' The princess, on his advice, began to dig the ground; when she had dug a yard in depth, behold, under the soil a door appeared. The princess cleared away the earth which lay before it; a large room filled with jewels and gold pieces appeared: she took four or five handfuls of gold and closed the door, and having filled up the place with earth, made level its surface. In the meantime the hermit returned. The princess said to him, "bring good masons and builders, and workmen of every kind, expert and masters in their craft, so that a grand palace may be erected on this spot equal to the palace of Kasra, and superior to the palace of Ni'man; and that the fortifications of the city, a fort, a garden, a well, and an unrivalled caravanserai be built as soon as possible; but first of all, draw out the plans on paper and bring them to me for approval."

"The hermit brought clever, skilful, intelligent workmen, and had them ready. The erection of the different buildings was soon begun according to the princess's directions, and clever and trusty servants for every office were chosen and entertained. The news of the erection of such princely buildings by degrees reached the king, the shadow of Omnipotence, who was the princess's father. On hearing it, he became greatly surprised, and asked everyone, 'Who is this person who has begun to erect such edifices?' No one knew anything of the matter to be able to give a reply. All put their hands on their ears and said, 'No one of your slaves knows who is the builder of them.' Then the king sent one of his nobles with this message, 'I wish to come and see those buildings, and to know also of what country you are the princess, and of what family; for I wish much to ascertain all these circumstances.'

"When the princess received this agreeable intelligence, she was greatly pleased in her mind, and wrote the following letter: 'To the protector of the world, prosperity! On hearing the intelligence of your majesty's visit, to my humble mansion, I am infinitely rejoiced; and it has been the cause of respect and dignity to me, the meanest of your slaves. How happy is the fate of that place where your majesty's footsteps are impressed, and on the inhabitants of which the shadow of the skirt of your prosperity is cast; may they both be dignified with the look of favour! This slave hopes that tomorrow, being Thursday, is a propitious day, and to me, it is more welcome than the day of *Nau Roz*, your majesty's person resembles the sun; by condescending to come here, be pleased to bestow, with your light, value and dignity on this worthless atom, and partake of whatever his humble slave can provide; this will be the essence of benevolence and courtesy, on the part of your majesty: to say more would exceed the bounds of respect.' To the nobleman who brought the message she made some presents, and dismissed him with the above reply.

"The king read the letter, and sent word, saying, 'We have accepted your invitation, and will certainly come.' The princess ordered the servants and all the attendants to get ready the necessary preparations for an entertainment, with such propriety and elegance, that the king, on seeing the banquet and eating thereof, might be highly pleased; and that all who came with the king, great and little, should be well entertained and return content. From the princess's strict directions, the dishes, of every kind, both salt and sweet, were so deliciously prepared, that if the daughter of a Brahman had tasted them, she would have become a Musalman. When the evening came, the king went to the princess's palace, seated on an uncovered throne; the princess, with her ladies in waiting, advanced to receive him; when she cast her eyes on the king's throne, she made the royal obeisance with such proper respect, that on seeing it, the king was still more surprised; with the same profound respect she accompanied the king to the throne, set with jewels, which she had erected for him. The princess had prepared a platform of 125,000 pieces of silver; a hundred and one trays of jewels and of gold pieces, and woollen shiffs, shawls, muslins, silk and brocades; two elephants and ten horses, of 'Irak and Yaman, with caparisons set with precious stones, were likewise prepared for the royal acceptance. She presented these to his majesty, and stood before him herself with folded arms. The king asked with great complacency, 'Of what country are you a princess, and for what reasons are you come here?'

"The princess, after making her obeisance, replied, 'This slave is that offender who, in consequence of the royal anger, was sent to this wilderness, and all these things which your majesty sees are the wonderful works of God.' On hearing these words, the king's blood glowed (with paternal warmth), and rising up, he pressed the princess fondly to his bosom, and seizing her hand, he ordered her to be seated on a chair that he had placed near the throne; but still the king was astonished and surprised at all he saw, and ordered that the queen, along with the princesses, should come thither with all speed. When they arrived, the mother and sisters recognized the princess, and, embracing her with fondness, wept over her, and praised God. The princess presented her mother and sisters with such heaps of gold and jewels, that the treasures of the world could not equal them in the balance. Then the king, having made them all sit in his company, partook of the feast which had been prepared.

"As long as the king lived, the time passed in this manner; sometimes the king came to visit the princess, and sometimes carried the princess with him to his own palaces. When the king died, the government of the kingdom descended to this princess; for, except herself, no other person of her family was fit for this office. O, youth, the history of the princess is what you have heard. Finally, heaven-bestowed wealth never fails, but the intentions of the possessor must at the same time be just; moreover, how much soever is spent out of this providential wealth so much also is the increase: to be astonished at the power of God, is not right in any religion." The female servant, after finishing this narrative, said "Now if you still intend to proceed to the country of Nimroz, and if you are determined in your mind to bring the requisite intelligence then depart soon." I replied, I am going this moment, and if God pleases I shall be back very soon. At last, taking leave of the princes and relying on the protection of God, I set out for that quarter.

In about a year's time, after encountering many difficulties, arrived at the city of Nimroz. All the inhabitants of that place tha I saw, noble or common, were dressed in black, and whatever I had heard, that I fully perceived. After some days, the evening of the new moon occurred. On the first day of the month, all the inhabitant of the city, little and great, children, nobles, prince, women and men, assembled on a large plain. I also, bewildered and distracted i my condition, went along with the vast concourse; separated from my country and possessions, in the garb of a pilgrim, I was standing to behold the strange sight, and to see what might result from the mysterious scene. In the meantime, a young man advanced from the woods, mounted on a bull, foaming at the mouth, and roaring and shouting in a frightful manner. I, miserable, who had undergone such labour, and overcome so many dangers, and had come there to ascertain the circumstances, yet on seeing the young man I was quite confounded and stood silent with astonishment. The young man, according to his usual custom, did what he used to do, and returned to the woods; and the concourse of people from the city likewise returned thither. When I had collected my senses, I then repented saying to myself, "What is this you have done? Now it is your lot to wait anxiously for another whole month." Having no remedy, I returned with the rest; and I passed that month like the month of *Ramadan*, counting one day after another. At last the new moon appeared, and was hailed by me as *'Id*. On the first of the month, the king and the inhabitants again assembled on that same plain; then I determined, that this time, let what will happen, I would be resolute, and propound this mysterious circumstance.

Suddenly the young man appeared, mounted, according to custom, on a yellow bull, and, dismounting, sat down on the ground; in one hand he held a naked sword, and in the other the bull's halter; he gave the vase to his attendant, who, as usual, showed it to everyone, and carried it back to his master. The crowd, on seeing the vase, began to weep; the young man broke the vase, and struck such a blow on the slave's neck as to sever his head from his body, and, he himself remounting the bull, returned towards the woods. I began to run after him, with all speed, but the inhabitants laid hold of my hand, and exclaimed, "What is this you are going to do?

why, knowingly, art thou about to perish? If thou art so tired of life, there are a great many ways of dying, by which thou mayest end thy existence." How much soever I beseeched them to let me go, and even had recourse to main force, in order that by some means I might escape from their hands, yet I could not release myself. Three or four men clung fast to me, and having seized me, led me towards the city. I again suffered for another whole month in a strange state of disquietude.

When that month passed also, and the last day of it had elapsed, all the inhabitants assembled on the plain on the following morning in the same manner. I, apart from all, arose at the hour of morning prayer. I went before all the others were astir into the woods, and there lay concealed, exactly on the road by which the young man was to pass; for no one could there restrain me from executing my project. The young man came in the usual manner, performed the same acts already described, re-mounted, and was returning. I followed him, and eagerly running up, I joined him. The young man, from the noise of my steps, perceived that somebody was coming after him. All at once, turning round the halter of his bull, he gave a loud shout, and threatened me; then drawing his sword, he advanced towards me, and was about to strike. I bent down with the utmost respect, and made him my *salam*, and joining both my hands together, I stood in silence. That person being a judge of respectful behaviour restraining his blow, said to me. "O pilgrim, thou wouldest have been killed for nothing, but thou hast escaped – thy life is prolonged; get away. Where art thou going?" He then drew a jewelled dagger, having a tassel set with pearls, from his waist, and threw it towards me, and added, "At this moment I have no money about me to give thee; carry this dagger to the king, and thou wilt get whatever thou askest." To such a degree did my fear and dread of him prevail, that I had not power to speak or ability to move; my voice was choked, and my feet became heavy.

After saying this, the brave young man, roaring aloud, went on. I said to myself, "let what will happen, to remain behind now is, in thy case, folly thou wilt never again get such an opportunity to execute thy project. Regardless, therefore, of my life, I also went on. He again turned round and forbade me in great wrath to follow him, and seemed determined to put me to death. I stretched forth my neck, and conjuring him by all that was sacred, I said, "O Rustam of these days, strike such a blow that I may be cut clean in two; let not a fibre remain together, and let me be released from this wandering and wretched state; I pardon you my blood." He replied, "O demon-faced! why dost thou for nothing bring thy blood on my head, and makest me criminal; go thy own way; what! is thy life become a burden to thee?" I did not mind what he said, but advanced; then he knowingly appeared not to regard me, and I followed him. Proceeding on about two *kos*, we passed the wood, and came to a square building; the young man went up to the door and gave a frightful scream; the door opened of itself; he entered, and I remained altogether outside. "O God," said I, "what shall I now do?" I was perplexed; at last, after a short delay, a slave came out and brought a message, saying, "Come in, he has called you to his presence; perhaps the angel of death hovers over your head; what evil fortune has befallen you?" I replied, "Verily it is good fortune;" and without fear, I entered along with him into the garden.

At last, he led me to a place where the young man was sitting; on seeing him, I made him a very low *salam*; he beckoned me to sit down; I sat down with respect. What do I see but the young man sitting alone on a *masnad*, with the tools of a goldsmith lying before him; and he had just finished a branch of emeralds. When the time came for him to rise up, all the slaves that were around the place concealed themselves in different rooms; I also from fear hid myself in a small closet. The young man rose up, and having fastened the chains of all the apartments, he went towards the corner of the garden, and began to beat the bull he usually rode. The noise of the animal's roaring reached my ear, and my heart quaked with fear; but as I had ran all these risks to develop this mystery, I forced the door, though trembling with fear, and under the screen of the trunk of a tree, I stood and saw what was going on. The young man threw down the club with which he was beating the bull, and unlocked a room and entered it. Then, instantly coming out, he stroked the bull's back with his hand, and kissed its mouth; and having given it some grain and grass, he came towards me. On perceiving this, I ran off quickly, and hid myself in the room.

The young man unfastened the chains of all the rooms, and the whole of the slaves came out, bringing with them a small carpet, a wash-hand basin, and a water pot. After washing his hands and face, he stood up to pray; when he had finished his prayers, he called out, "Where is the pilgrim?" On hearing myself called, I ran out and stood before him; he desired me to sit down; after making him a *salam*, I sat down; the dinner was served; he partook of it, and gave me some, which I also ate. When the dishes were removed, and we had washed our hands, he dismissed his slaves and told them to go to rest. When no one except ourselves remained in the apartment, he then spoke to me, and asked, "O friend, what great misfortune has befallen thee that thou goest about seeking thy death?" I related in full detail all the adventures of my life, from beginning to end, and added, that, "from your goodness, I have hopes of obtaining my wishes." On hearing this, he heaving a deep sigh, went raving mad, and began to say, "O God! who except thee is acquainted with the tortures of love! He whose chilblain has not yet broken out, how can he know the pains of others? he only knows the degree of this pain who has felt the pangs of love!

> *'The anguish of love, you must ask of the lover,*
> *Not of him who feigns, but of the true lover.'"*

A moment after, coming to himself, he heaved a heart-burning sigh; the room resounded with it; then I perceived that he was likewise tortured with the pangs of love, and was suffering from the same malady as myself. On this discovery, I plucked up courage and said, "I have related to you all my own adventures; now do me the favour to impart to me the past events of your life; I will then first of all assist you as far as I can, and by exerting myself obtain for you the desires of your heart." In short, that true lover, conceiving me his companion and fellow-sufferer, began the relation of his adventures in the following manner. "Hear, O friend! I whose heart is tortured with anguish, am the prince of this country of Nimroz; the king, that is to say, my father, at my birth, collected together all the fortune tellers, astrologers and learned men, and ordered them to cast and examine my horoscope, to fix my nativity, and to state in full to his majesty whatever was to befall me every individual moment, and hour, and *pahar*, and day, and month, and year, of my life. They all assembled according to the king's order, and consulting together, they, from their mystical science, ascertained my future fate, and said, 'By the blessing of God, the prince has been begotten and born under such a propitious planet, and in such a lucky moment, that he ought to be equal to Alexander in extent of dominion, and in justice equal to Naushirwan. He will be, moreover, proficient in every science, and every branch of learning, and towards whatever subject his heart is inclined, he will accomplish it with perfection. He will in generosity and bravery acquire such renown, that mankind will no longer remember Hatim and Rustam; but until he attains the age of fourteen, he is exposed to great danger if he sees the sun or moon; yea, it is to be feared he may become a mad demoniac, and shed the blood of many; and restless of living in society, he will fly to the woods, and associate with beasts and birds; great and strict pains must be taken that he should never behold the sun by day or the moon by night, or cast a look even towards the heavens. If this period of fourteen years pass away without danger and in safety, then for the rest of his life he will reign in peace and prosperity.'

"On hearing this prognostication, the king ordered this garden to be laid out, and caused to be built in it many apartments of various kinds. He gave an order for me to be brought up in a vault, lined on the inside with felt, so that not a single ray of light from the sun or moon might penetrate into my apartment. I had a wet nurse and all other kinds of female servants and attendants attached to me, and was brought up in this grand palace with this imagined security. A learned tutor, who was skilled in public affairs, was appointed to superintend my education; so that I might acquire every science and art, and the practice of the seven varieties of penmanship; and my father always looked after me; the occurrences of every day and every moment were told to the king. I considered that same place as the whole world, and amused myself with toys and flowers; and I had procured for me every delicacy the world could produce for my food; whatever I desired I had. By the age of ten years, I had acquired every species of learning, and every useful accomplishment.

"One day, beneath that dome, an astonishing flower appeared from the sky-light, which increased in size as I gazed upon it; I wished to seize it with my hands, but as I stretched them towards it, it ascended and eluded my grasp. I, having become astonished, was looking steadfastly at it, when the sound of a loud laugh reached my ear; I raised my head to look towards the dome from which the noise proceeded. Then I saw that a face, resplendent as the full moon, having rent the felt, continued issuing forth. On beholding it, my reason and senses vanished. On coming to myself, I looked up, and saw a throne of jewels raised on the shoulders of fairies; a person was seated on it, with a crown of precious stones on her head, and clothed in a superb dress; she held in her hand a cup made of ruby, and seated, was drinking wine. The throne descended by slow degrees from its height, and rested on the floor of the dome. Then the fairy called me, and placed me beside her on the throne; she began to make use of expressions of endearment, and having pressed her lips to mine, she made me drink a cup of rosy wine, and said, 'The human race is faithless, but my heart loves thee.' The expressions she uttered were so endearing and so fascinating, that in a moment my heart was enraptured, and I felt such pleasure as if I had tasted the supreme joys of life, and thus I conceived that I had only on that day entered the world of enjoyment.

"The result is my present state! but no one on earth hath ever seen, or heard such ecstatic pleasure! In that zest, with our hearts at ease, we both were seated, when all at once our joys were dashed to pieces! Now listen to the unlooked-for circumstance which produced this sudden change. At the moment, four fairies descended from the heavens, and whispered something in that beloved one's ear. On hearing it, her colour changed, and she said to me, 'O my beloved, I fondly wished to pass some moments with you, and regale my heart, and to repeat my visits in the same manner, or to take thee with me. But fate will not permit two persons like us to remain in one place in peace and felicity; farewell, my beloved! may God protect you!' On hearing these dreadful words, my senses vanished, and my bliss fled from my grasp. I cried, 'O my charmer, when shall we meet again? what dreadful words of wrath are these which you have made me hear? If you will return quickly, then you will find me alive, otherwise you will regret the delay; or else tell me your name and place of residence, that I may from those directions, by diligent search, conduct myself to you.' On hearing this she said, 'God forbid you should do so; may the ears of Satan be deaf; may your age amount to a hundred and twenty years; if we live we shall meet again; I am the daughter of the king of the Jinns, and I dwell in the mountain of Kaf. On saying this, she caused the throne to ascend, and it ascended in the same manner as it had descended.

"Whilst the throne was in sight, our eyes were fixed on each other; when it disappeared from my eyes, my state became such as if the shadow of a fairy had fallen on me; a strange sort of gloom was spread over my heart, and my understanding and consciousness left me; the world appeared dark under my eyes; distracted and confused, I wept bitterly, and scattered dust over my head, and tore my clothes; I became regardless of food and drink, nor cared for good or evil.

'What various evils result from this same love!
In the heart are produced sadness and impatience.'

"My misfortune was soon known to my nurse and preceptor; with fear and trembling they went before the king, and said, 'Such is the state of the prince of the people of the world; we do not know how this disaster has suddenly and of itself fallen upon him, so that rest, food, and drink have all on his part been abandoned.' On hearing these sad tidings the king immediately came to the garden where I resided, accompanied by the vizier, intelligent nobles, wise physicians, true astrologers, learned *mullas*, holy devotees, and men abstracted from worldly affairs. On seeing my distracted, sighing, weeping condition, his mind became also distracted; he wept, and with fond affection clasped me to his breast, and gave orders for my proper treatment. The physicians wrote out their prescriptions, in order to strengthen my heart and cure my brain, and the holy priests wrote out charms and amulets, some to be swallowed, and others to be worn on my person, and having each repeated prayers of exorcism, they began to blow upon me; the astrologers said this misfortune had happened owing to the revolution of the stars, for the averting of it, give pious donations. In short, everyone advised according to his science; but what was passing within me, my heart alone experienced; no one's assistance or remedy was of avail to my evil destiny; day after day my lunacy increased, and my body became emaciated from the want of nourishment. There remained for me only to shriek and moan, day and night. Three years passed away in this state. In the fourth year, a merchant, who was on his travels, arrived, and brought with him into the royal presence rare and valuable articles of different countries; he met with a gracious reception.

"The king favoured him greatly, and after enquiries respecting his health, he said to him, 'You have seen many countries; have you anywhere seen a truly learned physician, or have heard of such from anyone?' The merchant replied, 'Mighty sire, this slave has travelled a great deal; in the middle of the Ganges river in Hindustan there is a small mountain; there a Jata-dhari Gusa,in has built a large temple to Mahadev, together with a place of worship, and a garden of great beauty, and in that mountain-island he lives; and his custom is this, that once a year on the day of *Shevrat*, he comes out of his dwelling, swims in the river, and enjoys himself. After washing himself, when he is returning to his abode, then the sick and afflicted of various countries and regions, who come there from afar, assemble near his door. Of these a numerous crowd is formed.

'"The holy Gusa,in (who ought to be called the Plato of these days), moves along examining the urine, and feeling the pulse of each, and giving each a recipe. God has given him such healing power, that, on taking his medicines, their effects are instantaneous, and the disease utterly vanishes. These circumstances I have seen with my own eyes, and adored the power of God which has created such beings! If your majesty orders it, I will conduct the prince of the people of the world to that wonderful man, and show the prince to him; I firmly hope he will soon be completely cured; moreover, this scheme is externally beneficial, for from inhaling the air of various places, and from the diet and drink of different countries through which we shall pass, the prince's mind will be restored to cheerfulness.' The merchant's advice seemed very proper to the king, and being pleased, he said, 'Very well; perhaps the holy man's treatment may prove efficacious, and this melancholy may be removed from my son's mind.' The king appointed a confidential nobleman, who had seen the world, and had been tried on various occasions, together with the merchant, to attend me, and he furnished us with the requisite equipment. Having seen us embark on boats of every variety, together with our baggage, he dismissed us. Proceeding onwards, stage after stage, we arrived at the place where the holy Gusa,in lived. From change of air, and from living on a different diet, my mind became somewhat composed; but there still remained the same state of silence; and I wept incessantly. The recollection of the lovely fairy was not for a moment effaced from my mind; if I spoke sometimes, it was only to repeat these lines:

'I know not what fairy-faced one has glanced over me,
But my heart was sound and tranquil not long ago.'

At last, when two or three months had passed away, nearly four thousand sick had assembled on the rock, and all said, 'If God please, the Gusa,in will shortly come out of his abode, and bestow on us his advice, and we shall be perfectly cured.' In short, when that day arrived, the Gusa,in appeared in the morning, like the sun, and bathed and swam in the river; he crossed over it and returned, and rubbed ashes of cow-dung over his body, and hid his fair form like a live coal under the ashes. He made a mark with sandal wood on his forehead, girded on his *langoti*, threw a towel over his shoulders, tied his long hair up in a knot, twisted his mustachios, and put on his shoes. It appeared, from his looks, that the whole world possessed no value to him. Having put a small writing desk set with gems under his arm, and looking at each patient in turn, he gave them his recipes, and came to me. When our looks met, he stood still, paused for a moment, and then said to me, 'Come with me.' I went along with him.

"When he had done with all the rest, he led me into the garden, and into a neat and richly-ornamented private apartment, and he said to me, 'Do you make your residence here,' and went himself to his abode. When forty days had elapsed, he came to me, and found me better comparatively with what I had been before. He then, smiling, said, 'Amuse yourself by walking about in this garden, and eat whatever fruits you like.' He gave me a china pot filled with *ma'jun*, and added, 'Take without fail six *mashas* from this pot every morning, fasting.' Saying this, he went away, and I followed strictly his prescription. My body perceptibly gained strength daily, and my mind composure, but mighty love was still triumphant; that fairy's form ever wandered before my eyes.

"One day I perceived a book in a recess in the wall; I took it down, and saw that all the sciences relating to the future and the present world were comprised in it, as if the ocean had been compressed into a vase. I used to read it at all times; I acquired great skill in the science of physic, and the mystical art of philters. A year passed away in the meantime, and again that same day of joy returned; the Gusa,in, having arisen from his devotional posture, came out of his abode; I made him my *salam*; he gave me the writing case, and said, 'Accompany me.' I accordingly went along with him. When he came out of the gate a vast crowd showered blessings on him. The nobleman and the merchant, seeing me with the Gusa,in, fell at his feet, and began to pour forth their blessings on him, saying, "by the favour of your holiness, this much at least has been effected." The Gusa,in went to the *ghat* of the river, according to custom, and performed his ablutions and devotions, as he was wont to do every year; returning from thence, he was proceeding along the line and examining the sick.

"It happened, that in the group of lunatics, a handsome young man, who had scarce strength to stand up, attracted the Gusa,in's attention. He said to me, 'Bring him with you.' After delivering his prescriptions of cure to all, he went into his private apartment and opened a little of the young lunatic's skull; he attempted to seize with his forceps the centipede which was curled on his brain. An idea struck me, and I spoke out, saying, 'If you will heat the forceps in the fire, and then apply it to the centipede's back, it will be better, as it will then come out of its own accord; but if you thus attempt to pull it off, it will not quit its grasp on the brain, and the patient's life will be endangered.' On hearing this, the Gusa,in looked towards me; silently he rose up, and, without saying a word, he went to the corner of the garden, and seizing a tree in his grasp, he formed his long hair into a noose, and hanged himself. I went to the spot, and saw, alas! alas! that he was dead. I became quite afflicted at the strange and astonishing sight; but being helpless, I thought it best to bury him. The moment I began to take him down from the tree, two keys dropped from his locks; I took them up, and interred that treasure of excellence in the earth. Having taken with me the two keys, I began to apply them to all the locks. By chance I opened the locks of two rooms with these keys, and perceived that they were filled from the floor to the roof with precious stones; in one place I saw a chest covered with velvet, with clasps of gold, and locked. When I opened it, then I saw in it a book, in which was written the "Most awful of Names," and the mode of invoking the genii, and the fairies, and the holding of intercourse with spirits, and how to subdue them, also the mode of charming the sun.

"I became quite delighted at the idea of having acquired such a treasure, and began to put those charms in practice. I opened the garden door, and said to the nobleman, and to those who had come with me, 'Send for the vessels which had brought us, and embark in them all these jewels, specie, merchandise, and books,' and having embarked myself in a small vessel, I proceeded from thence to the main ocean. When sailing along, I approached my own country. The intelligence reached my father. He mounted his horse, and advanced to meet us; with anxious affection he clasped me to his bosom; I kissed his feet, and said, 'May this humble being be allowed to live in the former garden?'

"The king replied, 'O my son, that garden appears to me calamitous, and I have therefore forbidden its being kept up; that spot is not at present fit for the abode of man; reside in any other abode which your heart may desire. You had best choose some place in the fort, and live under my eyes; and having there formed such a garden as you wish, continue to walk about and to amuse yourself.' I strenuously resisted and caused the former garden to be repaired once more, and having embellished it like a perfect paradise, I went to reside in it. There, at my ease, I fasted forty days for the purpose of subduing the jinns to my will; and having abandoned living creatures, I began to practise my spells on the world of spirits.

"When the forty days were completed, such a terrible storm arose at midnight, that the very strongest buildings fell down, and trees were uprooted and scattered in all directions; an army of fairies appeared. A throne descended from the air, on which a person of dignified appearance was seated, richly dressed, with a crown of pearls on his head. On seeing him, I saluted him with great respect; he returned my salutation, and said, 'O friend, why hast thou raised this commotion for nothing? what dost thou want with me?' I replied, 'This wretch has been long in love with your daughter, and for her I have everywhere wandered about wretched, distracted, and am dead, though alive; I am now sick of existence, and have staked my life on this deed which I have done. All my hopes now rest on your benevolence, that you will exalt this unfortunate wanderer with your favour, and that you will bestow on me life and happiness, by allowing me to behold your fair daughter; it will be an act of great merit.'

"On hearing my wishes, he said, 'Man is made of earth, and we are formed of fire; connection between two such classes is very difficult.' I swore an oath, saying, 'I only desire to see her, and have no other purpose.' Again the king of the fairies replied, 'Man does not adhere to his promises; in time of need he promises everything, but he does not keep it in recollection. I say this for thy good; for if ever thou formest other wishes, then she and thou wilt be ruined and undone; moreover, it will endanger your lives.' I repeated my oaths, and added, that whatever could injure both of us, I would never do, and that all I desired was to see her sometimes. These words were passing between us, when suddenly, the fairy (of whom we were talking) appeared before us, with much splendour, and completely adorned; and the throne of the king of the fairies remounted thence. I then embraced the fairy with fond eagerness, and repeated this verse:

> *'Why should not she of the arched eyebrows come to my house,*
> *She for whose sake I have fasted for forty days.'*

In that state of felicity we resided together in the garden. I dreaded, through fear, to think of other joys; I only tasted the superficial pleasure of her roseate lips, and constantly gazed upon her charms. The lovely fairy, seeing me so true to my oath, was surprised within herself, and used sometimes to say, 'O my beloved, you are indeed strictly faithful to your promise; but I will give you, by the way of friendship, a piece of advice; take care of your mystical book; for the jinns, seeing you off your guard, will purloin it some day or other.' I replied, 'I guard this book as I would my life.'

"It so happened, that one night Satan led me astray; in a fit of overpowering passion, I said to myself, 'Let happen what will, how long can I restrain myself?' I clasped the lovely fairy to my bosom, and attempted to revel in ecstatic joys. Instantly, a voice came forth, saying, 'Give me the book, for the great name of God is written in it; do not profane it.' In that fervour of passion, I was insensible to every other consideration; I took the book from my bosom and delivered it, without knowing to whom I gave it, and plunged myself into the fervid joys of love. The beautiful fairy, seeing my foolish conduct, said, 'Alas! selfish man, thou hast at last transgressed, and forgotten my admonition.'

"On saying this, she became senseless, and I perceived a jinn standing at the head of the bed, who held the magical book in his hand; I attempted to seize him, and beat him severely, and snatch away the book, when in the meantime another appeared, took the book from his hand, and ran off. I began to repeat the incantations I had learnt. The jinn, who was still standing near me, became a bull; but, alas! the lovely fairy had not in the least recovered her senses, and that same state of stupor continued. Then my mind became distracted, and all my joys were turned into bitterness. From that day, man became my aversion. I live in a corner of this garden; and for the sake of agreeably occupying my mind, I made this emerald vase, ornamented with flowers, and every month I go to the plain, mounted on that same bull, break the vase, and kill a slave, with the hope that everyone may see my sad state and pity me; perhaps some creature of God may so far favour me and pray for me, that I even may regain the desire of my heart. O faithful friend, such as I have related to thee is the sad tale of my madness and lunacy."

I wept at hearing it, and said, "O prince, you have truly suffered greatly from love; but I swear here by God, that I will abandon my own wishes, and will now roam among woods and mountains for your good, and do all I can to find out your beloved fairy. Having made this promise, I took leave of the prince, and for five years wandered through the desert, sifting the dust, like a mad man, but found no trace of the fairy. At last, desponding of success, I ascended a mountain, and wished to throw myself down from its summit, so that neither bone nor rib in my frame might remain entire. The same veiled horseman, who saved you from destruction, came up to me and said, "Do not throw away thy life; in a few days thou wilt be in possession of the desires of thy heart." O holy Dervishes! I have at last seen you. I have now hopes that joy and happiness will be our lot, and all of us, now affected as we are, may attain our wished-for objects.

THE BAKHTYAR NAMA

A staple of Persian and Turkic literatures, the *Bakhtyār-nāma* shares motifs and themes with older Indian literary traditions. The story follows Prince Bakhtyār, a just and noble ruler, as he navigates the challenges of governance alongside his ten trusted viziers, who in fact conspire against him. Despite facing betrayal and treachery orchestrated by one of his viziers, Bakhtyār's unwavering commitment to justice and integrity ultimately leads to his triumph, reinforcing the principles of ethical leadership and moral courage. Through his journey Bakhtyār emerges not only as a victorious hero but also as a beacon of virtue, inspiring admiration and loyalty among his loyal subjects.

CHAPTER I

History of King Azad Bakht and the Vizier's Daughter

Thus it is recorded by the authors of remarkable histories, and the narrators of delightful tales, that there was once in the country of Sistan, a certain King, possessing a crown and a throne, whose name was Azad Bakht; and he had a Vizier entitled Sipahsalar, a person of such bravery and skill that the moon concealed herself among the clouds from fear of his scimitar. This Vizier had a daughter endowed with such exquisite beauty that the rose of the garden and the moon of the heavenly spheres were confounded at the superior lustre of her cheeks. Sipahsalar loved this daughter with excessive fondness, so that he could scarcely exist an hour without her. Having gone on an expedition to inspect the state of the country, it happened that he found himself under a necessity of passing some time from home. He immediately despatched confidential persons with orders to bring his daughter to him from the capital. These persons, having arrived at the Vizier's palace, paid their obeisance to the damsel, who ordered her attendants to prepare for the journey to her father. The horses were instantly caparisoned, and a litter provided with magnificence suitable to a princely traveller. The damsel, seated in this, commenced her journey, and went forth from the city.

It happened that the King, who had gone on a hunting-party, was at that moment returning from the chase. He beheld the litter with its ornaments and splendid decorations; and, whilst he gazed, it was borne quite out of the town. He sent to enquire about it; and the attendants said that it belonged to the daughter of Sipahsalar, who was going to her father. When the King's servants returned and reported to him this intelligence, he rode up to the litter that he might send his compliments to Sipahsalar. On his approach the attendants alighted from their horses, and kissed the ground of respectful obedience. The King, having desired that they would bear his salutations to the Vizier, and they having promised punctually to do so, was preparing to turn back, when suddenly, the wind lifting up a corner of the hangings which covered the litter, his eyes were fixed by the fascinating beauty of the damsel; and he who in the chase had sought for game became now the captive prey of this lovely maid, and fell into the snares of love.

At length he ordered the attendants to despatch a messenger to the north, where Sipahsalar was, and to inform him that the King would accept his daughter as a wife, hoping that he might not be esteemed an unworthy son-in-law.

When the attendants heard this, they kissed the ground of obedience, saying, "Long be the King's life! – the sovereign of the earth and of the age, and the ruler of the world! If Sipahsalar could even dream of this honour, he would be supreme in happiness. But, if the King permits, we will proceed with the damsel to her father, and inform him of what has happened, that he may prepare everything necessary for the occasion, and then send her back to the city." When the servant of the damsel had thus spoken, the King, who was displeased with his discourse, exclaimed, "How darest thou presume to counsel or advise me?" He would have punished the servant on the spot, but he feared lest the tender heart of his fair mistress should be distressed thereby. He accordingly remitted the punishment; and taking the reins into his own hands, he conducted the litter back towards the city, which he entered at the time when the shades of evening began to fall.

The next day he assembled the magistrates and chief men; and, having asked the damsel's consent to the marriage, he caused the necessary ceremonies to be performed. The secretaries were employed in writing letters of congratulation; and Sipahsalar was informed of the insult offered to him during his absence, which caused the tears to flow from his eyes whilst he perused the letters of congratulation. He dissembled, however; and, concealing his vexation, wrote letters to the King, and addressed him in language of the strongest gratitude, declaring himself at a loss for words whereby to express his sense of the honour conferred upon him.

Such was the purport of his letters; but in his mind he cherished hopes of revenge, and day and night were employed in devising stratagems by means of which he might obtain it.

After two or three months spent in this manner, Sipahsalar assembled all the chief officers of the army, and informed them that, confiding in their secrecy and fidelity, he would communicate to them an affair of considerable importance. They all assured him of their attachment and regard; and declared that the flourishing state of the empire was the result of his wisdom, prudent management, and bravery. To this Sipahsalar replied, "You all know what actions I have performed, and what troubles I have undergone, to raise the empire to its present state of glory and prosperity: but what has been my recompense? You have seen how the ungrateful monarch carried off my daughter." Having thus spoken, a shower of tears fell from his eyes; and the chiefs who were assembled about him said, "We have been acquainted with this matter for some time, and it has given us great concern. But now the moment is arrived when we may depose this king."

Then Sipahsalar threw open the doors of his treasury, and distributed considerable sums of money amongst the soldiers; so that in a little time he assembled a multitude of troops, almost innumerable. He then resolved to attack the King, and, with that intention, seized, during the night, upon all the avenues of the city, both on the right hand and on the left.

The King, astonished and alarmed at the tumult, consulted with the Queen, saying, "What can we do in this misfortune? For it is a night to which no morning shall succeed, and a war in which there is not any hope of peace." The Queen replied, "Our only remedy for this evil is to fly and seek protection in the dominions of some other prince, and solicit his assistance." Azad Bakht approved of this counsel, and resolved to seek an asylum from the King of Kirman, who was renowned for his generosity throughout the world.

In the palace there was a certain door which opened into a subterraneous passage leading towards the desert. The King gave orders that two horses should be instantly saddled; and having put on his armour, and taken from the royal treasury many precious jewels and fastened them in his girdle, he placed the Queen on one of the horses, and mounting the other himself, they went forth privately through the door above-mentioned, and directed their course towards the desert.

Now it happened that the Queen had been for nine months in a state of pregnancy; and, after travelling during a whole day and night in the desert, they arrived at the side of a well, whose waters were more bitter than poison, and unpleasant as the revolutions of inconstant Fortune. Here the Queen was affected by the pains of labour; whilst heat and thirst reduced both the King and her to despair: their mouths were parched up for want of water, and they had no hopes of saving their lives; for the sword of the enemy was behind them, and before them the sand of the desert. In this forlorn situation, the Queen said, "As it is impossible for me to proceed any farther, I entreat you to save your own life, and find out some place where water may be obtained. Though I must perish here, you may be saved; and a hundred thousand lives such as mine are not in value equal to a single hair of the King's head." Azad Bakht replied, "Soul of the world! I can relinquish riches and resign a throne; but it is impossible to abandon my beloved: her who is dearer to me than existence itself."

Thus were they engaged in conversation, when suddenly the Queen brought forth a son; in beauty he was lovely as the moon and from the lustre of his eyes the dreary desert was illumined. The Queen, pressing the infant to her bosom, began to perform the duties of a mother, when the King told her that she must not fix her affections on the child, as it would be impossible to take him with them, "We must, therefore," added the King, "leave the infant on the brink of this well, and commit him to the providence of the Almighty, whose infinite kindness will save him from destruction." They accordingly wrapped up the child in a cloak embroidered with gold and fastened a bracelet of ten large pearls round his shoulders; then, leaving him on the brink of the well, they both proceeded on their journey to Kirman, whilst their hearts were afflicted with anguish on account of their helpless infant. When they approached the capital of Kirman, the King of that place was informed of their arrival. He sent his servants to welcome them, and received them with the greatest respect and hospitality; he provided a princely banquet, and assembled all the minstrels, and sent his own son and two attendants to wait on Azad Bakht.

During the feast, whilst the musicians were employed in singing and playing, and the guests in drinking, whenever the wine came round to Azad Bakht, his eyes were filled with tears. The King of Kirman, perceiving this, desired him to banish sorrow, and to entertain a hope that Heaven might yet be propitious to him. Azad Bakht replied, "O King of the world! how can I be cheerful, whilst thus an exile from my home, and whilst my kingdom and my treasures are in the possession of my enemies?"

The King of Kirman then enquired into the particulars of Azad Bakht's misfortunes, which he related from beginning to end. The heart of the King of Kirman was moved with compassion; and during that whole day he endeavoured, by every sort of amusement, to divert the mind of his guest from dwelling on the past misfortunes.

The next day he ordered a powerful army to be led forth, and placed it under the command of Azad Bakht, who marched immediately towards the capital of his own dominions. On the King's approach, Sipahsalar, who had usurped his authority, fled in confusion, and all the troops, the peasants, and other inhabitants paid homage to Azad Bakht, and entreated his forgiveness. He pardoned them; and again ascending the royal throne, governed his people with justice and generosity; and having liberally rewarded the King of Kirman's soldiers, he sent them back with many rare and valuable presents for that monarch.

After these transactions, Azad Bakht and his Queen passed their time in a state of tranquillity, interrupted only by the remembrance of the child whom they had left in the desert, and whom, they were persuaded, wild beasts must have devoured the same hour in which they abandoned him: but they little knew the kindness which Providence had shown him.

It happened that the desert in which they had left the infant was frequented by a gang of robbers, the chief of whom was named Farrukhsuwar; and very soon after the King and Queen had departed, these robbers came to the well; there they discovered a beautiful infant crying bitterly. Farrukhsuwar alighted from his horse and took up the child; and his extraordinary beauty induced them to believe him the son of some prince or illustrious personage. In this opinion they were confirmed by the ten valuable pearls which were fastened on his shoulders. As Farrukhsuwar had not any child, he resolved to adopt this infant as his own, and accordingly bestowed on him the name of Khudadad; and having taken him to his home committed him to the care of a nurse. When he was of a proper age Farrukhsuwar instructed him in all necessary accomplishments, and in horsemanship and the use of arms, which rendered him, with hi natural bravery, when fifteen years of age, able to fight, alone, five hundred men. Farrukhsuwar loved this youth with such affection that he could not exist one moment without him, and took him along with him wheresoever he went. Whenever it happened that the robbers were proceeding to attack a caravan, Khudadad, who felt compassion for the merchants and travellers, and at all times disliked the profession of a robber, requested that Farrukhsuwar might dispense with his attendance, and leave him to guard the castle. Farrukhsuwar consented that he should not join in attacking the caravan; but entreated him to accompany the robbers to the scene of action. It happened, however, one day, that they attacked a caravan consisting of superior numbers, and of such brave men that they fought against the robbers with success, and took several of them prisoners. In this action, Farrukhsuwar received a wound, and was near falling into the hands of his enemies, when Khudadad, mounting his charger, galloped into the midst of the battle, and put many of them to death.

But it was so ordained that he should fall from his horse; in consequence of which, he was taken prisoner, and with many of the robbers, led in chains to the capital.

The chief of the caravan having brought them all before the tribunal of Azad Bakht, the King's eyes were no sooner fixed upon the countenance of Khudadad, than paternal affection began to stir his heart: he wept, and said, "Alas! if the infant whom I abandoned in the desert were now alive, he would probably appear such a youth as this!" He continued to gaze involuntarily upon him, and, desiring him to approach, enquired his name, and said, "Art thou not ashamed to have abused the favours of Heaven, which has endowed thee with so much beauty and strength, by plundering travellers, and seizing on the property to which thou hadst not any right?"

Khudadad, with tears, replied, "The Lord knows my innocence, and that I have never partaken of the plunder." Azad Bakht then granted him a free pardon, and took him into his service, desiring that his chains might be taken off; he also put on him his own robe, and said, "I now give you the name of Bakhtyar; from this time forth Fortune shall be your friend." The King then dismissed the other robbers; to whom, on condition that they would never again commit any depredations, he granted not only their lives, but a pension, by which he engaged them in his service.

After this, Bakhtyar continued day and night in attendance on the King, whose affection for him hourly increased. To his care were entrusted the royal stables, which he superintended with such skill and good management that in a few months the horses became fat and sleek; and the King, one day remarking their improved condition, understood that it was the result of Bakhtyar's care and attention, and conceiving that a person who evinced such abilities was capable of managing more important matters, he sent for Bakhtyar, at his return to the palace, and ordered that the keys of the treasury should be presented to him, and thus constituted him keeper of the treasures. Bakhtyar, having kissed the ground, was invested with a splendid robe of honour. He discharged the duties of his high station with such fidelity and attention that he every day increased in favour with the King, and at length was consulted on every measure, and entrusted with every secret of his royal master. If on any day it happened that Bakhtyar absented himself from the palace, on that day the King would not give audience to any person: and the advice of Bakhtyar was followed on every occasion of importance. In short, he was next in power to the King, and his conduct was discreet and skilful.

But there were ten viziers, who became envious of his exaltation, and conspired against him, resolving to devise some stratagem whereby they might deprive him of the King's esteem, and effect his degradation.

It happened one day that Bakhtyar, having indulged in the pleasures of wine beyond the bounds of moderation, lost the power of his reason, and continued in a state of sleepy intoxication until night came on and the world became dark; the porters fastened the gates, and the sentinels repaired to their respective stations. Bakhtyar, after some time, came forth from the treasury, but knew not whither he went, so completely had the wine deprived him of recollection: he wandered on, however, until he found himself in one of the King's private apartments, where he saw tapers burning, a couch with pillows and cushions, a splendid throne, or seat, and various embroidered robes and silken coverings. This was the apartment in which the King used to sleep. Here, from excessive intoxication, Bakhtyar flung himself upon the throne: after a little while the King entered, and discovering the unfortunate young man, enquired, with violent anger, his business in that place. Bakhtyar, roused by the noise, threw himself from the throne, and crept beneath it, where again he fell asleep.

The King, having called some attendants, ordered them to seize him, and, drawing his sword, hastened to the Queen, of whom he asked how Bakhtyar found admittance to the private apartments of the palace; and added, that he could not have come there without her knowledge. The Queen, shocked at such an imputation, declared herself ignorant of the whole transaction but desired the King, if he still entertained any suspicions, to confine her that night, and enquire into the matter on the next morning, when her innocence would appear, and the guilty might be punished. The King accordingly ordered her to be confined, and suspended the execution of vengeance during that night.

When morning came, being seated on the royal throne, he gave audience to his ten viziers. The first of these, having paid his respects to the King, enquired into the transactions of the preceding night, and was informed of all that had occurred. The enmity which this Vizier had long cherished in his heart against Bakhtyar induced him to conceive that a fair opportunity now offered of destroying that unfortunate young man; and he said within himself, "Though he may have a thousand lives, he shall not be able to save one of them." He then addressed the King, and said, "How could a person bred up in the desert, and by profession a robber and assassin, be fit for the service of a King? I well knew that his wickedness would appear, but durst not say so; now, however, that it is manifest, let the King ordain for him such a punishment as may be a lesson to all the world." The King gave orders that Bakhtyar should be brought before him. "Ungrateful wretch!" said he, "I forgave your offences; I spared your life; I raised you to dignities almost equal to my own; and you requite these favours by treason and perfidy: you have entered into the recesses of my harem, and have presumed to occupy my place." Bakhtyar on hearing this began to weep; declared himself ignorant of all those transactions, and that if he had been found in the royal apartments, he must have wandered there unconsciously.

The First Vizier solicited the King's permission that he might go to the harem, and enquire from the Queen all that she knew concerning this affair. Having obtained permission, he went to the Queen, and told her that there were various reports on the subject of that young robber Bakhtyar, in which she was implicated; that, as the King was exceedingly enraged against her, the only means whereby she could appease his anger would be to accuse Bakhtyar, and to say, "O King! thou hast brought hither the son of a robber; thou hast bestowed on him the name of 'Fortune's Favourite,' and hast exalted him to honours; but his baseness has at length appeared: he has presumed to make amorous proposals to me, and has threatened, should I not comply with his licentious desires, to use violence with me, to kill the King, and to seize upon the throne."

"This declaration," said the Vizier to the Queen, "will induce the King to order the immediate execution of Bakhtyar, and you will at the same time reestablish yourself in his good opinion." The Queen was astonished, and replied, "How can I, even to save myself, thus destroy the life of an innocent person by a false testimony?"

"The life of Bakhtyar," said the Vizier, "has long been forfeited to the laws, since he exercised the profession of a robber and a murderer; therefore, any scruples on that subject are vain; and I'll answer at the day of judgment for your share in this transaction."

The Queen at last consented to follow the Vizier's advice; and he returned to the presence of the King, who desired to know the result of his conference with the Queen. The artful Vizier replied, "That which I have heard, I have not the power of relating; but the Queen herself will tell it." The King, having retired, sent for the Queen, and she repeated to him all that the Vizier had instructed her to say. The King, acknowledging that he was himself to blame, as having bestowed favours on the base-born son of a robber, gave orders that heavy irons should be put on the feet of Bakhtyar, and sent him to prison; declaring that in due time he should suffer such a punishment as would strike terror into all men.

In the meantime, Bakhtyar languished in the prison, appealing to God for relief; and the Viziers returned to their homes, devising means whereby they might induce the King to hasten the execution of the young man.

CHAPTER II

On the following day, the Second Vizier came before the King, and, having paid his respects, recommended that Bakhtyar should be no longer kept in prison, but led out to execution. The King approved of this advice, and gave orders that Bakhtyar and the executioner should be brought before him. When they were come, he addressed the young man, and told him that he had directed the tree of his existence to be rooted out from the soil of his empire. Bakhtyar replied, "Long be the King's life! Such is my prayer, as I stand here on the eve of departure from this world; yet, as it is every man's duty to endeavour by honest means to save himself, I appeal to the Almighty, who knows my innocence. But alas! my situation is like that of the Merchant, whom good fortune constantly avoided, and evil fortune incessantly pursued, so that all his exertions ended in disappointment, and all his projects failed of success." The King desired to hear the story of this ill-fated Merchant, and Bakhtyar, after the usual compliments, began to relate it as follows:

Story of the Ill-Fated Merchant, and His Adventures

In the city of Basra there was a certain man, a merchant, who possessed immense riches; but it was decreed that the light of prosperity should be changed into the darkness of misfortune, so that in a short space of time very little of all his wealth remained, and whatsoever commercial projects he tried invariably terminated in loss.

It happened one year, that the price of corn was increased, and the Merchant thought that, by laying out what remained of his money in purchasing some loads of corn and keeping it till the next year, he might profit considerably. He therefore hired a granary, purchased some corn, and laid it by, in expectation that the price would rise.

But corn became more abundant, and consequently more cheap, the following season. When the Merchant perceived this, he resolved to keep that which he had in store until the next year, thinking it probable that a barren season might succeed a plentiful one. But it happened that the next year, so much rain fell, that most of the houses were washed away, and the water found its way into the Merchant's granary, where it spoiled all his corn, and caused it to send forth a smell so intolerable, that the people of the city compelled him to throw it away.

He was confounded by this misfortune; but after some time, finding that he could not derive any profit from idleness or inactivity, he sold his house, and joined a company of merchants, who were setting out on a voyage by sea. With them, he embarked on board a vessel, and after three days and three nights, the world became dark, the tempest arose, the billows rolled: at length the ship was wrecked, and many of the crew perished. The Merchant, with a few others, was saved on a plank, and cast on dry land.

Hungry and naked, he wandered into a desert, when, after advancing some leagues, he discovered a man at a little distance. Delighted to find that the country was inhabited, and hoping to be relieved from hunger and thirst, which had now become almost insupportable, he directed his course towards that man, and soon perceived an extensive and populous village, with trees and running streams. At the entrance to this village he stopped. The chief man, or dihkan, of the place was a person of considerable wealth, and of great generosity; he had erected in the outlets of this village, a summer-house, in which he happened to be when the Merchant arrived. As soon as he discovered the stranger, he ordered his servants to bring him into the summer-house. The stranger paid his respects, and was entertained by the dihkan with politeness and hospitality. Having satisfied his hunger and thirst, he related, at the desire of his host, all the circumstances of his past life, and all the misfortunes he had undergone. The story excited compassion in the breast of the generous dihkan, who gave the Merchant a suit of his own clothes, and bade him not despair, for he would keep him with himself until his affairs should be again in a prosperous condition.

After this, the dihkan gave into the Merchant's charge the account of his property and possessions, and said that he would allow him, for his own share, the eleventh part of all the corn. The Merchant, much delighted, was very diligent in superintending the concerns of his employer; and as the harvest proved very abundant, when the corn was gathered in, he found his portion so considerable, that he said within himself, "The dihkan most probably will not consent to allow me such a share; I shall therefore take it and conceal it, until the settlement of accounts, when, if he think proper to bestow so much on me, I shall give back this." He accordingly took this quantity of the corn, and concealed it in a cavern; but it happened that a thief discovered what he had done, and stole the corn away by night.

When the dihkan inspected the accounts of the harvest, and had made his calculation of the produce, he assigned to the Merchant the eleventh part of the corn. The Merchant returned him thanks, and acknowledged the doubts which he had entertained, and told him how he had set apart a certain portion of the corn, "which," said he, "I shall now go and cause to be deposited in the granary." The dihkan sent two of his people with him to the place where he had concealed the corn, but none could be found. They were astonished, and bit the finger of amazement. When the dihkan was informed of this circumstance, he became angry, and ordered that the Merchant should be driven forth out of the village.

In melancholy plight, the unlucky Merchant turned his face towards the road which led to the seashore. There he chanced to meet six of those persons who gain a livelihood by diving for pearls. They knew him, and enquired into his situation. He related to them all that had happened, and his story so much excited their compassion that they agreed to bestow on him, for the sake of God, whatsoever their next descent to the bottom of the sea should produce. They accordingly, with this charitable intention, plunged all six into the sea, and each brought up from the bottom a pearl of such exquisite beauty that its equal could not be found amongst the treasures of any monarch. The Merchant received from the divers those six precious pearls, and set forward with a joyful heart.

It happened that after some time he fell into company with certain robbers, whom he much feared, and he resolved to save part, at least, of his property, by concealing three of the pearls in his mouth, and the other three among his clothes; hoping that, if they should search him, they might be contented with these, and that he might save those concealed within his mouth. He accordingly put three of the pearls among his clothes, and the other three into his mouth, and went on for some time without exciting any suspicion, or attracting the notice of the robbers. But unluckily opening his mouth to address them, the pearls fell on the ground; and when the robbers saw them, they seized the Merchant, and so terrified him with their threats and violence that he became senseless. The robbers, perceiving this, took up the three pearls and went away. After some time the Merchant recovered his senses, and was overjoyed to find that he had still three of the pearls left.

Proceeding on his journey, he arrived by night at a certain city, where he slept; and next morning went to the shop of a jeweller, to whom he offered the pearls for sale. The jeweller, on beholding them, was astonished; for they far exceeded anything he had ever seen: then casting his eyes on the mean and squalid garments of the Merchant, he immediately seized him by the collar, and exclaimed with a loud voice, accusing the unfortunate stranger of having stolen the pearls from his shop: a violent struggle and dispute ensued, and at length they both proceeded to the tribunal of the King.

The jeweller was a man of some repute in the city, and that which he said was believed by the inhabitants. He accused the Merchant of having contrived a hole through which he stole away a casket of gold and jewels from his shop, and those three pearls were part of the contents of the casket. The Merchant declared himself innocent; but the King ordered him to deliver the pearls to the jeweller, and he was loaded with chains and thrown into prison.

There he pined in misery and affliction, until after some time those divers who had given him the pearls arrived in that city; and going to visit the prison, that they might benefit by seeing the punishment of vice and wickedness, they distributed some money among those who were confined, and at last discovered the Merchant in a corner, loaded with chains. They were astonished, and enquired into the occasion of his disgrace. He related the whole affair, and they, feeling great indignation on account of the injurious treatment which their friend had suffered, desired him not to despair, as they would soon procure him his liberty. They immediately hastened from the prison to the palace. The chief of them was a man whom the King much respected; and when he had related the story of the Merchant, and of the pearls which they had given him, the King became convinced of the jeweller's guilt, and instantly ordered him to be seized and brought before him, and at the same time that the Merchant should be released from prison. When the jeweller appeared before the King, his confusion and trembling betrayed his guilt. The King asked him why he had thus injured a stranger; but he remained silent; and was then led away to execution. The King caused to be proclaimed throughout the city, "Such is to be the punishment of those who shall injure or do wrong to strangers."

He directed also, that the property of the jeweller should be transferred to the Merchant. Supposing that a man who had seen so much of the world, both of prosperity and adversity, must be well qualified for the service of a King, he ordered a splendid robe to be given to the Merchant; and desired that he should be purified from the filth of the prison in a warm bath, and appointed him keeper of the treasury.

The Merchant employed himself diligently in the duties of his station; but there was a vizier who became envious of his good fortune, and resolved to devise some stratagem whereby to effect his ruin.

The King's daughter had a summer-house adjoining the treasury, and it was her custom to visit this summer-house during six months of the year, once every month. It happened that a mouse had made a hole quite through the wall of the treasury; and one day, the Merchant having reason to drive a nail into the wall, it entered into the hole which the mouse had made, and went through and caused a brick to fall out on the road which led to the Princess's summer-house. The Merchant went immediately and stopped up the hole with clay.

The malicious vizier, having discovered this circumstance, hastened to the King, and informed him that he had seen the Merchant making a hole through the wall of the summer-house, and that, when he had found himself detected, he had, in shame and confusion, stopped it up with clay. The King was astonished at this information: he arose and proceeded to the treasury, where finding the Merchant's hands yet dirty from the clay, he believed what the vizier had told him; and on returning to his palace, ordered his attendants to put out the Merchant's eyes, and to turn him out at the palace-gate. After this the King went to the summer-house, that he might pay a visit to his daughter; but he found that she had not been there for some time, having gone to amuse herself in the gardens. On proceeding to the treasury, the King discovered the hole, which had evidently been the work of a mouse. From these circumstances he began to suspect the truth of the vizier's information, and at last being convinced that the Merchant was innocent, he ordered the vizier to be punished. He lamented exceedingly the hard fate of the Merchant, and was much grieved at his own precipitancy; but his condolence and his sorrow were of no avail.

* * *

Having related this story, Bakhtyar observed, that the King would have prevented all this distress had he taken some time to enquire into the affair, and entreated a further respite, that he might be enabled to prove his innocence. The King, being pleased with the recital of this story, complied with Bakhtyar's request, and ordered him to be taken back to prison for that day.

CHAPTER III

On the following morning the Third Vizier presented himself before the King, and, having paid his respects, expressed many apprehensions that the indulgence shown to Bakhtyar might prove of dangerous consequences, by encouraging other criminals, and strongly advised his speedy execution. The King, having sent for Bakhtyar, the executioner prepared to blindfold him; but he petitioned for mercy, and said, "The imprisonment of suspected persons is certainly a just measure, as the guilt or innocence of the prisoner will probably be ascertained in the course of time; but if a King will not have patience, but punish without due investigation of the offence, what can result from such precipitancy but affliction and repentance? Thus it happened to a son of the King of Aleppo, whose impatience occasioned the loss of that kingdom, and infinite misery."

The King's curiosity being excited, he desired Bakhtyar to relate the story of the Impatient Prince of Aleppo; and Bakhtyar, having kissed the ground of obedience, thus began:

Story of the Impatient Prince of Aleppo

The King of Aleppo was an upright and generous monarch, who protected strangers and permitted not any person to oppress or insult another; and he had a son named Bihzad, a young man of excellent genius, polite accomplishments, and many good qualities; but so very impatient, that he would not admit a moment's delay in the gratification of any desire, whatsoever might be the consequences of his rash haste.

It happened once, that, being seated with several of his companions, he desired one of them to relate his adventures. The young man accordingly began his story in the following words:

"About two years ago, being in possession of considerable wealth, I purchased several beasts of burden, and, having loaded them with various commodities, I undertook a journey, but on the way was attacked by robbers, who plundered me of all my property, and I proceeded with a disconsolate heart until night came on, and I found myself in a place without any vestige of inhabitants. I took shelter beneath a great tree, and had remained there for some time, when I perceived a light, and several persons who passed by with much festivity and mirth. After them came some who held vessels full of burning incense, so very fragrant, that the desert was perfumed by its delightful odour. When they had passed on, a magnificent litter appeared, before which walked several damsels holding torches, scented with ambergris. In this litter was seated a fair one, of such exquisite beauty, that the radiance of her charms far exceeded the light of the torches, and quite dazzled my fascinated eyes."

When the young man had advanced thus far in his narrative, Bihzad began to show symptoms of impatience, having fallen in love with the lady, though unseen. The young man continued his story, and said:

"The next morning I proceeded on my journey, and arrived at the city of Rum, the capital and residence of the Kaisar, or Greek Emperor; and having made enquiries, I was informed that the beautiful damsel whom I had seen was the Princess Nigarin, daughter of the Kaisar, who had a villa at a little distance from the city, to which she sometimes went for recreation."

Here the young man concluded his narrative, and Prince Bihzad immediately arose and hastened to the house of the vizier, and said, "You must go this moment to my father, and tell him that if he is solicitous about my happiness, he will provide me a wife without delay." The vizier accordingly went to the palace and informed the King of Bihzad's wishes. The King desired the vizier to assure the prince that he only waited to find a suitable match for him; but that, if he had fixed his affections on any fair object, he would do everything in his power to obtain her for him.

This being reported to Bihzad, he sent back the vizier with another message to the King, informing him that the object of his choice was the Princess Nigarin, the lovely daughter of the Kaisar of Rum, and requesting that ambassadors might be sent to ask her in marriage for him. The King replied to this message, and said, "Tell Bihzad that it were in vain for me to send ambassadors on such an errand to the Kaisar: he is the powerful Emperor of Rum, and I am only a petty sovereign of Aleppo; we are of different religions and of different manners; and there is not any probability that he would comply with our demand."

The vizier returned to Bihzad, and delivered him this message from his father. The impatient Prince immediately declared that, if the King would not send ambassadors to solicit the Kaisar's daughter in marriage for him, he would set out on that errand himself.

The King, being informed of his son's resolution, sent for the prince, whom he loved with a tender affection, and at last consented that ambassadors should be despatched to Rum. The Kaisar received with due respect the ambassadors from the King of Aleppo; but when they disclosed the object of their mission, he replied, with great indignation, and informed them, that no one should obtain his daughter without paying the sum of one hundred lacs of dinars (or pieces of gold); and that whoever should consent to pay that sum might become her husband.

The ambassadors returned to Aleppo, and related to the King all that the Kaisar had said. "Did I not tell you," said the King to

Bihzad, "that the Greek Emperor would refuse his consent to so unequal a match?" – "He has not refused his consent," replied Bihzad; "but he requires money, which must be immediately sent." The King declared that he could not make up so considerable a sum; but, at Bihzad's request, having collected all his wealth, he found he possessed thirty lacs. Bihzad then urged him to sell his male and female slaves, and all his household goods. Having done so, he found that they produced twenty lacs.

Then Bihzad advised the King to make up the requisite sum, by compelling his subjects to contribute their money; but the King was not willing to distress his people. However, by the persuasion of Bihzad, he extorted from them an additional sum of twenty lacs. Having thus collected seventy lacs of dinars, Bihzad proposed that they should be immediately transmitted to the Kaisar of Rum. Letters were accordingly written, and messengers despatched with the money, who were instructed to say that the remaining sum of thirty lacs should speedily be sent after. When these messengers arrived at Rum, they presented the letters and gifts to the Kaisar, with the money. He treated the messengers with great respect, accepted the money, and agreed to the proposed conditions; after which they returned to Aleppo, and reported their success. Bihzad then urged his father to collect by any means the thirty lacs of dinars still deficient, either by a forced loan from the merchants, or by taxing the peasants of the country; but the King advised him to be patient, and wait until they should recover from the effects of the late exactions; and said, "You have already rendered me poor, and now you wish to complete my ruin, and occasion the loss of my kingdom."

Bihzad desired his father to keep his kingdom, and declared his intention of setting out immediately. The King, much afflicted at the thought of his son's departure, entreated him to wait one year, that the people might forget the sums they had already paid; but Bihzad would not consent. The King then begged that he would be patient for six months; this also he refused. "Wait even three months," said his father. "I cannot wait three days," said the impatient youth. On which the King, disgusted with such obstinacy, desired his son to go wherever he pleased. Bihzad immediately retired; and, having clothed himself in armour, with two confidential servants set out upon his journey.

It happened that one morning they overtook a caravan, consisting of a hundred camels loaded with valuable commodities, proceeding on the way to Rum. The chief of this caravan was a man of considerable wealth, with a numerous train of attendants, and he was held in great esteem by the Kaisar. When Bihzad and his two companions espied the caravan, they rushed forward with loud shouts, but were instantly seized, and their hands and feet bound: they were then brought before the chief, who ordered that they should be flung upon a camel. When they arrived at Rum, the chief took Bihzad to his own house, and kept him confined for three days.

On the third day, having looked attentively at his prisoner, he discovered in his air and manner something that bespoke his princely origin and education. He enquired into the circumstances of his adventure, but Bihzad answered only with tears. The chief then said, "If you tell me the truth of this affair, I will set you free; and if you do not, I shall inform the Kaisar of your offence, and he will cause you to be hanged."

Bihzad, not knowing what else to do, related his whole history to the chief of the caravan, who, moved with compassion, desired him not to despair, for he would lend him the thirty lacs of dinars, and procure him the Kaisar's daughter, on condition of his being repaid whenever Bihzad should become king.

To this Bihzad gladly consented; and the chief, having unloosed his fetters, clothed him in royal garments, and dressed his servants also in splendid attire; and having given him thirty lacs of dinars, he led him to the palace: then he left Bihzad at the door, whilst he himself went in and informed the Kaisar that the Prince of Aleppo was waiting for the honour of presenting to his Majesty the thirty lacs of dinars, which he had brought sealed up.

The Kaisar consented to receive Bihzad, who, on being introduced, paid due homage, and was treated with great kindness, and placed by the Kaisar's side. After much conversation, the Kaisar desired him to declare the object of his wishes, and promised that, whatever it might be, he would endeavour to procure it for him. Bihzad replied, that his only desire in this world was to obtain the princess for his wife. The Kaisar begged that he would wait ten days; but to this delay he would not consent. The Kaisar then entreated that he would be patient for five days; and this also he refused to do. "At least," said the Kaisar, "wait three days, that the women may have time to make the necessary preparations." But Bihzad would not consent. "This one day, however," then said the Kaisar, "you must be patient, and tomorrow you shall espouse my daughter." – "Since it must be so," replied Bihzad, "I'll wait this day, but no longer."

The Kaisar gave orders that the princess should be brought to the garden of the palace, and all the nobles assembled, and banquets provided for the entertainment of Bihzad. When night came, Bihzad, having indulged in wine, became impatient to behold the princess, and, going to the summer-house, in which she was, he discovered an aperture in the wall, to which he applied his eye. The princess at that moment happened to perceive the aperture, and found that some person was looking at her through it. She immediately ordered her attendants to burn out his eyes with red-hot irons.

This order was put in execution without delay. The unhappy Bihzad, crying aloud, fell on the ground, deprived of sight. His voice being at length recognized, the servants ran out and beheld him rolling in agony on the ground. They exclaimed, and tore their hair, but all in vain. The news was brought to the Kaisar, who said, "What can be done? This silly youth has brought the evil on himself by his own impatience, and has occasioned the loss of his own eyes." He then directed that Bihzad should be sent back to Aleppo, as he could not give his daughter to a person deprived of sight.

When the unhappy youth returned to Aleppo, his father and mother, and the inhabitants of the city, all wept at his misfortunes; but their compassion was of no avail. After some time the King died; but the people introduced a stranger, and placed him on the throne, saying that a blind man was not capable of governing. And the remainder of Bihzad's life passed away in misery, and in repentance for his rashness and impatience.

"Now," added Bakhtyar, "had that unfortunate young man waited until night, the Princess Nigarin would have been his, and he would have saved his eyes and his kingdom, and not have had occasion to repent of impatience. If the King will send me back to prison, he will not be sorry for the delay, as my innocence will hereafter appear; and if he hasten my execution, any future repentance will not avail."

The King ordered Bakhtyar to go back to prison for that day.

CHAPTER IV

On the following day, the Fourth Vizier presented himself before the King, and, having paid his respects, advised him not to defer any longer the execution of Bakhtyar. The King immediately gave orders that the young man should be brought from the prison; the executioner with a drawn sword stood ready to perform his part, when Bakhtyar exclaimed, "Long be the King's life! Let him not be precipitate in putting me to death; but as I have, in the story of Bihzad, described the fatal consequences of rashness, let me be permitted to celebrate the blessings attendant on forbearance, and recount the adventures of Abu Saber, the Patient Man."

The King's curiosity being excited, he desired Bakhtyar to relate the story, which he accordingly began in the following words:

Story of Abu Saber, or, The Patient Man

There lived in a certain village, a worthy man, whose principal riches consisted in a good understanding and an inexhaustible stock of patience. On account of those qualifications he was so much respected by all his neighbours, that his advice was followed on every occasion of importance.

It happened once that a tax-gatherer came to this village, and extorted from the poor peasants their miserable pittance, with such circumstances of cruelty and injustice that they could not any longer submit to the oppression: a number of the young men, having assembled in a body, slew the tax-gatherer and fled.

The other inhabitants, who had not been concerned in this transaction, came to Abu Saber, and begged that he would accompany them to the King, and relate to his Majesty the circumstances as they had happened; but Abu Saber told them, that he had drank of the sherbet of patience, and would not intermeddle in such affairs. When the King was informed of the tax-gatherer's death, he ordered his servants to punish the people of that village, and to strip them of all their property.

After two years it happened that a lion took up his abode in the neighbourhood, and destroyed so many children that no person would venture to cultivate the ground, or attend the harvest, from fear of being devoured. In this distress the villagers went to Abu Saber, and entreated him to associate with them in some measure for their relief; but he replied, that patience was his only remedy.

It happened soon after, that the King, being on a hunting-party, arrived in the vicinity of this place; and the inhabitants, presenting themselves before him, related the story of the tax-gatherer, the consequences of the King's anger, and their dread of the lion. The King, pitying them, asked why they had not sent some person to inform him of their distresses. They replied that Abu Saber, the chief man of the village, whose assistance they solicited, had declined interfering in the matter. The King, hearing this, was enraged, and gave orders that Abu Saber should be driven forth from the village. These orders were instantly put in execution, and the King sent people to destroy the lion.

With a heavy heart, Abu Saber commenced his journey, accompanied by his wife and two sons. It happened that they were soon overtaken by some robbers, who, not perceiving anything more valuable of which they might strip him, resolved to carry off the two boys and sell them; they accordingly seized the poor children and bore them away. The wife began to cry and weep most bitterly; but Abu Saber recommended patience. They then proceeded on their journey, and travelled all night and all day, till, faint from hunger and thirst, weary and fatigued, they at length approached a village, in the outlets of which Abu Saber left his wife, whilst he went to procure some food. He was employed on this business in the village, when a robber happened to discover the woman, and seeing that she was a stranger, handsome, and unprotected, he seized her with violence, and declared that he would take her as his wife. After many tears and supplications, finding the robber determined to carry her away, she contrived to write upon the ground with blood, which she had procured by biting her own finger. When Abu Saber returned from the village, and sought his wife in the spot where he had left her, the words which she had written sufficiently explained the occasion of her absence.

He wept at this new misfortune, and implored the Almighty to bestow patience on his wife, and enable her to bear whatever should befall her.

With a disconsolate heart, Abu Saber proceeded on his solitary journey, until he came to the gate of a certain city where a King resided, who was very tyrannical and impious. And it happened at this time that he had ordered a summer-house to be erected, and every stranger who approached the city was by his command seized and compelled to work, guarded day and night, and fed with a scanty portion of coarse black bread.

Abu Saber was immediately seized and dragged to the building; when a heavy load was placed upon his shoulders, and he was obliged to ascend a ladder of seventy steps. In this distress he consoled himself by reflections on the advantages of patience, the only remedy within his power, for the evils which had occurred.

It happened on this day, that the King was sitting in a corner of the building, superintending the work, when he overheard Abu Saber enquire of another man, what time they might expect to be relieved from this excessive fatigue. The man informed Abu Saber that it was three months since he had been thus laboriously employed, and languishing for a sight of his beloved wife and children. "During this space of time," added he, "I have not had any intelligence of them; and I long for permission to visit them, were it but for one night." Abu Saber desired him to be patient; for Providence would relieve him at last from the oppression under which he suffered.

All this conversation the King overheard. After some time Abu Saber, being faint from excessive fatigue, fell senseless from the steps of the ladder, by which accident his legs and arms were dislocated. The King, however, provoked to anger by what he had heard, ordered that Abu Saber should be brought before him, and, having upbraided him with inconsistency in recommending patience to another person, when he himself could not practise it, he ordered him to be punished with fifty stripes and thrown into prison. This sentence was immediately put into execution, and Abu Saber, supporting his head on the knees of patience, implored the protection of the Almighty, with perfect submission to His divine dispensations.

After some time had elapsed, it happened that the King was affected one night by a violent cholic, of which he died in excessive agony; and as he did not leave any heir to the crown, the people of the city assembled in order to elect a King.

It was resolved that they should go to the prison, and propose three questions to the criminals confined there; and that whoever gave the best answer should be chosen King. In consequence of this resolution, they proceeded to the prison, and asked the three questions, to which none of the prisoners replied, except Abu Saber, whose answers were so ingenious, that he was borne triumphantly away, washed in a warm bath, clothed in royal garments, and placed upon the throne; after which all the inhabitants came and paid him homage. And he governed with such mildness and wisdom, that the people night and day offered up their prayers for him; and the fame of his justice and liberality was spread all over the world.

One day it happened that two men attended at his tribunal and demanded an audience. Abu Saber caused them to be brought before him. One of those men was a merchant, and the other the robber who had carried off the sons of Abu Saber. The robber he immediately recognized, but was silent. The merchant then addressed him, and said, "Long be the King's life! This man sold to me two boys; and after some time these boys began to say, 'We are freemen – we are the sons of a Mussulman; and that man carried us away by force, and sold us, at which time, from fear of him, we were afraid to say that we were freemen.' Now," added the merchant, "let the King order this man to return me the money, and take back the boys."

Abu Saber then asked the robber what he had to say. The man answered that it was the merchant's fault, who had not taken good care of the boys; but that for his own part he had always treated them well, which induced them to make this complaint, in order that he might take them back. Abu Saber then sent for the two boys, who proved to be his own sons. He knew them, but they had not any recollection of him. He desired them to explain this matter; and they declared that the robber had carried them away from their father and mother to his own dwelling, and had desired them not to say, on any account, that they were freemen; but that when sold as slaves they could not any longer suppress their complaints.

Abu Saber, much affected by their story, ordered them to tell their names, and then sent them to his own apartments; after which he caused the robber to be imprisoned, and the merchant's money to be deposited in the public treasury.

On another day it happened that two persons in like manner solicited an audience of the King. When they were admitted, one proved to be the wife of Abu Saber, and the other the man who had taken her away by force. But Abu Saber did not know his wife, because she wore her veil. The robber, having paid his respects, informed the King that this woman, who had lived with him for some time, would not consent to perform the duties of a wife. Abu Saber addressed the woman, and asked her why she refused to obey her husband. She immediately answered, that this man was not her husband; that she was the wife of a person named Abu Saber; and that this man had taken her to his house against her inclination.

Abu Saber ordered his servants to take the woman to his harem; and, having made a proclamation and assembled all the inhabitants of the city, caused the robber who had taken away his sons and the man who had carried off his wife to be brought before them; and, having explained the nature of their offences and related the circumstances of his own story, he gave orders for their execution.

After this he passed the remainder of his life in peaceful enjoyment of the supreme power, which at his death devolved upon his son, and continued for many generations in the family, as the reward of his patience.

* * *

Here Bakhtyar concluded his story, and by order of the King was sent back to prison.

CHAPTER V

When the next morning arrived, the Fifth Vizier waited upon the King, and represented the danger that might attend any further delay in the execution of Bakhtyar, as the indulgence which had been shown to him would be an encouragement to others, and induce them to commit offences, by giving them hopes of impunity. In consequence of this, the King ordered everything to be prepared for the execution of the young man, who, being brought before him, entreated his Majesty for a longer respite, and assured him that he would, on a future day, be as rejoiced at having spared his life, as a certain King of Yemen was at having pardoned the offence of his slave.

The King desired Bakhtyar to relate the particular circumstances of this story; and he accordingly began it in the following manner:

Story of the King of Yemen and His Slave Abraha

In former times, the kingdom of Yemen was governed by a very powerful but tyrannical Prince, who, for the slightest offences, inflicted the most severe punishments. He had, however, a certain slave, named Abraha, of whom he was very fond. This young man was the son of the King of Zangibar, who by chance had fallen into slavery, and never disclosed the secret of his birth.

Abraha used frequently to attend the King of Yemen on his hunting parties. During one of these excursions, it happened that a deer bounded before the King's horse: he discharged some arrows at it without effect; when Abraha, who was close behind him, spurred on his horse, and aimed a broad-bladed arrow at the deer; but it so happened that the arrow passed by the side of the King's head, and cut off one of his ears. The King, in the first impulse of anger, ordered his attendants to seize Abraha; but afterwards declared that he pardoned his offence.

They then returned to the city; and, after some time had elapsed, having gone on board a vessel and sailed into the ocean, a tempest arose, and the ship was wrecked, and the King saved himself by clinging to a plank, and was driven on the coast of Zangibar.

Having returned thanks to Providence for his preservation, he proceeded till he reached the chief city of that country. As it was night, the doors of the houses and all the shops were shut; and, not knowing where he might find a better place of repose, he sheltered himself under the shade of a merchant's house. It happened that some thieves, in the course of the night, broke open the house, and having murdered the merchant and his servants, plundered it of everything that was valuable. The King of Yemen, overcome by fatigue, had slept the whole time, unconscious of this transaction; but some of the blood had by accident fallen on his clothes.

When morning came, everybody was employed in endeavouring to discover the murderers of the merchant; and the stranger, being found so near the house, with blood upon his clothes, was immediately seized and dragged before the tribunal of the King.

The King of Zangibar asked him why he had chosen his capital as the scene of such an infamous murder; and desired him to acknowledge who were his accomplices, and how he had disposed of the merchant's property. The King of Yemen declared that he was innocent, and perfectly ignorant of the whole transaction; that he was of a princely family; and, having been shipwrecked, was driven on the coast, and had by accident reposed himself under the shade of that house when the murder was committed.

The King of Zangibar then enquired of him by what means his clothes had become stained with blood, and finding that the stranger could not account for that circumstance, he ordered the officers of justice to lead him away to execution. The unfortunate King of Yemen entreated for mercy, and asserted that his innocence would on some future day become apparent. The King consented to defer his execution for a while, and he was sent to prison.

On one side of the prison there was an extensive plain, with a running stream, to which every day the prisoners were brought, that they might wash themselves; and it was the custom that once every week the King resorted to that plain, where he gave public audience to persons of all ranks. On one of those days, the King of Zangibar was on the plain, surrounded by his troops, and the prisoners were sitting by the side of the stream, along which ran a wall of the prison. It happened that Abraha, who had been the King of Yemen's slave, was standing near this wall, but his former master did not recognize him, as they had been separated for some time, Abraha having found means to return to Zangibar, his native country.

At this moment a crow chanced to light upon the wall, which the King of Yemen perceived, and taking up a large flat bone, he threw it with his utmost strength, and exclaimed, "If I succeed in hitting that crow, I shall obtain my liberty," but he missed his aim; the bone passed by the crow, and striking the cheek of Abraha, cut off one of his ears. Abraha immediately caused an enquiry to be made, and the person who had thrown the bone to be brought before the King, who called him a base-born dog, and ordered the executioner to cut off his head. The King of Yemen sued for mercy, and requested that at most he might be punished according to the law of retaliation, which would not award a head for an ear. The King gave orders that one of his ears should be cut off; and the executioner was preparing to fulfil this sentence when he perceived that the prisoner had already lost an ear.

This circumstance occasioned much surprise, and excited the King's curiosity. He told the prisoner that he would pardon him, on condition of his relating the true story of his adventures.

The King of Yemen immediately disclosed his real name and rank, described the accident by which he lost his ear, the shipwreck which he suffered, and the circumstances which occasioned his imprisonment.

At the conclusion of his narrative, Abraha, having recognized his former master, fell at his feet, embraced him, and wept. They mutually forgave each other; and the King of Yemen, being taken to a warm bath, was clothed in royal garments, mounted on a noble charger, and conducted to the palace; after which he was furnished with a variety of splendid robes and suits of armour, horses, slaves, and damsels. During two months he was feasted and entertained with the utmost hospitality and magnificence, attended constantly by Abraha. In the course of this time, the robbers who had murdered the merchant were discovered and punished; and after that the King of Yemen returned to his own country.

* * *

Bakhtyar having thus demonstrated that appearances might be very strong against an innocent person, the King resolved to defer his execution for another day, and he was accordingly led back to prison.

CHAPTER VI

On the following day, the Sixth Vizier, having paid his respects to the King, represented the danger of letting an enemy live when in one's power, and, by many artful speeches, induced his Majesty to order the execution of Bakhtyar, who was immediately brought from the prison. When he came before the King, he persisted in declaring his innocence, and advised him not to be precipitate, like King Dadin, in putting to death a person on the malicious accusation of an enemy. The King, desirous of hearing the story to which Bakhtyar alluded, ordered him to relate it; and he began as follows:

Story of King Dadin and His Two Viziers

There was a certain King named Dadin, who had two viziers, Kardar and Kamgar; and the daughter of Kamgar was the most lovely creature of the age. It happened that the King, proceeding on a hunting excursion, took along with him the father of this beautiful damsel, and left the charge of government in the hands of Kardar.

One day, during the warm season, Kardar, passing near the palace of Kamgar, beheld this fair damsel walking in the garden, and became enamoured of her beauty; but having reason to believe that her father would not consent to bestow her on him, he resolved to devise some stratagem whereby he might obtain the object of his desires. "At the King's return from the chase," said he, "I'll represent the charms of this damsel in such glowing colours, that he will not fail to demand her in marriage; and I'll then contrive to excite his anger against her, in consequence of which he shall deliver her to me for punishment; and thus my designs shall be accomplished."

One day after the King's return from the hunting party, he desired Kardar to inform him of the principal events which had occurred during his absence. Kardar replied that his Majesty's subjects had all been solicitous for his prosperity; but that he had himself seen one of the most astonishing objects of the universe. The King's curiosity being thus excited, he ordered Kardar to describe what he had seen; and Kardar dwelt with such praises on the fascinating charms of Kamgar's daughter, that the King became enamoured of her, and said, "But how is this damsel to be obtained?" Kardar replied, "There is not any difficulty in this business; it is not necessary to employ either money or messengers: your Majesty needs only to acquaint her father with your wishes."

The King approved of this counsel, and having sent for Kamgar, mentioned the affair to him accordingly. Kamgar, with due submission, declared that if he possessed a hundred daughters they should all be at his Majesty's command; but begged permission to retire and inform the damsel of the honour designed for her. Having obtained leave, he hastened to his daughter, and related to her all that had passed between the King and him. The damsel expressed her dislike to the proposed connection; and her father, dreading the King's anger in case of a refusal, knew not how to act. "Contrive some delay," said she, "solicit leave of absence for a few days, and let us fly from this country!" Kamgar approved of this advice; and having waited on the King, obtained leave to absent himself from court for ten days, under pretence of making the preparations necessary for a female on the eve of matrimony; and when night came on, he fled from the city with his daughter.

Next day, the King was informed of their flight; in consequence of which he sent off two hundred servants to seek them in various directions, and the officious Kardar set out also in pursuit of them.

After ten days they were surprised by the side of a well, taken and bound, and brought before the King, who, in his anger, dashed out the brains of Kamgar; then looking on the daughter of the unfortunate man, her beauty so much affected him, that he sent her to his palace, and appointed servants to attend her, besides a cook, who, at his own request, was added to her establishment. After some time Kardar became impatient, and enraged at the failure of his project; but he resolved to try the success of another scheme.

It happened that the encroachments of a powerful enemy rendered the King's presence necessary among the troops; and on setting out to join the army, he committed the management of affairs and the government of the city to Kardar, whose mind was wholly filled with stratagems for getting the daughter of Kamgar into his power.

One day he was passing near the palace, and discovered her sitting alone on the balcony; to attract her attention, he threw up a piece of brick or tile, and on her looking down to see from whence it came, she beheld Kardar. He addressed her with the usual salutation, which she returned. He then began to declare his admiration of her beauty, and the violence of his love, which deprived him of repose both day and night; and concluded by urging her to elope with him, saying that he would take as much money as they could possibly want; or, if she would consent, he was ready to destroy the King by poison, and seize upon the throne himself.

The daughter of Kamgar replied to this proposal by upbraiding Kardar with his baseness and perfidy. When he asked her how she could ever fix her affections on the man who had killed her father, she answered, that such had been the will of God, and she was resolved to submit accordingly. Having spoken thus, she retired. Kardar, fearing lest she should relate to the King what had passed between them, hastened to meet him as he returned in triumph after conquering his enemies; and whilst walking along by the side of the King's horse, began to inform his Majesty of all that had happened in his absence. Having mentioned several occurrences, he added, that one circumstance was of such a nature that he could not prevail on himself to relate it, for it was such as the King would be very much displeased at hearing.

The King's curiosity being thus excited, he ordered Kardar to relate this occurrence; and he, declaring that it was a most ungrateful task, informed him that it was a maxim of the wise men, "When you have killed the serpent, you should also kill its young." He then proceeded to relate that, one day during the warm season, being seated near the door of the harem, he overheard some voices, and his suspicions being excited, he concealed himself behind the hangings, and listened attentively, when he heard the daughter of Kamgar express her affection for the cook, who, in return, declared his attachment; and they spoke of poisoning the King in revenge for his having killed her father. "I had not patience," added Kardar, "to listen any longer." At this intelligence the King changed colour with rage and indignation, and on arriving at the palace, ordered the unfortunate cook to be instantly cut in two. He then sent for the daughter of Kamgar, and upbraided her with the intention of destroying him by poison. She immediately perceived that this accusation proceeded from the malevolence of Kardar, and was going to speak in vindication of herself, when the King ordered her to be put to death; but being dissuaded by an attendant from killing a woman, he revoked the sentence of death; and she was tied hands and feet, and placed upon a camel, which was turned into a dreary wilderness, where there was neither water nor shade, nor any trace of cultivation.

Here she suffered from the intense heat and thirst, to such a degree that, expecting every moment to be her last, she resigned herself to the will of Providence, conscious of her own innocence. Just then the camel lay down, and on that spot where they were a fountain of delicious water sprang forth; the cords which bound her hands and feet dropped off: she refreshed herself by a hearty draught of the water, and fervently returned thanks to Heaven for this blessing and her wonderful preservation. On this the most verdant and fragrant herbage appeared around the borders of the fountain; it became a blooming and delightful spot, and the camel placed himself so as to afford his lovely companion a shade and shelter from the sunbeams.

It happened that one of the King's camel-keepers was at this time in pursuit of some camels which had wandered into the desert, and without which he dared not return to the city. He had sought them for several days amidst hills and forests without any success. At length, on coming to this spot, he beheld the daughter of Kamgar and the camel, which at first he thought was one of those he sought, and the clear fountain with the verdant banks, where neither grass nor water had ever been seen before. Astonished at this discovery, he resolved not to interrupt the lady, who was engaged in prayer; but when she had finished, he addressed her, and was so charmed by her gentleness and piety, that he offered to adopt her as his child, and expressed his belief that, through the efficacy of her prayers, he should recover the strayed camels.

This good man's offer she thankfully accepted; and having partaken of a fowl and some bread which he had with him, at his request she prayed for the recovery of his camels. As soon as she had concluded her prayer, the camels appeared on the skirts of the wilderness, and of their own accord approached the camel-keeper.

He then represented to the daughter of Kamgar the danger of remaining all night in the wilderness, which was the haunt of many wild beasts; and proposed that she should return with him to the city, and dwell with him in his house, where he would provide for her a retired apartment, in which she might perform her devotions without interruption. To this proposal she consented, and being mounted on her camel, she returned to the city, and arrived at the house of her companion at the time of evening prayer. Here she resided for some time, employing herself in exercises of piety and devotion.

One day the camel-keeper, being desired by the King to relate his past adventures, mentioned, among other circumstances, the losing of his camels, the finding of them through the efficacy of a young woman's prayers, the discovery of a spring where none had been before, and his adopting the damsel as his daughter: he concluded by telling the King that she was now at his house, and employed day and night in acts of devotion.

The King, on hearing this, expressed an earnest wish that he might be allowed to see this young woman, and prevail on her to intercede with Providence on his behalf. The camel-keeper, having consented, returned at once to his house accompanied by the King, who waited at the door of the apartment where the daughter of Kamgar was engaged in prayer. When she had concluded he approached, and with astonishment recognized her. Having tenderly embraced her, he wept, and entreated her forgiveness. This she readily granted, but begged that he would conceal himself in the apartment whilst she should converse with Kardar, whom she sent for.

When he arrived, and beheld her with a thousand expressions of fondness, he enquired the means whereby she had escaped; and he told her that on the day when the King had banished her into the wilderness, he had sent people to seek her, and to bring her to him. "How much better would it have been," added he, "had you followed my advice, and agreed to my proposal of poisoning the King, who, I said, would endeavour to destroy you, as he had killed your father! But you rejected my advice, and declared yourself ready to submit to whatsoever Providence should decree. Hereafter," continued he, "you will pay more attention to my words. But now let us not think of what is past: I am your slave, and you are dearer to me than my own eyes!" So saying, he attempted to clasp the daughter of Kamgar in his arms, when the King, who was concealed behind the hangings, rushed furiously on him, and put him to death. After this he conducted the damsel to his palace, and constantly lamented his precipitancy in having killed her father.

* * *

Here Bakhtyar concluded the story; and having requested a further respite, that he might have an opportunity of proving his innocence, he was sent back to prison by order of the King.

CHAPTER VII

The Seventh Vizier, on the following day, approached the King, and having told him that his lenity towards Bakhtyar was made the subject of public conversation, added many arguments to procure an order for the execution of that unfortunate young man. The King, changing colour with anger, sent immediately for the Queen, and asked her advice concerning Bakhtyar. She declared that he deserved death; in consequence of which the King ordered his attendants to bring him from the prison. When he came into the royal presence, he begged for mercy, saying, "My innocence will appear hereafter; and though your Majesty can easily put to death a living man, you cannot restore a dead man to life." – "How," said the King, "can you deny your guilt, since the women of the harem all bear witness against you?" Bakhtyar replied, "Women, for their own purposes, often devise falsehoods, and are very expert in artifice and fraud, as appears from the story of the daughter of the King of `Irak and her adventures with the King of Abyssinia, which, if your Majesty permit, I shall briefly relate." Having obtained permission, he began the story as follows:

Story of the King of Abyssinia, Showing the Artifice of Women

It is related that Abyssinia was once governed by a certain monarch, whose armies were very numerous, and his treasury well filled; but not having any enemy to engage him in war, he neglected his troops, and withheld their pay, so that they were reduced to great distress, and began to murmur, and at last made their complaints to the Vizier. He, pitying their situation, promised that he would take measures for their relief, and desired them to be patient for a little while. He then considered within himself what steps he should take; and at length, knowing the King's inclination to women, and understanding that the Princess of `Irak was uncommonly beautiful, he resolved to praise her charms in such extravagant language before the King, as to induce him to demand her from her father, who, from his excessive fondness, would not probably consent to bestow her on him, and thus a war would ensue, in which case the troops should be employed, and their arrears paid off.

Pleased with the ingenuity of this stratagem, the vizier hastened to the King, and after conversing for some time on various subjects, he contrived to mention the King of `Irak, and immediately described the beauty of his daughter in such glowing colours, that the King became enamoured, and consulted the vizier on the means whereby he might hope to obtain possession of that lovely Princess. The vizier replied, that the first step was to send ambassadors to the King of `Irak, soliciting his daughter in marriage. In consequence of this advice, some able and discreet persons were despatched as ambassadors to `Irak. On their arrival in that country, the King received them courteously; but when they disclosed the object of their mission he became angry, and declared that he would not comply with their demand.

The ambassadors returned to Abyssinia, and having reported to the King the unsuccessful result of their negotiation, he vowed that he would send an army into `Irak, and lay that country waste, unless his demands were complied with.

In consequence of this resolution, he ordered the doors of his treasury to be thrown open, and caused so much money to be distributed among the soldiers that they were satisfied. From all quarters the troops assembled, and zealously prepared for war. On the other hand, the King of `Irak levied his forces, and sent them to oppose the Abyssinians, who invaded his dominions; but he did not lead them to the field himself, and they were defeated and put to flight. When the account of this disaster reached the King of `Irak, he consulted his vizier, and asked what was next to be done. The vizier candidly declared that he did not think it necessary to prolong the war on account of a woman, and advised his Majesty to send ambassadors with overtures of peace, and an offer of giving the princess to the King of Abyssinia. This advice the King of `Irak followed, although reluctantly. Ambassadors were despatched to the enemy with offers of peace, and a declaration of the King's consent to the marriage of his daughter.

These terms being accepted, the princess was sent with confidential attendants to the King of Abyssinia, who retired with her to his own dominions, where he espoused her; and some time passed away in festivity and pleasure. But it happened that the King of `Irak had some years before given his daughter in marriage to another man, by whom she had a son; and this boy was now grown up, and accomplished in all sciences, and such a favourite with the King of `Irak, that he would never permit him to be one hour absent from him. The princess, when obliged to leave him, felt all the anxiety of a mother, and resolved to devise some stratagem whereby she might enjoy his society in Abyssinia.

One day the King of Abyssinia, on some occasion, behaved harshly to the Queen, and spoke disrespectfully of her father. She in return said, "Your kingdom, it is true, is most fertile and abundant; but my father possesses such a treasure as no other monarch can boast of – a youth sent to him by the kindness of Heaven, skilled in every profound science, and accomplished in every manly exercise; so that he rather seems to be one of the inhabitants of Paradise than of this earth." These praises so excited the curiosity of the King, that he vowed he would bring this boy to his court, were he even obliged to go himself for him. The Queen replied, "My father would be like a distracted person were he deprived, even for an hour, of this boy's society; but some intelligent person must be sent to `Irak in the character of a merchant, and endeavour by every means to steal him away."

The King approved of this advice, and chose a person well skilled in business, who had experienced many reverses of fortune, and seen much of the world. To this man he promised a reward of a hundred male slaves and a hundred beautiful damsels, if he should succeed in bringing away this boy from the King of `Irak's court. The man enquired the name of the boy, which was Farrukhzad, and, disguised as a merchant, set out immediately for `Irak.

Having arrived there, he presented various offerings to the King; and one day found an opportunity of conversing with the boy. At last he said, "With such accomplishments as you possess, were you in Abyssinia for one day, you would be rendered master of slaves and damsels, and riches of every kind." He then described the delights of that country, which made such an impression on Farrukhzad, that he became disgusted with `Irak, and attached himself to the merchant, and said, "I have often heard of Abyssinia, and have long wished to enjoy the pleasures which it yields. The King's daughter is now in that country, and if I could contrive to go there, my happiness would be complete. But I know not how to escape from this place, as the King will not permit me to be one hour absent from him."

The merchant gladly undertook to devise some means for the escape of Farrukhzad; and at last having put him into a chest, and placed him upon a camel, he contrived one evening to carry him off unnoticed. The next day, the King of `Irak sent messengers in all directions to seek him. They enquired of all the caravans and travellers, but could not obtain any intelligence concerning him. At last the merchant brought him to Abyssinia, and the King, finding that his accomplishments and talents had not been over-rated, was much delighted with his society; and as he had not any child, he bestowed on him a royal robe and crown, a horse, a sword, and a shield, and adopted him as his son, and brought him into the harem.

When the Queen beheld Farrukhzad, she wept for joy, embraced him, and kissed him with all the fondness of a mother. It happened that one of the servants was a witness, unperceived, of this interview. He immediately hastened to the King, and represented the transaction in such a manner as to excite all his jealousy and rage. However, he resolved to enquire into the matter; but Farrukhzad did not acknowledge that the Queen was his mother; and when he sent for her, she answered his questions only by her tears. From these circumstances he concluded that they were guilty; and accordingly he ordered one of his attendants to take away the young man to a burying-ground without the city, and there to cut off his head.

The attendant led Farrukhzad away, and was preparing to put the King's sentence into execution, but when he looked in the youth's face, his heart was moved with compassion, and he said, "It must have been the woman's fault, and not his crime;" and he resolved to save him. When he told Farrukhzad that he would conceal him in his own house, the boy was delighted, and promised that if ever it was in his power he would reward him for his kindness. Having taken him to his house, the man waited on the King, and told him that he had, in obedience to his orders, put Farrukhzad to death.

After this the King treated his wife with the utmost coldness; and she sat melancholy, lamenting the absence of her son. It happened that an old woman beheld the Queen as she sat alone, weeping, in her chamber. Pitying her situation, she approached, and humbly enquired the occasion of her grief. The Queen made no reply; but when the old woman promised, not only to observe the utmost secrecy, if entrusted with the story of her misfortunes, but to find a remedy for them, she related at length all that had happened, and disclosed the mystery of Farrukhzad's birth.

The old woman desired the Queen to comfort herself, and said, "This night, before the King retires to rest, you must lay yourself down, and close your eyes, as if asleep; he will then place something, which I shall give him, on your bosom, and will command you, by the power of the writing contained in that, to reveal the truth. You must then begin to speak, and, without any apprehension, repeat all that you have now told me."

The old woman, having then found that the King was alone in his summer-house, presented herself before him, and said, "O King, this solitary life occasions melancholy and sadness!" The King replied that it was not solitude which rendered him melancholy, but vexation on account of the Queen's infidelity, and the ingratitude of Farrukhzad, on whom he had heaped so many favours, and whom he had adopted as his own son. "Yet," added he, "I am not convinced of his guilt; and since the day that I caused him to be killed, I have not enjoyed repose, nor am I certain whether the fault was his or the Queen's."

"Let not the King be longer in suspense on this subject," said the old woman, "I have a certain talisman, one of the talismans of Solomon, written in Grecian characters, and in the Syrian language; if your Majesty will watch an opportunity when the Queen shall be asleep, and lay it on her breast, and say: 'O thou that sleepest! by virtue of the talisman, and of the name of God, which it contains, I conjure thee to speak to me, and to reveal all the secrets of thy heart,' she will immediately begin to speak, and will declare everything that she knows, both true and false."

The King, delighted at the hopes of discovering the truth by means of this talisman, desired the old woman to fetch it. She accordingly went home, and taking a piece of paper, scrawled on it some unmeaning characters, folded it up, and tied it with a cord, and sealed it with wax; then hastened to the King, and desired him to preserve it carefully till night should afford an opportunity of trying its efficacy.

When it was night, the King watched until he found that the Queen was in bed; then gently approaching, and believing her to be asleep, he laid the talisman on her breast, and repeated the words which the old woman had taught him. The Queen, who had also received her lesson, still affecting the appearance of one asleep, immediately began to speak, and related all the circumstances of her story.

On hearing this, the King was much affected, and tenderly embraced the Queen, who started from her bed as if perfectly unconscious of having revealed the secrets of her breast. He then blamed her for not having candidly acknowledged the circumstance of Farrukhzad's birth, who, he said, should have been considered as his own son.

All that night they passed in mutual condolence, and on the next morning the King sent for the person to whom he had delivered Farrukhzad, and desired him to point out the spot where his body lay, that he might perform the last duty to that unfortunate youth, and ask forgiveness from his departed spirit. The man replied, "It appears that your Majesty is ignorant of Farrukhzad's situation: he is at present in a place of safety; for although you ordered me to kill him, I ventured to disobey, and have concealed him in my house, from whence, if you permit, I shall immediately bring him." At this information the King was so delighted that he rewarded the man with a splendid robe, and sent with him several attendants to bring Farrukhzad to the palace.

On arriving in his presence, Farrukhzad threw himself at the King's feet, but he raised him in his arms and asked his forgiveness, and thus the affair ended in rejoicing and festivity.

* * *

"Now," said Bakhtyar, having concluded his story, "it appears that women are expert in stratagems; and if Farrukhzad had been put to death, according to the King's command, what grief and sorrow would have been the consequence! To avoid such," added he, "let not your Majesty be precipitate in ordering my execution."

The King resolved to wait another day, and Bakhtyar was sent back to prison.

CHAPTER VIII

On the next morning, the Eighth Vizier, having paid his compliments to the King, addressed him on the subject of Bakhtyar, and said, "Government resembles a tree, the root of which is legal punishment. Now, if the root of a tree becomes dry, the leaves will wither: why then should the punishment of Bakhtyar be any longer deferred?"

In consequence of this discourse, the King ordered the executioner to prepare himself, and Bakhtyar was brought from prison. When the unfortunate young man came before the King, he addressed him, and said, "If your Majesty will consider the consequences of haste and precipitancy, it will appear that they are invariably sorrow and repentance; as we find confirmed in the Story of the Jewel-Merchant."

The King expressed his desire of hearing the story to which he alluded; and Bakhtyar began it accordingly, in the following manner:

Story of the Jewel-Merchant

There was a certain jewel-merchant, a very wealthy man, and eminently skilled in the knowledge of precious stones. His wife, a very prudent and amiable woman, was in a state of pregnancy when it happened that the King sent a messenger to her husband, desiring his attendance at court, that he might consult him in the choice of jewels. The merchant received the King's messenger with all due respect, and immediately prepared to set out on his journey to the capital. When taking leave of his wife, he desired her to remember him in her prayers; and, in case she should bring forth a boy, to call his name Bihruz.

After this injunction he departed from his house, and at length arrived in the capital, where he waited on the King, and having paid his respects, was employed in selecting from a box of pearls those that were most valuable. The King was so much pleased with his skill and ingenuity, that he kept him constantly near his own person, and entrusted to him the making of various royal ornaments, crowns, and girdles studded with jewels.

At length the wife of this jewel-merchant was delivered of two boys; one of whom, in compliance with her husband's desire, she called Bihruz, the other Ruzbih; and she sent intelligence of this event to the father, who solicited permission from the King that he might return home for a while and visit his family; but the King would not grant him this indulgence. The next year he made the same request, and with the same success. Thus, during eight years he as often solicited leave to visit his wife and sons, but could not obtain it.

In the course of this time, the boys had learned to read the Qur'an, and were instructed in the art of penmanship and other accomplishments; and they wrote a letter to their father, expressing their sorrow and anxiety on account of his absence. The jewel-merchant, no longer able to resist his desire of seeing his family, represented his situation to the King in such strong colours that he desired him to send for his wife and children, and allowed him an ample sum of money to defray the expenses of their journey.

A trusty messenger was immediately despatched to the jewel-merchant's wife, who, on receipt of her husband's letter, set out with her two sons on their way to the capital. One evening, after a journey of a month, they arrived at the seaside. Here they resolved to wait until morning; and, being refreshed with a slight repast, the boys amused themselves in wandering along the shore.

It happened that the jewel-merchant, in expectation of meeting his wife and children, had come thus far on the way; and having left his clothes and money concealed in different places, he bathed himself in the sea, and on returning to the shore put on his clothes, but forgot his gold. Having taken some refreshment, he was proceeding on his journey, when he thought of his money, and went back to seek it, but could not find it. At this moment he perceived the two boys, who had wandered thus far, amusing themselves playing along the shore. He immediately suspected that these boys had discovered and taken the gold, and accused them accordingly. They declared their ignorance of the matter, which so enraged the jewel-merchant, that he seized them both, and cast them headlong into the sea.

After this he proceeded on his way; whilst the wife was so unhappy at the long absence of her sons, that the world became dark in her eyes, and she raised her voice and called upon the boys. When the jewel-merchant heard the voice of his wife, he hastened to meet her, and enquired after his two sons, expressing his eager desire of seeing them. The wife told him that they had left her some time before, and had wandered along the seaside. At this intelligence the jewel-merchant began to lament, and tore his clothes, and exclaimed, "Alas, alas, I have drowned my sons!" He then related what had happened, and proceeded with his wife along the shore in search of the boys, but they sought in vain. Then they smote their breasts and wept. And when the next morning came, they said, "From this time forth, whatsoever happens must be to us a matter of indifference;" and they set out on their journey towards the city, with afflicted bosoms and bleeding hearts, being persuaded that their sons had perished in the water.

But they were ignorant of the wonderful kindness of Providence, which rescued the two boys from destruction; for it happened that the King of that country, being on a hunting excursion, passed along the shore on that side where Bihruz had fallen. When he perceived the boy, he ordered his attendants to take him up, and finding him of a pleasing countenance, although pale from the terror of the water and the danger he had escaped, he enquired into the circumstances which had befallen him. The boy informed him, that with his brother he had been walking on the shore, when a stranger seized upon them, and flung them into the water. The King, not having any child, enquired the name of the boy; and when he answered, that his name was Bihruz, he exclaimed, "I accept it as a favourable omen, and adopt you as my own son." After this, Bihruz, mounted on a horse, accompanied the King to his capital, and all the subjects were enjoined to obey him as heir to the crown. After some time, the King died, and Bihruz reigned in his place, with such wisdom, liberality, and uprightness, that his fame resounded through all quarters of the world.

It happened in the meantime, that the other boy, whose name was Ruzbih, had been rescued from the water by some robbers, who agreed to sell him as a slave, and divide the price amongst them. The jewel-merchant and his wife had reached the city and purchased a house, where they resolved to pass the remainder of their lives in prayer and exercises of devotion. But finding it necessary to procure an attendant, the jewel-merchant purchased a young boy at the slave-market, whom he did not know, but whom natural affection prompted him to choose. On bringing home the young slave, his wife fainted away, and exclaimed, "This is your son Ruzbih!" The parents as well as the child wept with joy, and returned thanks to Heaven for such an unexpected blessing.

After this the jewel-merchant instructed Ruzbih in his own profession, so that in a little time he became perfectly skilled in the value of precious stones; and having collected a very considerable number, he expressed a wish of turning them to profit, by selling them to a certain King in a distant country, one who was celebrated for his generosity and kindness to strangers.

The father consented that he should visit the court of this monarch, on condition that he would not afflict his parents by too long an absence. Ruzbih accordingly set out, and arrived at the capital of that King, who happened to be his own brother Bihruz. Him, however, after the lapse of many years, he did not recognize. The King, having graciously received the present which Ruzbih offered, purchased of him all the jewels, and conceived such an affection for him that he kept him constantly in the palace, day and night.

At this time a foreign enemy invaded the country; but the King thought the matter of so little importance, that he contented himself with sending some troops to the field, and remained at home carousing and drinking with Ruzbih. At length, one night, at a very late hour, all the servants being absent, the King became intoxicated, and fell asleep. Ruzbih, not perceiving any of the guards or attendants, resolved that he would watch the King until morning; and accordingly, taking a sword, he stationed himself near the King's pillow.

After some time had elapsed, several of the soldiers who had gone to oppose the enemy returned, and, entering the palace, discovered Ruzbih and the King in this situation. They immediately seized Ruzbih; and when the King awoke, they told him that, by their coming, they had saved his Majesty from assassination, which the jeweller, with a drawn sword, had been ready to perpetrate. The King, at first, ordered his immediate execution; and as day was beginning to dawn, and the approach of the enemy required his presence at the head of his troops, he sent for the executioner, who, having bound the eyes of Ruzbih and drawn his sword, exclaimed, "Say, King of the world, shall I strike or not?"

The King, considering that it would be better to enquire more particularly into the affair, and, knowing that, although it is easy to kill, it is impossible to restore a man to life, resolved to defer the punishment until his return, and sent Ruzbih to prison.

After this he proceeded to join the army, and having subdued his enemies, returned to the capital; but, during the space of two years, forgot the unfortunate Ruzbih, who lingered away his life in confinement. In the meantime his father and mother, grieving on account of his absence, and, ignorant of what had befallen him, sent a letter of enquiry by a confidential messenger to the money-changers (or bankers) of that city. Having read this, they wrote back, in answer, that Ruzbih had been in prison for two years.

On receiving this information, the jewel-merchant and his wife resolved to set out and throw themselves at the feet of this King, and endeavour to obtain from him the pardon and liberty of their son. With heavy hearts they accordingly proceeded on their journey, and having arrived at the capital, presented themselves before the King, and said, "Be it known unto your exalted Majesty, that we are two wretched strangers, oppressed by the infirmities of age, and overwhelmed by misfortune. We were blessed with two sons, one named Bihruz, the other Ruzbih; but it was the will of Heaven that they should fall into the sea, where one of them perished, but the other was restored to us. The fame of your Majesty's generosity and greatness induced our son to visit this imperial court; and we are informed that, by your orders, he is now in prison. The object of our petition is, that your Majesty might take compassion on our helpless situation, and restore to us our long-lost son."

The King, on hearing this, was astonished, and for a while imagined that it was all a dream. At length, when convinced that the old man and woman were his own parents, and that Ruzbih was his own brother, he sent for him to the prison, embraced them and wept, and placed them beside him on the throne; and for the sake of Ruzbih, set at liberty all those who had been confined with him. After this he divided the empire with his brother, and their time passed away in pleasure and tranquillity.

* * *

This story being concluded, Bakhtyar observed, that the jewel-merchant, by his precipitancy, had nearly occasioned the death of his two sons; and that Bihruz, by deferring the execution of his brother, had prevented an infinity of distress to himself and his parents. This observation induced the King to grant Bakhtyar another day's reprieve, and he was taken back to prison.

CHAPTER IX

When the next morning came, the Ninth Vizier appeared before the King and said that his extraordinary forbearance and lenity in respect to Bakhtyar had given occasion to much scandal; as every criminal, however heinous his offence, began to think that he might escape punishment by amusing the King with idle stories.

The King, on hearing this, sent to the prison for Bakhtyar, and desired the executioner to attend. When the unfortunate young man came before the King, he requested a respite only of two days, in the course of which he hoped his innocence might be proved; "although," said he, "I know that the malice of one's enemies is a flame from which it is almost impossible to escape: as appears from the story of Abu Temam, who, on the strength of a false accusation, was put to death by the King, and his innocence acknowledged when too late."

"Who was that Abu Temam?" demanded the King, "and what were those malicious accusations which prevailed against him?"

Story of Abu Temam

Abu Temam (said Bakhtyar) was a very wealthy man, who resided in a city, the King of which was so tyrannical and unjust, that whatever money anyone possessed above five direms he seized on for his own use. Abu Temam was so disgusted and terrified by the oppressions and cruelties of this King, that he never enjoyed one meal in peace or comfort, until he had collected all his property together and contrived to escape from that place. After some time, he settled in the capital of another King, a city adorned with gardens, and well supplied with running streams. This King was a man of upright and virtuous principles, renowned for hospitality and kindness to strangers. In this capital Abu Temam purchased a magnificent mansion, in which he sumptuously entertained the people of the city, presenting each of them, at his departure, with a handsome dress suited to his rank. The inhabitants were delighted with his generosity, and his hospitality was daily celebrated by the strangers who resorted to his house. He also expended considerable sums in the erection of bridges, caravanseries, and mosques. At last the fame of his liberality and munificence reached the King, who sent to him two servants with a very flattering message and an invitation to court. This Abu Temam thankfully accepted; and having prepared the necessary presents for the King, he hastened to the palace, where he kissed the ground of obedience and was graciously received.

In a short time he became so great a favourite that the King would not permit him to be one day absent, and heaped on him so many favours that he was next in power to his royal master; and his advice was followed in all matters of importance.

But this King had ten viziers, who conceived a mortal hatred against Abu Temam, and said, one to another, "He has robbed us of all dignity and power, and we must devise some means whereby we may banish him from this country." The chief vizier proposed that, as the King was a very passionate admirer of beauty, and the Princess of Turkestan one of the loveliest creatures of the age, they should so praise her charms before him as to induce him to send Abu Temam to ask her in marriage; and as it was the custom of the King of Turkestan to send all ambassadors who came on that errand to his daughter, who always caused their heads to be cut off, so the destruction of Abu Temam would be certain.

This advice all the other viziers approved of; and, having proceeded to the palace, they took an opportunity of talking on various subjects, until the King of Turkestan was mentioned, when the chief vizier began to celebrate the charms of the lovely Princess.

When the King heard the extravagant praises of her beauty, he became enamoured, and declared his intention of despatching an ambassador to the court of Turkestan, and demanding the princess in marriage. The viziers immediately said that no person was so properly qualified for such an embassy as Abu Temam. The King accordingly sent for him, and, addressing him as his father and friend, informed him that he had now occasion for his assistance in the accomplishment of a matter on which his heart was bent. Abu Temam desired to know what his Majesty's commands might be, and declared himself ready to obey them. The King having communicated his design, all the necessary preparations were made, and Abu Temam set out on his journey to the court of Turkestan. In the meantime the viziers congratulated one another on the success of their stratagem.

When the King of Turkestan heard of Abu Temam's arrival, he sent proper officers to receive and compliment him, and on the following day gave him a public audience; and when the palace was cleared of the crowd, and Abu Temam had an opportunity of speaking with the King in private, he disclosed the object of his mission, and demanded the princess for his master. The King acknowledged himself highly honoured by the proposal of such an alliance, and said, "I fear that my daughter is not qualified for so exalted a station as you offer; but if you will visit her in the harem, and converse with her, you may form an opinion of her beauty and accomplishments; and if you approve of her, preparations for the marriage shall be made without delay."

Abu Temam thanked his Majesty for this readiness in complying with his demands; but said that he could not think of profaning the beauty of her who was destined for his sovereign by gazing on her, or of allowing his ears to hear the forbidden sounds of her voice; besides, his King never entertained a doubt on the subject of her charms and qualifications: the daughter of such a monarch must be worthy of any King, but he was not sent to make any enquiry as to her merits, but to demand her in marriage.

The King of Turkestan, on hearing this reply, embraced Abu Temam, and said, "Within this hour I meditated thy destruction; for of all the ambassadors who have hitherto come to solicit my daughter, I have tried the wisdom and talents, and have judged by them of the Kings who employed them, and finding them deficient, I have caused their heads to be cut off." On saying this, he took from under his robe a key, with which he opened a lock, and going into another part of the palace, he exhibited to Abu Temam the heads of four hundred ambassadors.

After this the King directed the necessary preparations for the departure of his daughter, and invested Abu Temam with a splendid robe of honour, who, when ten days had elapsed, embarked in a ship with the princess, her damsels, and other attendants. The news of his arrival with the fair Princess of Turkestan being announced, the King, his master, was delighted, and the viziers, his mortal enemies, were confounded at the failure of their stratagems. The King, accompanied by all the people, great and small, went two stages to meet Abu Temam and the princess, and, having led her into the city, after three days celebrated their marriage by the most sumptuous feasts and rejoicings, and bestowed a thousand thanks on Abu Temam, who every day became a greater favourite.

The ten viziers, finding, in consequence of this, their own importance and dignity gradually reduced, consulted one with another, saying, "All that we have hitherto done only tends to the exaltation of Abu Temam; we must devise some other means of disgracing him in the King's esteem, and procuring his banishment from this country."

After this they concerted together, and at length resolved to bribe two boys, whose office was to rub the King's feet every night after he lay down on his bed; and they accordingly instructed these boys to take an opportunity, when the King should close his eyes, of saying that Abu Temam had been ungrateful for the favours bestowed on him; that he had violated the harem, and aspired to the Queen's affections, and had boasted that she would not have come from Turkestan had she not been enamoured of himself. This lesson the viziers taught the boys, giving them a thousand dinars, and promising five hundred more.

When it was night the boys were employed as usual in their office of rubbing the King's feet; and when they perceived his eyes to be closed, they began to repeat all that the viziers had taught them to say concerning Abu Temam.

The King, hearing this, started up, and dismissing the boys, sent immediately for Abu Temam, and said to him, "A certain matter has occurred, on the subject of which I must consult you; and I expect that you will relieve my mind by answering the question that I shall ask." Abu Temam declared himself ready to obey. "What, then," demanded the King, "does that servant merit, who, in return for various favours, ungratefully attempts to violate the harem of his sovereign?" – "Such a servant," answered Abu Temam, "should be punished with death: his blood should expiate his offence." When Abu Temam had said this, the King drew his scimitar, and cut off his head, and ordered his body to be cast into a pit.

For some days he gave not audience to any person, and the viziers began to exult in the success of their stratagem; but the King was melancholy, and loved to sit alone, and was constantly thinking of the unfortunate Abu Temam.

It happened, however, that one day the two boys who had been bribed by the viziers were engaged in a dispute one with the other on the division of the money, each claiming for himself the larger share. In the course of their dispute they mentioned the innocence of Abu Temam, and the bribe which they had received for defaming him in the King's hearing.

All this conversation the King overheard; and trembling with vexation, rage, and sorrow, he compelled the boys to relate all the circumstances of the affair; in consequence of which the ten viziers were immediately seized and put to death, and their houses levelled with the ground; after which the King passed his time in fruitless lamentation for the loss of Abu Temam.

* * *

"Thus," said Bakhtyar, "does unrelenting malice persecute unto destruction; but if the King had not been so hasty in killing Abu Temam, he would have spared himself all his subsequent sorrow."

The King, affected by this observation, resolved to indulge Bakhtyar with another day, and accordingly sent him back to prison.

CHAPTER X

Early on the next morning, the Tenth Vizier sent a woman to the Queen with a message, urging her to exert her influence over the King, and induce him to give orders for the execution of Bakhtyar. The Queen, in consequence of this, addressed the King on the subject before he left the palace, and he replied, that Bakhtyar's fate was now decided, and that his execution should not be any longer deferred. The King then went forth, and the Viziers attended in their proper places. The Tenth Vizier was rising to speak, when the King informed him of his resolution to terminate the affair of Bakhtyar by putting him to death on that day.

He was brought accordingly from the prison; and the King on seeing him said, "You have spoken a great deal of your innocence, yet have not been able to make it appear; therefore no longer entertain any hopes of mercy, for I have given orders for your execution." On hearing this, Bakhtyar began to weep, and said, "I have hitherto endeavoured to gain time, conscious of my innocence, and hoping that it might be proved, and a guiltless person saved from an ignominious death; but I now find it vain to struggle against the decrees of Heaven. Thus the King of Persia foolishly attempted to counteract his destiny, and triumph over the will of Providence, but in vain."

The King expressed a desire of hearing the story to which Bakhtyar alluded, and the young man began to relate it as follows:

Story of the King of Persia

There was a certain King of Persia, a very powerful and wealthy monarch, who, not having any child, employed all the influence of prayers and of alms to procure the blessing of a son from Heaven. At length one of his handmaids became pregnant, and the King was transported with joy; but one night, in a dream, he was addressed by an old man, who said, "The Lord has complied with your request, and tomorrow you shall have a son; but in his seventh year a lion shall seize and carry off this son to the top of a mountain, from which he shall fall, rolling in blood and clay." When the King awoke, he assembled the viziers, and related to them the horrors of his dream. They replied, "Long be the King's life! If Heaven has decreed such a calamity who can oppose or control it?" The King presumptuously declared that he would struggle against and counteract it; but one of his viziers, eminently skilled in astrology, discovered one day, by the power of his science, that the King would, after twenty years, perish by the hand of his own son. In consequence of this, he immediately waited on the King, and informed him that he had to communicate a certain matter, for the truth and certainty of which he would answer with his life. The King desired him to reveal it; and he, falling on the knees of obedience, related all that he had discovered in the stars. "If it happens not according to what you predict," said the King, "I shall certainly put you to death."

In the meantime, however, he caused a subterraneous dwelling to be constructed, to which he sent the boy, with a nurse. There they remained during the space of seven years, when, in compliance with the heavenly decree, a lion suddenly rushed into the cave, and devoured the nurse, and having wounded the child, carried him up to the summit of a neighbouring mountain, from which he let him fall to the bottom, covered with blood and earth. It happened that one of the King's secretaries came by, in pursuit of game, and perceived the boy in this situation, and the lion standing on the summit of the mountain. He immediately resolved to save the child; and having taken him to his own house, he healed his wounds, and instructed him in various accomplishments.

On the day after the nurse had been devoured and the child carried away by the lion, the King resolved to visit the cave, and finding it deserted, he concluded that the nurse had escaped to some other place. He instantly despatched messengers to seek her in every quarter, but in vain.

In process of time the boy grew up, and acted as keeper of pen and ink to the secretary. In this situation, having been employed at the palace, it happened that the King saw and was much pleased with him, and felt within his bosom the force of paternal affection. In consequence of this, he demanded him of the secretary, and clothed him in splendid garments; and after some time, when an enemy invaded the country, and required the King's presence with his army, he appointed the young man to be his armour-bearer; and, accompanied by him, proceeded to battle.

After a bloody conflict, the troops of the enemy were victorious, and those of the King began to fly; but he, in the impulse of rage and fury, threw himself into the midst of his adversaries, fighting with the most desperate valour. In this state of confusion it was impossible to know one person from another; the young armour-bearer, who fought also with the utmost bravery, no longer distinguishing the King, rushed into a crowd of combatants, and striking furiously on all sides, cut off the hand of one man whom he supposed to be of the enemy's side; but this person was the King, who, on recognising the armour-bearer, upbraided him with this attempt upon his life, and being unable to remain any longer in the field, he retired, with his troops, to the capital, and the next day concluded a peace with the enemy, on condition of paying a considerable sum of money. He then gave orders that the armour-bearer should be arrested, and although he persevered in declarations of innocence, they availed him not; he was thrown into prison, and loaded with chains.

In the meantime the King was reposing on the pillow of death; and when he found that all hopes of recovery were vain, he resolved to punish the vizier who had told him that his son should be torn by a lion, and that he should fall by the hand of that son. "Now," said the King, "my son has been carried away to some other country by his nurse, and I have been wounded by the hand of a different person." Having said this, he sent for the vizier, and desired him to prepare for death. "This armour-bearer," added he, "and not my own son, has wounded me, contrary to your prediction; and, as you consented to be punished in case your prediction should not be accomplished, I have resolved to put you to death." – "Be it so," replied the vizier, "but let us first enquire into the birth of this young armour-bearer."

The King immediately sent for the young man, and asked him concerning his parents and his country. He answered that of the country which gave him birth he was ignorant; but that he had been with his mother in a subterraneous place, and that she had informed him of his father's being a king, but he had never seen his father; that one day a lion carried him away to the summit of a mountain, from which he fell, and was taken up by the secretary, by whom he was instructed in various accomplishments, and from whose service he passed into that of the King.

When the King heard this, he was amazed, and his hair stood on end; and he sent for the viziers and secretary, who confirmed what the young man had said.

Having thus ascertained that the armour-bearer was his own son, he resigned to him the crown and throne; and having invested the vizier with the robe of prime-minister, he expired in the course of three days.

* * *

Here Bakhtyar concluded his narrative, and observed, that he had struggled against his evil destiny, like that king, but in vain. Having said this, the King wished to send him back to prison; but the ten viziers unanimously declared that they would leave the country if Bakhtyar's punishment was any longer deferred.

The King then acknowledged that he could not bear to behold the execution of the young man; in consequence of which the Viziers led him away, and assembled all the people by proclamation, that they might see him put to death.

CONCLUSION

It happened at this time that Farrukhsuwar, who had found Bakhtyar at the side of the well, came with some of his companions to the city, and was wrapped in that embroidered cloak which the King and Queen had left with the infant. In passing by the place of execution he beheld the guards leading out Bakhtyar to punishment, on which he rushed amongst them with his companions, and rescued the young man from their hands, and then solicited an audience of the King.

On coming into the royal presence Farrukhsuwar exclaimed, "This young man is my son; I cannot bear to see him executed: if he must perish, let me also be put to death." – "Your wish in this respect," said the King, "may be easily gratified." – "Alas!" cried Farrukhsuwar, "if the father of this youth, who was a king, or his mother, who was a queen, were informed of his situation, they would save him from this ignominious death!" The King laughed at the seeming inconsistency of Farrukhsuwar, and said, "You told me at one time that Bakhtyar was your son, yet now you describe him as the child of royal parents."

Farrukhsuwar, in reply, told all the circumstances of his finding Bakhtyar near the well, and showed the cloak in which he had been wrapped. The King immediately knew it to be the same which he had left with the infant, and asked whether Farrukhsuwar had found anything besides. He produced the bracelet of pearls, and the King, now convinced that Bakhtyar was not the son of Farrukhsuwar, but his own, took the cloak and the bracelets to the Queen, and asked her if she had ever before seen them. She instantly exclaimed, "They were my child's! What tidings do you bring of him?" – "I shall bring himself," replied the King; and he immediately sent an order to the Viziers that they should conduct Bakhtyar to the palace.

When he arrived, the King, with his own hands, took off his chains, placed a royal turban on his head, and covered him with the embroidered cloak, and then led him to the Queen, saying, "This is our son, whom we left on the brink of the well." When the Queen heard this, and beheld Bakhtyar, the tears gushed forth from her eyes, and she embraced him with the greatest emotion. Bakhtyar then asked the Queen why she had endeavoured to destroy him by a false accusation, and she confessed that the Viziers had induced her; on which the King ordered their immediate execution, and then resigned the throne to Bakhtyar, who was acknowledged sovereign by all the people. Farrukhsuwar was invested with the dignity of chief Vizier, and his companions rewarded with honourable appointments; and Bakhtyar continued for many years to govern with justice, wisdom, and generosity.

THE BAKHTYAR NAMA

THE SEVEN VIZIERS

Known as the *Seven Wise Masters* in Europe, this narrative framework is likely to trace its origins to ancient India before spreading across cultures, notably through the Middle East into Europe. Like the *Bakhtyār-nāma*, it consists of moralistic tales framed around a king and his seven viziers, each sharing a story to impart wisdom to the king's son. Each vizier tells a story to the prince, employing allegory to explore themes of loyalty, betrayal, friendship and justice. These tales remain influential across cultures today. They serve as both entertainment and moral education, reflecting the values of their societies and offering timeless insights into human nature.

INTRODUCTION

There lived in ancient days a powerful and mighty sultan, who was a wise sovereign, just to his subjects, bountiful to his dependants, and beloved by the whole empire; but he was become grey-bearded and stricken in years, and there had not been allotted to him a son, who might preserve his memory, and inherit the kingdom after him. On this account uneasiness assailed him, and such depression of spirits, that he secluded himself from society, and passed whole days in his private apartments.

At length his subjects began to murmur concerning him. Some said he was dead; others, that an accident had befallen him. On a certain day, his queen entered his chamber, and found him thoughtful, reclining his head towards the earth, like one plunged in sorrow.

She approached, and, kissing his hand, said, "Fortune has not persecuted thee, nor have the evils of chance reached thee. God has bestowed upon thee enjoyments, and given thee every delight. What, then, is the cause that I find thee so pensive?"

He replied, "Alas! my years are advanced, my age is drawing to its end, and my kingdom will pass to another family; for I am not blessed with a son, with whom my eyes might be delighted, and who might succeed me in my dominions. On this account extreme sorrow has overcome me."

The queen said, "God will remove thy grief and thy sorrow. The same thoughts which afflicted thy heart have afflicted mine, and what had invaded thy mind was invading mine, when, lo! drowsiness overcame me, and I fell asleep. I dreamt, and saw in my vision a phantom, which revealed to me, saying: 'If the sultan shall be blessed with a son by almighty God, he will with difficulty be preserved from death at a certain period. After that, prosperity will attend him. But if a daughter is born, her father will not love her; and if she lives, she will occasion the ruin of his kingdom. He must not, however, think of a child by any other woman than thyself, and thou shalt be the cause of his having one when the moon and the sign Gemini shall be in conjunction.' I now awoke from sleep, and became thoughtful, reflecting on what I had heard in my vision."

When the sultan heard these words, he said to her, "By God's permission, all will be well;" and the queen did not fail to comfort him until his gloom had passed away. He now quitted his retirement, sat upon the throne of his kingdom, summoned his nobles and his subjects, and entreated their prayers, that God would bless him with a son; when they prayed, and God accepted their prayers.

The night being arrived in which the moon and Gemini entered into conjunction, the queen became pregnant. She informed the sultan of her condition, and he rejoiced with exceeding great joy, and did not refrain, until she had borne her months, and brought forth a son, beautiful as the full moon. Then the sultan made rejoicings from evening till morning, gave alms, and released the prisoners. The infant was suckled nearly two years, when the mother returned to the mercy of God, and they lamented over her with great mourning.

The child did not cease to remain on the bosoms of the nurses and female attendants until he had completed his second year, when his father entrusted him to tutors, that they might teach him what was necessary for princes to acquire. The eighth year of his age passed over, but he had learnt nothing, for every book was to him too difficult. When the tutors represented this to the sultan, he was enraged against his son, and commanded him to be put to death, saying, "This is a disgraceful child, from whom there can no advantage arise."

There was at the court a man of wisdom, learning, and penetration, deeply versed in every science. When he found that the sultan intended to kill his son, he advanced, and kissing the ground before him, said, "O sovereign, be not grieved on account of thy son. Entrust him to me, and I will teach him whatever is necessary in two years. I will not deceive you, but instruct him in the sciences, philosophy, and princely accomplishments." The sultan exclaimed, "How canst thou make him learn, when every book has been too difficult for him, and his tutors have been wearied out?" The sage replied, "I pledge myself to do it; and if I do not perfect him in what I have mentioned, act by me as thou shalt think proper."

Upon this the sultan delivered his son to the sage, who took him to his house, prepared for him a chamber, and wrote upon the walls in yellow and white what he wished him to learn. Then he carried to him what was necessary for him of carpets, food, and utensils, and left him alone in the apartment. He did not permit any person to visit him but himself. Every third day the tutor entered, that he might teach him what was necessary from those books, the contents of which he had written on the walls, and depict for him fresh lessons; after which he placed round him provisions, locked the door upon him, and departed.

Now it came to pass that the boy, when his mind was at a loss for amusement, studied the lessons written on the walls, which he learnt in a short time. When the tutor found his sense and understanding on every point equal to what was necessary for him, he took him from the apartment, and instructed him in horsemanship and archery; after which he sent to his father, and informed him that his son had learnt whatever was becoming his condition in one year.

The sultan rejoiced exceedingly, and informed his viziers of it, who were, in number, seven. Then he wished to examine his son, and commanded the tutor to bring him with him, in order that he might question him. The tutor consulted the horoscope of the youth, and foresaw that if he should speak before there should pass over his head seven days and nights, there would occur to him imminent danger of death. Upon this the sage addressed the prince, saying, "I have inspected thy nativity, and if from this time thou speakest before seven days are expired, great hazard of life will befall thee." The prince replied, "What can ensure my safety?" The tutor answered, "Repair to thy father, but when he speaketh to thee, utter not a word." The youth exclaimed, "I swear by God, that if thou hadst commanded me that I should not breathe, I would have obeyed thee, on account of what thou hast done for me of kindness and favour." The tutor replied, "Go, and speak not, though they beat thee with scourges, for thou wilt recover of thy wounds, there will be in store for thee great glory, and thou shalt rule the kingdom after thy father." Then the prince said, "Remember thy speech to my father before thou lookedst at my nativity." The tutor replied, "What must be must be; further conversation will not profit. Nothing will occur but felicity to thee, whatever may become of me. Be firm, and trust in God; for whoever trusteth in God is secure."

The prince departed, and repaired to his father, when the viziers, with the nobles, officers of state, and the men of science met him on his way. They placed before him a herb, that he might describe its genus and properties; but he did not speak. They importuned him to answer, but he would not utter a word.

Upon this the sultan was affected with grief, and sent for the tutor to punish him; when some of the assembly said, the sage had deserted his house in the night; some, that he had taken poison; and others contradicted this last assertion. There was much disputation among them, but still the prince would not speak. At length the assembly broke up, and there remained only the prince and his father.

The sultan had a concubine, of beautiful person and very young, with the love of whom he was dotingly fascinated. She now entered, and saw the prince sitting near his father, like an affrighted fawn. She approached near, and said to the sultan, "I perceive thee, my lord, overcome with affliction;" when he related to her the conduct of his son. She replied, "I desire that thou wouldst commit him to my charge, for perhaps he will be affable to me and speak, and I shall discover the cause of his silence."

He replied, "Take him with thee." Upon which she led him by the hand, conducted him to her chamber, caressed him, and explained to him her wishes, clasped him to her bosom, and attempted to kiss him; but he rejected her advances. She exclaimed, "I am a young damsel, and thou a young man; I will be thine, and thou shalt be mine. Thy father is become superannuated, must soon depart this life, when thou wilt govern the kingdom after him, and shalt espouse me; but if thou wilt not comply with my desires, I will effect thy destruction. Choose, then, one or the other – happiness or death."

When the prince heard this, he was exceedingly enraged against her, and thought within himself, "I will speedily repay thee for thy crimes, when after seven days I shall be able to speak." The artful damsel, when she perceived his anger, hastened to contrive his ruin. She beat her cheeks, tore her garments, dishevelled her hair, and went before the sultan in that manner. He said, "What can have happened to thee?" She exclaimed, "He, whom thou seest, hath done this, even thy own son, who has plotted the destruction of thy life, and feigned himself dumb. When I entered with him into my chamber, he declared to me his love; and when I refused him, he said: 'I cannot live without thee, and if thou dost not comply with my desires, I will kill thee, and murder my father.'"

When the sultan heard these words, his wrath was violent against his son, and he gave orders to have him put to death. He sent for his viziers; but the tutor had informed them of the circumstances, and why the prince was prevented from speaking for seven days. Upon this the viziers assembled together, and consulted, saying, "The sultan intends to put his son to death, but there may not be in him any fault, so that when he is dead, our master may repent, when repentance will not avail." Then the prime vizier said, "Let us each take charge of him for a day during the seven days, till the whole are expired, and I will be responsible for you all at the conclusion of that period."

The First Vizier, having contrived thus, repaired to the sultan, kissed the ground, and said, "O sultan, if there were to thee a thousand sons, far be it from thee the death of one of them! Alas, then, when thou hast one only, with whom thou wast blessed after much anxiety and expectation, that thou shouldst command his execution upon the bare assertion of a woman! God only knoweth whether she hath spoken truly or accused him falsely; for there are among the sex women artfully malicious."

STORY OF AHMED THE ORPHAN

I have heard, O my sovereign, that a certain sultan resolved to educate those unfortunate children who are sometimes abandoned on the highways. As he was passing one day, behold, he saw a male infant upon a heap of rubbish, who appeared beautiful as the moon at the full. He commanded his attendants to convey him to the palace; and they took him up, and committed him to nurses till he grew up, when they placed him at school. The boy learnt the Qur'an and the sciences and languages. When he had finished his education, the sultan committed to him the care of his treasury; and it came to pass that at length he did nothing but with his advice, and the youth attended in his private chambers.

As he was in waiting one day, the sultan said, "Go to the apartment of Hayatu-'n-nufus, and bring me a medicine from her closet." The youth passed through the chamber of the concubine, and found her with a slave. He took up the medicine, but did not seem to attend to her actions, and returned with haste to the sultan. The name of this youth was Ahmed Yetlm. Then the sultan said, "What has happened to thee, that I perceive thy colour changed?" Ahmed replied, "My lord, because I came with hurry and precipitation;" but he did not inform the sultan of what he had discovered.

The concubine Hayatu-'n-nufus, being convinced that Ahmed must have beheld herself and her paramour, hastily contrived a scheme against him. She scarred her face, and rent her garments. When the sultan entered, and found her in that situation, he said, "What is thy condition?" She exclaimed, "From him who is the offspring of adultery no good can proceed." The sultan, understanding her meaning, replied, "Conceal this affair, and within this hour I will bring thee his head." He departed from her, filled with indignation, and ascended his throne.

Ahmed attended, according to custom, but did not suspect what was plotted against him. The sultan beckoned to one of his slaves, and said privately to him, "Go to the house of such a person, and remain there. When anyone shall say unto thee: 'Thus saith the sultan, Do that which thou wast commanded to execute,' strike off his head, place it in this basket, and fasten over it the cover. When I shall send to thee a messenger who will say: 'Hast thou performed the business?' commit to him the basket." The slave replied, "To hear is to obey," and retired. Soon after, the sultan called to Ahmed Yetim, and said: "Hasten to a certain house, and say unto such a slave, 'Execute the commands of the sultan.'"

Ahmed departed, but on the way he saw the man who had been criminal with the concubine, with a number of other slaves, sitting down, drinking and. feasting. As they saw Ahmed approaching, they stood up; and the guilty slave thought that if he could detain him from the business of the sultan, he might procure his death. He stopped him, paid obeisance to him, and entreated that he would sit down with them a little while. But Ahmed said, "The sultan hath sent me upon business to a certain house, and I cannot stay." Upon this the guilty slave replied, "I will perform the commission." Ahmed answered, "If so, hasten, and say to a slave whom thou wilt find there, that he must execute the orders of the sultan." The slave said, "To hear is to obey," and departed.

Ahmed sat down with the rest, while the other proceeded to the house, and said to the person in waiting, "Thus saith the sultan, 'Complete thy orders.'" He replied, "Most readily," and drawing his scimitar, struck off the head of the guilty slave, washed it from the blood, placed it in the basket, tied the cover on it, and sat down.

When Ahmed had waited some time for the return of his messenger, he took leave of his company, went to the house, and said to the slave in waiting, "Hast thou performed thy orders?" He replied, "Yes," and committed the basket to Ahmed, who took it up, and went with it to the sultan; but he did not suspect what was within the basket, nor did curiosity lead him to open it.

When the sultan saw him, he said, "Ahmed, I sent thee upon a commission, but thou hast entrusted it to another." He replied, "My lord, it is true." The sultan exclaimed, "Hast thou seen what is contained in this basket?" Ahmed answered, "No; I swear by thy head, I do not know what is within it, nor have I opened it." The king was astonished, and said, "Take off the covering." He lifted it up, and, behold! in it was the head of the slave who had done evil with Hayatu-'n-nufus.

The sultan exclaimed, "I cannot suppose, Ahmed, that it should be concealed from thee, whether or not this slaughtered man was guilty of a crime which rendered him worthy of death." Ahmed replied, "Know, my lord, when thou didst send me for the medicine to the chamber of Hayatu-'n-nufus, I found this slave in her embraces; I took up the medicine, but did not disclose what I had beheld. When despatched to the house, I found on the way this guilty slave, sitting with his fellows eating and drinking. He stood up, and entreated me to stay among them. I replied: 'The sultan hath sent me to execute a commission,'

Upon which he said: 'Sit down – I will perform this business,' and departed." He then related the other circumstances, until he was entrusted with the basket.

Then the sultan exclaimed, "O Ahmed! none is discerning but God;" related to him the behaviour of the damsel, and what she had accused him of, and said, "I resign her unto thee." Ahmed replied, "I cannot repay the bounties of the sultan with ingratitude; I can have no concern with her." When the sultan heard these words, he commanded her to be put to death.

"This, O sultan," continued the vizier, "is only one instance of the deceitfulness of women. Trust not to their declarations, for their artful malice is great. Another example of their arts hath reached me."

STORY OF THE MERCHANT, HIS WIFE, AND THE PARROT

There was a merchant, who traded largely, and travelled much abroad; he had a wife whom he loved, and to her he was constant. A journey became necessary for him, and he bought for a hundred dinars a parrot, that could speak like a human being, that it might inform him of what passed in the house.

Before he departed upon his journey, he committed to the parrot the charge of watching his wife's conduct. When he was gone, the lady sent to her lover, who was a soldier; and he came, and abode with her during the time of her husband's absence. The parrot observed all that was done. On the merchant's return, he called for the bird, and asked him what had passed, and was informed of his wife's misconduct. When the merchant heard this intelligence, he was enraged against his wife, beat her severely, and kept himself from her. The wife supposed that her neighbours had accused her; but they declared, upon oath, that they had not spoken to him. Then she said, "None can have informed him but the parrot."

Upon a certain night, the merchant went to visit a friend. Then the wife took a coarse cloth, and put it upon the parrot's cage, and placed over it, on the floor above, the grinding-stones; after which she ordered her slave-girls to grind, throw water over the cloth, and raise a great wind with a fan. Then she took a looking glass, and made it dazzle in the light of the lamp, by a quick motion.

The bird (being in the dark) supposed that the noise of the grinding was thunder; the gleams from the mirror, lightning; the blasts from the fan, wind; and the water, hard rain. In the morning, when the merchant returned to his house, the parrot said, "How fared my lord last night, during the wind, the rain, and the dreadful lightning?" The merchant exclaimed, "Villain, thou liest; for I did not see anything of it;" and the parrot replied, "I only tell thee what I experienced."

The merchant now disbelieved the bird, and put confidence in his wife. He went to her, and sought to be reconciled, but she said, "I will not be reconciled, unless you destroy the mischief-making parrot, who belied me." He killed the bird, and after that remained some time happy with his wife. At length the neighbours informed him of her crimes, when he concealed himself, and detected the soldier with her. The fidelity of the parrot was apparent, but the merchant repented of putting him to death, when repentance would not avail him. He divorced his wife, and took an oath never to marry.

"I have thus informed thee, O sultan," added the vizier, "of the artfulness of women, and proved that rashness produces only fruitless remorse." The sultan, upon this, refrained from the execution of his son.

When night set in, the Damsel came to the sultan, and said, "Why hast thou delayed doing me justice? Hast thou not heard that sovereigns should be obeyed in whatever they command, and that an order not enforced is a sign of weakness? Everyone knows what must follow. Do me justice, then, upon thy son, or it will happen to you both, as it happened to the fuller and his son." Then the king said, "What befell the fuller and his son?" She replied with the…

STORY OF THE FULLER AND HIS SON

Know O sultan, that there was a fuller who went daily to wash his cloths on the bank of a river, and with him his son, who used to venture far into the water and swim; which his father forbade, but he would not be prevented. On a certain day, the youth went into a deep part, and his arms became cramped. When the father beheld his situation, he threw himself into the river, hoping to save him; but the youth hung upon his legs, and they were both drowned.

"Do me justice, then, upon thy son. Thy viziers pretend that the art of our sex is greater than that of men; but the fact is the contrary, as you will see from the following tale:

STORY OF THE SULTAN AND THE VIZIER'S WIFE

It has been related to me, my lord, that there was a certain sultan much addicted to the love of women, of violent passions. Being one day upon the terrace of his palace, he saw a lady upon the platform of her house, beautiful and elegant; his soul desired her, and he was told that she was the wife of his vizier. Upon this he sent for the minister, and despatched him on a distant expedition, with orders not to return till he had executed his commission. The vizier attended to his sovereign's commands, and departed.

When the sultan knew of his departure, he was impatient to see the lady, and repaired to her house. She received him standing, and kissed the ground before him; but she was virtuous, and had no inclination to immodesty. She then said, "Why, O my lord, is this auspicious visit?" He replied, "From the excess of my love and passion for thee." Upon which she kissed the ground, and said, "It is not befitting that I should be thy partner; my heart has never aspired to such an honour."

Then the sultan extended his hands upon her, and tempted her; when she cried, "My lord, this must never be." Observing that he was enraged at her refusal, she dissembled, and said, "Wait, O my lord, until I have prepared a supper, which when thou hast partaken of, I shall be honoured with thy commands." She then seated the sultan upon the sofa of her husband, and brought him a book from which the vizier was used to read to her. In it were written admonitions and warnings against adultery, and commands to his wife not to admit anyone within doors without his orders. On the perusal of it, the sultan's mind was diverted from the pursuit of his guilty passion.

At length the lady placed a supper before him, consisting of ninety and nine dishes; when the sultan ate a mouthful from every dish. Each was of a different colour, but all of the same sort of food. Then he said to her, "How is this?" She replied, "My lord, I have set a parable before thee. In thy palace are ninety and nine concubines, of different stature and complexion; who, however, form but one kind of food."

The sultan was confounded, and did not importune her. Rising up, he went to perform his ablutions, but left his ring under a cushion of the sofa; and on his return to the palace, forgot to take it with him.

When the vizier returned from his journey, and had visited the sultan, he repaired to his own house, and sat down upon the sofa; and, behold! under the cushion he discovered the sultan's ring, which he knew. Becoming jealous of his wife, he was enraged against her, and secluded himself from her for a whole year; during which he did not go near, nor even enquire after her. When the coolness of her husband became intolerable, the lady complained to her father, and informed him of his neglect of her for a whole year; upon which the father repaired to the sultan, when the vizier was present, and said:

"May God preserve the sultan! I had an elegant garden, which was formed by my own hand, and I watered it until it was the season of its fruits. Then I presented it to thy vizier, and he ate of its productions until he was satiated, when he deserted and neglected it; and it was spoiled, and reptiles overran it; its flowers were injured, and its condition was changed."

The sultan said to the vizier, "How sayest thou?" The vizier replied, "He speaketh the truth in what he hath related. But one day, when I entered the garden, I saw the track of a lion in it; my mind was alarmed, and I refrained from visiting it."

On hearing this parable, the sultan understood it, recollected that he had forgotten his ring in the house of the vizier, and knew that by it was meant the track of the lion. He then said, "It is true, O vizier, that the lion did enter without the consent of the owner's wife; but the lion did not compel her to commit evil. She is a virtuous woman, and of chaste desires."

Then the vizier said, "To hear is to obey;" and he was now convinced that the sultan had not compelled her to dishonour. He returned to his wife, who related to him all that had passed; and he relied upon her truth, her honour, and her fidelity.

"Had she been vicious," continued the Damsel, "she would have complied with the sultan, when he disclosed his wishes; but know, my lord, that men are more deceitful than women."

Next morning, the sultan commanded the execution of his son; when the Second Vizier entered, and, kissing the ground, said, "Be not rash in executing thy son. Thou wast not blessed with him till after despairing of issue, and could scarcely credit his existence. He may yet prove to thee the preserver of thy kingdom, and a guardian of thy memory. Be patient, then, my lord, until he shall find a proper opportunity to speak for himself. If thou puttest him to death, thou wilt repent when repentance will not avail. I have heard, O sultan, much of the female sex, of their arts and their stratagems, especially in the…

STORY OF THE OFFICER AND THE MERCHANT'S WIFE

There was an officer belonging to the bodyguard of his prince, who admired a merchant's wife, and was passionately beloved by her. On a certain day he sent his slave to see whether her husband was at home or absent. When the slave came, not finding her husband, he would have returned; but the lady, on seeing him, would not let him go.

While they were conversing, the officer came up, and she took the slave and locked him in an inner chamber. And, while the officer was with her, suddenly her husband knocked at the door. Upon this the lady said to the officer, who was much alarmed, "Draw thy scimitar, and go down to the entry, abuse me, and revile me, and say: 'He certainly is with thee, and thou hast concealed him.' When my husband enters, go out, and pursue thy way."

Her husband, on coming in, saw the officer standing in the entry, with a drawn sword in his hand, exclaiming, "Thou wretch! thou hast hidden the lad near thee," and he then hastened home. The merchant said to his wife, "What has been the matter?" She replied, "Thou hast this day saved an unfortunate Mussulman from being murdered." He asked her how that was, and she replied, "I was sitting, thinking upon thee, when a young lad rushed in, and cried: 'Save me from death, and God will save thee from the fire! An officer would murder me without a fault.' Then I took him, and concealed him in my chamber; after which the officer entered, and began to abuse me, and would have killed me, saying, 'He is with thee.' God be praised that you came in, or I should have been a corpse." Her husband said, "God preserve thee from the fire, for what thou hast done – I doubt not but he will."

Then she took the lad from the chamber, and he pretended to weep, and thanked her for her kindness; but the husband did not guess the least of the disgrace that had befallen his head from his wife's intrigues.

"This, O sultan, is only one instance of the art of women; alas, that thou shouldst give credit to their accusations!"

When the third night was arrived, the Damsel entered, and kissing the ground, wept, and said, "Wilt thou not, my lord, do me justice upon thy son? And wilt thou not refrain from attending to the stories of thy viziers? They are full of wickedness. I have heard, O sultan, of a vizier who would have murdered the son of his master." He enquired, "In what manner?" She replied with the…

STORY OF THE PRINCE AND THE GHUL

There was a certain sultan who had a son, whom he loved with ardent affection. The prince one day begged permission of his father to hunt; upon which the sultan ordered preparations, commanded his vizier to attend him, and sent with him slaves, domestics, and troops. They advanced towards the chase, and passed through a verdant plain, having groves and rivulets, among which the antelopes sported. The prince pursued and ran down much game of various kinds, and remained long, diverting himself with the sport, in great spirits and enjoyment.

As he was returning homewards, there bounded across the plain an antelope, brilliant as the sun shining in a serene sky; and the vizier said, "Let us pursue this deer, for my heart longs to take her." When the prince heard this, he followed her; and the attendants would have accompanied him, but the vizier forbade them. The antelope did not cease to gain ground, nor the prince to pursue her, till the evening overshadowed, when she disappeared, and darkness came on.

The prince would have returned, but could not find his path, and he fainted with terror; nor could he move from the thirsty desert until the morning. He then prayed to God for deliverance, and travelled on, oppressed with hunger, until midday; when, lo! he came to a ruined town, in which owls and ravens had their abodes. While he stopped, astonished at their screaming, a female voice struck his ear, and he beheld a beautiful girl sitting under one of the mouldering walls, weeping bitterly. He addressed her, and said, "Why dost thou lament, and who art thou?" She replied, "Know that I am the daughter of a certain sultan of the north. My father espoused me to the son of my uncle, and detached troops to escort me to him, and we began our journey. When we arrived here, I fell from my carriage, as you see, and my attendants went on, and left me, thinking I was still upon the camel. I have remained here three days, famishing and thirsty, and was despairing of life, when I saw thee." The prince mounted her behind him, and said, "Comfort thy heart, and dry thine eyes, and say, God be praised, for thy deliverance from this desert."

They now proceeded, and besought assistance from the Almighty. When they had journeyed some time, they reached a city, ruinous like the first, and the damsel said to him, "Remain here, while I retire a little; I will soon return." The prince helped her down, and waited with his horse, when, behold! the ghul (for such was the pretended damsel) cried to two others, saying, "I have brought a prey to feast upon." When the prince heard this, his heart was chilled. The ghul came out, and found him pale and trembling. She said, "Prince, why do I behold thy colour changed?" He answered, "I was reflecting on the cause of my sorrows." She exclaimed, "Seek a remedy for them in the treasures of thy father." He replied, "They are not to be remedied by treasure or hoards." She said, "Remedy them by your armies and troops." He replied, "They are not to be remedied by them." She continued, "Ask help of the God of power and might; for ye pretend that ye have in the heavens a God who, when ye call upon him, will be gracious, and that he is absolute over all things." The prince replied, "It is true; and we have no other help but him." Then he lifted up his face towards heaven, and said,

"O Lord, I humbly beseech thee, and implore aid from thee in this crisis, which grieveth and afflicteth me;" at the same time catching the pretended princess in his arms. Scarcely had he concluded his prayer, when an angel descended from the sky, with a sword of flame, and smote her with it, and destroyed her. For this miracle may the Almighty be glorified! The prince after this returned safely to the capital of his father.

"All this danger," continued the damsel, "occurred from the schemes of the vizier; and I inform thee, O sultan, that thy viziers are also treacherous. Be, then, watchful of their arts." Upon this the sultan gave orders for the execution of his son.

On the next day the Third Vizier entered, kissed the ground before the sultan, and said, "Know, O sultan, I would advise thee candidly, and am faithful to thyself and thy son. Be not violent against thy child, the light of thine eyes. It is possible the damsel's desire of his death may proceed from malice; and I have heard that two great tribes were destroyed for the sake of a drop of honey." The sultan enquired, upon what occasion, and the vizier said:

STORY OF THE DROP OF HONEY

It has been related to me that there was a hunter, who chased every species of wild animals. One day, in his excursion to the mountains, he found a hollow in the rocks, full of honey, with which he filled a vessel he had with him, and returned to the city. He chanced to stop at the door of an oil merchant, when a little of the honey happening to drop, the merchant's cat licked it up, and was killed by the hunter's dog. Upon this, the merchant killed the dog, at which the hunter was enraged, and having wounded the merchant, went to his quarter, and raised his friends. The merchant also raised his friends, and when the parties met, they fought till they were all destroyed – for the sake of a drop of honey.

I have also heard, continued the Third Vizier, among instances of female artifice, the...

STORY OF THE WOMAN AND THE RICE-SELLER

A man one day gave his wife a dirham to buy rice, and she went to the shop of the rice-seller, and said to him, "Give me rice for this dirham." When he saw that she was possessed of beauty and an elegant form, he began cajoling her, and said to her, "Rice is not good unless with sugar; come within, and I will give thee some." The woman consented, and the dealer ordered his slave to measure a quantity of rice and sugar, but accompanied the order with a private sign, which the youth understood; and while his master was engaged with the woman, he filled her towel with earth and stones. After this the woman took the towel, and went off, thinking that it contained sugar and rice; and when she arrived at her house she placed it before her husband, and went to fetch the cauldron. In the meantime her husband opened the towel, and discovered the earth and the stones, and when she came back, he said to her, "Did I tell thee that we had a house to build, that thou hast brought earth and stones?" She then perceived that the dealer had tricked her, and said, "O my husband, see what I have done in my confusion: I went for the sieve, and have brought the cauldron! For the dirham you gave me dropped from my hand in the marketplace, and I was ashamed before the people to look around for it; so I brought back earth and stones, that you might sift them." The husband then arose, and took the sieve, and he sat down sifting the earth until his face and his beard were covered with dust; and the poor man knew not what had happened to him.

On the fourth night the Damsel entered to the sultan, kissed the ground before him, and said, "My lord, you have rejected my cause, delayed my claims, and will not do me justice upon thy son. But God will assist me, as he assisted the son of a certain sultan against his father's vizier." The sultan enquired in what manner that happened, and she related the…

STORY OF THE TRANSFORMED PRINCE

There was a sultan, who had an only son, whom he betrothed to the daughter of a great monarch. She was very beautiful, and passionately beloved by the son of her uncle; but her father would not consent to give her to him in marriage, on account of his prior engagement to the sultan. When the young man found that his uncle had affianced her to another, he was exceedingly afflicted, and had no other resource but to send rich presents to the vizier of the intended bridegroom's father, and entreat him that he would deceive the prince by some stratagem, so that the match might be broken off. The vizier accepted the bribe, and promised compliance.

The father of the princess, after some time, wrote to the sultan, requesting that he would send his son, to celebrate the marriage at his court; after which he might return home with his bride. The sultan consented, and despatched the prince under care of his vizier, with attendants and slaves, and an escort of a thousand horse; he also sent by him a rich present of camels, and horses, and tents, and valuable curiosities.

The vizier departed with the prince, but resolved to betray him, on account of the bribes he had received from the cousin of the princess. At length they entered a desert, where the vizier bethought himself of a fountain, named the White Fountain, of which but few persons knew the properties; these were, that if a man drank of the water, he became a woman; and if a woman drank of it, she became a man. The vizier encamped at some distance from it, and invited the prince to ride out with him; when he mounted, but did not suspect what the vizier had devised. They did not cease riding in the wilderness till sunset, when the prince complained that he was overcome with thirst, and unable to converse from the parching of his mouth. The vizier then brought him to the fountain, and said, "Dismount, and drink."

The prince alighted from his horse, and drank, when lo! he instantly became a woman. On perceiving his condition, he wept aloud, and was overcome with shame, and fainted. On his recovery, the vizier came up to him with pretended condolements, and said, "What has befallen thee? And whence is this sorrow?" The prince having related what had occurred to him, the vizier said, "Thy enemies must have done this. A great misfortune and a heavy calamity have certainly come upon thee; for how can the object of our journey be performed when thou art thyself become a bride? I would advise that we return to thy father, and inform him of what has happened." The prince replied, "I swear by the Almighty, that I will not return, until he shall remove from me this affliction, though I should die under it." The vizier then returned to his troops, and left the prince; who walked onwards, not knowing whither he should proceed.

On the way there met him a horseman, beautiful as the full moon, who saluted him, and said, "Lady, who art thou, and why behold I thee alone in this frightful desert? For I perceive upon thee the marks of distinction, and that thou art sorrowful and afflicted." When the prince heard these kind expressions from the horseman, he put confidence in him, and related what had befallen him. The cavalier said, "Hast thou drank of the White Fountain?" He answered, "Yes;" and the other rejoined, "Comfort thyself, and dry thine eyes, for I will attempt thy delivery." The prince then fell at his feet, and would have kissed them, but he forbade him; when the prince said, "I conjure thee by Allah, tell me, how can relief come to me through thee?" He replied, "I am a jinni, but will not injure thee."

They travelled all night, and at dawn reached a verdant plain, abounding in trees and rivulets, and upon it lofty edifices; and there they dismounted, and entered one of the palaces. The jinni welcomed him, and they remained all day feasting in mirth and gladness. At night the jinni mounted his horse, and taking the prince behind him, travelled through the dark until daylight, when, lo! they beheld a black plain, frightful and gloomy, which might be compared to the confines of hell. The prince enquired the name of the country, and the jinni replied, "This country is called the Black Region, and is governed by a prince of the jinn, without whose permission no one dare enter it. Remain here, while I ask for leave, and return." The prince remained a little while, when the jinni appeared, and conducted him onwards; and they did not stop till they came to a stream of water flowing from a rock, of which the jinni commanded him to drink. He dismounted, and drank, and his sex returned to him as before.

The prince now praised God, and prayed, and he thanked the jinni and kissed his hands, and enquired the name of the well. The jinni replied, "This is the Fountain of Women. If a woman drink of it she becomes a man, by the decree of God. Praise the Lord, then, O my brother, for thy welfare and deliverance."

They travelled the remainder of the day, till they arrived at the dwelling of the jinni, where the prince remained with him in mirth and festivity all that night and the following day; in the evening of which the jinni said, "Dost thou wish to spend this night with thy bride?" The prince replied, "Certainly; but how, my lord, can I effect it?" The jinni then called to one of his attendants, whose name was Jazur, and said, "Take this youth upon thy back, and do not descend anywhere but upon the terrace of his father-in-law's palace, near the apartment of his bride." Jazur replied, "To hear is to obey."

When a third of the night remained, Jazur appeared. He was an 'Ifrit of monstrous size, so that the prince was alarmed; but the jinni said, "He will not injure thee; fear him not." He then embraced the prince, took leave, and mounting him upon the back of the 'Ifrit, said, "Bind something over thine eyes." The prince having done so, the 'Ifrit soared with him between heaven and earth; but he perceived no motion, till he was set down on the terrace of his father-in-law's palace, when the 'Ifrit disappeared. The prince slept till near daylight, when his spirits revived, and he descended towards the apartments. The female attendants met him, and saluted him, and conducted him to the sultan, who knew him, and stood up and embraced him, and welcoming him, said, "My son, they usually bring the bridegroom by the gate, but thou comest from the terrace; truly I am astonished at thy proceedings." The prince answered, "If that seems strange, I have still more wonderful events to detail;" and he then related his adventures from first to last, at which the sultan was astonished, and praised God for his deliverance.

The nuptial ceremonies were now commenced, and when the rites were concluded the prince was admitted to his bride, and remained with her a whole month. He then requested leave to return home; upon which his father-in-law presented him with rich gifts, and furnished him with an escort. The cousin of the princess died of disappointment. The prince arrived with his bride at the capital of his father in safety; and the sultan rejoiced with exceeding great joy, after being in despair for his son.

"I hope," said the Damsel, "that God will also revenge me upon thy viziers and upon thy son." The sultan replied, "I will do thee justice immediately," and issued orders for the execution of the prince.

On the fourth day the Fourth Vizier came to the sultan, kissed the ground before him, and said, "O sultan, kill not thy son, or thou wilt repent when repentance will not profit thee. A wise man will not act until he hath considered the consequences. I have heard the following anecdote."

The vizier then related, as an example of the artifice and duplicity of women, the…

STORY OF THE OLD WOMAN AND THE SHE-DOG

There was a certain merchant's son, who had a handsome wife, and it happened that a libertine, accidentally beholding her, fell in love with her. While the husband was absent on a journey of business, the youth went to an old woman of the neighbourhood, who was on intimate terms with the wife, and disclosed to her his passion, offering her ten dinars for her assistance.

The cunning old woman went several times to visit the merchant's wife, and always took with her a little she-dog. One day she contrived the following stratagem. She took flour and minced meat, and kneaded them into a cake, with a good deal of pepper. Then she forced the cake down the animal's throat, and when the pepper began to heat her stomach, her eyes became wet, as if with tears. The merchant's wife, observing this, said to the old woman, "My good mother, this dog daily follows you, and seems as if she wept. What can be the cause?" The old woman replied, "My dear mistress, the circumstance is wonderful; for she was formerly a beautiful girl, straight as the letter *alif*, and made the sun ashamed by her superior radiance. A Jewish sorcerer fell in love with her, whom she refused; and when he despaired of obtaining her, he was enraged, and by magic transformed her into a she-dog, as thou seest. She was a friend of mine; she loved me, and I loved her; so that, in her new form, she took to following me wherever I went, for I have always fed her, and taken care of her, on account of our friendship. She weeps often when reflecting on her unfortunate condition."

When the merchant's wife heard this, she trembled for herself, and said, "A certain man hath professed love to me, and I did not intend to gratify his criminal passion. But thou hast terrified me with the story of this unhappy damsel, so that I am alarmed lest the man should transform me in like manner." – "My dear daughter," said the wicked old woman, "I am your true friend, and advise you that if any man makes love to you not to refuse him." The wife then said, "How shall I find out my lover?" – "For the sake of thy peace," replied the old wretch, "for the love I bear thee, and for fear lest thou shouldst also be transformed, I will go and seek him."

She then went out, rejoicing that she had gained her ends, and sought the young man, but did not find him at home. So she said to herself, "I will not let this day pass, however, without gaining a reward for my trouble. I will introduce someone else to her, and obtain from him a second present." She then walked through the streets in search of a proper man; when, behold! she met the husband just returning from his journey, whom she did not know. She went up to him, and saluted him, and said, "Hast thou any objection to a good supper and a handsome mistress?" He replied, "I am ready;" upon which she took him by the hand, and leading him to his own house, desired him to wait at the door.

When the man reached his own dwelling, jealousy overcame him, and the world became dark to his eyes. The old woman went to the wife, to inform her of the coming of her lover; whom, when she saw him from the window, she knew, and exclaimed, "Why, mother, thou hast brought my husband!" The old woman, hearing this, replied, "There remains nothing now but to deceive him." The wife took the hint, and said, "I will meet him, and abuse him for his intrigues, and will say, 'I sent this old woman as a spy upon thee.'"

She then began to exclaim against the infidelity of her husband, took a sheet of paper, and descended the staircase, and said to him, "Thou shameless man, there was a promise of constancy between us, and I swore unto thee that I would not love another. Luckily, however, I suspected thy falsehood, and when I knew thou wast returning from thy journey, sent this old woman to watch thee, that I might discover thy proceedings, and whether thou wast faithful to thy agreement or not. It is now clear that thou frequentest the dwellings of courtesans, and I have been deceived. But since I know thy falsehood, there can be no cordiality between us; therefore write me a divorce, for I can no longer love thee."

The husband, on hearing this, was alarmed, and remained for a time in astonishment. He took a solemn oath that he had not been unfaithful to her, and had not been guilty of what she had accused him. He did not cease to soothe her till she was somewhat pacified, when the old woman interfered, and effected a reconciliation between them, for which kindness she was handsomely rewarded. The unfortunate husband little suspected the disgrace he had so narrowly escaped.

"This, O sultan," said the vizier, "is only one instance of the art and deceit of women." The sultan then countermanded the execution of his son.

On the fifth evening the Damsel came to the sultan, holding a cup of poison in her hand, and said, "If thou wilt not do me justice upon thy son, I will drink this poison, and my crime will rest upon thy shoulders. Thy viziers say that women are cunning and deceitful, but there is no creature in the universe more crafty than man. For instance, this tale…

STORY OF THE GOLDSMITH AND THE SINGING-GIRL

I have heard that a goldsmith, who was passionately fond of women, one day entered a friend's house, and saw upon the wall of an apartment the portrait of a beautiful girl, with which he became enraptured; and love so overcame his heart that his friends said to him, "Thou foolish man, how couldst thou think of loving a figure depicted on a wall, of the original of which thou hast never heard or seen?" He replied, "A painter could not have drawn this portrait unless he had seen the original." One of his friends observed, that perhaps the painter might have formed it merely from his imagination. He answered, "I hope from heaven comfort and relief; but what you say cannot be proved except by the painter." They then told him that he lived in a certain town; and the young man wrote to enquire whether he had seen the original of the picture he had painted, or had drawn it from fancy. The answer was that the portrait was that of a singing-girl belonging to a vizier of Ispahan. Encouraged by this intelligence, the young man made preparations for a journey, and having departed, travelled night and day until he reached the city, where he took up his abode.

In a few days he made acquaintance with an apothecary, and became intimate with him. Talking upon various subjects, at length they conversed regarding the sultan of Ispahan and his disposition; when the apothecary said, "Our sovereign bears inveterate hatred to all practitioners of magic, and if they fall into his hands, he casts them into a deep cave without the city, where they die of hunger and thirst." Next they conversed about the famous singing-girl of the vizier, and the young man learned that she was still with him.

The young goldsmith now began to plan his stratagems. On the first moonlight night he disguised himself as a robber, and repairing to the palace of the vizier, fixed a ladder of ropes, by which he gained the terrace, from whence he descended into the court; when lo! a light gleamed from one of the apartments. He entered it, and beheld a throne of ivory, inlaid with gold, on which reposed a lady bright as the sun in a serene sky. At her head and feet were placed lamps, the splendour of which her countenance outshone. He approached, and gazed upon her, and saw that she was the object of his desires. Near the pillow was a rich veil, embroidered with pearls and precious stones. He drew a knife from his girdle, and wounded her slightly on the palm of her hand. The pain awakened the lady, but she did not scream from alarm, believing him to be only a robber in search of plunder; she said, "Take this embroidered veil, but do not injure me." He took the veil, and departed by the same way that he had entered.

When daylight appeared, he disguised himself in white vestments, like a holy pilgrim; visited the sultan, and having saluted him, and the sultan having returned the salutation, he thus addressed him, "O sultan, I am a pilgrim devoted to religion, from the country of Khurasan, and have repaired to thy presence because of the report of thy virtues and thy justice to thy subjects, intending to remain under the shade of thy protection. I reached thy capital at the close of day, when the gates were shut. Then I lay down to repose, and was in slumber, when, behold! four women issued from a grove, one mounted upon a hyaena, another upon a ram, a third upon a black she-dog, and the fourth upon a leopard. When I saw them, I knew they must be sorceresses. One of them having approached me, began to kick me with her feet, and to strike me with a whip, which appeared like a flame of fire. I then repeated the names of God, and struck at her hand with my knife, which wounded her, but she escaped from me. There dropped from her this veil, which I took up, and found it embroidered with valuable jewels; but I have no occasion for them, for I have given up the world." Having thus spoken, he laid the veil at the sultan's feet, and departed.

On examining the veil, the sultan recognized it as one which he had presented to his vizier, of whom he demanded, "Did I not bestow upon thee this veil?" The vizier replied, "You did, my lord; and I gave it to a favourite singing-girl of my own." – "Let her be sent for immediately," exclaimed the sultan; "for she is a wicked sorceress." The vizier went to his palace, and brought the girl before the sultan, who, on seeing the slight wound on her hand, was convinced of the pretended pilgrim's assertion, and commanded her to be cast into the cave of sorcerers.

When the goldsmith found that his stratagem had succeeded, and that the girl was thrown into the cave, he took a purse of a thousand dinars, and went to the keeper of the cave, and said to him, "Accept this purse, and listen to my story." After relating his adventures, the goldsmith said, "This poor girl is innocent, and I am the person who has plunged her into misfortune. If thou wilt release her, it will be a merciful action, and I will convey her privately to my own country. Should she remain here, she will soon be among the number of the dead. Pity, then, her condition and my own, and repay thy generosity with this purse." The keeper accepted the present, and released the girl; and the goldsmith took her with him, and returned to his own city.

"This, O sultan," said the Damsel, "is but one example of the craft of men." The sultan then gave orders for the execution of his son.

Next day, the Fifth Vizier presented himself before the sultan, and said, "O my lord, reprieve thy son, and be not hasty in his death, lest thou repent, as the man repented, who never afterwards smiled." The sultan enquired his history, and the vizier proceeded with the...

STORY OF THE YOUNG MAN WHO WAS TAKEN TO THE LAND OF WOMEN

There was a man, possessed of great wealth and master of many slaves, who died, leaving his estates to an infant son. When he reached manhood, he engaged in pleasure and amusements, in feasting and drinking, in music and dancing, with profusion and extravagance, until he had expended the riches his father had left him. He then took to selling his effects and slaves and concubines, till at length, through distress, he was obliged to ply as a porter in the streets for a subsistence.

As he one day waited for an employer, an old man of portly and respectable appearance stopped, and looked earnestly at him for some time. At length the young man said, "Why, sir, do you so earnestly gaze at my countenance? Have you any occasion for my services?" The old man replied, "Yes, my son. We are ten old men, who live together in the same house, and have at present no person to attend us. If thou wilt accept the office, I trust (God willing) it will afford thee much advantage." The youth replied, "Most willingly and readily." Then said the old man, "You shall serve us, but upon condition that you conceal our situation; and when you see us weeping and lamenting, that you ask not the cause." The young man consented, whereupon his new master took him to a bath, and when he was cleansed, presented him with a handsome dress, and repaired with him to his own house. This proved to be a magnificent palace; its courts surrounded by galleries, and adorned with basins and fountains. All sorts of birds fluttered in the lofty trees which ornamented the gardens, and overshadowed the apartments.

The old man conducted him into one of the pavilions, which was laid over with silken carpets, rich masnads (a kind of counterpane, spread on the carpet where the master of the house sits and receives company), and superb cushions. In this pavilion sat nine venerable old men, all weeping and lamenting, at which he was astonished, but asked no questions. His master then took him to a large chest, pulled out of it a bag containing a thousand dinars, and said, "My son, thou art entrusted by God with this treasure, to expend it upon us and thyself with integrity." The young man replied, "To hear is to obey." He now busied himself in providing for their wants, what was necessary for victuals and raiment, during three years. At length one of the old men died, and they washed his corpse, and buried it in the garden of the palace.

The young man continued to serve them, and the old men died one after another, until nine had departed, and he only remained who had hired him. At last he also fell sick, and the young man despaired of his recovery. So he said to himself, "My master will surely die, and why should I not ask him the cause of their bewailings?" Approaching the couch of the old man, who groaned in the agonies of death, he said, "O my master, I conjure thee by God to acquaint me with the reason of your constant lamentations." "My son," he replied, "there is no occasion for thee to know it, so do not importune me for what will not profit thee. Believe me, I have ever loved and compassionated thee. I dread lest thou shouldst be punished as we have been punished, but wish thou mayest be preserved. Be advised, therefore, my son, and open not yonder locked door." He then pointed out the door to him; after which his agonies increased, and he exclaimed, "I testify that there is no god but God, and that Muhammad is his servant and prophet!" Then his soul fluttered, he turned upon his side, and he was joined to his Lord. The young man washed the corpse, enshrouded it, and buried him by the side of his companions.

After this, he took possession of the palace, and diverted himself for some time in examining the treasures it contained. At length his mind became restless for want of employment. He reflected upon the fate of the old men, and on the dying words of his master, and the charge he had given him. He examined the door; his mind was overcome by curiosity to see what could be within it, and he did not weigh the consequences. Satan tempted him to open the door, and he exclaimed with the poet, "What is not to happen cannot be effected by human contrivance; but what is to be will be." He now unlocked the door. It opened into a long dark passage, in which he wandered for three hours, when he came out upon the shore of the ocean. He was astonished, and gazed with wonder on all sides. He would have returned, but lo! a black eagle of monstrous size darted from the air, and seizing him in her talons, soared for some time between heaven and earth. At length it descended with him upon a small island in the ocean, and fled away.

The young man remained a while motionless with terror; but recovering, began to wander about the island. Suddenly a sail arose to his view on the waters, resembling a fleeting cloud in the heavens. He gazed, and the sail approached, till it reached the beach of the island, when he beheld a boat formed of ivory, ebony, and sandal, the oars of which were made of aloes-wood of Comorin, the sails were of white silk, and it was navigated by beautiful maidens, shining like moons. They advanced from the boat, and kissing his hands, said, "Our souls are refreshed at seeing thee, for thou art the master of our country and of our queen." One of the ladies approached him with a parcel wrapped in rich damask, in which was a royal dress most superbly embroidered, and a crown of gold splendidly set with diamonds and pearls. She assisted him to dress; during which the youth said to himself, "Do I see this in a dream? or am I awake? The old man mentioned nothing of this. He must surely have forbade my opening the door out of envy."

The ladies then conducted him to the boat, which he found spread with elegant carpets and cushions of brocade. They hoisted the sails, and rowed with their oars, while the youth could not divine what would be the end of his adventure. He continued in a state of bewilderment till they reached land, when, behold! the beach was crowded with troops and attendants, gallant in appearance, and of the tallest stature. When the boat anchored, five principal officers of the army advanced to the young man, who was at first alarmed, but they paid their obeisance profoundly, and welcomed him in a tone shrill as the sound of silver. Then the drums beat, the trumpets sounded, and the troops arranged themselves on his right hand and on his left. They proceeded till they reached an extensive and verdant meadow, in which another detachment met them, numerous as the rolling billows or waving shadows.

Lastly appeared a young prince, surrounded by the nobles of his kingdom, but all wore veils, so that no part of them could be seen but their eyes. When the prince came near the young man, he and his company alighted, some of them embraced each other, and after conversing a while, remounted their horses. The cavalcade then proceeded, and did not halt till it came to the royal palace, when the young man was helped from his horse, and the prince conducted him into a splendid hall, in which was the royal throne. The seeming prince ascended it and sat down; and on removing the veil from his face, the young man beheld a beautiful damsel in the supposed prince. While he gazed in astonishment, she said, "Young man, this country is mine, the troops are mine, and I am their queen; but when a man arriveth amongst us, he becomes my superior, and governs in my place." The youth, upon hearing this, was wrapt still more in wonder. And while they were conversing, the vizier entered, who was a stately looking matron, to whom the queen said, "Call the qazi and the witnesses." She replied, "To hear is to obey."

The queen then said to the young man, "Art thou willing that I should be thy wife, and to be my husband?" Hearing this, and beholding her condescending demeanour, he rose up, and kissing the ground, said (as she would have prevented his prostration), "I am not worthy of such high honour, or even to be one of thy humblest attendants." She replied, "My lord, all that thou hast beheld, and what remains unseen by thee of this country, its provinces, people, and treasures are thine, and I am thy handmaiden. Avoid only yonder door, which thou must not open: if thou dost, thou wilt repent when repentance will not avail." The vizier, qazi, and witnesses, who were all women, now entered, and they were married; after which the courtiers and people were introduced, and congratulated them.

The young man remained for seven months in the height of enjoyment, when one day he recollected his old master, and how he had warned him not to open the door in his palace, which though he had done, yet from his disobedience such unexpected good fortune had befallen him. His curiosity and Satan whispered to him, that within the door which the queen had forbidden him to open, some important scenes must also be concealed. He advanced, opened it, and entered; but found a gloomy passage, in which he had not walked more than twenty steps, when light gleamed upon him. He advanced, and beheld the same eagle that had borne him away. He would now have retreated, but the monster darted upon him, seized him in its talons, ascended, and put him down on the spot where it had first taken him up.

He regretted his lost grandeur, power, and dominion, exclaiming, "When I rode out, a hundred beautiful damsels surrounded me, and were flattered by being permitted to attend me. Alas! I was living in honour, until I rashly ventured upon what I have committed!" For two full months he lamented, crying out, "Alas! alas! if the bird would but once again return!" but in vain. Night and day, weeping, he would exclaim, "I was enjoying my ease until my imprudence ruined me." At length one night, in a restless slumber, he heard a voice saying, "Alas! alas! What is past cannot be recovered," upon which he despaired of seeing again his queen or his kingdom. He then entered the palace of his old masters by the dark passage, fatally convinced of what had occasioned their incessant lamentations. He employed himself in praying for their souls; and, like them, wept and lamented, until he died.

"Observe, therefore, O sultan," said the vizier, "that precipitancy is of ill consequence, and I advise thee from experience." The sultan then refrained from executing his son.

On the sixth night the Damsel entered with a dagger in her hand, and said, "O sultan, wilt thou revenge me of thy son? If not, I will instantly put myself to death. Thy viziers pretend that woman is more artful than man, wishing to destroy my rights; but I assure thee that man is far more deceitful than woman, which is clear from what passed between a prince and a merchant's wife.

STORY OF THE LOVER IN THE CHEST

A merchant, who was exceedingly jealous, had a very beautiful wife. From suspicion of her fidelity, he would not dwell in a city among men, but built a house in a most retired situation, that no one might visit her. It was surrounded by lofty walls, and had a strong gateway. Every morning he locked the door, took the key with him, and proceeded to the city to transact business. until the evening.

One day, the sultan's son, riding out for amusement, passed by the house, and cast his eyes on the merchant's wife, who was walking on the terrace. He was captivated by her beauty, and she was no less charmed with his appearance. He tried the gate, but it was securely fastened. At length he wrote a declaration of his love, and fixed it on an arrow, which he shot upon the terrace. The merchant's wife read the letter, and returned a favourable answer. He then took the key of a chest, tied it to a note, in which was written, "I will come to thee in a chest, of which this is the key," and threw it up to her. The prince after this took his leave, and returning to the city, sent for his father's vizier, to whom he communicated what had happened, requesting his assistance. "My son," said the vizier, "what can I do? I tremble for my character in such a business, and what plan can we pursue?" The prince answered, "I only require thy help in what I have contrived. I mean to place myself in a large chest, which thou must lock upon me, and convey at night to the merchant's house, and say to him: 'This chest contains my jewels and treasure, which I am afraid the sultan may seize, and must for a time entrust to thy care.'"

The vizier having consented to the proposal, the prince entered the chest, which was then locked and conveyed privately to the townhouse of the merchant. The vizier knocked at the door, and the merchant appearing, made a profound obeisance to so honourable a visitant, who requested to leave the chest with him for some days, till the alarm of the sultan's displeasure should be over. The merchant readily consented, and had the chest for security carried to his country house, and placed in the apartments of his wife. In the morning he went about his affairs to the city, when his wife, having adorned herself in her richest apparel, opened the chest. The prince came out, embraced her, and kissed her. They passed the day together in merriment, till the merchant's return, when the prince repaired to his place of concealment.

Seven days had passed in this manner, when it chanced that the sultan enquired for his son, and the vizier went hastily to the merchant to reclaim the chest. The merchant had returned earlier than usual to his country house, and was overtaken on his way by the vizier. The lady and the prince, who had been amusing themselves in the court of the house, were suddenly disturbed by a knocking at the gate, and the prince betook himself to the chest, which the wife in her confusion forgot to lock. The merchant entered with his servants, who took up the chest to deliver to the vizier; when lo!

the lid opened, and the prince was discovered, half intoxicated with wine. The poor merchant durst not revenge himself upon the son of his sovereign. He conducted him to the vizier, who was overwhelmed with shame at the disgraceful discovery. The merchant, convinced of his own dishonour, and that his precautions had been in vain, divorced his wife, and took an oath never to marry again.

"Such is the wiliness of men," added the Damsel, "but thy viziers cannot escape my penetration." After hearing this story, the sultan, who dotingly loved the Damsel, gave orders for the execution of his son.

On the sixth day the Sixth Vizier came before the sultan, and said, "Be cautious, my lord, in the execution of your son; be not rash, for rashness is sinful, and the artfulness of women is well known, for God has declared, in the Qur'an, that their craftiness is beyond all measure.

STORY OF THE MERCHANT'S WIFE AND HER SUITORS

It has been reported to me that there was a woman who had a husband accustomed to travel much on business to distant countries. During one of his journeys, his wife became enamoured of a young man, who returned her fondness. It happened one day that this youth, having been engaged in a brawl, was apprehended by the police, and carried before the wali (chief of police) of the city, when it was proved that he was the transgressor, and the wali sentenced him to be imprisoned.

When the lady heard of her lover's confinement, her mind was employed from hour to hour devising means for his release. At length she dressed herself in her richest apparel, repaired to the wali, made obeisance to him, and complained that her brother, having had a scuffle with another youth, hired witnesses had sworn falsely against him, and he had been wrongfully cast into prison. She added that she could not remain safe without the protection of her brother, and begged that he should be set at liberty. The lady had a great share of beauty, which when the wali perceived, he desired her to enter his apartment while he gave orders for her brother's release. She guessed his design, and said, "My lord, I am an honourable and reputable woman, and cannot enter any apartments but my own. But if you desire it, you may visit me;" she then mentioned where she resided, and appointed the day when he should come. The wali was enraptured, and gave her twenty dinars, saying, "Expend this at the bath." She then left him, his heart busy in thinking of her beauty.

The lady next went to the venerable qazi, and said, "My lord, look upon me," and removed her veil from her face. "What has happened to thee?" enquired the qazi. She replied, "I have a younger brother, and none but him, for a protector, whom the wali has imprisoned wrongfully, and whom I beseech thee out of thy compassion to release from his confinement." The qazi said, "Step in, while I order his release." She answered, "If you mean that, my lord, it must be at my house;" and she made an assignation for the same day she had appointed to the wali. The qazi then presented her with twenty dinars, saying, "Purchase provisions and sherbets with part of this sum, and pay for the bath with the remainder."

From the qazi's house the lady repaired to that of the vizier, repeated her story, and besought his interference with the wali for the release of her brother. The vizier also, smitten with her beauty, made proposals of love, which she accepted, but said he must visit her at her own house, and fixed the same day she had named to the wali and the qazi. The vizier then gave her twenty dinars, saying,

"Expend part of this money at the bath, and with the rest prepare for us a supper and wine." She replied, "To hear is to obey."

From the vizier she proceeded to the hajib (governor of the city), and said, "My lord, the wali has imprisoned my brother, who is but a stripling, on the evidence of false witnesses, and I humbly beseech thee for his release." The hajib replied, "Step in, while I send for thy brother." She suspected his designs, and rejoined, "If my lord has business with me – in his house is a constant assemblage of persons – rather let him honour my humble dwelling with his footsteps." Then she assigned the same day she had appointed for the others, informing him of the situation of her house; and the hajib gave her fifty dinars, saying, "Prepare a supper for us with part, and lay out the remainder at the bath."

The lady took the gold, and went to a joiner's shop, and said, "I desire that you will make me a large cabinet, with four compartments, so strong that no single person could burst it open. When thou hast finished it, I will pay thee ten dinars." The joiner agreed, and she hurried him daily till it was finished, when he carried it to her house upon a camel, and set it up in its place. She offered him the price agreed upon, but the joiner refused it, saying, "My dear lady, I will not take anything, and only desire that I may pass an evening with you." She replied, "If that be the case, you must add a fifth compartment to the cabinet." He readily consented, and she fixed the same evening she had appointed for the wali, the qazi, the vizier, and the hajib.

She now went to market, and bought some old garments, which she dyed red, yellow, black, and blue, and made to them whimsical caps of various colours. Then she cooked flesh and fowl, bought wine, and prepared everything for the appointed evening; when she attired herself in her richest apparel, and sat down, expecting her guests.

First the wali knocked at the door, and she rose and opened it, and said, "My lord, the house of your slave is yours, and I am your handmaid." Then, having feasted him till he was satisfied, she took off his robes, and, bringing a black vest and a red cap, said, "Put on the dress of mirth and pleasure;" after which she made him drink wine till he was intoxicated, when lo! there was a knocking at the door, and she said, "My lord, I cannot be cheerful till you have released my brother." He immediately wrote an order to the jailor to give the young man his freedom, which she gave to a servant to deliver, and had no sooner returned to the wali when the knocking became louder. "Who is coming?" he enquired. "It is my husband," replied the lady, "get into this cabinet, and I will return presently and release thee." Having locked the wali in the cabinet, she went to the door.

The qazi now entered, whom she saluted, led in, and seated respectfully. She first filled a cup with wine, and drank to him; and then presented him with meat and wine. The qazi said gravely, "I have never drunk wine during all my life;" but she persuaded him to drink, saying that company was always dull without wine. After this, she pulled off his magisterial robes, and saying, "My lord, put on the garments of mirth and pleasure," dressed him in a robe of yellow and red, with a black cap. Suddenly the door resounded, and the qazi, alarmed for his reputation, asked, "Who is at the door? what shall we do?" She replied, "I fear it is my husband. Go into this cabinet, until he goes away, when I will release thee, and we shall pass the evening pleasantly together."

Having locked the qazi in the cabinet, the lady admitted the vizier, and, kissing his hand, she said, "Thou hast highly honoured me, my lord, by thy auspicious approach." Then she set supper before him, and cajoled him to drink till he was merry and frolicsome, when she said, "Disrobe yourself, my lord, put on the vesture of pleasure, and leave the habit of the vizier for its proper offices." Smiling at her playfulness, the vizier undressed, and put on, at the lady's request, a red vest and a green cap tufted with wool, after which they began to drink and sing, when there was a knocking at the door, and the vizier, in terror, enquired the cause. "It is my husband," said the lady, "step into this cabinet, till he is gone." The vizier quickly slipped in, upon which she locked the compartment, and hastened to the door.

The hajib now entered, according to appointment, and having seated him, the lady said courteously, "My lord, you have honoured me by your kindness and condescension." Then she began to undress him, and his robes were worth at least four thousand dinars. She brought him a parti-coloured vest, and a copper cap set with shells, saying, "These, my lord, are the garments of festivity and mirth." The hajib, having put them on, began to toy and kiss, and she plied him with wine till he was intoxicated. A knocking was again heard at the gate, when the hajib cried out, "Who is this?" and she replied, "My husband; hide in this cabinet, until I can send him away, and I will immediately return to thee."

The poor joiner was next admitted, and the lady plied him so freely with wine, after he had supped, that he was ready for any kind of foolery; so she bade him take off his clothes, and left him, to fetch a dress, when once more the door resounded, and she exclaimed, "Run into this cabinet, even as thou art, for here is my husband." He entered, and having locked him in, the lady then admitted her lover, just released from prison by the wali's order. She informed him of her stratagem, and said, "We must not remain longer here;" upon which the lover went out and hired camels, and they loaded them with all the effects of the house, leaving nothing but the cabinet, strongly secured with five locks, and within it the worthy officers of government and the poor joiner.

The lady and her lover set off without further delay, and travelled to another city, where they could be secure from discovery.

Meanwhile the unfortunate lovers in the cabinet were in a woeful condition. At length they became aware of each other's presence, and began to converse, and, notwithstanding their distress, could not refrain from laughing at each other. In the morning the landlord of the house, finding the gate open, entered, but hearing voices from the cabinet, he was alarmed, and summoned a number of the neighbours. Then the landlord exclaimed, "Are you men or jinn that are in this cabinet?" They replied, "If we were jinn, we should not remain here, nor should we want anyone to open the doors. We are only men." The neighbours cried out, "Let us not open the cabinet, but in presence of the sultan;" upon which the qazi exclaimed, "O my people, let us out – 'Conceal what God has concealed!' and do not disgrace us. I am the qazi." They replied, "Thou liest, and it is impossible. For if thou art the qazi, how earnest thou to be confined here? Thou art an impostor; for our worthy qazi, thou impious wretch, is a man who subdueth his passions. Be silent, lest he hear thee, and bring thee to punishment." After this the qazi durst not speak, and was silent.

Then they brought several porters, who took up the great cabinet, and carried it to the palace of the sultan, who, on being informed of the affair, sent for carpenters and smiths, and caused it to be broken open in his presence, when lo! he discovered the wali, the qazi, the vizier, the hajib, and the poor joiner. "What brought thee here, O reverend qazi?" enquired the sultan. The qazi exclaimed, "God be praised, who hath providentially saved thee, O sultan, from what hath befallen us!" He then issued from the cabinet in his coloured vest and fool's cap, as did the rest of his companions in their ridiculous dresses, but the poor joiner in his birthday habit. The sultan laughed till he almost fainted, and commanded the adventures of each to be written, from first to last. He also ordered search to be made for the merchant's wife, but in vain, for she had escaped with the robes, valuables, and weapons of the foolish gallants.

"From this story," said the vizier, "consider, O sultan, how deep is the artifice of women, and how little dependence should be placed upon their declarations."

On the seventh night the Damsel kindled a funeral pile, and affected to cast herself into it, when her attendants prevented her, and carrying her forcibly to the sultan, informed him of her attempt on her own life. The sultan exclaimed, "What could have induced thee to such rashness?" She replied, "If thou wilt not credit my assertions, I will certainly throw myself into the fire, when thou wilt be too late regretful on my account, as the prince repented of having unjustly punished the religious woman." The sultan desired to know the particulars, and the Damsel replied with the…

STORY OF THE DEVOUT WOMAN AND THE MAGPIE

A certain pious woman, who made pilgrimages to various parts of the world, in the course of one of them came to the court of a sultan, who received her with welcome reverence. One day his queen took the good woman with her to the bath, and handed her a string of jewels, worth two thousand gold dinars, to take charge of while she bathed. The religious woman placed it upon the sajjada (a prostration cloth, mat, or carpet), and began to say her prayers. Suddenly a magpie alighted from the roof of the palace, and fled away with the string of jewels in its claws, unobserved by the pilgrim, and ascended to one of the turrets.

When the queen came from the bath, she searched for the string of jewels, but not finding it, demanded it of the pilgrim, who said, "It was here this instant, and I have not moved from this place. Whether any of your domestics may have taken it up or not, I cannot tell." The queen was enraged, and complained to the sultan, who commanded the pilgrim to be scourged till she should discover the jewels. She was beaten severely, but confessed nothing; after which she was imprisoned, and remained a long time in durance; till one day the sultan, sitting upon the terrace of the palace, beheld a magpie, with the string of jewels twisted round its claws. He commanded the bird to be caught, released the pilgrim, of whom he entreated pardon, kissed her hands, begged forgiveness of God for what he had done, and would have made atonement to her by a valuable present, but she would not accept it. She left the court; and having resolved in her mind, for the remainder of her life, not to enter the house of anyone, retired to the mountains, till she died. May God have mercy upon her!

The Damsel then related, as an example of the crafty disposition of men, the…

STORY OF PRINCE BAHRAM AND PRINCESS ED-DETMA

There was formerly a princess, than whom no one of her time was more skilful in horsemanship and throwing the lance and javelin. Her name was Ed-Detmà. Many powerful princes demanded her in marriage, but she would not consent, having resolved to wed only him who should overcome her in combat, saying, "Whoever worsts me, I will be his; but should I prove victorious, he shall forfeit his weapons and his horse, and I will stamp upon his forehead with a hot iron this inscription: 'The Freedman of Ed-Detmà.'

Many princes attempted to gain her, but she foiled them, seized their weapons, and marked them as she had signified. At length the Prince of Persia, named Bahram, hearing of her charms, resolved to obtain her; for which purpose he quitted his kingdom, and underwent many difficulties on his journey, until he reached his destination. He then entrusted his property to a respectable inhabitant, and visited the sultan; to whom he presented a valuable offering. The sultan seated him respectfully, and enquired the object of his visit. "I am come from a distant country," replied the prince, "anxiously desirous of an alliance with thy daughter." The sultan said, "My son, I have no power over her; for she has resolved not to wed, unless her suitor shall vanquish her in combat." The prince answered, "I accept the conditions;" upon which the sultan informed his daughter, who accepted the challenge.

On the appointed day, a numerous crowd assembled in the maydan (an open space for martial exercises and sports), where the sultan with his nobles appeared in great pomp. Ed-Detmà advanced, arrayed in dazzling habiliments; and the prince came forth, elegant in person, and superbly accoutred. They immediately encountered; the earth vibrated from the shock of their horses, and violent was the charge of weapons on both sides. The sultan viewed with admiration the majestic demeanour of the prince; and Ed-Detmà, perceiving his superior valour and agility, dreaded being vanquished. She artfully withdrew her veil, when her countenance appeared as the resplendent moon suddenly emerging from a dark cloud. The prince was fascinated with her beauty, and his whole frame trembled. The princess, observing his confusion, threw her javelin at his breast, and he fell from his horse, and she returned exulting to the palace.

The prince rose up, much mortified at his discomfiture, and returned to the city, pondering upon the deceit she had practised, and resolved to try a stratagem upon her. After some days, he fixed to his face a long white beard, like that of a venerable old man, clothed himself in the dress of a devotee, and repaired to a garden which he was informed the princess visited every month. He formed an intimacy with the keeper of it, by making him presents, till he had drawn him over to his interest. He then pretended to understand the cultivation of a garden, and the management of plants. The keeper therefore entrusted them to his care, and he watered them carefully, so that the shrubs became fresher and the blossoms more beautiful under his management.

At the usual time, the ferashes (servants, who have charge of tents, etc.) came, and spread carpets, and made other preparations for the reception of the princess. Bahram, on her approach, took some jewels and scattered them in the walks, when the princess and her attendants, seeing an old man, apparently trembling with age, stopped and enquired what he was doing with the jewels. He replied, "I would purchase a wife with them, and would have her from among you." At this the ladies laughed heartily, and said, "When thou art married, how wilt thou behave to thy wife?" He said, "I would just give her one kiss, and divorce her." Then said the princess jestingly, and pointing to one of her ladies, "I will give thee this girl for a wife," upon which he advanced, kissed the damsel in a tremulous manner, and gave her the jewels. After laughing at him for some time, the princess and her attendants quitted the garden.

The like scene was enacted for several days, the prince every time giving richer jewels to the lady he espoused; till at length the princess thought to herself, "Every one of my maidens has obtained from this dotard jewels richer than is in the possession of most sovereigns, and I certainly am more worthy of them than my attendants. He is a decrepid wretch, and can do me no harm." She then went alone to the garden, where she beheld the old man scattering jewels which were invaluable, and said, "I am the sultan's daughter, wilt thou accept me as a wife?" He advanced, and presented her with such a number of jewels that she was delighted beyond measure, and became anxious that he should give her one kiss, and let her depart like the other ladies. The prince, suddenly clasping her in his arms, exclaimed, "Dost thou not know me? I am Bahram, son of the sultan of Persia, whom thou overcamest only by stratagem, and I have now vanquished thee in the same manner. On thy account I exiled myself from my friends and country, but I have now obtained my desires."

The princess remained silent, not being able to utter a word from confusion. She retired in anger to the palace; but, upon reflection, did not disclose what had passed, through fear of disgrace. She said to herself, "If I have him put to death, what will it profit me? I can now do nothing wiser than marry him, and repair with him to his own country." Having thus resolved, she sent a trusty messenger to inform him of her intentions, and appointed a night to meet him.

At the time fixed upon, the prince was ready to receive her; they mounted their horses under cover of the night, and by daylight had travelled a great distance. They did not slacken their speed day or night until they were beyond the reach of pursuit, and arrived at the capital of Persia in safety. The prince then despatched rich presents by an ambassador to the sultan her father, entreating that he would send an envoy to ratify the marriage of his daughter. The sultan having duly complied, the qazi and proper witnesses attended; and they were married amid the greatest rejoicings, and the prince lived long with her in perfect felicity.

"Such," said the Damsel, "is the artfulness of men." When the sultan had heard these stories, he again gave orders that his son should be put to death.

On the following day the Seventh Vizier approached the sultan, and, after the usual obeisance, said, "Forbear, my lord, to shed the blood of thy innocent son; for thou hast none but him, and may not have another, when thou hast put him to death. Attend not to the malicious accusations of concubines, for the deceit of bad women is astonishing, and is exemplified in the…

STORY OF THE BURNT VEIL

There was a certain merchant, very rich, who had an only son, whom he loved exceedingly. One day he said to the young man, "My son, tell me whatever thou desirest of the pleasures of life, that I may gratify thee." The youth replied, "I long for nothing so much as to visit the city of Bagdad, and see the palaces of the khalif and the viziers – that I may behold what so many merchants and travellers have so rapturously described." The merchant observed, "I do not approve of such an excursion, because it would occasion your absence from me." – "My dear father," said the young man, "you enquired my wish, and this is it, and I cannot willingly give it up." When the father heard this, being unwilling to vex his son, he prepared for him an adventure of merchandise of the value of thirty thousand dinars, and recommended him to the care of some eminent merchants, his particular friends.

The youth was amply provided with requisites for the journey, and, attended by many slaves and domestics, he travelled unceasingly till he reached the celebrated capital of Islam, where he hired a handsome house near the grand market. For several days he rode about the city, and beheld such splendid scenes that his mind was bewildered amidst the magnificence of the buildings, the richness of the shops, and the spaciousness of the markets, He admired the dome-crowned palaces, their extensive courts, and regular arcades; the pavements of variously coloured marbles, the ceilings adorned with gold and azure, the doors studded with nails of silver, and painted in fanciful devices.

At length, he stopped at a mansion of this description, and enquired the rent by the month; and the neighbours told him that the monthly hire was ten dirhams. The young merchant exclaimed in astonishment, "Are ye speaking the truth, or do ye only jeer me?" They replied, "We swear, my lord, that we speak the truth exactly; but it is impossible to reside in that house more than a week or a fortnight, without being in hazard of death – a circumstance well known in Bagdad. The rent originally was twenty gold dinars monthly, and is now reduced to ten silver dirhams."

The young man was now still more surprised, and said to himself, "There must be some reason for this, which I wish to find out, and am resolved to hire the house." He did so; and, casting all fear from his mind, took possession, brought his goods, and resided some time in it, employed in business and amusement. At length, sitting one day at his gate, he beheld an old woman (may God's vengeance rest upon her!), who was a cunning go-between under a religious garb. When the old jade saw the young man reclining upon a mastaba (a platform, of stone or brick, built against the front wall of a house or shop) spread with nice carpets, and that he had every appearance of affluence around him, she bowed to him, and he returned her salute. She then gazed steadfastly at him, upon which he said, "Dost thou want my services, good mother? Dost thou know me, or mistake me for one whom I may resemble?" She answered, "My lord, and my son, I know thee not; but when I beheld thy beauty and manliness, I thought upon a circumstance, which, with God's blessing, I will relate." The youth exclaimed, "God grant it may be a fortunate one!" She said, "How long hast thou resided in this house?" On his replying, two months, she exclaimed, "That is wonderful, my son! For everyone who before resided in it for more than a week or a fortnight either died or, being taken dangerously ill, gave it up. I suppose thou hast not opened the prospect room or ascended the terrace?" When she had thus spoken, she went away, and left the young man astonished at her questions.

Curiosity made him immediately examine closely all the upper apartments of the mansion, till at length he found a secret door, almost covered with cobwebs, which he wiped away. He then opened the door, and, hesitating to proceed, said to himself, "This is wonderful! What if I should meet my death within?" Relying, however, upon God, he entered, and found an apartment having windows on every side, which overlooked the whole neighbourhood. He opened the shutters, and sat down to amuse himself with the prospect. His eyes were speedily arrested by a palace more elegant than the others, and while he surveyed it, a lady appeared upon the terrace, beautiful as a huri; her charms would have ravished the heart, changed the love of Majnun, torn the continence of Joseph, overcome the patience of Job, and assuaged the sorrow of Jacob: the chaste and devout would have adored her, and the abstinent and the pilgrim would have longed for her company.

When the merchant's son beheld her, love took possession of his heart. He sank down on the carpet, and exclaimed, "Well may it be said that whoever resides in this mansion will soon die from hopeless love of this beautiful damsel!" He quitted the apartment, locked the door, and descended the staircase. The more he reflected the more he was disturbed, and both rest and patience forsook him. Then he went and sat down at his gate, when, lo! after a short interval, the old woman appeared, devoutly counting her beads, and mumbling prayers. When she came near, he saluted her, and said, "I was at ease and contented until I looked out of the apartment you mentioned, and beheld a young lady, whose beauty has distracted me; and if thou canst not procure me her company, I shall die with disappointment." She replied, "My son, do not despair on her account, for I will accomplish thy desires." Then she consoled him, and he gave her fifty dinars, with many thanks for her kindness, saying, "My dear mother, assist me to the purpose, and you may demand what you please." The old woman replied, "My son, go to the great market, and enquire for the shop of our lord Abu-'l Fat-h the son of Qaydam, the great silk merchant, whose wife this lady is. Approach him with all civility, and say that you want a rich veil, embroidered with gold and silver, for your concubine. Return with it to me, and your desires shall be gratified." The young man hastened to the bazaar of the chief merchants, and was soon directed to the person he enquired after, who was also a broker of merchandise to the khalif Harunu-'r-Rashid. He easily found such a veil as he was directed to purchase, for which he paid a hundred gold dinars, and returned home with it to the old woman, who took a live coal, and with it burned three holes in the veil, which she then took away with her.

She then proceeded to the young lady's house, and knocked at the gate. When the lady enquired who was there, the old woman said, "It is I, Ummu Maryam," on which the merchant's wife, knowing her to be a humble acquaintance of her mother, said, "My dear aunt, my mother is not here, but at her own house." The old woman said, "Daughter, the hour of prayer approaches, and I cannot reach my house in time to perform my ablutions. I request, therefore, that I may make them in your house, as I am secure of having pure water here."

The door was now opened, and the hypocritical jade entered, counting her beads, and mumbling her prayers for the welfare of the young lady, her husband, and her mother. She then took off her drawers, girded her vest round her waist, and a vessel of water being brought, performed her ablutions; after which she said, "Show me, good daughter, a pure spot, free from pollution, to pray upon." The young lady replied, "You may pray upon my husband's carpet." The old woman now muttered her prayers, during which, unperceived by the merchant's wife, she slipped the burnt veil under the cushion at the head of the husband's carpet, and then, rising up from her devotions, she thanked the young lady, warned her against meeting the eyes of licentious men, and took her leave.

Soon after this, the merchant returned home, sat down upon his carpet to repose himself, and his wife brought him a collation, of which he ate. She then set before him water, and he washed his hands, after which he turned to take a napkin from under his cushion to wipe them, when, lo! he discovered the veil which he had that day sold to the young man, and instantly became suspicious of his wife's fidelity. For some time he was unable to speak. On reflection, he resolved that his disgrace should not become public among his brother merchants, or reach the ears of the khalif, whose agent and broker he was, lest he should be dishonoured at court. He kept the discovery of the veil to himself; but, in a little time, addressing his wife, desired that she would go and visit her mother.

The lady, supposing from this that she was indisposed, put on her veil, and hastened to the house of her mother, whom, however, she found in good health, and that no ill had befallen her. The mother and daughter sat down, and were talking of indifferent matters, when suddenly several porters entered the house, loaded with the wife's effects, her marriage dower, and a writing of divorce. The old lady in alarm exclaimed, "Knowest thou not, daughter, the cause of thy husband's displeasure?" The wife replied, "I can safely swear, my dear mother, that I know not of any fault of which I can have been guilty, deserving this treatment." The mother wept bitterly for the disgrace of her daughter, and the wife lamented her separation from her husband, whom she ardently loved. She continued to grieve night and day; her appetite failed her, and her beauty began to decay.

In this manner a month passed away. At the expiry of this period, the old woman Ummu Maryam came to visit the young lady's mother, and after many fawning caresses sat down. When she had told the common news, she said, "I heard, sister, that my lord Abu-l Fat-h had divorced your daughter his wife, on which account I have fasted some days and spent the nights in prayer, in hopes that God may restore her condition." The mother replied, "May God grant us that blessing!" The old woman then enquired after her daughter, and the mother said, "She is grieving for the loss of her husband; her heart is breaking; she feels no pleasure in company, which is disgustful to her, and I fear that, should her lamentations and sorrow continue, they will occasion her death." Then the old woman asked, "Does thy daughter wish to be reconciled to her husband?" The mother replied, that she did. "If so," said the old woman, "let her abide with me for a night or two. She will see proper company; her heart will be refreshed; and society will relieve her depression of mind." The mother assented to the propriety of her observations, gained the consent of her daughter, prevailed upon her to dress herself, and sent her home with Ummu Maryam, who conducted her to the house of the merchant's son.

The young man, when he saw his beloved, rejoiced as if he had gained possession of the world. He ran to her, saluted her, and kissed her between the eyes. The affrighted lady was overcome with shame and confusion; but he addressed her with such tenderness, made such ardent professions, and repeated so many elegant verses, that at length her fears were dispelled. She partook of a collation, and drank of various wines. Every now and then she looked at the young man, who was beautiful as the full moon, and love for him at length fascinated her mind. She took up a lute, and played and sang in praise of his accomplishments, so that he was in such ecstasies that he would have sacrificed his life and property to her charms.

In the morning the old woman returned, and said, "My children, how passed you the evening?" The young lady replied, "In ease and happiness, my dear aunt, by virtue of your supplications and midnight prayers." On this the old woman said roughly, "Thou must now accompany me to thy mother." The young merchant flattered her, and giving her ten gold dinars, said, "I pray thee let her remain with me this day." She took the gold, and then repaired to the mother of the young lady, to whom, after the usual salutations, she said, "Sister, thy daughter bids me inform thee that she is better, and her grief is removed; so that I hope you will not take her from me." The mother replied, "Since my daughter is happy, why should I deny thee, even should she remain a month; for I know that thou art an honest and pious woman, and that thy dwelling is auspicious."

After this the young lady remained seven days at the house of the young merchant, during which on each morning Ummu Maryam appeared; saying to her, "Return with me to thy mother;" and the young man entreated for another day, giving her regularly ten gold dinars. Having received the present, she always visited the mother, and gave her agreeable tidings of her daughter's health. On the eighth day, however, the mother said to the old woman, "My heart is anxious about my daughter; and truly her long absence seems extraordinary;" and Ummu Maryam, pretending to be affronted, replied, "Sister, dost thou cast reflections upon me?" She then repaired to the house of the young merchant, brought away the lady, and conducted her to her mother, but did not enter the house.

When the mother saw that her health and beauty were restored, she was delighted, and said, "Truly, daughter, my heart was anxious concerning thee; and I began to suspect Ummu Maryam, and treated her unkindly because of thy long absence." – "I was not with her," replied the young lady, "but in pleasure and happiness, and in repose and safety. I have obtained through her means health and contentment; so that I conjure thee, my dear mother, to ease her mind, and be grateful for her kindness." Hearing this, the mother arose, and went immediately to the house of the old woman, entreated her pardon, and thanked her for her kindness to her daughter. Ummu Maryam accepted her excuses, and the old lady returned home with her mind relieved.

Next morning, the wily Ummu Maryam visited the young merchant, and said, "My son, I wish you to repair the mischief you have done, and to reconcile a wife to her husband." – "How can that be effected?" he asked. "Go to the warehouse of Abu-'l Fat-h the son of Qaydam," she replied, "and enter into conversation with him, till I shall appear before you; then start up, and lay hold of me, abuse me roundly, and say: 'Where is the veil I gave thee to darn, which I bought of my lord Abu-'l Fat-h, the son of Qaydam?' If he asks thee the cause of thy claim upon me, answer him thus: 'You may recollect that I bought a veil of you for a hundred gold dinars, as a present to my concubine. I gave it to her, and she put it on, but soon after, while she was carrying a lamp, some sparks flew from the wick, and burnt it in three places. This old woman was present, and said that she would take it to the lace-darner, to which I consented, and I have never seen her since till this moment.'"

The young merchant accordingly went to the great market, and coming to the shop of my lord Abu-'l Fat-h, the son of Qaydam, he made him a profound obeisance, which Abu-'l Fat-h returned, but in a gloomy and sulky manner. The youth, however, seated himself, and began to address him on various subjects, when Ummu Maryam appeared, with a long rosary in her hands, the beads of which she counted, while repeating aloud the attributes of the Deity. He immediately started up, ran and laid hold of her, and began to abuse her, when she exclaimed, "I am innocent, and thou art innocent!" A crowd soon gathered around them, and Abu-'l Fat-h, coming from his shop, seized the young man, and demanded, "What is the cause of this rude behaviour to a poor old woman?" He replied, "You must recollect, sir, that I bought of you a rich veil for a hundred dinars. I gave it to my concubine, who shortly afterwards dropped some sparks from a lamp, which burnt the veil in three places. This cursed hypocritess was present at the time, and offered to carry it immediately to the lace-darner. She took it, accordingly, and I have not set eyes upon her again till now, though more than a month has elapsed."

Ummu Maryam assented to the veracity of this statement, and said, "My son, I honestly intended to get the veil mended; but, calling at some houses on my way to the darner, I left it behind me, but where I cannot recollect. I am, it is true, a poor woman, but of pure reputation, and have nothing wherewith to make up the loss of the veil. 'Let the owner, then,' said I to myself, 'believe that I have cheated him, for that is better than that I should occasion disturbances among families by endeavouring to recover the veil.'

This is the whole matter; 'God knows the truth, and God will release from difficulty the true speaker.'"

When Abu-'l Fat-h heard these words his countenance changed from sorrowful to glad. He thought tenderly of his divorced wife, and said in his mind, "Truly I have treated her harshly." He then begged pardon of God for his jealousy, and blessed him for restoring to him again his happiness. To his enquiry of the old woman, whether she frequented his house, she replied, "Certainly; and also the houses of your relations. I eat of your alms, and pray that you may be rewarded both in this world and the next. I have enquired for the veil at all the houses I visit, but in vain." – "Did you enquire at my house?" said the merchant. "My lord," replied the old woman, "I went yesterday, but found no one at home, when the neighbours informed me that my lord had for some cause divorced his wife."

Addressing the young man, Abu-'l Fat-h said, "Sir, I pray you, let this poor old woman go, for your veil is with me, and I will take care that it shall be properly repaired;" on which Ummu Maryam fell down before the merchant and kissed his hands, and then went her way. Abu-'l Fat-h now took out the veil in the presence of the young man, and gave it to a darner; and was convinced that he had treated his wife cruelly, which indeed was the case, had she not afterwards erred through the temptations of that wicked old woman. He then sent to his wife, requesting her to return, and offered her what terms she pleased; and she complied with his desire, and was reconciled; but my lord Abu-'l Fat-h the son of Qaydam little knew what had befallen him from the arts of Ummu Maryam.

When the vizier had ended his story, "Consider, O sultan," he said, "the cunning of bad women, their wiles, and their artful contrivances." The sultan again gave orders to stay the execution of his son.

On the eighth morning, when the impediment was done away against his speaking, the prince sent to the viziers and his tutor, who had concealed himself, and desired them to come to him. On their arrival, he thanked them for their services to his father, and what they had done to prevent his own death, adding, "By God's help, I will soon repay you."

The viziers now repaired to the sultan, informed him of the cause of his son's obstinate silence, and of the arts of the damsel. The sultan rejoiced exceedingly, and ordered a public audience to be held, at which the viziers, the officers of state, and the learned men appeared. The prince entered, with his tutor, and, kissing the ground before his father, prayed eloquently for his welfare and that of his viziers and his tutor. The whole assembly were astonished at his fluency of speech, his propriety of diction, and his accomplished demeanour. The sultan was enraptured, and ran to him, kissed him between the eyes, and clasped him to his bosom. He did the same to the tutor, and thanked him for his care of the prince. The tutor said, "I only commanded him to be silent, fearful for his life during these seven days, which were marked in his horoscope as unfortunate, but have ended happily." Then the sultan said, "Had I put him to death, in whom would have been the crime – myself, thee, or the damsel?" On this question the assembly differed much in their opinions, and the prince, observing their altercations, said, "I will solve this difficulty." The assembly with one voice exclaimed, "Let us hear," and the prince told the…

STORY OF THE POISONED FOOD

I have heard of a certain merchant to whom there came unexpectedly a visitor; upon which he sent a female domestic to buy laban in the market. As she was returning with it upon her head in an uncovered vessel, she passed under a tree, on which was a serpent, from whose mouth fell some drops of venom into the laban. Her master and his guest ate of it, and both died.

"Whose, then, was the fault?" asked the prince, "the girl's, who left the vessel uncovered? or her master's, who gave the laban to his guest?"

Some said it was the master's fault, because he did not examine the laban first. The prince replied, "No one was in fault; their time was come and their residence in this world at an end. Had my death taken place, no one would have been guilty but my father's concubine."

When the assembly heard this, all were astonished at the prince's eloquence and wisdom, and raised their voices in applause, saying, "O sultan, thy son is most accomplished!" Then the sultan commanded a ponderous stone to be tied to the feet of the artful and wicked concubine, and she was cast into the sea. The tutor was rewarded, and invested with an embroidered robe of great value. The sultan delighted in his son, and abdicating his throne, gave it up to the prince, who made all happy by his justice and clemency.

THE SEVEN VIZIERS

A GLOSSARY OF MYTH & FOLKLORE

Aaru Heavenly paradise where the blessed went after death.

Ab Heart or mind.

Abiku (Yoruba) Person predestined to die. Also known as ogbanje.

Absál Nurse to Saláman, who died after their brief love affair.

Achilles The son of Peleus and the sea-nymph Thetis, who distinguished himself in the Trojan War. He was made almost immortal by his mother, who dipped him in the River Styx, and he was invincible except for a portion of his heel which remained out of the water.

Acropolis Citadel in a Greek city.

Adad-Ea Ferryman to Ut-Napishtim, who carried Gilgamesh to visit his ancestor.

Adapa Son of Ea and a wise sage.

Adar God of the sun, who is worshipped primarily in Nippur.

Aditi Sky goddess and mother of the gods.

Adityas Vishnu, children of Aditi, including Indra, Mitra, Rudra, Tvashtar, Varuna and Vishnu.

Aeneas The son of Anchises and the goddess Aphrodite, reared by a nymph. He led the Dardanian troops in the Trojan War. According to legend, he became the founder of Rome.

Aengus Óg Son of Dagda and Boann (a woman said to have given the Boyne river its name), Aengus is the Irish god of love whose stronghold is reputed to have been at New Grange. The famous tale 'Dream of Aengus' tells of how he fell in love with a maiden he had dreamt of. He eventually discovered that she was to be found at the Lake of the Dragon's Mouth in Co. Tipperary, but that she lived every alternate year in the form of a swan. Aengus plunges into the lake, transforming himself also into the shape of a swan. Then the two fly back together to his palace on the Boyne where they live out their days as guardians of would-be lovers.

Aesir Northern gods who made their home in Asgard; there are twelve in number.

Afrásiyáb Son of Poshang, king of Túrán, who led an army against the ruling shah Nauder. Afrásiyáb became ruler of Persia on defeating Nauder.

Afterlife Life after death or paradise, reached only by the process of preserving the body from decay through embalming and preparing it for reincarnation.

Agamemnon A famous King of Mycenae. He married Helen of Sparta's sister Clytemnestra. When Paris abducted Helen, beginning the Trojan War, Menelaus called on Agamemnon to raise the Greek troops. He had to sacrifice his daughter Iphigenia in order to get a fair wind to travel to Troy.

Agastya A rishi (sage). Leads hermits to Rama.

Agemo (Yoruba) A chameleon who aided Olorun in outwitting Olokun, who was angry at him for letting Obatala create life on her lands without her permission. Agemo outwitted Olokun by changing colour, letting her think that he and Olorun were better cloth dyers than she was. She admitted defeat and there was peace between the gods once again.

Aghasur A dragon sent by Kans to destroy Krishna.

Aghríras Son of Poshang and brother of Afrásiyáb, who was killed by his brother.

Agni The god of fire.

Agora Greek marketplace.

Ahura-Mazda Supreme god of the Persians, god of the sky. Similar to the Hindu god Varuna.

Ajax Ajax of Locris was another warrior at Troy. When Troy was captured, he committed the ultimate sacrilege by seizing Cassandra from her sanctuary with the Palladium.

Ajax Ajax the Greater was the bravest, after Achilles, of all warriors at Troy, fighting Hector in single combat and distinguishing himself in the Battle of the Ships. He was not chosen as the bravest warrior and eventually went mad.

Aje (Igbo) Goddess of the earth and the underworld.

Aje (Yoruba) Goddess of the River Niger, daughter of Yemoja.

Akhet Season of the year when the River Nile traditionally flooded.

Akkadian Person of the first Mesopotamian empire, centred in Akkad.

Akwán Diw An evil spirit who appeared as a wild ass in the court of Kai-khosráu. Rustem fought and defeated the demon, presenting its head to Kai-khosráu.

Alba Irish word for Scotland.

Alberich King of the dwarfs.

Alcinous King of the Phaeacians.

Alf-heim Home of the elves, ruled by Frey.

All Hallowmass All Saints' Day.

Allfather Another name for Odin; Yggdrasill was created by Allfather.

Alsvider Steed of the moon (Mani) chariot.

Alsvin Steed of the sun (Sol) chariot.

Amado Outer panelling of a dwelling, usually made of wood.

Ama-no-uzume Goddess of the dawn, meditation and the arts, who showed courage when faced with a giant who scared the other deities, including Ninigi. Also known as Uzume.

Amaterasu Goddess of the sun and daughter of Izanagi after Izanami's death; she became ruler of the High Plains of Heaven on her father's withdrawal from the world. Sister of Tsuki-yomi and Susanoo.

Ambalika Daughter of the king of Benares.

Ambika Daughter of the king of Benares.

Ambrosia Food of the gods.

Amemet Eater of the dead, monster who devoured the souls of the unworthy.

Amen Original creator deity.

Amen-Ra A being created from the fusion of Ra and Osiris. He champions the poor and those in trouble. Similar to the Greek god Zeus.

Ananda Disciple of Buddha.

Anansi One of the most popular African animal myths, Anansi the spider is a clever and shrewd character who outwits his fellow animals to get his own way. He is an entertaining but morally dubious character. Many African countries tell Anansi stories.

Ananta Thousand-headed snake that sprang from Balarama's mouth, Vishnu's attendant, serpent of infinite time.

Andhrímnir Cook at Valhalla.

Andvaranaut Ring of Andvari, the King of the dwarfs.

Angada Son of Vali, one of the monkey host.

Anger-Chamber Room designated for an angry queen.

Angurboda Loki's first wife, and the mother of Hel, Fenris and Jormungander.

Aniruddha Son of Pradyumna.

Anjana Mother of Hanuman.

Anunnaki Great spirits or gods of Earth.

Ansar God of the sky and father of Ea and Anu. Brother-husband to Kishar. Also known as Anshar or Asshur.

Anshumat A mighty chariot fighter.

Anu God of the sky and lord of heaven, son of Ansar and Kishar.

Anubis Guider of souls and ruler of the underworld before Osiris;

he was one of the divinities who brought Osiris back to life. He is portrayed as a canid, African wolf or jackal.

Apep Serpent and emblem of chaos.

Apollo One of the twelve Olympian gods, son of Zeus and Leto. He is attributed with being the god of plague, music, song and prophecy.

Apsaras Dancing girls of Indra's court and heavenly nymphs.

Apsu Primeval domain of fresh water, originally part of Tiawath with whom he mated to have Mummu. The term is also used for the abyss from which creation came.

Aquila The divine eagle.

Arachne A Lydian woman with great skill in weaving. She was challenged in a competition by the jealous Athene who destroyed her work and when she killed herself, turned her into a spider destined to weave until eternity.

Aralu Goddess of the underworld, also known as Eres-ki-Gal. Married to Nergal.

Ares God of War, 'gold-changer of corpses', and the son of Zeus and Hera.

Argonauts Heroes who sailed with Jason on the ship Argo to fetch the golden fleece from Colchis.

Ariki A high chief, a leader, a master, a lord.

Arjuna The third of the Pandavas.

Aroha Affection, love.

Artemis The virgin goddess of the chase, attributed with being the moon goddess and the primitive mother-goddess. She was daughter of Zeus and Leto.

Arundhati The Northern Crown.

Asamanja Son of Sagara.

Asclepius God of healing who often took the form of a snake. He is the son of Apollo by Coronis.

Asgard Home of the gods, at one root of Yggdrasill.

Ashvatthaman Son of Drona.

Ashvins Twin horsemen, sons of the sun, benevolent gods and related to the divine.

Ashwapati Uncle of Bharata and Satrughna.

Asipû Wizard.

Asopus The god of the River Asopus.

Assagai Spear, usually made from hardwood tipped with iron and used in battle.

Astrolabe Instrument for making astronomical measurements.

Asuras Titans, demons, and enemies of the gods possessing magical powers.

Atef crown White crown made up of the Hedjet, the white crown of Upper Egypt, and red feathers.

Atem The first creator-deity, he is also thought to be the finisher of the world. Also known as Tem.

Athene Virgin warrior-goddess, born from the forehead of Zeus when he swallowed his wife Metis. Plays a key role in the travels of Odysseus, and Perseus.

Atlatl Spear-thrower.

Atua A supernatural being, a god.

Atua-toko A small carved stick, the symbol of the god whom it represents. It was stuck in the ground whilst holding incantations to its presiding god.

Augeas King of Elis, one of the Argonauts.

Augsburg Tyr's city.

Avalon Legendary island where Excalibur was created and where Arthur went to recover from his wounds. It is said he will return from Avalon one day to reclaim his kingdom.

Ba Dead person or soul. Also known as ka.

Bairn Little child, also called bairnie.

Balarama Brother of Krishna.

Balder Son of Frigga; his murder causes Ragnarok. Also spelled as Baldur.

Bali Brother of Sugriva and one of the five great monkeys in the Ramayana.

Balor The evil, one-eyed King of the Fomorians and also grandfather of Lugh of the Long Arm. It was prophesied that Balor would one day be slain by his own grandson, so he locked his daughter away on a remote island where he intended that she would never fall pregnant. But Cian, father of Lugh, managed to reach the island disguised as a woman, and Balor's daughter eventually bore him a child. During the second battle of Mag Tured (or Moytura), Balor was killed by Lugh, who slung a stone into his giant eye.

Ban King of Benwick, father of Lancelot and brother of King Bors.

Bannock Flat loaf of bread, typically of oat or barley, usually cooked on a griddle.

Banshee Mythical spirit, usually female, who bears tales of imminent death. They often deliver the news by wailing or keening outside homes. Also known as bean sí.

Bard Traditionally a storyteller, poet or music composer whose work often focused on legends.

Barû Seer.

Basswood Any of several North American linden trees with a soft light-coloured wood.

Bastet Goddess of love, fertility and sex and a solar deity. She is often portrayed with the head of a cat.

Bateta (Yoruba) The first human, created alongside Hanna by the Toad and reshaped into human form by the Moon.

Bau Goddess of humankind and the sick, and known as the 'divine physician'. Daughter of Anu.

Bawn Fortified enclosure surrounding a castle.

Beaver Largest rodent in the United States of America, held in high esteem by the native American people. Although a land mammal, it spends a great deal of time in water and has a dense waterproof fur coat to protect it from harsh weather conditions.

Behula Daughter of Saha.

Bel Name for the god En-lil, the word is also used as a title meaning 'lord'.

Belus Deity who helped form the heavens and earth and created animals and celestial beings. Similar to Zeus in Greek mythology.

Benten Goddess of the sea and one of the Seven Divinities of Luck. Also referred to as the goddess of love, beauty and eloquence and as being the personification of wisdom.

Bere Barley.

Berossus Priest of Bel who wrote a history of Babylon.

Berserker Norse warrior who fights with a frenzied rage.

Bestla Giant mother of Aesir's mortal element.

Bhadra A mighty elephant.

Bhagavati Shiva's wife, also known as Parvati.

Bhagiratha Son of Dilipa.

Bharadhwaja Father of Drona and a hermit.

Bharata One of Dasharatha's four sons.

Bhaumasur A demon, slain by Krishna.

Bhima The second of the Pandavas.

Bhimasha King of Rajagriha and disciple of Buddha.

Bier Frame on which a coffin or dead body is placed before being carried to the grave.

Bifrost Rainbow bridge presided over by Heimdall.

Big-Belly One of Ravana's monsters.

Bilskirnir Thor's palace.

Bodach The term means 'old man'. The Highlanders believed that the Bodach crept down chimneys in order to steal naughty children. In other territories, he was a spirit who warned of death.

Bodkin Large, blunt needle used for threading strips of cloth or tape through cloth; short pointed dagger or blade.

Boer Person of Dutch origin who settled in southern Africa in the late seventeenth century. The term means 'farmer'. Boer people are often called Afrikaners.

Bogle Ghost or phantom; goblin-like creature.

Boliaun Ragwort, a weed with ragged leaves.

Book of the Dead Book for the dead, thought to be written by Thoth, texts from which were written on papyrus and buried with the dead, or carved on the walls of tombs, pyramids or sarcophagi.

Bors King of Gaul and brother of King Ban.

Bothy Small cottage or hut.

Brahma Creator of the world, mythical origin of colour (caste).

Brahmadatta King of Benares.

Brahman Member of the highest Hindu caste, traditionally a priest.

Bran In Scottish legend, Bran is the great hunting hound of Fionn Mac Chumail. In Irish mythology, he is a great hero.

Branstock Giant oak tree in the Volsung's hall; Odin placed a sword in it and challenged the guests of a wedding to withdraw it.

Brave Young warrior of native American descent, sometimes also referred to as a 'buck'.

Bree Thin broth or soup.

Breidablik Balder's palace.

Brigit Scottish saint or spirit associated with the coming of spring.

Brisingamen Freyia's necklace.

Britomartis A Cretan goddess, also known as Dictynna.

Brocéliande Legendary enchanted forest and the supposed burial place of Merlin.

Brokki Dwarf who makes a deal with Loki, and who makes Miolnir, Draupnir and Gulinbursti.

Brollachan A shapeless spirit of unknown origin. One of the most frightening in Scottish mythology, it spoke only two words, 'Myself' and 'Thyself', taking the shape of whatever it sat upon.

Brownie A household spirit or creature which took the form of a small man (usually hideously ugly) who undertakes household chores, and mill or farm work, in exchange for a bowl of milk.

Brugh Borough or town.

Brunhilde A Valkyrie found by Sigurd.

Buddha Founder of buddhism, Gautama, avatar of Vishnu in Hinduism.

Buddhism Buddhism arrived in China in the first century BC via the silk trading route from India and Central Asia. Its founder was Guatama Siddhartha (the Buddha), a religious teacher in northern India. Buddhist doctrine declared that by destroying the causes of all suffering, mankind could attain perfect enlightenment. The religion encouraged a new respect for all living things and brought with it the idea of reincarnation; i.e. that the soul returns to the earth after death in another form, dictated by the individual's behaviour in his previous life. By the fourth century, Buddhism was the dominant religion in China, retaining its powerful influence over the nation until the mid-ninth century.

Buffalo A type of wild ox, once widely scattered over the Great Plains of North America. Also known as a 'bison', the buffalo was an important food source for the Indian tribes and its hide was also used in the construction of tepees and to make clothing. The buffalo was also sometimes revered as a totem animal, i.e. venerated as a direct ancestor of the tribesmen, and its skull used in ceremonial fashion.

Bull of Apis Sacred bull, thought to be the son of Hathor.

Bulu Sacrificial rite.

Bundles, sacred These bundles contained various venerated objects of the tribe, believed to have supernatural powers. Custody or ownership of the bundle was never lightly entered upon, but involved the learning of endless songs and ritual dances.

Bushel Unit of measurement, usually used for agricultural products or food.

Bushi Warrior.

Byre Barn for keeping cattle.

Byrny Coat of mail.

Cacique King or prince.

Cailleach Bheur A witch with a blue face who represents winter. When she is reborn each autumn, snow falls. She is mother of the god of youth (Angus mac Og).

Calabash Gourd from the calabash tree, commonly used as a bottle.

Calchas The seer of Mycenae who accompanied the Greek fleet to Troy. It was his prophecy which stated that Troy would never be taken without the aid of Achilles.

Calpulli Village house, or group or clan of families.

Calumet Ceremonial pipe used by the north American Indians.

Calypso A nymph who lived on the island of Ogygia.

Camaxtli Tlascalan god of war and the chase, similar to Huitzilopochtli.

Camelot King Arthur's castle and centre of his realm.

Caoineag A banshee.

Caravanserai Traveller's inn, traditionally found in Asia or North Africa.

Carle Term for a man, often old; peasant.

Cat A black cat has great mythological significance, is often the bearer of bad luck, a symbol of black magic, and the familiar of a witch. Cats were also the totem for many tribes.

Cath Sith A fairy cat who was believed to be a witch transformed.

Cazi Magical person or influence.

Ceasg A Scottish mermaid with the body of a maiden and the tail of a salmon.

Ceilidh Party.

Cerberus The three-headed dog who guarded the entrance to the Underworld.

Chalchiuhtlicue Goddess of water and the sick or newborn, and wife of Tlaloc. She is often symbolized as a small frog.

Changeling A fairy substitute-child left by fairies in place of a human child they have stolen.

Channa Guatama's charioteer.

Chaos A state from which the universe was created – caused by fire and ice meeting.

Charon The ferryman of the dead who carries souls across the River Styx to Hades.

Charybdis **See** Scylla and Charybdis.

Chicomecohuatl Chief goddess of maize and one of a group of deities called Centeotl, who care for all aspects of agriculture.

Chicomoztoc Legendary mountain and place of origin of the Aztecs. The name means 'seven caves'.

Chinawezi Primordial serpent.

Chinvat Bridge Bridge of the Gatherer, which the souls of the righteous cross to reach Mount Alborz or the world of the dead. Unworthy beings who try to cross Chinvat Bridge fall or are dragged into a place of eternal punishment.

Chitambaram Sacred city of Shiva's dance.

Chrysaor Son of Poseidon and Medusa, born from the severed neck of Medusa when Perseus beheaded her.

Chryseis Daughter of Chryses who was taken by Agamemnon in the battle of Troy.

Chullasubhadda Wife of Buddha-elect (Sumedha).

Chunda A good smith who entertains Buddha.

Churl Mean or unkind person.

Circe An enchantress and the daughter of Helius. She lived on the island of Aeaea with the power to change men to beasts.

Citlalpol The Mexican name for Venus, or the Great Star, and one of the only stars they worshipped. Also known as Tlauizcalpantecutli, or Lord of the Dawn.

Cleobis and Biton Two men of Argos who dragged the wagon carrying their mother, priestess of Hera, from Argos to the sanctuary.

Clio Muse of history and prophecy.

Clytemnestra Daughter of Tyndareus, sister of Helen, who married Agamemnon but deserted him when he sacrificed Iphigenia, their daughter, at the beginning of the Trojan War.

Coatepetl Mythical mountain, known as the 'serpent mountain'.

Coatl Serpent.

Coatlicue Earth mother and celestial goddess, she gave birth to Huitzilopochtli and his sister, Coyolxauhqui, and the moon and stars.

Codex Ancient book, often a list with pages folded into a zigzag pattern.

Confucius (Kong Fuzi) Regarded as China's greatest sage and ethical teacher, Confucius (551–479 BC) was not especially revered during his lifetime and had a small following of some three thousand people. After the Burning of the Books in 213 BC, interest in his philosophies became widespread. Confucius believed that mankind was essentially good, but argued for a highly structured society, presided over by a strong central government which would set the highest moral standards. The individual's sense of duty and obligation, he argued, would play a vital role in maintaining a well-run state.

Coracle Small, round boat, similar to a canoe. Also known as curragh or currach.

Coyolxauhqui Goddess of the moon and sister to Huitzilopochtli, she was decapitated by her brother after trying to kill their mother.

Creel Large basket made of wicker, usually used for fish.

Crodhmara Fairy cattle.

Cronan Musical humming, thought to resemble a cat purring or the drone of bagpipes.

Crow Usually associated with battle and death, but many mythological figures take this form.

Cu Sith A great fairy dog, usually green and oversized.

Cubit Ancient measurement, equal to the approximate length of a forearm.

Cuculain Irish warrior and hero. Also known as Cuchulainn.

Cutty Girl.

Cyclopes One-eyed giants who were imprisoned in Tartarus by Uranus and Cronus, but released by Zeus, for whom they made thunderbolts. Also a tribe of pastoralists who live without laws, and on, whenever possible, human flesh.

Daedalus Descendant of the Athenian King Erechtheus and son of Eupalamus. He killed his nephew and apprentice. Famed for constructing the labyrinth to house the Minotaur, in which he was later imprisoned. He constructed wings for himself and his son to make their escape.

Dagda One of the principal gods of the Tuatha De Danann, the father and chief, the Celtic equivalent of Zeus. He was the god reputed to have led the People of Dana in their successful conquest of the Fir Bolg.

Dagon God of fish and fertility; he is sometimes described as a sea-monster or chthonic god.

Daikoku God of wealth and one of the gods of luck.

Daimyō Powerful lord or magnate.

Daksha The chief Prajapati.

Dana Also known as Danu, a goddess worshipped from antiquity by the Celts and considered to be the ancestor of the Tuatha De Danann.

Danae Daughter of Acrisius, King of Argos. Acrisius trapped her in a cave when he was warned that his grandson would be the cause of his ultimate death. Zeus came to her and Perseus was born.

Danaids The fifty daughters of Danaus of Argos, by ten mothers.

Daoine Sidhe The people of the Hollow Hills, or Otherworld.

Dardanus Son of Zeus and Electra, daughter of Atlas.

Dasharatha A Manu amongst men, King of Koshala, father of Santa.

Deianeira Daughter of Oeneus, who married Heracles after he won her in a battle with the River Achelous.

Deirdre A beautiful woman doomed to cause the deaths of three Irish heroes and bring war to the whole country. After a soothsayer prophesied her fate, Deidre's father hid her away from the world to prevent it. However, fate finds its way and the events come to pass before Deidre eventually commits suicide to remain with her love.

Demeter Goddess of agriculture and nutrition, whose name means earth mother. She is the mother of Persephone.

Demophoon Son of King Celeus of Eleusis, who was nursed by Demeter and then dropped in the fire when she tried to make him immortal.

Dervish Member of a religious order, often Sufi, known for their wild dancing and whirling.

Desire The god of love.

Deva A god other than the supreme God.

Devadatta Buddha's cousin, plots evil against Buddha.

Dhrishtadyumna Twin brother of Draupadi, slays Drona.

Dibarra God of plague. Also a demonic character or evil spirit.

Dik-dik Dwarf antelope native to eastern and southern Africa.

Dilipa Son of Anshumat, father of Bhagiratha.

Dionysus The god of wine, vegetation and the life force, and of ecstasy. He was considered to be outside the Greek pantheon, and generally thought to have begun life as a mortal.

Dioscuri Castor and Polydeuces, the twin sons of Zeus and Leda, who are important deities.

Distaff Tool used when spinning which holds the wool or flax and keeps the fibres from tangling.

Divan Privy council.

Divots Turfs.

Dog The dog is a symbol of humanity, and usually has a role helping the hero of the myth or legend. Fionn's Bran and Grey Dog are two examples of wild beasts transformed to become invaluable servants.

Dōshin Government official.

Dossal Ornamental altar cloth.

Doughty Persistent and brave person.

Dragon Important animal in Japanese culture, symbolizing power, wealth, luck and success.

Draiglin' Hogney Ogre.

Draupadi Daughter of Drupada.

Draupnir Odin's famous ring, fashioned by Brokki.

Drona A Brahma, son of the great sage Bharadwaja.

Druid An ancient order of Celtic priests held in high esteem who flourished in the pre-Christian era. The word 'druid' is derived from an ancient Celtic one meaning 'very knowledgeable'. These individuals were believed to have mystical powers and in ancient Irish literature possess the ability to conjure up magical charms, to create tempests, to curse and debilitate their enemies and to perform as soothsayers to the royal courts.

Drupada King of the Panchalas.

Dryads Nymphs of the trees.

Dun A stronghold or royal abode surrounded by an earthen wall.

Durga Goddess, wife of Shiva.

Durk Knife. Also spelled as dirk.

Duryodhana One of Drona's pupils.

Dvalin Dwarf visited by Loki; also the name for the stag on Yggdrasill.

Dwarfie Stone Prehistoric tomb or boulder.

Dwarfs Fairies and black elves are called dwarfs.

Dwarkanath The Lord of Dwaraka; Krishna.

Dyumatsena King of the Shalwas and father of Satyavan.

Ea God of water, light and wisdom, and one of the creator deities. He brought arts and civilization to humankind. Also known as Oannes and Nudimmud.

Eabani Hero originally created by Aruru to defeat Gilgamesh, the two became friends and destroyed Khumbaba together. He personifies the natural world.

Each Uisge The mythical water-horse which haunts lochs and appears in various forms.

Ebisu One of the gods of luck. He is also the god of labour and fishermen.

Echo A nymph who was punished by Hera for her endless stories told to distract Hera from Zeus's infidelity.

Ector King Arthur's foster father, who raised Arthur to protect him.

Edda Collection of prose and poetic myths and stories from the Norsemen.

Eight Immortals Three of these are reputed to be historical: Han Chung-li, born in Shaanxi, who rose to become a Marshal of the Empire in 21 BC. Chang Kuo-Lao, who lived in the seventh to eighth century AD, and Lü Tung-pin, who was born in AD 755.

Einheriear Odin's guests at Valhalla.

Eisa Loki' daughter.

Ekake (Ibani) Person of great intelligence, which means 'tortoise'. Also known as Mbai (Igbo).

Ekalavya Son of the king of the Nishadas.

Electra Daughter of Agamemnon and Clytemnestra.

Eleusis A town in which the cult of Demeter is centred.

Elf Sigmund is buried by an elf; there are light and dark elves (the latter called dwarfs).

Elokos (Central African) Imps of dwarf-demons who eat human flesh.

Elpenor The youngest of Odysseus's crew who fell from the roof of Circe's house on Aeaea and visited with Odysseus at Hades.

Elysium The home of the blessed dead.

Emain Macha The capital of ancient Ulster.

Emma Dai-o King of hell and judge of the dead.

En-lil God of the lower world, storms and mist, who held sway over the ghostly animistic spirits, which at his bidding might pose as the friends or enemies of men. Also known as Bel.

Eos Goddess of the dawn and sister of the sun and moon.

Erichthonius A child born of the semen spilled when Hephaestus tried to rape Athene on the Acropolis.

Eridu The home of Ea and one of the two major cities of Babylonian civilization.

Erin Term for Ireland, originally spelled Éirinn.

Erirogho Magical mixture made from the ashes of the dead.

Eros God of Love, the son of Aphrodite.

Erpa Hereditary chief.

Erysichthon A Thessalian who cut down a grove sacred to Demeter, who punished him with eternal hunger.

Eshu (Yoruba) God of mischief. He also tests people's characters and controls law enforcement.

Eteocles Son of Oedipus.

Eumaeus Swineherd of Odysseus's family at Ithaca.

Euphemus A son of Poseidon who could walk on water. He sailed with the Argonauts.

Europa Daughter of King Agenor of Tyre, who was taken by Zeus to Crete.

Eurydice A Thracian nymph married to Orpheus.

Excalibur The magical sword given to Arthur by the Lady of the Lake. In some versions of the myths, Excalibur is also the sword that the young Arthur pulls from the stone to become king.

Fabulist Person who composes or tells fables.

Fafnir Shape-changer who kills his father and becomes a dragon to guard the family jewels. Slain by Sigurd.

Fairy The word is derived from 'Fays' which means Fates. They are immortal, with the gift of prophecy and of music, and their role changes according to the origin of the myth. They were often considered to be little people, with enormous propensity for mischief, but they are central to many myths and legends, with important powers.

Faro (Mali, Guinea) God of the sky.

Fates In Greek mythology, daughters of Zeus and Themis, who spin the thread of a mortal's life and cut it when his time is due. Called Norns in Viking mythology.

Fenris A wild wolf, who is the son of Loki. He roams the earth after Ragnarok.

Ferhad Sculptor who fell in love with Shireen, the wife of Khosru, and undertook a seemingly impossible task to clear a passage through the mountain of Beysitoun and join the rivers in return for winning Shireen's hand.

Fialar Red cock of Valhalla.

Fianna/Fenians The word 'fianna' was used in early times to describe young warrior-hunters. These youths evolved under the leadership of Finn Mac Cumaill as a highly skilled band of military men who took up service with various kings throughout Ireland.

Filheim Land of mist, at the end of one of Yggdrasill's roots.

Fingal Another name for Fionn Mac Chumail, used after MacPherson's Ossian in the eighteenth century.

Fionn Mac Chumail Irish and Scottish warrior, with great powers of fairness and wisdom. He is known not for physical strength but for knowledge, sense of justice, generosity and canny instinct. He had two hounds, which were later discovered to be his nephews transformed. He became head of the Fianna, or Féinn, fighting the enemies of Ireland and Scotland. He was the father of Oisin (also called Ossian, or other derivatives), and father or grandfather of Osgar.

Fir Bolg One of the ancient, pre-Gaelic peoples of Ireland who were reputed to have worshipped the god Bulga, meaning god of lighting. They are thought to have colonized Ireland around 1970 BC, after the death of Nemed and to have reigned for a short period of thirty-seven years before their defeat by the Tuatha De Danann.

Fir Chlis Nimble men or merry dancers, who are the souls of fallen angels.

Flitch Side of salted and cured bacon.

Folkvang Freyia's palace.

Fomorians A race of monstrous beings, popularly conceived as sea-pirates with some supernatural characteristics who opposed the earliest settlers in Ireland, including the Nemedians and the Tuatha De Danann.

Frey Comes to Asgard with Freyia as a hostage following the war between the Aesir and the Vanir.

Freyia Comes to Asgard with Frey as a hostage following the war between the Aesir and the Vanir. Goddess of beauty and love.

Frigga Odin's wife and mother of gods; she is goddess of the earth.

Fuath Evil spirits which lived in or near the water.

Fulla Frigga's maidservant.

Furies Creatures born from the blood of Cronus, guarding the greatest sinners of the Underworld. Their power lay in their ability to drive mortals mad. Snakes writhed in their hair and around their waists.

Furoshiki Cloths used to wrap things.

Gae Bolg Cuchulainn alone learned the use of this weapon from the woman-warrior, Scathach and with it he slew his own son Connla and his closest friend, Ferdia. Gae Bolg translates as 'harpoon-like javelin' and the deadly weapon was reported to have been created by Bulga, the god of lighting.

Gaea Goddess of Earth, born from Chaos, and the mother of Uranus and Pontus. Also spelled as Gaia.

Gage Object of value presented to a challenger to symbolize good faith.

Galahad Knight of the Round Table, who took up the search for the Holy Grail. Son of Lancelot, Galahad is considered the purest and most perfect knight.

Galatea Daughter of Nereus and Doris, a sea-nymph loved by Polyphemus, the Cyclops.

Gandhari Mother of Duryodhana.

Gandharvas Demi-gods and musicians.

Gandjharva Musical ministrants of the upper air.

Ganesha Elephant-headed god of scribes and son of Shiva.

Ganges Sacred river personified by the goddess Ganga, wife of Shiva and daughter of the mount Himalaya.

Gareth of Orkney King Arthur's nephew and knight of the Round Table.

Garm Hel's hound.

Garuda King of the birds and mount Vishnu, the divine bird, attendant of Narayana.

Gautama Son of Suddhodana and also known as Siddhartha.

Gawain Nephew of King Arthur and knight of the Round Table, he is best known for his adventure with the Green Knight, who challenges one of Arthur's knights to cut off his head, but only if he agrees to be beheaded in turn in a year and a day, if the Green Knight survives. Gawain beheads the Green Knight, who simply replaces his head. At the appointed time, they meet, and the Green Knight swings his axe but merely nicks Gawain's skin instead of beheading him.

Geisha Performance artist or entertainer, usually female.

Geri Odin's wolf.

Ghommid (Yoruba) Term for mythological creatures such as goblins or ogres.

Giallar Bridge in Filheim.

Giallarhorn Heimdall's trumpet – the final call signifies Ragnarok.

Giants In Greek mythology, a race of beings born from Gaea, grown from the blood that dropped from the castrated Uranus. Usually represent evil in Viking mythology.

Gilgamesh King of Erech, known as a half-human, half-god hero similar to the Greek Heracles, and often listed with the gods. He is the personification of the sun and is protected by the god Shamash, who in some texts is described as his father. He is also portrayed as an evil tyrant at times.

Gillie Someone who works for a Scottish chief, usually as an attendant or servant; guide for fishing or hunting parties.

Gladheim Where the twelve deities of Asgard hold their thrones. Also called Gladsheim.

Gled Bird of prey.

Golden Fleece Fleece of the ram sent by Poseidon to substitute for Phrixus when his father was going to sacrifice him. The Argonauts went in search of the fleece.

Goodman Man of the house.

Goodwife Woman of the house.

Gopis Lovers of the young Krishna and milkmaids.

Gorgon One of the three sisters, including Medusa, whose frightening looks could turn mortals to stone.

Graces Daughters of Aphrodite by Zeus.

Gramercy Expression of surprise or strong feeling.

Great Head The Iroquois Indians believed in the existence of a curious being known as Great Head, a creature with an enormous head poised on slender legs.

Great Spirit The name given to the Creator of all life, as well as the term used to describe the omnipotent force of the Creator existing in every living thing.

Great-Flank One of Ravana's monsters.

Green Knight A knight dressed all in green and with green hair and skin who challenged one of Arthur's knights to strike him a blow with an axe and that, if he survived, he would return to behead the knight in a year and a day. He turned out to be Lord Bertilak and was under an enchantment cast by Morgan le Fay to test Arthur's knights.

Gruagach Mythical creature, often a giant or ogre similar to a wild man of the woods. The term can also refer to other mythical creatures such as brownies or fairies. As a brownie, he is usually dressed in red or green as opposed to the traditional brown. He has great power to enchant the hapless, or to help mortals who are worthy (usually heroes). He often appears to challenge a boy-hero, during his period of education.

Gudea High priest of Lagash, known to be a patron of the arts and a writer himself.

Guebre Religion founded by Zoroaster, the Persian prophet.

Gugumatz Creator god who, with Huracan, formed the sky, earth and everything on it.

Guha King of Nishadha.

Guidewife Woman.

Guinevere Wife of King Arthur; she is often portrayed as a virtuous lady and wife, but is perhaps best known for having a love affair with Lancelot, one of Arthur's friends and knights of the Round Table. Her name is also spelled Guenever.

Gulistan *Rose Garden*, written by the poet Sa'di

Gungnir Odin's spear, made of Yggdrasill wood, and the tip fashioned by Dvalin.

Gylfi A wandering king to whom the Eddas are narrated.

Haab Mayan solar calendar that consisted of eighteen twenty-day months.

Hades One of the three sons of Cronus; brother of Poseidon and Zeus. Hades is King of the Underworld, which is also known as the House of Hades.

Haere-mai Maori phrase meaning 'come here, welcome.'

Haere-mai-ra, me o tatou mate Maori phrase meaning 'come here, that I may sorrow with you.'

Haere-ra Maori phrase meaning 'goodbye, go, farewell.'

Haji Muslim pilgrim who has been to Mecca.

Hakama Traditional Japanese clothing, worn on the bottom half of the body.

Hanuman General of the monkey people.

Harakiri Suicide, usually by cutting or stabbing the abdomen. Also known as seppuku.

Hari-Hara Shiva and Vishnu as one god.

Harmonia Daughter of Ares and Aphrodite, wife of Cadmus.

Hatamoto High-ranking samurai.

Hathor Great cosmic mother and patroness of lovers. She is portrayed as a cow.

Hati The wolf who pursues the sun and moon.

Hatshepsut Second female pharaoh.

Hauberk Armour to protect the neck and shoulders, sometimes a full-length coat of mail.

Hector Eldest son of King Priam who defended Troy from the Greeks. He was killed by Achilles.

Hecuba The second wife of Priam, King of Troy. She was turned into a dog after Troy was lost.

Heimdall White god who guards the Bifrost bridge.

Hel Goddess of death and Loki's daughter. Also known as Hela.

Helen Daughter of Leda and Tyndareus, King of Sparta, and the most beautiful woman in the world. She was responsible for starting the Trojan War.

Heliopolis City in modern-day Cairo, known as the City of the Sun and the central place of worship of Ra. Also known as Anu.

Helius The sun, son of Hyperion and Theia.

Henwife Witch.

Hephaestus or **Hephaistos** The Smith of Heaven.

Hera A Mycenaean palace goddess, married to Zeus.

Heracles An important Greek hero, the son of Zeus and Alcmena. His name means 'Glory of Hera'. He performed twelve labours for King Eurystheus, and later became a god.

Hermes The conductor of souls of the dead to Hades, and god of trickery and of trade. He acts as messenger to the gods.

Hermod Son of Frigga and Odin who travelled to see Hel in order to reclaim Balder for Asgard.

Hero and Leander Hero was a priestess of Aphrodite, loved by Leander, a young man of Abydos. He drowned trying to see her.

Hestia Goddess of the hearth, daughter of Cronus and Rhea.

Hieroglyphs Type of writing that combines symbols and pictures, usually cut into tombs or rocks, or written on papyrus.

Himalaya Great mountain and range, father of Parvati.

Hiordis Wife of Sigmund and mother of Sigurd.

Hoderi A fisher and son of Okuninushi.

Hodur Balder's blind twin; known as the personification of darkness.

Hoenir Also called Vili; produced the first humans with Odin and Loki, and was one of the triad responsible for the creation of the world.

Hōichi the Earless A biwa hōshi, a blind storyteller who played the biwa or lute. Also a priest.

Holger Danske Legendary Viking warrior who is thought to never die. He sleeps until he is needed by his people and then he will rise to protect them.

Homayi Phoenix.

Hoodie Mythical creature which often appears as a crow.

Hoori A hunter and son of Okuninushi.

Horus God of the sky and kinship, son of Isis and Osiris. He captained the boat that carried Ra across the sky. He is depicted with the head of a falcon.

Hotei One of the gods of luck. He also personifies humour and contentment.

Houlet Owl.

Houri Beautiful virgin from paradise.

Hrim-faxi Steed of the night.

Hubris Presumptuous behaviour which causes the wrath of the gods to be brought on to mortals.

Hueytozoztli Festival dedicated to Tlaloc and, at times, Chicomecohuatl or other deities. Also the fourth month of the Aztec calendar.

Hugin Odin's raven.

Huitzilopochtli God of war and the sun, also connected with the summer and crops; one of the principal Aztec deities. He was born a full-grown adult to save his mother, Coatlicue, from the jealousy of his sister, Coyolxauhqui, who tried to kill Coatlicue. The Mars of the Aztec gods. In some origin stories he is one of four offspring of Ometeotl and Omecihuatl.

Hurley A traditional Irish game played with sticks and balls, quite similar to hockey.

Hurons A tribe of Iroquois stock, originally one people with the Iroquois.

Huveane (Pedi, Venda) Creator of humankind, who made a baby from clay into which he breathed life. He is known as the High God or Great God. He is also known as a trickster god.

Hymir Giant who fishes with Thor and is drowned by him.

Iambe Daughter of Pan and Echo, servant to King Celeus of Eleusis and Metaeira.

Icarus Son of Daedalus, who plunged to his death after escaping from the labyrinth.

Ichneumon Mongoose.

Idunn Guardian of the youth-giving apples.

Ifa (Yoruba) God of wisdom and divination. Also the term for a Yoruban religion.

Ife (Yoruba) The place Obatala first arrived on Earth and took for his home.

Igigi Great spirits or gods of Heaven and the sky.

Igraine Wife of the duke of Tintagel, enemy of Uther Pendragon, who marries Uther when her first husband dies. She is King Arthur's mother.

Ile (Yoruba) Goddess of the earth.

Imhetep High priest and wise sage. He is sometimes thought to be the son of Ptah.

Imam Person who leads prayers in a mosque.

Imana (Banyarwanda) Creator or sky god.

In The male principle who, joined with Yo, the female side, brought about creation and the first gods. In and Yo correspond to the Chinese Yang and Yin.

Inari God of rice, fertility, agriculture and, later, the fox god. Inari has both good and evil attributes but is often presented as an evil trickster.

Indra The King of Heaven.

Indrajit Son of Ravana.

Indrasen Daughter of Nala and Damayanti.

Indrasena Son of Nala and Damayanti.

Inundation Annual flooding of the River Nile.

Iphigenia The eldest daughter of Agamemnon and Clytemnestra who was sacrificed to appease Artemis and obtain a fair wind for Troy.

Iris Messenger of the gods who took the form of a rainbow.

Iseult Princess of Ireland and niece of the Morholt. She falls in love with Tristan after consuming a love potion but is forced to marry King Mark of Cornwall.

Ishtar Goddess of love, beauty, justice and war, especially in Ninevah, and earth mother who symbolizes fertility. Married to Tammuz, she is similar to the Greek goddess Aphrodite. Ishtar is sometimes known as Innana or Irnina.

Isis Goddess of the Nile and the moon, sister-wife of Osiris. She and her son, Horus, are sometimes thought of in a similar way to Mary and Jesus. She was one of the most worshipped female

Egyptian deities and was instrumental in returning Osiris to life after he was killed by his brother, Set.

Istakbál Deputation of warriors.

Izanagi Deity and brother-husband to Izanami, who together created the Japanese islands from the Floating Bridge of Heaven. Their offspring populated Japan.

Izanami Deity and sister-wife of Izanagi, creator of Japan. Their children include Amaterasu, Tsuki-yomi and Susanoo.

Jade It was believed that jade emerged from the mountains as a liquid which then solidified after ten thousand years to become a precious hard stone, green in colour. If the correct herbs were added to it, it could return to its liquid state and when swallowed increase the individual's chances of immortality.

Jambavan A noble monkey.

Jason Son of Aeson, King of Iolcus and leader of the voyage of the Argonauts.

Jatayu King of all the eagle-tribes.

Jesseraunt Flexible coat of armour or mail.

Jimmo Legendary first emperor of Japan. He is thought to be descended from Hoori, while other tales claim him to be descended from Amaterasu through her grandson, Ninigi.

Jizo God of little children and the god who calms the troubled sea.

Jord Daughter of Nott; wife of Odin.

Jormungander The world serpent; son of Loki. Legends tell that when his tail is removed from his mouth, Ragnarok has arrived.

Jorō Geisha who also worked as a prostitute.

Jotunheim Home of the giants.

Ju Ju tree Deciduous tree that produces edible fruit.

Jurasindhu A rakshasa, father-in-law of Kans.

Jyeshtha Goddess of bad luck.

Ka Life power or soul. Also known as ba.

Kai-káús Son of Kai-kobád. He led an army to invade Mázinderán, home of the demon-sorcerers, after being persuaded by a demon. Known for his ambitious schemes, he later tried to reach Heaven by trapping eagles to fly him there on his throne.

Kaikeyi Mother of Bharata, one of Dasharatha's three wives.

Kai-khosrau Son of Saiawúsh, who killed Afrásiyáb in revenge for the death of his father.

Kai-kobád Descendant of Feridún, he was selected by Zál to lead an army against Afrásiyáb. Their powerful army, led by Zál and Rustem, drove back Afrásiyáb's army, who then agreed to peace.

Kailyard Kitchen garden or small plot, usually used for growing vegetables.

Kali The Black, wife of Shiva.

Kalindi Daughter of the sun, wife of Krishna.

Kaliya A poisonous hydra that lived in the jamna.

Kalki Incarnation of Vishnu yet to come.

Kalnagini Serpent who kills Lakshmindara.

Kal-Purush The Time-man, Bengali name for Orion.

Kaluda A disciple of Buddha.

Kalunga-ngombe (Mbundu) Death, also depicted as the king of the netherworld.

Kama God of desire.

Kamadeva Desire, the god of love.

Kami Spirits, deities or forces of nature.

Kamund Lasso.

Kans King of Mathura, son of Ugrasena and Pavandrekha.

Kanva Father of Shakuntala.

Kappa River goblin with the body of a tortoise and the head of an ape. Kappa love to challenge human beings to single combat.

Karakia Invocation, ceremony, prayer.

Karna Pupil of Drona.

Kaross Blanket or rug, also worn as a traditional garment. It is often made from the skins of animals which have been sewn together.

Kasbu A period of twenty-four hours.

Kashyapa One of Dasharatha's counsellors.

Kauravas or Kurus Sons of Dhritarashtra, pupils of Drona.

Kaushalya Mother of Rama, one of Dasharatha's three wives.

Kay Son of Ector and adopted brother to King Arthur, he becomes one of Arthur's knights of the Round Table.

Keb God of the earth and father of Osiris and Isis, married to Nut. Keb is identified with Kronos, the Greek god of time.

Kehua Spirit, ghost.

Kelpie Another word for each uisge, the water-horse.

Ken Know.

Keres Black-winged demons or daughters of the night.

Keshini Wife of Sagara.

Khalif Leader.

Khara Younger brother of Ravana.

Khepera God who represents the rising sun. He is portrayed as a scarab. Also known as Nebertcher.

Kher-heb Priest and magician who officiated over rituals and ceremonies.

Khnemu God of the source of the Nile and one of the original Egyptian deities. He is thought to be the creator of children and of other gods. He is portrayed as a ram.

Khosru King and husband to Shireen, daughter of Maurice, the Greek Emperor. He was murdered by his own son, who wanted his kingdom and his wife.

Khumbaba Monster and guardian of the goddess Irnina, a form of the goddess Ishtar. Khumbaba is likened to the Greek gorgon.

Kia-ora Welcome, good luck. A greeting.

Kiboko Hippopotamus.

Kikinu Soul.

Kimbanda (Mbundu) Doctor.

Kimono Traditional Japanese clothing, similar to a robe.

King Arthur Legendary king of Britain who plucked the magical sword from the stone, marking him as the heir of Uther Pendragon and 'true king' of Britain. He and his knights of the Round Table defended Britain from the Saxons and had many adventures, including searching for the Holy Grail. Finally wounded in battle, he left Britain for the mythical Avalon, vowing to one day return to reclaim his kingdom.

Kingu Tiawath's husband, a god and warrior who she promised would rule Heaven once he helped her defeat the 'gods of light'. He was killed by Merodach who used his blood to make clay, from which he formed the first humans. In some tales, Kingu is Tiawath's son as well as her consort.

Kinnaras Human birds with musical instruments under their wings.

Kinyamkela (Zaramo) Ghost of a child.

Kirk Church, usually a term for Church of Scotland churches.

Kirtle One-piece garment, similar to a tunic, which was worn by men or women.

Kis Solar deity, usually depicted as an eagle.

Kishar Earth mother and sister-wife to Anshar.

Kist Trunk or large chest.

Kitamba (Mbundu) Chief who made his whole village go into mourning when his head-wife, Queen Muhongo, died. He also pledged that no one should speak or eat until she was returned to him.

Knowe Knoll or hillock.

Kojiki One of two myth-histories of Japan, along with the *Nihon Shoki*.

Ko-no-Hana Goddess of Mount Fuji, princess and wife of Ninigi.

Kore 'Maiden', another name for Persephone.

Kraal Traditional rural African village, usually consisting of huts surrounded by a fence or wall. Also an animal enclosure.

Krishna The Dark one, worshipped as an incarnation of Vishnu.

Kui-see Edible root.

Kumara Son of Shiva and Paravati, slays demon Taraka.

Kumbha-karna Ravana's brother.

Kunti Mother of the Pandavas.

Kura Red. The sacred colour of the Maori.

Kusha or Kusi One of Sita's two sons.

Kvasir Clever warrior and colleague of Odin. He was responsible for finally outwitting Loki.

Kwannon Goddess of mercy.

Labyrinth A prison built at Knossos for the Minotaur by Daedalus.

Lady of the Lake Enchantress who presents Arthur with Excalibur.

Laertes King of Ithaca and father of Odysseus.

Laestrygonians Savage giants encountered by Odysseus on his travels.

Laili In love with Majnun but unable to marry him, she was given to the prince, Ibn Salam, to marry. When he died, she escaped and found Majnun, but they could not be legally married. The couple died of grief and were buried together. Also known as Laila.

Laird Person who owns a significant estate in Scotland.

Lakshmana Brother of Rama and his companion in exile.

Lakshmi Consort of Vishnu and a goddess of beauty and good fortune.

Lakshmindara Son of Chand resurrected by Manasa Devi.

Lancelot Knight of the Round Table. Lancelot was raised by the Lady of the Lake. While he went on many quests, he is perhaps best known for his affair with Guinevere, King Arthur's wife.

Land of Light One of the names for the realm of the fairies. If a piece of metal welded by human hands is put in the doorway to their land, the door cannot close. The door to this realm is only open at night, and usually at a full moon.

Lang syne The days of old.

Lao Tzu (Laozi) The ancient Taoist philosopher thought to have been born in 571 BC, a contemporary of Confucius with whom, it is said, he discussed the tenets of Tao. Lao Tzu was an advocate of simple rural existence and looked to the Yellow Emperor and Shun as models of efficient government. His philosophies were recorded in the Tao Te Ching. Legends surrounding his birth suggest that he emerged from the left-hand side of his mother's body, with white hair and a long white beard, after a confinement lasting eighty years.

Laocoon A Trojan wiseman who predicted that the wooden horse contained Greek soldiers.

Laomedon The King of Troy who hired Apollo and Poseidon to build the impregnable walls of Troy.

Lava Son of Sita.

Leda Daughter of the King of Aetolia, who married Tyndareus. Helen and Clytemnestra were her daughters.

Legba (Dahomey) Youngest offspring of Mawu-Lisa. He was given the gift of all languages. It was through him that humans could converse with the gods.

Leman Lover.

Leprechaun Mythical creature from Irish folk tales who often appears as a mischievous and sometimes drunken old man.

Lethe One of the four rivers of the Underworld, also called the River of Forgetfulness.

Lif The female survivor of Ragnarok.

Lifthrasir The male survivor of Ragnarok.

Lil Demon.

Liongo (Swahili) Warrior and hero.

Lofty mountain Home of Ahura-Mazda.

Logi Utgard-loki's cook.

Loki God of fire and mischief-maker of Asgard; he eventually brings about Ragnarok. Also spelled as Loptur.

Lotus-Eaters A race of people who live a dazed, drugged existence, the result of eating the lotus flower.

Ma'at State of order meaning truth, order or justice. Personified by the goddess Ma'at, who was Thoth's consort.

Macha There are thought to be several different Machas who appear in quite a number of ancient Irish stories. For the purposes of this book, however, the Macha referred to is the wife of Crunnchu. The story unfolds that after her husband had boasted of her great athletic ability to the King, she was subsequently forced to run against his horses in spite of the fact that she was heavily pregnant. Macha died giving birth to her twin babies and with her dying breath she cursed Ulster for nine generations, proclaiming that it would suffer the weakness of a woman in childbirth in times of great stress. This curse had its most disastrous effect when Medb of Connacht invaded Ulster with her great army.

Machi-bugyō Senior official or magistrate, usually samurai.

Macuilxochitl God of art, dance and games, and the patron of luck in gaming. His name means 'source of flowers' or 'prince of flowers'. Also known as Xochipilli, meaning 'five-flower'.

Madake Weapon used for whipping, made of bamboo.

Maduma Taro tuber.

Mag Muirthemne Cuchulainn's inheritance. A plain extending from River Boyne to the mountain range of Cualgne, close to Emain Macha in Ulster.

Magni Thor's son.

Mahaparshwa One of Ravana's generals.

Maharaksha Son of Khara, slain at Lanka.

Mahasubhadda Wife of Buddha-select (Sumedha).

Majnun Son of a chief, who fell in love with Laili and followed her tribe through the desert, becoming mad with love until they were briefly reunited before dying.

Makaras Mythical fish-reptiles of the sea.

Makoma (Senna) Folk hero who defeated five mighty giants.

Mana Power, authority, prestige, influence, sanctity, luck.

Manasa Devi Goddess of snakes, daughter of Shiva by a mortal woman.

Manasha Goddess of snakes.

Mandavya Daughter of Kushadhwaja.

Man-Devourer One of Ravana's monsters.

Mandodari Wife of Ravana.

Mandrake Poisonous plant from the nightshade family which has hallucinogenic and hypnotic qualities if ingested. Its roots resemble the human form and it has supposedly magical qualities.

Mani The moon.

Manitto Broad term used to describe the supernatural or a potent spirit among the Algonquins, the Iroquois and the Sioux.

Man-Slayer One of Ravana's counsellors.

Manthara Kaikeyi's evil nurse, who plots Rama's ruin.

Mantle Cloak or shawl.

Manu Lawgiver.

Manu Mythical mountain on which the sun sets.

Mara The evil one, tempts Gautama.

Markandeya One of Dasharatha's counsellors.

Mashu Mountain of the Sunset, which lies between Earth and the underworld. Guarded by scorpion-men.

Matali Sakra's charioteer.

Mawu-Lisa (Dahomey) Twin offspring of Nana Baluka. Mawu (female) and Lisa (male) are often joined to form one being. Their own offspring populated the world.

Mbai (Igbo) Person of great intelligence, also known as Ekake (Ibani), which means 'tortoise'.

Medea Witch and priestess of Hecate, daughter of Aeetes and sister of Circe. She helped Jason in his quest for the Golden Fleece.

Medusa One of the three Gorgons whose head had the power to turn onlookers to stone.

Melpomene One of the muses, and mother of the Sirens.

Menaka One of the most beautiful dancers in Heaven.

Menat Amulet, usually worn for protection.

Mendicant Beggar.

Menelaus King of Sparta, brother of Agamemnon. Married Helen and called war against Troy when she eloped with Paris.

Menthu Lord of Thebes and god of war. He is portrayed as a hawk or falcon.

Mere-pounamu A native weapon made of a rare green stone.

Merlin Wizard and advisor to King Arthur. He is thought to be the son of a human female and an incubus (male demon). He brought about Arthur's birth and ascension to king, then acted as his mentor.

Merodach God who battled Tiawath and defeated her by cutting out her heart and dividing her corpse into two pieces. He used these pieces to divide the upper and lower waters once controlled by Tiawath, making a dwelling for the gods of light. He also created humankind. Also known as Marduk.

Merrow Mythical mermaid-like creature, often depicted with an enchanted cap, called a cohuleen driuth, which allows it to travel between land and the depths of the sea. Also known as murúch.

Metaneira Wife of Celeus, King of Eleusis, who hired Demeter in disguise as her nurse.

Metztli Goddess of the moon, her name means 'lady of the night'. Also known as Yohualtictl.

Michabo Also known as Manobozho, or the Great Hare, the principal deity of the Algonquins, maker and preserver of the earth, sun and moon.

Mictlan God of the dead and ruler of the underworld. He was married to Mictecaciuatl and is often represented as a bat. He is also the Aztec lord of Hades. Also known as Mictlantecutli. Mictlan is also the name for the underworld.

Midgard Dwelling place of humans (Earth).

Midsummer A time when fairies dance and claim human victims.

Mihrab Father of Rúdábeh and descendant of Zohák, the serpent-king.

Milesians A group of iron-age invaders led by the sons of Mil, who arrived in Ireland from Spain around 500 BC and overcame the Tuatha De Danann.

Mimir God of the ocean. His head guards a well; reincarnated after Ragnarok.

Minos King of Crete, son of Zeus and Europa. He was considered to have been the ruler of a sea empire.

Minotaur A creature born of the union between Pasiphae and a Cretan Bull.

Minúchihr King who lives to be one hundred and twenty years old. Father of Nauder.

Miolnir *See* Mjolnir.

Mithra God of the sun and light in Iran, protector of truth and guardian of pastures and cattle. Alo known as Mitra in Hindu mythology and Mithras in Roman mythology.

Mixcoatl God of the chase or the hunt. Sometimes depicted as the god of air and thunder, he introduced fire to humankind. His name means 'cloud serpent'.

Mjolnir Hammer belonging to the Norse god of thunder, which is used as a fearsome weapon which always returns to Thor's hand, and as an instrument of consecration.

Mnoatia Forest spirits.

Moccasins One-piece shoes made of soft leather, especially deerskin.

Modi Thor's son.

Moly A magical plant given to Odysseus by Hermes as protection against Circe's powers.

Montezuma Great emperor who consolidated the Aztec Empire.

Mordred Bastard son of King Arthur and Morgawse, Queen of Orkney, who, unknown to Arthur, was his half-sister. Mordred becomes one of King Arthur's knights of the Round Table before betraying and fatally wounding Arthur, causing him to leave Britain for Avalon.

Morgan le Fay Enchantress and half-sister to King Arthur, Morgan was an apprentice of Merlin's. She is generally depicted as benevolent, yet did pit herself against Arthur and his knights on occasion. She escorts Arthur on his final journey to Avalon. Also known as Morgain le Fay.

Morholt, the Knight sent to Cornwall to force King Mark to pay tribute to Ireland. He is killed by Tristan.

Morongoe the brave (Lesotho) Man who was turned into a snake by evil spirits because Tau was jealous that he had married the beautiful Mokete, the chief's daughter. Morongoe was returned to human form after his son, Tsietse, returned him to their family.

Mosima (Bapedi) The underworld or abyss.

Mount Fuji Highest mountain in Japan, on the island of Honshū.

Mount Kunlun This mountain features in many Chinese legends as the home of the great emperors on Earth. It is written in the *Shanghaijing* (*The Classic of Mountains and Seas*) that this towering structure measured no less than 3300 miles in circumference and 4000 miles in height. It acted both as a central pillar to support the heavens, and as a gateway between Heaven and Earth.

Moving Finger Expression for taking responsibility for one's life and actions, which cannot be undone.

Moytura Translated as the 'Plain of Weeping', Mag Tured, or Moytura, was where the Tuatha De Danann fought two of their most significant battles.

Mua An old-time Polynesian god.

Muezzin Person who performs the Muslim call to prayer.

Mugalana A disciple of Buddha.

Muilearteach The Cailleach Bheur of the water, who appears as a witch or a sea-serpent. On land she grew larger and stronger by fire.

Mul-lil God of Nippur, who took the form of a gazelle.

Muloyi Sorcerer, also called mulaki, murozi, ndozi or ndoki.

Mummu Son of Tiawath and Apsu. He formed a trinity with them to battle the gods. Also known as Moumis. In some tales, Mummu is also Merodach, who eventually destroyed Tiawath.

Munin Odin's raven.

Murile (Chaga) Man who dug up a taro tuber that resembled his baby brother, which turned into a living boy. His mother killed the baby when she saw Murile was starving himself to feed it.

Murtough Mac Erca King who ruled Ireland when many of its people – including his wife and family – were converting to Christianity. He remained a pagan.

Muses Goddesses of poetry and song, daughters of Zeus and Mnemosyne.

Musha Expression, often of surprise.

Muskrat North American beaver-like, amphibious rodent.

Muspell Home of fire, and the fire-giants.

Mwidzilo Taboo which, if broken, can cause death.

Nabu God of writing and wisdom. Also known as Nebo. Thought to be the son of Merodach.

Nahua Ancient Mexicans.

Nakula Pandava twin skilled in horsemanship.

Nala One of the monkey host, son of Vishvakarma.

Nana Baluka (Dahomey) Mother of all creation. She gave birth to an androgynous being with two faces. The female face was Mawu, who controlled the night and lands to the west. The male face was Lisa and he controlled the day and the east.

Nanahuatl Also known as Nanauatzin. Presided over skin diseases and known as Leprous, which in Nahua meant 'divine'.

Nandi Shiva's bull.

Nanna Balder's wife.

Nannar God of the moon and patron of the city of Ur.

Naram-Sin Son or ancestor of Sargon and king of the Four Zones or Quarters of Babylon.

Narcissus Son of the River Cephisus. He fell in love with himself and died as a result.

Narve Son of Loki.

Nataraja Manifestation of Shiva, Lord of the Dance.

Natron Preservative used in embalming, mined from the Natron Valley in Egypt.

Nauder Son of Minúchihr, who became king on his death and was tyrannical and hated until Sám begged him to follow in the footsteps of his ancestors.

Nausicaa Daughter of Alcinous, King of Phaeacia, who fell in love with Odysseus.

Nebuchadnezzar Famous king of Babylon. Also known as Nebuchadrezzar.

Necromancy Communicating with the dead.

Nectar Drink of the gods.

Neith Goddess of hunting, fate and war. Neith is sometimes known as the creator of the universe.

Nemesis Goddess of retribution and daughter of night.

Neoptolemus Son of Achilles and Deidameia, he came to Troy at the end of the war to wear his father's armour. He sacrificed Polyxena at the tomb of Achilles.

Nephthys Goddess of the air, night and the dead. Sister of Isis and sister-wife to Seth, she is also the mother of Anubis.

Nereids Sea-nymphs who are the daughters of Nereus and Doris. Thetis, mother of Achilles, was a Nereid.

Nergal God of death and patron god of Cuthah, which was often known as a burial place. He is also known as the god of fire. Married to Aralu, the goddess of the underworld.

Nestor Wise King of Pylus, who led the ships to Troy with Agamemnon and Menelaus.

Neta Daughter of Shiva, friend of Manasa.

Ngai (Gikuyu) Creator god.

Ngaka (Lesotho) Witch doctor.

Niflheim The underworld. In Norse mythology, ruled over by Hel.

Night Daughter of Norvi.

Nikumbha One of Ravana's generals.

Nila One of the monkey host, son of Agni.

Nin-Girsu God of fertility and war, patron god of Girsu. Also known as Shul-gur.

Ninigi Grandson of Amaterasu, Ninigi came to Earth bringing rice and order to found the Imperial family. He is known as the August Grandchild.

Niord God of the sea; marries Skadi.

Nippur The home of En-lil and one of the two major cities of Babylonian civilization.

Nirig God of war and storms, and son of Bel. Also known as Enu-Restu.

Nirvana Transcendent state and the final goal of Buddhism.

Nis Mythological creature, similar to a brownie or goblin, usually harmless or even friendly, but can be easily offended. They are often associated with Christmas or the winter solstice.

Noatun Niord's home.

Noisy-Throat One of Ravana's counsellors.

Noondah (Zanzibar) Cannibalistic cat which attacked and killed animals and humans.

Norns The fates and protectors of Yggdrasill. Many believe them to be the same as the Valkyries.

Norvi Father of the night.

Nott Goddess of night.

Nsasak bird Small bird who became chief of all small birds after winning a competition to go without food for seven days. The

Nsasak bird beat the Odudu bird by sneaking out of his home to feed.

Nü Wa The Goddess Nü Wa, who in some versions of the Creation myths is the sole creator of mankind, and in other tales is associated with the God Fu Xi, also a great benefactor of the human race. Some accounts represent Fu Xi as the brother of Nü Wa, but others describe the pair as lovers who lie together to create the very first human beings. Fu Xi is also considered to be the first of the Chinese emperors of mythical times who reigned from 2953 to 2838 BC.

Nuada The first king of the Tuatha De Danann in Ireland, who lost an arm in the first battle of Moytura against the Fomorians. He became known as 'Nuada of the Silver Hand' when Diancecht, the great physician of the Tuatha De Danann, replaced his hand with a silver one after the battle.

Nunda (Swahili, East Africa) Slayer that took the form of a cat and grew so big that it consumed everyone in the town except the sultan's wife, who locked herself away. Her son, Mohammed, killed Nunda and cut open its leg, setting free everyone Nunda had eaten.

Nut Goddess of the sky, stars and astronomy. Sister-wife of Keb and mother of Osiris, Isis, Set and Nephthys. She often appears in the form of a cow.

Nyame (Ashanti) God of the sky, who sees and knows everything.

Nymphs Minor female deities associated with particular parts of the land and sea.

Obassi Osaw (Ekoi) Creator god with his twin, Obassi Nsi. Originally, Obassi Osaw ruled the skies while Obassi Nsi ruled the Earth.

Obatala (Yoruba) Creator of humankind. He climbed down a golden chain from the sky to the earth, then a watery abyss, and formed land and humankind. When Olorun heard of his success, he created the sun for Obatala and his creations.

Oberon Fairy king.

Odin Allfather and king of all gods, he is known for travelling the nine worlds in disguise and recognized only by his single eye; dies at Ragnarok.

Oduduwa (Yoruba) Divine king of Ile-Ife, the holy city of Yoruba.

Odur Freyia's husband.

Odysseus Greek hero, son of Laertes and Anticleia, who was renowned for his cunning, the master behind the victory at Troy, and known for his long voyage home.

Oedipus Son of Leius, King of Thebes and Jocasta. Became King of Thebes and married his mother.

Ogdoad Group of eight deities who were formed into four male–female couples who joined to create the gods and the world.

Ogham One of the earliest known forms of Irish writing, originally used to inscribe upright pillar stones.

Oiran Courtesan.

Oisin Also called Ossian (particularly by James Macpherson who wrote a set of Gaelic Romances about this character, supposedly garnered from oral tradition). Ossian was the son of Fionn and Sadbh, and had various brothers, according to different legends. He was a man of great wisdom, became immortal for many centuries, but in the end he became mad.

Ojibwe Another name for the Chippewa, a tribe of Algonquin stock.

Okuninushi Deity and descendant of Susanoo, who married Suseri-hime, Susanoo's daughter, without his consent. Susanoo tried to kill him many times but did not succeed and eventually forgave Okuninushi. He is sometimes thought to be the son or grandson of Susanoo.

Olokun (Yoruba) Most powerful goddess who ruled the seas and marshes. When Obatala created Earth in her domain, other gods began to divide it up between them. Angered at their presumption, she caused a great flood to destroy the land.

Olorun (Yoruba) Supreme god and ruler of the sky. He sees and controls everything, but others, such as Obatala, carry out the work for him. Also known as Olodumare.

Olympia Zeus's home in Elis.

Olympus The highest mountain in Greece and the ancient home of the gods.

Omecihuatl Female half of the first being, combined with Ometeotl. Together they are the lords of duality or lords of the two sexes. Also known as Ometecutli and Omeciuatl or Tonacatecutli and Tonacaciuatl. Their offspring were Xipe Totec, Huitzilopochtli, Quetzalcoatl and Tezcatlipoca.

Ometeotl Male half of the first being, combined with Omecihuatl.

Ometochtli Collective name for the pulque-gods or drink-gods. These gods were often associated with rabbits as they were thought to be senseless creatures.

Onygate Anyway.

Opening the Mouth Ceremony in which mummies or statues were prayed over and anointed with incense before their mouths were opened, allowing them to eat and drink in the afterlife.

Oracle The response of a god or priest to a request for advice – also a prophecy; the place where such advice was sought; the person or thing from whom such advice was sought.

Oranyan (Yoruba) Youngest grandson of King Oduduwa, who later became king himself.

Orestes Son of Agamemnon and Clytemnestra who escaped following Agamemnon's murder to King Strophius. He later returned to Argos to murder his mother and avenge the death of his father.

Orpheus Thracian singer and poet, son of Oeagrus and a Muse. Married Eurydice and when she died tried to retrieve her from the Underworld.

Orunmila (Yoruba) Eldest son of Olorun, he helped Obatala create land and humanity, which he then rescued after Olokun flooded the lands. He has the power to see the future.

Osiris God of fertility, the afterlife and death. Thought to be the first of the pharaohs. He was murdered by his brother, Set, after which he was conjured back to life by Isis, Anubis and others before becoming lord of the afterworld. Married to Isis, who was also his sister.

Otherworld The world of deities and spirits, also known as the Land of Promise, or the Land of Eternal Youth, a place of everlasting life where all earthly dreams come to be fulfilled.

Owuo (Krachi, West Africa) Giant who personifies death. He causes a person to die every time he blinks his eye.

Palamedes Hero of Nauplia, believed to have created part of the ancient Greek alphabet. He tricked Odysseus into joining the fleet setting out for Troy by placing the infant Telemachus in the path of his plough.

Palermo Stone Stone carved with hieroglyphs, which came from the Royal Annals of ancient Egypt and contains a list of the kings of Egypt from the first to the early fifth dynasties.

Palfrey Docile and light horse, often used by women.

Palladium Wooden image of Athene, created by her as a monument to her friend Pallas who she accidentally killed. While in Troy it protected the city from invaders.

Pallas Athene's best friend, whom she killed.

Pan God of Arcadia, half-goat and half-man. Son of Hermes. He is connected with fertility, masturbation and sexual drive. He is also associated with music, particularly his pipes, and with laughter.

Pan Gu Some ancient writers suggest that this God is the offspring of the opposing forces of nature, the yin and the yang. The yin (female) is associated with the cold and darkness of the earth, while the yang (male) is associated with the sun and the warmth of the heavens. 'Pan' means 'shell of an egg' and 'Gu' means 'to secure' or 'to achieve'. Pan Gu came into existence so that he might create order from chaos.

Pandareus Cretan King killed by the gods for stealing the shrine of Zeus.

Pandavas Alternative name for sons of Pandu, pupils of Drona.

Pandora The first woman, created by the gods, to punish man for Prometheus's theft of fire. Her dowry was a box full of powerful evil.

Papyrus Paper-like material made from the pith of the papyrus plant, first manufactured in Egypt. Used as a type of paper as well as for making mats, rope and sandals.

Paramahamsa The supreme swan.

Parashurama Human incarnation of Vishnu, 'Rama with an axe'.

Paris Handsome son of Priam and Hecuba of Troy, who was left for dead on Mount Ida but raised by shepherds. Was reclaimed by his family, then brought them shame and caused the Trojan War by eloping with Helen.

Parsa Holy man. Also known as a zahid.

Parvati Consort of Shiva and daughter of Himalaya.

Passion Wife of desire.

Pavanarekha Wife of Ugrasena, mother of Kans.

Peerie Folk Fairy or little folk.

Pegasus The winged horse born from the severed neck of Medusa.

Peggin Wooden vessel with a handle, often shaped like a tub and used for drinking.

Peleus Father of Achilles. He married Antigone, caused her death, and then became King of Phthia. Saved from death himself by Jason and the Argonauts. Married Thetis, a sea nymph.

Penelope The long-suffering but equally clever wife of Odysseus who managed to keep at bay suitors who longed for Ithaca while Odysseus was at the Trojan War and on his ten-year voyage home.

Pentangle Pentagram or five-pointed star.

Pentecost Christian festival held on the seventh Sunday after Easter. It celebrates the holy spirit descending on the disciples after Jesus's ascension.

Percivale Knight of the Round Table and original seeker of the Holy Grail.

Persephone Daughter of Zeus and Demeter who was raped by Hades and forced to live in the Underworld as his queen for three months of every year.

Perseus Son of Danae, who was made pregnant by Zeus. He fought the Gorgons and brought home the head of Medusa. He eventually founded the city of Mycenae and married Andromeda.

Pesh Kef Spooned blade used in the Opening the Mouth ceremony.

Phaeacia The Kingdom of Alcinous on which Odysseus landed after a shipwreck which claimed the last of his men as he left Calypso's island.

Pharaoh King or ruler of Egypt.

Philoctetes Malian hero, son of Poeas, received Heracles's bow and arrows as a gift when he lit the great hero's pyre on Mount Oeta. He was involved in the last part of the Trojan War, killing Paris.

Philtre Magic potion, usually a love potion.

Pibroch Bagpipe music.

Pintura Native manuscript or painting.

Pipiltin Noble class of the Aztecs.

Pismire Ant.

Piu-piu Short mat made from flax leaves and neatly decorated.

Po Gloom, darkness, the lower world.

Polyphemus A Cyclops, but a son of Poseidon. He fell in love with Galatea, but she spurned him. He was blinded by Odysseus.

Polyxena Daughter of Priam and Hecuba of Troy. She was sacrificed on the grave of Achilles by Neoptolemus.

Pooka Mythical creature with the ability to shapeshift. Often appears as a horse, but also as a bull, dog or in human form, and has the ability to talk. Also known as púca.

Popol Vuh Sacred 'book of counsel' of the Quiché or K'iche' Maya people.

Poseidon God of the sea, and of sweet waters. Also the god of earthquakes. His is brother to Zeus and Hades, who divided the earth between them.

Pradyumna Son of Krishna and Rukmini.

Prahasta (Long-Hand) One of Ravana's generals.

Prajapati Creator of the universe, father of the gods, demons and all creatures, later known as Brahma.

Priam King of Troy, married to Hecuba, who bore him Hector, Paris, Helenus, Cassandra, Polyxena, Deiphobus and Troilus. He was murdered by Neoptolemus.

Pritha Mother of Karna and of the Pandavas.

Prithivi Consort of Dyaus and goddess of the earth.

Proetus King of Argos, son of Abas.

Prometheus A Titan, son of Iapetus and Themus. He was champion of mortal men, which he created from clay. He stole fire from the gods and was universally hated by them.

Prose Edda Collection of Norse myths and poems, thought to have been compiled in the 1200s by Icelandic historian Snorri Sturluson.

Proteus The old man of the sea who watched Poseidon's seals.

Psyche A beautiful nymph who was the secret wife of Eros, against the wishes of his mother Aphrodite, who sent Psyche to perform many tasks in hope of causing her death. She eventually married Eros and was allowed to become partly immortal.

Ptah Creator god and deity of Memphis who was married to Sekhmet. Ptah built the boats to carry the souls of the dead to the afterlife.

Puddock Frog.

Pulque Alcoholic drink made from fermented agave.

Purusha The cosmic man, he was sacrificed and his dismembered body became all the parts of the cosmos, including the four classes of society.

Purvey To provide or supply.

Pushkara Nala's brother.

Pushpaka Rama's chariot.

Putana A rakshasi.

Pygmalion A sculptor who was so lonely he carved a statue of a beautiful woman, and eventually fell in love with it. Aphrodite brought the image to life.

Quauhtli Eagle.

Quern Hand mill used for grinding corn.

Quetzalcoatl Deity and god of wind. He is represented as a feathered or plumed serpent and is usually a wise and benevolent god. Offspring of Ometeotl and Omecihuatl, he is also known as Kukulkan.

Ra God of the sun, ruling male deity of Egypt whose name means 'sole creator'.

Radha The principal mistress of Krishna.

Ragnarok The end of the world.

Rahula Son of Siddhartha and Yashodhara.

Raiden God of thunder. He traditionally has a fierce and demonic appearance.

Rakshasas Demons and devils.

Ram of Mendes Sacred symbol of fatherhood and fertility.

Rama or **Ramachandra** A prince and hero of the Ramayana, worshipped as an incarnation of Vishnu.

Ra-Molo (Lesotho) Father of fire, a chief who ruled by fear. When trying to kill his brother, Tau the lion, he was turned into a monster with the head of a sheep and the body of a snake.

Rangatira Chief, warrior, gentleman.

Regin A blacksmith who educated Sigurd.

Reinga The spirit land, the home of the dead.

Reservations Tracts of land allocated to the native American people by the United States Government with the purpose of bringing the many separate tribes under state control.

Rewati Daughter of Raja, marries Balarama.

Rhadha Wife of Adiratha, a gopi of Brindaban and lover of Krishna.

Rhea Mother of the Olympian gods. Cronus ate each of her children, but she concealed Zeus and gave Cronus a swaddled rock in his place.

Rill Small stream.

Rimu (Chaga) Monster known to feed off human flesh, which sometimes takes the form of a werewolf.

Rishis Sacrificial priests associated with the devas in Swarga.

Rituparna King of Ayodhya.

Rohini The wife of Vasudeva, mother of Balarama and Subhadra, and carer of the young Krishna. Another Rohini is a goddess and consort of Chandra.

Rōnin Samurai whose master had died or fallen out of favour.

Rubáiyát Collection of poems written by Omar Khayyám.

Rúdábeh Wife of Zál and mother of Rustem.

Rudra Lord of Beasts and disease, later evolved into Shiva.

Rukma Rukmini's eldest brother.

Rustem Son of Zál and Rúdábeh, he was a brave and mighty warrior who undertook seven labours to travel to Mázinderán to rescue Kai-káús. Once there, he defeated the White Demon and rescued Kai-káús. He rode the fabled stallion Rakhsh and is also known as Rustam.

Ryō Traditional gold currency.

Sabdh Mother of Ossian, or Oisin.

Sabitu Goddess of the sea.

Sagara King of Ayodhya.

Sahadeva Pandava twin skilled in swordsmanship.

Sahib diwan Lord high treasurer or chief royal executive.

Saiawúsh Son of Kai-káús, who was put through trial by fire when Sudaveh, Kai-káús's wife, told him that Saiawúsh had taken advantage of her. His innocence was proven when the fire did not harm him. He was eventually killed by Afrásiyáb.

Saithe Blessed.

Sajara (Mali) God of rainbows. He takes the form of a multi-coloured serpent.

Sake Japanese rice wine.

Sakuni Cousin of Duryodhana.

Salam Greeting or salutation.

Saláman Son of the Shah of Yunan, who fell in love with Absál, his nurse. She died after they had a brief love affair and he returned to his father.

Salmali tree Cotton tree.

Salmon A symbol of great wisdom, around which many Scottish legends revolve.

Sám Mighty warrior who fought and won many battles. Father of Zál and grandfather to Rustem.

Sambu Son of Krishna.

Sampati Elder brother of Jatayu.

Samurai Noblemen who were part of the military in medieval Japan.

Sanehat Member of the royal bodyguard.

Sango (Yoruba) God of war and thunder.

Sangu (Mozambique) Goddess who protects pregnant women, depicted as a hippopotamus.

Santa Daughter of Dasharatha.

Sarapis Composite deity of Apis and Osiris, sometimes known as Serapis. Thought to be created to unify Greek and Egyptian citizens under the Greek pharaoh Ptolemy.

Sarasvati The tongue of Rama.

Sarcophagus Stone coffin.

Sargon of Akkad Raised by Akki, a husbandman, after being hidden at birth. Sargon became King of Assyria and a great hero. He founded the first library in Babylon. Similar to King Arthur or Perseus.

Sarsar Harsh, whistling wind.

Sasabonsam (Ashanti) Forest ogre.

Sassun Scottish word for England.

Sati Daughter of Daksha and Prasuti, first wife of Shiva.

Satrughna One of Dasharatha's four sons.

Satyavan Truth speaker, husband of Savitri.

Satyavati A fisher-maid, wife of Bhishma's father, Shamtanu.

Satyrs Elemental spirits which took great pleasure in chasing nymphs. They had horns, a hairy body and cloven hooves.

Saumanasa A mighty elephant.

Scamander River running across the Trojan plain, and father of Teucer.

Scarab Dung beetle, often used as a symbol of the immortal human soul and regeneration.

Scylla and Charybdis Scylla was a monster who lived on a rock of the same name in the Straits of Messina, devouring sailors. Charybdis was a whirlpool in the Straits which was supposedly inhabited by the hateful daughter of Poseidon.

Seal Often believed that seals were fallen angels. Many families are descended from seals, some of which had webbed hands or feet. Some seals were the children of sea-kings who had become enchanted (selkies).

Seelie-Court The court of the Fairies, who travelled around their realm. They were usually fair to humans, doling out punishment that was morally sound, but they were quick to avenge insults to fairies.

Segu (Swahili, East Africa) Guide who informs humans where honey can be found.

Sekhmet Solar deity who led the pharaohs in war. She is goddess of healing and was sent by Ra to destroy humanity when people turned against the sun god. She is portrayed with the head of a lion.

Selene Moon-goddess, daughter of Hyperion and Theia. She was seduced by Pan, but loved Endymion.

Selkie Mythical creature which is seal-like when in water but can shed its skin to take on human form when on land.

Seneschal Steward of a royal or noble household.

Sensei Teacher.

Seriyut A disciple of Buddha.

Sessrymnir Freyia's home.

Set God of chaos and evil, brother of Osiris, who killed him by tricking him into getting into a chest, which he then threw in the Nile, before cutting Osiris's body into fourteen separate pieces. Also known as Seth.

Sgeulachd Stories.

Shah Nameh *The Book of Kings* written by Ferdowski, one of the world's longest epic poems, which describes the mythology and history of the Persian Empire.

Shaikh Respected religious man.

Shaivas or Shaivites Worshippers of Shiva.

Shakti Power or wife of a god and Shiva's consort as his feminine aspect.

Shaman Also known as the 'Medicine Men' of Indian tribes, it was the shaman's role to cultivate communication with the spirit world. They were endowed with knowledge of all healing herbs, and learned to diagnose and cure disease. They could foretell the future, find lost property and had power over animals, plants and stones.

Shamash God of the sun and protector of Gilgamesh, the great Babylonian hero. Known as the son of Sin, the moon god, he is also portrayed as a judge of good and evil.

Shamtanu Father of Bhishma.

Shankara A great magician, friend of Chand Sadagar.

Shashti The Sixth, goddess who protects children and women in childbirth.

Sheen Beautiful and enchanted woman who casts a spell on Murtough, King of Ireland, causing him to fall in love with her and cast out his family. He dies at her hands, half burned and half drowned, but she then dies of grief as she returns his love. Sheen is known by many names, including Storm, Sigh and Rough Wind.

Shesh A serpent that takes human birth through Devaki.

Shi-en Fairy dwelling.

Shinto Indigenous religion of Japan, from the pre-sixth century to the present day.

Shireen Married to Khosru. Her beauty meant that she was desired by many, including Khosru's own son by his previous marriage. She killed herself rather than give in to her stepson.

Shitala The Cool One and goddess of smallpox.

Shiva One of the two great gods of post-Vedic Hinduism with Vishnu.

Shogun Military ruler or overlord.

Shoji Sliding door, usually a lattice screen of paper.

Shu God of the air and half of the first divine couple created by Atem. Brother and husband to Tefnut, father to Keb and Nut.

Shubistán Household.

Shudra One of the four fundamental colours (caste).

Shuttle Part of a machine used for spinning cloth, used for passing weft threads between warp threads.

Siddhas Musical ministrants of the upper air.

Sif Thor's wife; known for her beautiful hair.

Sigi Son of Odin.

Sigmund Warrior able to pull the sword from Branstock in the Volsung's hall.

Signy Volsung's daughter.

Sigurd Son of Sigmund, and bearer of his sword. Slays Fafnir the dragon.

Sigyn Loki's faithful wife.

Símúrgh Griffin, an animal with the body of a lion and the head and wings of an eagle. Known to hold great wisdom. Also called a symurgh.

Sin God of the moon, worshipped primarily in Ur.

Sindri Dwarf who worked with Brokki to fashion gifts for the gods; commissioned by Loki.

Sirens Sea nymphs who are half-bird, half-woman, whose song lures hapless sailors to their death.

Sisyphus King of Ephrya and a trickster who outwitted Autolycus. He was one of the greatest sinners in Hades.

Sita Daughter of the earth, adopted by Janaka, wife of Rama.

Skadi Goddess of winter and the wife of Niord for a short time.

Skanda Six-headed son of Shiva and a warrior god.

Skraeling Person native to Canada and Greenland. The name was given to them by Viking settlers and can be translated as 'barbarian'.

Skrymir Giant who battled against Thor.

Sleipnir Odin's steed.

Sluagh The host of the dead, seen fighting in the sky and heard by mortals.

Smote Struck with a heavy blow.

Sohráb Son of Rustem and Tahmineh, Sohráb was slain in battle by his own father, who killed him by mistake.

Sol The sun-maiden.

Soma A god and a drug, the elixir of life.

Somerled Lord of the Isles, and legendary ancestor of the Clan MacDonald.

Soothsayer Someone with the ability to predict or see the future, by the use of magic, special knowledge or intuition. Known as seanagal in Scottish myths.

Squaw North American Indian married woman.

Squint-Eye One of Ramana's monsters.

Squire Shield- or armour-bearer of a knight.

Srutakirti Daughter of Kushadhwaja.

Stirabout Porridge made by stirring oatmeal into boiling milk or water.

Stone Giants A malignant race of stone beings whom the Iroquois believed invaded Indian territory, threatening the Confederation of the Five Nations. These fierce and hostile creatures lived off human flesh and were intent on exterminating the human race.

Stoorworm A great water monster which frequented lochs. When it thrust its great body from the sea, it could engulf islands and whole ships. Its appearance prophesied devastation.

Stot Bullock.

Styx River in Arcadia and one of the four rivers in the Underworld. Charon ferried dead souls across it into Hades, and Achilles was dipped into it to make him immortal.

Subrahmanian Son of Shiva, a mountain deity.

Sugriva The chief of the five great monkeys in the Ramayana.

Sukanya The wife of Chyavana.

Suman Son of Asamanja.

Sumantra A noble Brahman.

Sumati Wife of Sagara.

Sumedha A righteous Brahman who dwelt in the city of Amara.

Sumitra One of Dasharatha's three wives, mother of Lakshmana and Satrughna.

Suniti Mother of Dhruva.

Suparshwa One of Ravana's counsellors.

Supranakha A rakshasi, sister of Ravana.

Surabhi The wish-bestowing cow.

Surcoat Loose robe, traditionally worn over armour.

Surtr Fire-giant who eventually destroys the world at Ragnarok.

Surya God of the sun.

Susanoo God of the storm. He is depicted as a contradictory character with both good and bad characteristics. He was banished from Heaven after trying to kill his sister, Amaterasu.

Sushena A monkey chief.

Svasud Father of summer.

Swarga An Olympian paradise, where all wishes and desires are gratified.

Sweating A ritual customarily associated with spiritual purification and prayer, practised by most tribes throughout North America prior to sacred ceremonies or vision quests. Steam was produced within a 'sweat lodge', a low, dome-shaped hut, by sprinkling water on heated stones.

Syrinx An Arcadian nymph who was the object of Pan's love.

Tablet of Destinies Cuneiform clay tablet on which the fates were written. Tiawath had given this to Kingu, but it was taken by Merodach when he defeated them. The storm god Zu later stole it for himself.

Taiaha A weapon made of wood.

Tailtiu One of the most famous royal residences of ancient Ireland. Possibly also a goddess linked to this site.

Tall One of Ravana's counsellors.

Tammuz Solar deity of Eridu who, with Gishzida, guards the gates of Heaven. Protector of Anu.

Tamsil Example or guidance.

Tangi Funeral, dirge. Assembly to cry over the dead.

Taniwha Sea monster, water spirit.

Tantalus Son of Zeus who told the secrets of the gods to mortals and stole their nectar and ambrosia. He was condemned to eternal torture in Hades, where he was tempted by food and water but allowed to partake of neither.

Taoism Taoism (or Daoism) came into being at roughly the same time as Confucianism, although its tenets were radically different and were largely founded on the philosophies of Lao Tzu (Laozi). While Confucius argued for a system of state discipline, Taoism strongly favoured self-discipline and looked upon nature as the architect of essential laws. A newer form of Taoism evolved after the Burning of the Books, placing great emphasis on spirit worship and pacification of the gods.

Tapu Sacred, supernatural possession of power. Involves spiritual rules and restrictions.

Tara Also known as Temair, the Hill of Tara was the popular seat of the ancient High-Kings of Ireland from the earliest times to the sixth century. Located in Co. Meath, it was also the place where great noblemen and chieftains congregated during wartime, or for significant events.

Tara Sugriva's wife.

Tartarus Dark region, below Hades.

Tau (Lesotho) Brother to Ra-Molo, depicted as a lion.

Taua War party.

Tefnut Goddess of water and rain. Married to Shu, who was also her brother. She, like Sekhmet, is portrayed with the head of a lion. Also known as Tefenet.

Telegonus Son of Odysseus and Circe. He was allegedly responsible for his father's death.

Telemachus Son of Odysseus and Penelope, who was aided by Athene in helping his mother to keep away the suitors in Odysseus's absence.

Temu The evening form of Ra, the Sun God.

Tengu Goblin or gnome, often depicted as bird-like. A powerful fighter with weapons.

Tenochtitlán Capital city of the Aztecs, founded around AD 1350 and the site of the 'Great Temple'. Now Mexico City.

Teo-Amoxtli Divine book.

Teocalli Great temple built in Tenochtitlán, now Mexico City.

Teotleco Festival of the Coming of the Gods; also the twelfth month of the Aztec calendar.

Tepee A conical-shaped dwelling constructed of buffalo hide stretched over lodge-poles. Mostly used by native American tribes living on the plains.

Tepeyollotl God of caves, desert places and earthquakes, whose name means 'heart of the mountain'. He is depicted as a jaguar, often leaping at the sun. Also known as Tepeolotlec.

Tepitoton Household gods.

Tereus King of Daulis who married Procne, daughter of Pandion King of Athens. He fell in love with Philomela, raped her and cut out her tongue.

Tezcatlipoca Supreme deity and Lord of the Smoking Mirror. He was also patron of royalty and warriors. Invented human sacrifice to the gods. Offspring of Ometeotl and Omecihuatl, he is known as the Jupiter of the Aztec gods.

Thalia Muse of pastoral poetry and comedy.

Theia Goddess of many names, and mother of the sun.

Theseus Son of King Aegeus of Athens. A cycle of legends has been woven around his travels and life.

Thetis Chief of the Nereids, loved by both Zeus and Poseidon. They married her to a mortal, Peleus, and their child was Achilles. She tried to make him immortal by dipping him in the River Styx.

Thialfi Thor's servant, taken when his peasant father unwittingly harms Thor's goat.

Thiassi Giant and father of Skadi, he tricked Loki into bringing Idunn to him. Thrymheim is his kingdom.

Thomas the Rhymer Also called 'True Thomas', he was Thomas of Ercledoune, who lived in the thirteenth century. He met with the Queen of Elfland, and visited her country, was given clothes and a tongue that could tell no lie. He was also given the gift of prophecy, and many of his predictions were proven true.

Thor God of thunder and of war (with Tyr). Known for his huge size, and red hair and beard. Carries the hammer Miolnir. Slays Jormungander at Ragnarok.

Thoth God of the moon. Invented the arts and sciences and regulated the seasons. He is portrayed with the head of an ibis or a baboon.

Three-Heads One of Ravana's monsters.

Thrud Thor's daughter.

Thrudheim Thor's realm. Also called Thrudvang.

Thunder-Tooth Leader of the rakshasas at the siege of Lanka.

Tiawath Primeval dark ocean or abyss, Tiawath is also a monster and evil deity of the deep. She took the form of a dragon or sea serpent and battled the gods of light for supremacy over all living beings. She was eventually defeated by Merodach, who used her body to create Heaven and Earth.

Tiglath-Pileser I King of Assyria, who made it a leading power for centuries.

Tiki First man created, a figure carved of wood, or other representation of man.

Tirawa The name given to the Great Creator (**see** Great Spirit) by the Pawnee tribe who believed that four direct paths led from his house in the sky to the four semi-cardinal points: north-east, north-west, south-east and south-west.

Tiresias A Theban who was given the gift of prophecy by Zeus. He was blinded for seeing Athene bathing. He continued to use his prophetic talents after his death, advising Odysseus.

Tirfing Sword made by dwarves which was cursed to kill every time it was drawn, be the cause of three great atrocities, and kill Suaforlami (Odin's grandson), for whom it was made.

Tisamenus Son of Orestes, who inherited the Kingdom of Argos and Sparta.

Titania Queen of the fairies.

Tlaloc God of rain and fertility, so important to the people, because he ensured a good harvest, that the Aztec heaven or paradise was named Tlalocan in his honour.

Tlazolteotl Goddess of ordure, filth and vice. Also known as the earth-goddess or Tlaelquani, meaning 'filth-eater'. She acted as a confessor of sins or wrongdoings.

Tohu-mate Omen of death.

Tohunga A priest; a possessor of supernatural powers.

Toltec Civilization that preceded the Aztecs.

Tomahawk Hatchet with a stone or iron head used in war or hunting.

Tonalamatl Record of the Aztec calendar, which was recorded in books made from bark paper.

Tonalpohualli Aztec calendar composed of twenty thirteen-day weeks called trecenas.

Totec Solar deity known as Our Great Chief.

Totemism System of belief in which people share a relationship with a spirit animal or natural being with whom they interact. Examples include Ea, who is represented by a fish.

Toxilmolpilia The binding up of the years.

Tristan Nephew of King Mark of Cornwall, who travels to Ireland to bring Iseult back to marry his uncle. On the way, he and Iseult consume a love potion and fall madly in love before their story ends tragically.

Triton A sea-god, and son of Poseidon and Amphitrite. He led the Argonauts to the sea from Lake Tritonis.

Trojan War War waged by the Greeks against Troy, in order to reclaim Menelaus's wife Helen, who had eloped with the Trojan prince Paris. Many important heroes took part, and form the basis of many legends and myths.

Troll Unfriendly mythological creature of varying size and strength. Usually dwells in mountainous areas, among rocks or caves.

Truage Tribute or pledge of peace or truth, usually made on payment of a tax.

Tsuki-yomi God of the moon, brother of Amaterasu and Susanoo.

Tuat The other world or land of the dead.

Tupuna Ancestor.

Tvashtar Craftsman of the gods.

Tyndareus King of Sparta, perhaps the son of Perseus's daughter Grogphone. Expelled from Sparta but restored by Heracles. Married Leda and fathered Helen and Clytemnestra, among others.

Tyr Son of Frigga and the god of war (with Thor). Eventually kills Garm at Ragnarok.

Tzompantli Pyramid of Skulls.

Uayeb The five unlucky days of the Mayan calendar, which were believed to be when demons from the underworld could reach Earth. People would often avoid leaving their houses on uayeb days.

Ubaaner Magician, whose name meant 'splitter of stones', who created a wax crocodile that came to life to swallow up the man who was trying to seduce his wife.

Uile Bheist Mythical creature, usually some form of wild beast.

Uisneach A hill formation between Mullingar and Athlone said to mark the centre of Ireland.

uKqili (Zulu) Creator god.

Uller God of winter, whom Skadi eventually marries.

Ulster Cycle Compilation of folk tales and legends telling of the Ulaids, people from the northeast of Ireland, now named Ulster. Also known as the *Uliad Cycle*, it is one of four Irish cycles of mythology.

Unseelie Court An unholy court comprising a kind of fairies, antagonistic to humans. They took the form of a kind of Sluagh, and shot humans and animals with elf-shots.

Urd One of the Norns.

Urien King of Gore, husband of Morgan le Fey and father to Yvain.

Urmila Second daughter of Janaka.

Usha Wife of Aniruddha, daughter of Vanasur.

Ushas Goddess of the dawn.

Utgard-loki King of the giants. Tricked Thor.

Uther Pendragon King of England in sub-Roman Britain; father of King Arthur.

Utixo (Hottentot) Creator god.

Ut-Napishtim Ancestor of Gilgamesh, whom Gilgamesh sought out to discover how to prevent death. Similar to Noah in that he was sent a vision warning him of a great deluge. He built an ark in seven days, filling it with his family, possessions and all kinds of animals.

Uz Deity symbolized by a goat.

Vach Goddess of speech.

Vajrahanu One of Ravana's generals.

Vala Another name for Norns.

Valfreya Another name for Freyia.

Valhalla Odin's hall for the celebrated dead warriors chosen by the Valkyries.

Vali The cruel brother of Sugriva, dethroned by Rama.

Valkyries Odin's attendants, led by Freyia. Chose dead warriors to live at Valhalla. Also spelled as Valkyrs.

Vamadeva One of Dasharatha's priests.

Vanaheim Home of the Vanir.

Vanir Race of gods in conflict with the Aesir; they are gods of the sea and wind.

Varuna Ancient god of the sky and cosmos, later, god of the waters.

Vasishtha One of Dasharatha's priests.

Vassal Person under the protection of a feudal lord.

Vasudev Descendant of Yadu, husband of Rohini and Devaki, father of Krishna.

Vasudeva A name of Narayana or Vishnu.

Vavasor Vassal or tenant of a baron or lord who himself has vassals.

Vedic Mantras, hymns.

Vernandi One of the Norns.

Vichitravirya Bhishma's half-brother.

Vidar Slays Fenris.

Vidura Friend of the Pandavas.

Vigrid The plain where the final battle is held.

Vijaya Karna's bow.

Vikramaditya A king identified with Chandragupta II.

Vintail Moveable front of a helmet.

Virabhadra A demon that sprang from Shiva's lock of hair.

Viradha A fierce rakshasa, seizes Sita, slain by Rama.

Virupaksha The elephant who bears the whole world.

Vishnu The Preserver, Vedic sun-god and one of the two great gods of post-Vedic Hinduism.

Vision Quest A sacred ceremony undergone by Native Americans to establish communication with the spirit set to direct them in life. The quest lasted up to four days and nights and was preceded by a period of solitary fasting and prayer.

Vivasvat The sun.

Vizier High-ranking official or adviser. Also known as vizir or vazir.

Volsung Family of great warriors about whom a great saga was spun.

Vrishadarbha King of Benares.

Vrishasena Son of Karna, slain by Arjuna.

Vyasa Chief of the royal chaplains.

Wairua Spirit, soul.

Wanjiru (Kikuyu) Maiden who was sacrificed by her village to appease the gods and make it rain after years of drought.

Weighing of the heart Procedure carried out after death to assess whether the deceased was free from sin. If the deceased's heart weighed less than the feather of Ma'at, they would join Osiris in the Fields of Peace.

Whare Hut made of fern stems tied together with flax and vines, and roofed in with raupo (reeds).

White Demon Protector of Mázinderán. He prevented Kai-káús and his army from invading.

Withy Thin twig or branch which is very flexible and strong.

Wolverine Large mammal of the musteline family with dark, very thick, water-resistant fur, inhabiting the forests of North America and Eurasia.

Wroth Angry.

Wyrd One of the Norns.

Xanthus & Balius Horses of Achilles, immortal offspring of Zephyrus the west wind. A gift to Achilles's father Peleus.

Xipe Totec High priest and son of Ometeotl and Omecihuatl. Also known as the god of the seasons.

Xiupohualli Solar year, composed of eighteen twenty-day months. Also spelt Xiuhpōhualli.

Yadu A prince of the Lunar dynasty.

Yakshas Same as rakshasas.

Yakunin Government official.

Yama God of Death, king of the dead and son of the sun.

Yamato Take Legendary warrior and prince. Also known as Yamato Takeru.

Yashiki Residence or estate, usually of a daimyō.

Yasoda Wife of Nand.

Yemaya (Yoruba) Wife of Obatala.

Yemoja (Yoruba) Goddess of water and protector of women.

Yggdrasill The World Ash, holding up the Nine Worlds. Does not fall at Ragnarok.

Ymir Giant created from fire and ice; his body created the world.

Yo The female principle who, joined with In, the male side, brought about creation and the first gods. In and Yo correspond to the Chinese Yang and Yin.

Yomi The underworld.

Yudhishthira The eldest of the Pandavas, a great soldier.

Yuki-Onna The Snow-Bride or Lady of the Snow, who represents death.

Yvain Son of Morgan le Fay and knight of the Round Table, who goes on chivalric quests with a lion he rescued from a dragon.

Zahid Holy man.

Zál Son of Sám, who was born with pure white hair. Sám abandoned Zál, who was raised by the Símúrgh, or griffins. Zal became a great warrior, second only to his son, Rustem. Also known as Ním-rúz and Dustán.

Zephyr Gentle breeze.

Zeus King of gods, god of sky, weather, thunder, lightning, home, hearth and hospitality. He plays an important role as the voice of justice, arbitrator between man and gods, and among them. Married to Hera, but lover of dozens of others.

Zohák Serpent-king and figure of evil. Father of Mihrab.

Zu God of the storm, who took the form of a huge bird. Similar to the Persian símúrgh.

Zukin Head covering.

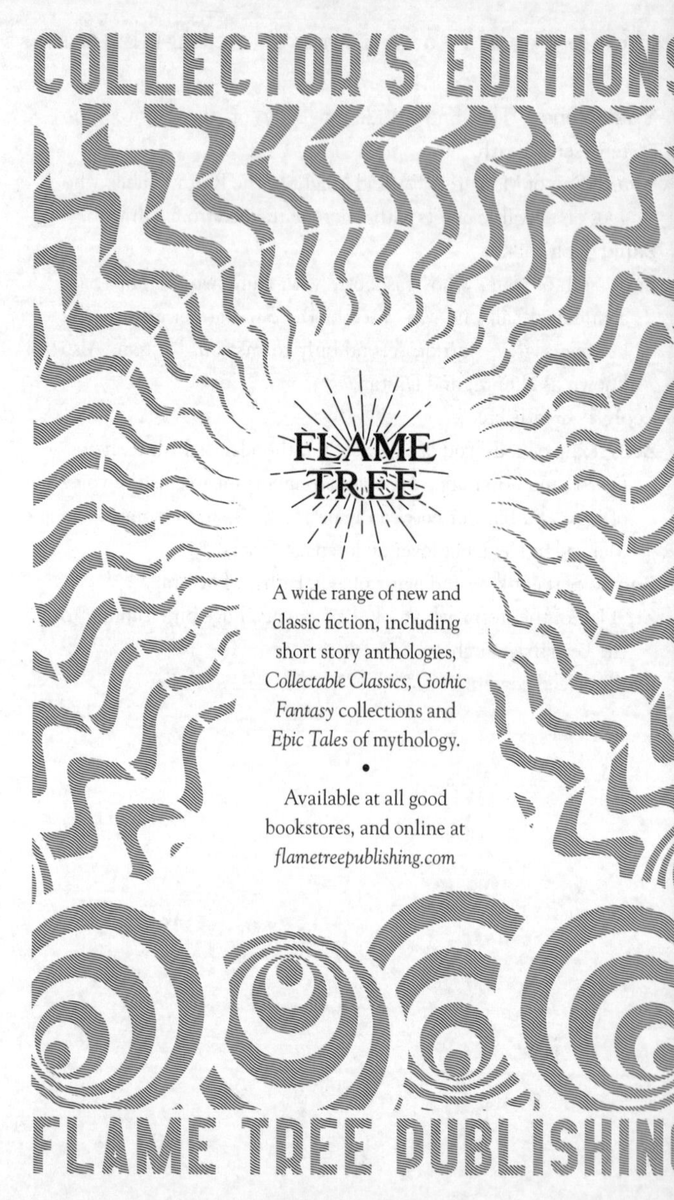
COLLECTOR'S EDITIONS
FLAME TREE
A wide range of new and classic fiction, including short story anthologies, *Collectable Classics*, *Gothic Fantasy* collections and *Epic Tales* of mythology.
•
Available at all good bookstores, and online at *flametreepublishing.com*
FLAME TREE PUBLISHING